Embrace Me at Dawn

BY

Shayla Black

EMBRACE ME AT DAWN

SHAYLA BLACK

Edited by Chloe Vale & Amy Garvey
Published by Shelley Bradley LLC
ISBN: 978-1-936596-13-3

Bonus Material and Excerpts at the end of the book

\

Dedication and Acknowledgements

A book doesn't happen by one person alone, at least not in my world. A book takes a village for me, so I've got many people to thank.

First, I wouldn't have even considered undertaking this project on my own without Sylvia Day and Sophie Oak encouraging me. I still might not have done it without my husband's support. So I dedicate this to you. Courage isn't always easy, but somehow you all make me find some just when I need it.

The army of cheerleaders helped me so much with the actual tasks around writing a book, and I can't not thank you all from the bottom of my heart. To Rhyannon Byrd and Angel Payne, I SO appreciate your enthusiasm and kind words as I fed you chapters. I know I've got true friends in you both. Laurie, what would I have done if you hadn't bought that damn timer and told me to go write for twenty minutes at a stretch every freaking day for weeks? I NEEDED that. Bless you. And to Pearl, you don't know how much you improved my mood just when I had to have a pick-me-up. A HUGE shout out to Rich for writing me a killer blurb! It's epic, and I owe you. The book would NEVER have made its way into reader's hands without the help of my editors, Amy Garvey and Chloe Vale. Your feedback and last minute dedication to help me, even as I was running behind, enabled me to get this book out on time. Lastly, I can't even begin to thank Christie Von Ditter, my assistant, enough to cover everything she's done to make this book a reality. Your feedback on this book while still juggling all my other projects was crucial. I wouldn't still be standing without you. Finally, to the fans of this series who encouraged me to keep going and the Doomsday Brethren players who write diligently on Facebook every day to keep the stories and the excitement alive, you have really touched me. Thanks much to you all!

Chapter One

Present day - England

Anka MacTavish held her breath as the most beautiful man she'd ever seen stormed toward her, one heavy footstep after another. Lucan, her mate.

Former mate, she reminded herself. He hated her now, with good reason. She could have blamed a number of people for that. She mostly blamed herself.

His full mouth thinned into a grim line, blue eyes narrowing as he drew closer. At the sight of his obvious anger, she turned away toward the surprising warmth of the rare January sun, praying the golden rays would chase away the perpetual chill that had plagued her these last three months.

It almost worked. Then Lucan grabbed her arm and spun her around to face him, dragging her so close to the familiar heat of his body. Suddenly, she didn't need the sun at all. Finally, she was warm. Their gazes connected, and heat seeped into her veins. Her heart lurched in her chest. A jolt of connection grabbed her all the way to her soul.

As quickly as he'd grabbed her, Lucan yanked his hand back. Sadly, the connection she felt was all one-sided now.

"Are you out of your mind?" he growled. "No. The answer is absolutely no."

Anka let her lashes flutter down, breaking the pull of his furious stare, then forcing herself to step away from his beloved warmth. She didn't pretend to misunderstand. "I suppose you heard that I intend to ask Bram to let me fight with the Doomsday Brethren."

Admittedly, asking the leader of the warrior wizards dedicated to ridding magickind of the evil Mathias d'Arc to allow a witch to join their ranks had been a long shot. But damn it, she had a personal stake in this fight. Those males who followed Bram into this terrible magical war all sought peace, to make magickind safe again. Admirable. Once upon a time, she'd wanted that, too.

Now, the need for vengeance beat in her chest even stronger than her own heart. She wanted nothing more than revenge against the malicious wizard who had forced her to break her sacred bond with Lucan. Mathias had ravaged her body until she barely knew her own name, and in doing so, had destroyed her once-beautiful life.

"Yes." Lucan leaned into her personal space, his glare intimidating, as he, no doubt, meant it to be. "He'd better not agree. It's mad! I won't have it."

That familiar woodsy-musky scent of his hadn't once failed to arouse her in the century they'd lived and loved together. It didn't fail today, either.

Inching back, Anka sent Lucan a sad smile. Not for one second did she imagine that he refused her because he loved her enough to be concerned for her safety. Three months ago, before her world had shattered, yes. No mate had been more caring than Lucan. Today? She winced. He didn't want to see her, much less fight beside her. Bloody hell, after Mathias had taken her captive, then plundered her mind and body, she'd eventually fled to her former suitor, Shock Denzell—Lucan's enemy—for protection and succor. For that, her former mate hated her.

This was the most conversation they'd had in weeks, maybe even since Mathias had abducted her from the home she'd shared with Lucan.

Even thoughts of the harrowing days that had followed as the madman's captive made her want to crumble. For a long time, she'd done nothing more than hide while fighting off one nightmare after another, and licking her wounds.

No more.

Shoving aside both regret and tears, she tossed her head back and met Lucan's damning stare. "It's no longer your decision."

Instantly, his jaw clenched. His fingers plowed through his dark hair. Those blue eyes of his could look so tender. Now they glowed with fury and condemnation. "You're right; it's not. And as much as I hate Shock, I know him. There is no way he'll allow you to fight with us."

It's none of his business, either. Anka kept the thought to herself. The last thing she wanted to discuss with her former mate was her current lover. At least, Shock was her lover when he was sober. Lately, that was never. More and more, Shock had begun grabbing a bottle and escaping into the bottom of it. Anka hadn't tried to stop him.

Lucan wouldn't care about her personal drama with Shock. The only thing that mattered to him was that she hadn't returned home after escaping Mathias and his torture. In fact, Lucan probably thought she'd willfully betrayed him, doing her utmost to rub salt into his wound by running to Shock. Never mind that breaking the mate bond had obliterated her memories of Lucan for weeks afterward. Never mind that she'd been barely alive and instinctively sought a safe haven in case Mathias hunted her again. When she'd first reached Shock, she'd been dangerously low on life energy. And he'd been more than happy to share hot exchanges of frequent, raw sex with her to repower her magic and keep her alive—at least at first. Her former mate didn't know or care that, for weeks now, Shock had only touched her enough for brief energy exchanges, or that, for the most part, Anka didn't mind.

Lucan only cared that she had betrayed him. And as much as she wanted to rail, she understood completely. In his place, she would feel utterly stabbed in the heart. Still, she would tell Lucan right now that she still loved him and always would—if she thought for a second that there wasn't too much water under the bridge between them or that he'd give a damn.

"Shock's opinion on the matter shouldn't concern you," she returned softly. "I've offered to lend my wand to a fight that's desperately outnumbered. The decision to accept or not is Bram's. If you're so against me joining, talk to him."

A muscle ticked in his jaw. "The second Sabelle gave me the news, that went on my agenda."

Anka pressed her lips together to hold in a curse. Of course, her old friend and Bram's sister would spill the secret. Sabelle was worried about her and still believed that Lucan cared enough to stop Anka from putting herself in harm's way. In a fashion, Sabelle's attempt was sweet, if futile.

"Be my guest." Anka gestured across the expanse of Bram's winter-brown lawn, dormant roses swaying with the slight breeze. The Doomsday Brethren's leader's massive new house beckoned, carpenters and masons in the distance adding finishing touches to the structure built directly over the site of the original estate, which Mathias had recently destroyed. "You won't stop me from trying to convince Bram that I can be an asset to your fight."

Lucan scowled at her as if she'd lost her mind. "After what Mathias did to you? Why? You're still healing."

"I'm better," she argued.

"That's crap. You look tired. Are you going to lie and tell me you're not having nightmares, Anka? I know you..."

He would always have an intimate knowledge of her, and one undeniable fact was that she often took the stress in her life and played it out in terrible detail in her dreams. Lucan could have no doubt that she was plagued by nightmares. Or that she avoided sleep because of them.

"I'm all right."

"You're not," he growled. "It's obvious. Why would you imagine that you'd be doing anything more than putting yourself—and the rest of us trying to save you—in more danger?"

It was a fair question, but she refused to back down. "I'm not the same woman I once was."

Lucan clenched massive fists at his sides. "Clearly."

He was trying to restrain his temper. Anka had seen this behavior more than once during their mating. She bit her lip to hold in a bittersweet smile. How much she missed his face and every one of those expressions she knew so well. If Bram refused to allow her to join the Doomsday Brethren, would she ever see them again?

Despair spread a heavy pain through her chest. It was unreasonable to assume that she would forget a century of happiness in mere months. Even tragedy and rape couldn't obliterate love.

"I have to go." Anka couldn't bear to look at him again and wonder if this would be the last time.

But when she turned toward Bram's home, she saw a familiar narrow-hipped giant sauntering her way. Shock. He wore black leather from top to bottom, like something out of a motorcycle gang—or a fetish club. A goatee framed his full mouth and square chin. Sunglasses covered his inscrutable eyes. She knew without question that he glared at Lucan.

Her former mate shifted his weight to the balls of his feet, clearly itching for any reason to punch Shock. "Why are you here?"

It was a fair question, given the fact that Shock, the Doomsday Brethren's supposed double agent, had behaved like Mathais's right hand more than once recently. Shock made a natural second to the evil wizard, as the Denzells had long been Mathias supporters. It was his role as an alleged informant and member of the Doomsday Brethren that everyone doubted. Despite living with him, even Anka didn't know exactly where his allegiance lay. She'd tried not to think about her lover helping her rapist tear magickind apart, but ignoring that possibility was becoming more and more difficult.

The arch of Shock's black brow popped above his dark-tinted glasses. "You think I need your permission to be here?"

Lucan hesitated. Anka hadn't thought it possible, but his body grew more taut. "After you dragged Tynan away last week, took him to your boss, then dumped him when he was only suitable for a body bag, you have the devil's audacity to show your face."

"Could you read Tynan's mind?"

No, but Shock could. And everyone knew that, upon returning to magickind months ago Mathias had murdered Auropha, the love of Tynan's life. Since then, the wizard had had a death wish. Shock had done nothing more than help Mathias grant it.

The night of Tynan's death, Shock sank farther than ever into a bottle. Given the depth of his black mood, Anka was surprised to see that he'd crawled out at all.

"You could have saved him," Lucan growled. "And you didn't."

"You think Tynan would have thanked me if I had?"

Shock crossed his arms over his chest and waited for Lucan to concede. That was never going to happen. These two together had always been like oil and water. She'd cared for them both deeply. Now, as always, divided loyalties were tearing her up inside.

"I'm leaving." She spun away from the two men.

"Where are you going?" Lucan demanded, grabbing her arm, his hold sizzling though her entire body, settling with a gentle ache right between her legs.

Shock took hold of the other in an equally tight grip. "Where have you been?"

They were both aggressive, demanding. She knew better than to jerk away. Either—or both—would do everything in his power to hold her until they got answers.

"I'm here to talk to Bram. Let go." She glared at them both.

Lucan flinched, yanking his hand away with a curse. Satisfied, Shock slowly unwound his fingers from her wrist. Anka knew that if she turned her back on them, it wouldn't be long before they began to argue—with their wands and their fists. Neither man was her responsibility any longer. By looking at Lucan's magical signature, she could see that he was brimming with energy, and wondering who he'd been taking to his bed to generate it was killing her. If she stayed to ponder the question longer, she would only cry.

A few days ago, she'd left Shock. This was likely the first time he'd been sober enough to notice her absence. Something was eating at him, and he wouldn't share it with her. She wanted to help him. God knew, she owed Shock. But she couldn't live with him anymore. Though he gave her the protection and occasional energy she desperately needed, in every other way they were slowly killing one another.

Anka turned toward the house again, this time to see Bram striding toward them, grim purpose filling his sharp blue eyes. In a glance, he took in the scene. His tawny hair moved with the breeze, mussing the strands in a very uncharacteristic fashion. He was so focused, he didn't notice or care.

"Shock?" The Doomsday Brethren's leader stopped in front of the other wizard, his brow lifted as if to ask, *Why the hell are you here?*

Clearly, Shock wasn't popular among the Doomsday Brethren. Then again, he never had been. No one trusted him. Anka only did because he'd kept her terrible secret for so long—just as she'd kept his. She'd always known that if one of them went down in flames, they'd likely be going together.

Smirking at Bram's arrogance, Shock pretended he didn't see the other wizard's impatient expression. "Yes?"

"No bloody stupid games. I hear you've come to see me. Out with it, then. And this had better be about stopping Mathias and Morganna le Fay's antics. That bitch especially has been so busy of late that everyone in England thinks the sky is going to fucking fall months before the Mayans supposed."

A chunk of the chip on Shock's shoulder seemed to fall away. His posture lost some starch. "That's exactly why I've come. When Mathias resurrected Morganna in her tomb, he planned to meld her power to his and—"

"Be magickind's most dastardly super villain or some such, I'm sure." Bram raked a hand though his already mussed hair. "But did he have to take all that energy and direct it against humans? My

God, if humankind discovers that we truly exist, the Inquisition will look like a friendly game of croquet."

"Did you bloody want him to direct his power at magickind?" Lucan glowered.

"It's only a matter of time before Mathias comes after us, too," Anka murmured. "We all know that."

She knew that better than most.

Shock growled, "Fucking listen! Mathias had nothing to do with the massacre at Stonehenge last week or the death of all those humans. Morganna is beyond control."

"Even Mathias's?" Bram quizzed.

"Completely." Nodding, his dark waves brushing his shoulders, Shock confirmed what some of the Doomsday Brethren had long suspected: Morganna wouldn't be tamed. "And she is obsessed."

"With what?" Bram looked skeptical.

A gruff laugh slipped from Shock's throat. "Do I look stupid enough to spend more time with the shrew than I must? Fuck, no. According to Mathias, she is completely absorbed in looking for something. He has no idea what."

"Or claims he has no idea." Bram put his hands on his narrow hips, skepticism hanging heavily around him. "So you're saying that he has no sway over her actions and no idea what she's seeking? Convenient, isn't it?" Bram mused.

Shock rolled his eyes. "Focus, you bloody stubborn wanker. I'm telling you the truth."

"Maybe I should fetch Felicia to see if that's the case?" Bram threatened slyly. "The Untouchable will know if you're lying."

Indeed. The beautiful Felicia could sniff out any lie, and Anka knew that Bram had come to rely on her skill, made only stronger by her recent mate bond with another Doomsday Brethren member, Duke.

"Feel free." Shock shrugged his massive, leather-clad shoulders. "I've nothing to hide."

Bram pulled out his mobile phone and sent a quick text. In less than thirty seconds, Duke and Felicia appeared on the dormant lawn, the stylish wizard's arm protectively around his mate's small waist, her long golden hair brushing his shoulder and chest.

"Say it again," Bram insisted.

"Mathias has no control over Morganna and no idea what she's searching for."

Every eye turned to Felicia. "He's telling the truth. Or…at least the truth as he knows it."

So if Mathias had lied to him—or Shock had intentionally allowed Mathias to do so—Felicia had no way of knowing. Bram sighed, and Duke shuffled his mate behind his body, out of Shock's path. Even in a suit that cost probably upwards of £1,000, Duke still looked every inch the protector.

The big, leather-clad wizard shook his head at Bram with a sigh. "I'm telling you the absolute truth. And despite your derision, I'm going to do you a huge fucking favor and tell you that Morganna is determined to kill you and your sister."

Felicia nodded, biting her lip anxiously.

Fear gripped Anka's throat. For Bram, yes. But he was one of magickind's most capable and talented wizards. Her fear was mostly for Sabelle. She was a gifted witch, but in Morganna's league? No one was. Bram, along with Sabelle's devoted mate, Ice, would both willingly give their lives to keep her safe. And still it might not be enough. If Mathias couldn't handle Morganna, and Bram died trying, who would save magickind? A bigger force might be their only means of defeating the evil witch—another reason Anka hoped that Bram let her join.

Bram frowned. "Morganna wants us dead because we have Merlin's blood in our veins?"

"Exactly." Shock crossed his arms over his chest. "This is merely a guess, mind you, but I suspect she sees it as payback because Merlin managed to keep her soul imprisoned for the last fifteen centuries. By the way, she's more than a bit vocal about the fact that she could feel pain, thirst, depravation, and agony while trapped in that cave."

Payback, indeed. Anka swallowed. Morganna had never been

known for restraint. Saddled with this sort of fury, what would the witch be capable of?

"I understand. Warning received. Thank you." Bram sounded almost grateful. "So this going after humankind instead of coming straight here? To draw us out?"

"You want me to guess Morganna's motives?" Shock's tone asked if Bram was out of his mind. "I don't fucking know why Morganna does anything. I just know she must be stopped. And Mathias wishes like hell that he'd never resurrected the bitch."

Shock drew in a big breath that lifted his massive shoulders. Anka frowned. He was never nervous, but whatever he hadn't yet said unnerved him.

"Go on," Bram demanded.

"Mathias has tried to put that genie back in the bottle, but he can't do it alone."

As the ramifications of Shock's visit sank in, everyone froze. Felicia didn't refute him. Anka merely gaped. How was it possible that she'd lived with this man, yet knew nothing of this revelation? Then again, Shock had never been one to share. Plus, they'd hardly spoken—or anything else—of late.

Their last coupling had been so rushed. Shock had barely touched her, instead just unzipping his leathers and shoving his cock inside. It had taken everything inside her not to push him away, but she'd needed energy as badly as he had—and the guilt for being in his bed was still festering in her heart. Sharing Shock's sheets at this point shouldn't matter. But with every moment, she'd thought of Lucan—and barely managed to hold her tears at bay until Shock had forced an orgasm from her and groaned out in completion. Then he'd immediately zipped up and left her sprawled in their bed.

Though hidden behind his sunglasses, Shock turned his eyes on her now. Anka felt his gaze sharpen, as if he was dissecting her. *Crap*! He knew exactly what she was thinking. She winced and intentionally turned her thoughts to the situation at hand.

Bram narrowed his eyes at Shock. "Are you telling me that Mathias wants *our* help to end Morganna?"

"What do you think? Either the bitch will go on the sort of rampage that will bring human authorities down around magickind's ears or she'll come after you and your sister with every twisted trick she's got. Deal with those issues yourselves or help Mathias kill her. Your choice."

"No, there's another." Lucan surged at Shock, shoving his face directly into the other wizard's. "You and your boss have cooked up this elaborate scheme to lead us into a trap and straight to our demise. That would leave Mathias and Morganna free to live creepily ever after, with you as their trusted advisor."

Shock stared back at Lucan as if the barb hadn't bothered him a bit, but Anka sensed the fury he barely kept on its leash. A moment later, he wrapped an arm around her waist. Horror spread over her as she realized he was publicly staking his claim on her—in front of Lucan. Her gaze flew to her former mate's, and his blue eyes turned hard. Shame and guilt doused Anka. She looked away.

"Bitter much?" Shock taunted.

The two caustic words barely left his mouth before all hell broke loose. Lucan rushed Shock with a growl that said he was going to tear the big wizard's head off. Shock roared in response, pushing her behind him, readying to fight like he was going to enjoy it. Duke hustled Felicia away, teleporting out.

Anka jumped between Lucan and Shock. It wasn't like her former mate to lose his temper so quickly. Sabelle had more than hinted that Lucan wasn't himself anymore. Anka's heart wept with concern. She didn't dare hope that longing for her had put him on edge. She didn't know how to make him understand the hows or whys of the past three months. And now that she'd graced the bed of his enemy willingly, she doubted he'd want to hear them. She only wanted him well and happy, and it hurt deeply to know he'd find those things without her.

Both wizards urged her out of their way, then charged at one another again. Thankfully Bram stepped between them this time and threw a force field between both, keeping them apart.

"I have precious little energy for this shit, children," Bram groused. "The clock is ticking down until Morganna's next trick, whatever that may be. I have no mate to replenish me. We can't afford this fighting amongst ourselves."

Lucan drew in a deep, shuddering breath, jaw clenched, eyes narrowed. God, she'd rarely seen him so angry. But with a roll of his wide shoulders, he backed away, still looking murderous. She wished she could help him. Shock clenched a meaty fist at his side but dropped an expression onto his face that looked to all the world like he didn't give a fuck. Anka knew better, and she had a feeling she'd have to deal with whatever was eating at him soon.

After a long pause, Bram finally dropped his hands and the force fields. After a sharp glance at both, he nodded. "Shock, you can tell Mathias we'll consider his request. I'm not ready to commit to anything."

"Are you out of your fucking mind?" Shock looked at Bram as if someone had beaten the Doomsday Brethren's leader with a stupid stick. "Do you have any bloody idea what else Morganna can do to expose us while you sit with your thumb up your arse?"

Bram grabbed Shock's leather jacket with one hand. "I don't trust you for shit. And I'm hardly sitting around with my thumb up my arse. This isn't just my decision; it's everyone's. I'm not making a move until I talk to them all, so you can run along and tell your boss that once we've talked, I'll be in touch."

Shock looked like he wanted to argue, but he jerked out of Bram's hold and straightened his jacket with a shrug. "Stupid fuck. More deaths will be on your conscience."

"I'm tired of your shit. Get off my property." Bram tossed his head in the direction of the gate.

Anka bit her lip. She wanted to ask Bram if he could live with those deaths, but before she could, Shock growled, grabbing her arm. "Let's go."

"She stays here," Bram demanded. "She came to me for a favor, and I haven't heard it yet. I'll do that now."

Shock's gaze bounced between her and Bram. Anka thought of anything and everything other than the topic of her business with

Bram. She felt him probe into her mind with a hard shove. It hurt, and she glared at him and winced, raising her hand to her abused forehead.

Lucan charged over to Anka, hovering protectively. "You're hurting her. Get the hell out of her head!"

After a moment's hesitation, Shock shrugged. "I'll figure it out when I fuck her later."

With a hard slap of his hand on her backside that tingled across her skin and fired her nerve endings, Shock walked away and left the grounds with a slam of the gate before teleporting out.

Lucan stared at her like he didn't understand. No, like he didn't know her at all. Having him near brought out the very worst in Shock, and Anka wished to hell the floor would open up and swallow her whole. The silence almost weighed too much for her slender shoulders. God, what must her former mate be thinking? She drew in a deep breath and shook the thought away. Lucan was no longer her concern—even if she missed him until insanity seemed just a breath away.

"Why are you with him?" Lucan demanded.

There was nothing she could say that he'd truly understand. Certainly nothing that would change their situation. So she remained mute.

"Goddamn it! If it's for protection, you're deluding yourself. Mathias knows exactly where to find you. If he wants you again, Shock won't be able to stop him."

Likely so. But Mathias didn't really want her, merely to weaken the Doomsday Brethren. He'd nearly driven Lucan mad with mate mourning after forcibly severing her bond with him. She couldn't risk Mathias targeting Lucan again. She alone had healed him from that terrible, mad state. It had cost her nearly every bit of her magic. Neither of them would survive that again.

She forced herself to face Bram, square her shoulders, and look him in the eyes. "You know what I want. I'm sure Sabelle has told you."

"Goddamn it, Bram. No!" Lucan snapped.

Bram turned a gaze to his friend. "Go get the others. We have bigger matters to discuss."

"This matter is vital to us all. Having Anka fighting with us will affect the entire group."

"You more than the rest. And still, this isn't your decision. Go."

Lucan whipped his gaze to her, jaw clenched. "Anka…"

She swallowed. She wanted to soothe him, reach out and brush back his too-long hair, caress his troubled brow. Their past, this… thing still between them, it couldn't matter anymore.

Resolutely, she ignored him.

He cursed a blue streak, grabbing a chair in one hand and flinging it across the lawn as he made for the house with giant stomping steps. At the door, he paused, staring a hole through her. "We're not done with this conversation, Anka."

She didn't look his way. "Yes, we are."

A pause. She felt his rage building. Then she heard him curse again. The door slammed. She and Bram were finally alone. Anka clasped her hands together to keep them from visibly shaking.

Bram raised a brow at her. "Certainly you can see that you fighting with us will present obstacles."

"I'm determined. That bastard Mathias took *everything* from me. My life, my mate, my dignity, my sense of security. He tortured me. He tortured Lucan. I deserve revenge."

"The Doomsday Brethren isn't here for your personal vendetta."

The truth stung. "You need more wands, both to destroy him and bring about Morganna's demise. You need strong magic and fighters who will not waver when things become difficult. I've already endured the worst Mathias can give me. He can't possibly hurt me more."

"Is that what you think?" Bram challenged.

"I think you can't afford to be picky. You must contend with two of the most evil villains to ever disgrace magickind, and you think to fight them with six wizards of varying abilities and a human? Really?" She cut Bram with a skeptical stare. "At the very least, I think you need to consider that Tynan's death leaves a hole among the ranks that I could fill."

Bram hesitated. "As long as we understand that the greater good of the mission and magickind comes before your revenge, I'll let you in."

She cocked her head at him. "You were always going to accept me, weren't you?"

A smile played at his lips. "Probably. I had to hear you argue your side to see if you were dedicated enough to take the hard work this will require."

"Sneaky bastard." She smiled. It was hard to stay mad at Bram.

"I've heard that before," he drawled. "I've got a few conditions before I'll allow you to join this fight, however."

And this was where Bram could truly trip her up. He was a master negotiator, and all she wanted was to jump in and rip out Mathias's throat now. "What?"

"You must appear every morning with the sun for training. You'll learn to fight in every way Marrok and I insist. You'll stay each day until we release you. No complaints. It's hard, sweaty work, and this is no time to worry about your hair."

"I'm not vain," she protested.

"No," he agreed. "But I guarantee you'll never work harder in your life. Marrok is relentless, and I encourage it. We don't have the advantage of a bigger fighting force or the element of surprise. We have to be better prepared."

"I'll be here every day, as long as you need me to be."

"What will Shock say to that?"

"Nothing. I moved out. I don't even think he knows it. Sabelle said I could adopt a spare bedroom here."

"No. That's another condition. You return to Shock."

"*What*?" She would have thought that Bram would applaud her for leaving a man no one liked or trusted.

"You're going to need energy far more frequently. He'll give it to you."

Anka hesitated. She remembered those first few days after the formation of the Doomsday Brethren. Lucan had returned home from Marrok's drills completely exhausted. He'd tumbled her into bed every evening, spending hours working her body into a sweet froth of need, then making love to her until they'd both been brimming and smiling. They'd fallen asleep in exhaustion, curled up around one another. Those had been some troubling days, but ones of great personal happiness, so filled with Lucan and his need for her.

The smile that had crept over her face faded. Now she was going to join the fight, expend the energy to train—and she would need to replenish her energy as frequently as Lucan once had. Did he still require that much energy? She winced at the pain of that thought.

"I'll find a surrogate." Though she found that thought distasteful, too. Letting some strange wizard paw her… Unlike most of her kind, she'd only ever taken two lovers. Shock had been her first, had seen her though the transition into magic, and cared for her until she'd mated with Lucan. After Mathias's brutal, repeated assault and a hundred years of mating, she didn't know how she'd accept another wizard's touch.

Bram shook his head. "Whatever Shock's issues, he'll keep you safe when you're not here. I don't have the resources or energy to expend worrying about you alone at night or with some strange wizard who might deliver you up to Mathias. I might hate Shock, but he'd never want to see you hurt. Besides, I know Shock is capable of giving you what you need."

Anka swallowed. If Bram only knew the half of it… Shock not only gave her what she needed—and now craved in order to cleanse her soul—but he wielded it like a weapon, doling it out sparingly, withholding it until she caved into whatever his demands of the moment were and she begged sweetly. No surrogate could give her what Shock could. They'd probably be horrified if she asked.

If she wanted to fight Mathias and get her revenge, she would have to swallow her pride.

"All right, then. I'll return to Shock."

"I'll allow you to train with us. As to whether you fight…that will be up to me, Marrok, and whoever teaches you. If we think you're not ready, you'll stay behind. This isn't a democracy."

Nothing with Bram ever was. She'd have to earn the right to fight. "No coddling me because I'm female or because I'm your best friend's former mate."

He smiled. "No mercy asked, no mercy given."

Anka sent him a sharp nod, and Bram looked her over. She was aware of her demure beige skirt, delicate heels, silk blouse, riot of curls. Without a word, he cataloged everything wrong with her wardrobe and general appearance.

"I'll be dressed in something appropriate."

He nodded as if that was a given. "And come with energy. If you're not ready, you're out."

Energy. From Shock. Tonight. Right, then.

Bram stared with a raised brow, and it took Anka a moment to realize that she'd been dismissed. She turned and made her way off of Bram's estate, then teleported back to the one place—to the one man—she dreaded having to beg again. But she had no doubt Shock would make her plead for everything he gave her. And he'd enjoy the hell out of it. Tears fell as she opened his door.

The summons to join Bram in his office had come not a moment too soon. Lucan had been ready to lose his mind. What the hell had Bram said to Anka?

Before he could confront his friend, the rest of the Doomsday Brethren filed in, many joined by their mates. Olivia curled up on Marrok's lap on a sofa in the corner, the human warrior no doubt enjoying a rare opportunity to touch her in the middle of the day. Ice filed in, holding Sabelle's hand. She looked pink and flushed and deliriously happy. Envy pierced Lucan—and a strange relief. He wanted what they had, but was glad that Sabelle had refused to mate with him after Anka had been lost. The move would have been politically expedient, yes. It would have helped magickind. But they would have made one another miserable.

Raiden and Ronan both filed in with a fist bump for him.

"Where are Kari and Tabitha?" he asked.

"Kari is at The Witch's Brew, preparing for the Friday night crowd," said Ronan, the woman's mate, of the bar she owned and ran in London.

"And Tabby isn't feeling well. I think the youngling growing inside my she-cat is already giving her hell."

"It will serve you right if it's a girl," Ronan snickered to his twin.

Raiden punched his brother's shoulder a bit harder than playfully. Bram broke it up by clearing his throat and sending them a pointed look.

Duke led Felicia in. He propped his length against the wall, drew his lovely wife's back to his chest, and whispered something in her ear that made her blush. Finally, his own brother strolled in with his mate, fiery-haired Sydney. The couple's eyes met and held, and Lucan could actually feel the love flowing between them. It was tender and passionate and so thick it damn near choked him.

He'd had that once. But he hadn't protected Anka. Now she was lost to him forever, warming that motherfucker Shock's bed. He had no one to blame but himself. Of course she'd be terrified to come home to the man who had failed her. In her shoes, he'd avoid himself, too.

That fact hurt like hell.

Caden and Sydney stood beside him, a silent show of support. She cupped his shoulder. "You know I love you, but you look ghastly."

No doubt. Anka's visit here had truly riled his temper. How could he want someone so badly who had chosen to give herself and her love to one of the worst wankers ever to disgrace magickind? Who had chosen his rival, his enemy?

"Thanks, Syd. I can always trust you to sugarcoat things." He smiled wryly.

"That's my mate." Caden slipped an arm around her waist.

"Thank you for coming so quickly," Bram said to everyone. "And thanks to you lovely ladies for being here on short notice. We have several situations you should know about. I'll need to ask you for help."

"You don't have to ask," Olivia assured, still perched on Marrok's lap.

"Of course not, brother." Sabelle smiled from Ice's embrace. "We'll help however we can."

"I'll hold you to that. It may be dull work, indeed. But I need you to pour through every one of Merlin's tomes and any Morganna folklore you can. It may not only mean the difference between life and death, but between our civilization and extinction."

Beside him, Sydney sucked in a breath. "Of course we're going to help."

Lucan only wished that Anka wanted to assist their cause in that capacity. But no. She wanted to fight. He could only hope that Bram had refused her.

"I daresay, with stakes that high, even these big wizards wouldn't object to cracking a book," Sabelle murmured.

"Normally, yes. But we'll have other pressing matters," Bram corrected. "According to Shock, Mathias regrets Morganna's resurrection and can't put the bitch down by himself. We've been asked to help."

"Is he fucking serious?" Ice growled, his nearly-shaved head giving his hollow cheeks an even starker, angrier appearance.

Bram sighed. "Yes. I didn't give him an answer yet. I want to see what we can do without his 'help' first. So if you ladies will search, we'll keep training and start scouting for Morganna's location. If we can get to her when she's resting, powering up, somehow vulnerable…"

Bram didn't finish the sentence, but Lucan could finish it for him. Even if they managed to find Morganna, she wasn't going to be put down easily. Finding her might just be their death sentence.

"You're seriously going to trust information coming from the bastard who recently killed one of our own?" Caden challenged him, then looked at Lucan. "Who took my brother's mate and—"

"I know. But it's not as if we can't read about Morganna's exploits ourselves." Bram reached behind him and picked up the latest copies of *The Sun* and *Out of This Realm*. "Her antics are front-page news. She is dangerous and doesn't seem to care if she exposes us all to humankind. That cannot happen, no matter what the cost."

No one argued with that. No one could.

"And we're still one less warrior since Mathias killed Tynan," Bram pointed out.

"He's ready for burial," Sabelle said sadly. "I've contacted his younger brother, Asher. He should be here soon. He's asking questions about the Council and the Doomsday Brethren."

"I'll deal with him," Bram promised. "But as I've said, we're still a fighter short and—"

"Anka is *not* replacing him." Lucan had only meant to think the words, but they came out in a roar. Suddenly, he was inches from Bram's face, and Caden was holding him back with a tight grip.

"Down, brother." Caden jerked on his arm.

Inside, he was seething, ready to beat Bram to a bloody pulp. Instead, he stood and dragged in huge breaths, trying to get his temper under control.

"And you wonder why I think you're not quite ready to fight?" Bram raised a brow.

Lucan bristled. Damn it, he hated feeling this on edge, off balance. Ever since Anka... *No*. He shoved the thought away. She was gone. Blaming her for his lack of self-control was foolish.

Finally, he rocked back on his heels and unclenched his fists. Slowly, Caden let go.

Bram's expression softened. "I appreciate that this is hard for you. I love Anka like a sister, but I've spoken to her. She knows the risks. She's agreed to the conditions I've attached. If Marrok, her trainer, and I think she can't function as a fighter, she never makes it into battle."

Relief poured through Lucan, and he smiled wide. Leave it to Bram to find the loophole. Then his eyes narrowed. "Her trainer?"

Now it was Bram's turn to smile. "You."

At that, Lucan laughed. She'd never see a moment of combat. Even if Bram and Marrok didn't back him on this, he'd simply say Anka wasn't ready to fight, and she'd stay behind, tucked away safely from Mathias. Because he'd do anything to keep her from harm's way again.

"Perfect."

Bram shook his head. "You actually have to train her—hand to hand, martial arts, weaponry and the like—and you must do it thoroughly. Anka has fight in her. I think she's smart enough. She's agile. You could help her to be strong and prepared."

"Fuck no! I'll do it in name only. I'll put her through her paces, teach her to defend herself. All the women should know that, but there's no damn way—"

"This isn't your choice, Lucan. As I told Anka earlier when she protested my conditions, this isn't a democracy. You must prepare her for battle. We might genuinely need her."

In combat? He wanted to swear again. No, he wanted to throw something at Bram and hit him in his perfectly implacable face.

"Don't look at me like that. I'm giving you a choice: I can find another to work with her closely every…single…day. Or you can take advantage of this opportunity to spend time with her again and see what comes of it. Your choice. But frankly, I think you need it. You need her. I'm giving you what might be your last chance. I suggest you take it.

Chapter Two

Anka was shaking by the time she reached Shock's house. Not at the idea of training or fighting or sweaty, hard work. She relished those opportunities. But being so close to Lucan every day. She sighed. She'd have to tamp down her yearning, try to steer clear of him. With a magical war to fight and not one, but two, rapaciously evil villains trying to tear down humankind and enslave everyone magical, her personal desires simply weren't important. If she angered or distracted Lucan, he wouldn't be as focused on fighting—or protecting himself—as he must be. She had to keep everything inside. At least for now. Shock would drag it out of her eventually. Of that, she had no doubt.

As she wiped her tears away, Anka glanced through the little house she shared with Shock. It was empty. Not that she actually needed to look. The dead silence hanging over the place told her that instantly. When Shock was here, he filled the space with his big presence. The still air around her told her that, after leaving Bram's, Shock hadn't returned here.

Damn. She needed energy before she appeared for her first training session tomorrow. Marrok and Bram would be taskmasters, and she had to prove herself up for the challenge. But that wasn't all. The trembling, the nightmares, the fury roiling inside her… She needed the emotional release Shock could give her. At least when he chose to. When she begged prettily enough to suit him.

Sifting mentally through a list of his haunts, Anka finally settled on the most likely. She teleported to the alley behind The Witch's Brew, then emerged from between a dumpster and some wooden pallets. Once inside the cheery, dark-wood pub, she glanced around. Kari, Ronan's pretty mate, stood behind the bar, drying glasses. The human swung her long blonde hair behind her shoulder. She wore a checked shirt knotted above her pierced navel and a pair of low-rise jeans around her narrow hips. When she smiled, her blue eyes turned warm.

"Anka!" she greeted. "What brings you to the Brew? Can I get you something?"

"Hi, Kari." She looked around the pub with a frown. "Have you seen Shock today?"

She shook her head, waves of her pale hair brushing her bare waist. "Not yet, dear. But it's early for him. You can take a seat and wait, if you'd like."

She probably should just move on to search another of Shock's haunts, but sooner or later, he usually turned up here.

"Sure. Can I have a…" A request for white wine sat on the tip of her tongue. Warriors didn't sip chardonnay. But she didn't care for ale or bitter. "Vodka, the good kind. On the rocks."

Kari raised a brow. The barkeep knew very well what she usually drank. But bless her, she didn't say a word, just poured and handed her the glass. "How are you?"

She tossed the vodka back in two swallows—and barely managed not to choke. Strong stuff. She winced, and Kari smiled.

"Better." It wasn't a total lie. In some ways, she had improved. The physical wounds had healed, though she'd been left with some scars. She'd managed not to cringe or panic every time a man touched her even casually or she climbed into bed with Shock for energy. But she was still desperately unhappy and tired of feeling useless. Vulnerable. Of replaying each and every one of the times Mathias had raped her over and over in her head. She shoved her memories of pleading with the monster aside. "You?"

"Great." The woman frowned. "Don't take this badly, but you don't look better."

Anka smiled. "I will, starting tomorrow."

Kari sent her an inquisitive glance at that, but didn't press her. "More?"

With a glance at her empty glass, Anka shook her head. "Um… no. How about a bit of water? I'll need to find a table and stay sober while I wait for Shock."

In moments, Kari poured a fresh glass of water and whisked the vodka away. Anka took it gratefully and ambled to a table in a dark corner. Hopefully, no one else would notice her. Or care. But a pair of human men in denim, work shirts, and discarded hard hats were already eyeing her in a manner that made her tremble. She looked away, using her magic to put off an unwelcoming vibe.

As she sat with her back to the wall—another paranoid trick of Shock's she'd picked up—she nursed her water, wondering exactly how she was going to ask him for the sort of sex she needed. In his perverse way, the more she wanted it, the more he withheld it—until it suited his purposes.

This time, she had a weapon. She'd be unable to hide her purpose for visiting Bram for long, but Anka had no doubt Shock would be desperate to know by now. He hadn't been kidding when he'd told Lucan that he'd fuck it out of her. Sex his way meant that she went to a mental place where she let go of all her worries, fears, and inadequacies. Shock took them, along with every thought running through her head. In return, he gave her permission to seek release and comfort. Anka had no illusions; he hadn't liked what he'd found in her head recently. He was going to like today's developments even less.

The door opened, and with a steadying breath, she looked up. It wasn't Shock, but a lovely brunette. Tall, lithe, with silky straight hair, a short skirt that flirted with indecent, perky breasts nearly falling out of a brief white shirt that flashed a lot of tanned cleavage. Her red stilettos didn't say 'fuck me'; they shouted it. A surrogate.

Anka had seen the woman before, and her magical signature displayed not only her colors, but those of many others in a swirl more complicated than any prism.

Kari got the woman a drink, and they chatted a bit. Once the barmaid walked away, the surrogate stared at the door, clearly waiting for a client.

Sauntering Anka's way with a tentative expression, Kari wrung her hands. "It's about to get crowded in here. I'll text you if Shock shows up."

The usually polite blonde was throwing her out? "You're asking me to leave?"

"No, but I think you'll want to." Kari glanced the brunette's way.

"She's a surrogate."

"Right. Not a prostitute, which Ronan has to remind me constantly. It's so different for humans. I know surrogates provide sexual service, but since it's medicinal for magickind…"

"Exactly. One of her kind is keeping Bram alive. He's mated, but with his mate missing, he can't shag someone else, so she's helping him generate energy—"

"That isn't who she's here for tonight," Kari cut in quietly. "Really, you'll want to—damn, it's too late."

Anka frowned and looked at the door when it opened again. Lucan strolled through and made his way directly to the surrogate with a smile. Suddenly, Anka couldn't breathe, especially when Lucan dropped into the chair beside the woman and brushed a kiss across her lush, red mouth.

That one simple buss of his lips over the other woman's was a chainsaw to Anka's heart. Tears burned the backs of her eyes. Yes, she'd known Lucan would be using surrogates for energy now that they were no longer mated, but she never imagined having to *see* him with another. Did he feel even a tenth of this agony when he saw her with Shock?

"I tried," Kari said by way of apology.

She had. And Anka regretted that she'd been too preoccupied

to catch on quickly enough to save herself this heartache.

"I have to go." But she couldn't walk past Lucan now. He and the gorgeous surrogate currently rifling her fingers through his dark hair sat at the table right beside the door. There was no way she could leave without them seeing. "Help me."

Kari bit her lip. "He doesn't usually stay long when he meets one of them here."

Of course not. He led them from here, straight to his bed. Their bed. And the way his lips were trailing up the brunette's neck and he was whispering something into her ear that made her laugh, Anka had no doubt he was eager to get this woman naked and supine.

"You could just stay and wait," Kari suggested. "They'll be gone soon."

Anka shook her head. No, she couldn't watch another moment of this. "Is there another exit?"

God, that sounded cowardly. But right now, she'd rather run past Mathias than Lucan cozying up to his surrogate for the night.

Pity softened Kari's expression as she stood directly in front of Anka. "Yes. Stand up and round that corner to your right. Behind that is my office. There's a door out back from there. I'll stay right behind you."

"Thank you," Anka said gratefully, doing her best not to fall apart now.

Kari nodded softly. "Listen, I spent two years watching Ronan charm other women to his bed nearly every night before we mated. I understand quite well how you feel."

On wobbling legs, Anka rose. The barkeep's taller frame blocked her view of Lucan, and him of her, she presumed. She managed one quick peek at her former mate, whose lips hovered right over the surrogate's. He never noticed her. That chainsaw sliced through Anka's chest again, rending her heart in two.

Once in Kari's office, she sagged into the barkeep's desk chair. Tears stabbed at her eyes again. Alone now, she let them fall, but nothing was going to cleanse her brain after seeing Lucan's hands, lips, and smile directed at another woman. As hard as he trained and fought, she knew he needed new energy frequently. There were other ways to power up his magic, but none more effective than a rousing romp between the sheets. Without energy, he would wither, die. And unlike Bram, who was mated, Lucan didn't have to rely on mutual self-pleasure to power up. He could—and probably would—have sex with that woman any way he pleased.

She had to focus on her desire to see him alive and happy, not on the fact that, right now, he was probably sweeping his lips across the surrogate's, tongue sinking deep, dragging her nubile body—one that hadn't been ravaged and scarred—against his. He was likely readying her so he could sink into her bed and into her body.

Anka bit her lip to hold in another cry. She had to get out of here and go home.

Stumbling into the back alley, behind the dumpster again, she teleported with the thoughts of home resonating through her brain. But it wasn't the little house she'd shared with Shock these past months that came into view.

Anka found herself directly in front of the house she'd shared for over one hundred years with Lucan.

Home.

The familiar warmth of its brown walls made her pine for the days and nights she spent here. Lovingly, her gaze traced the stately roof, the arched windows, and the long lawn, surrounded by the gardens she used to love keeping. In January, most everything lay dormant. Surprisingly, nothing looked neglected or overgrown. Even the same little wooden picket fence stood guard at the front of the yard. Downstairs was the same cozy sofa she'd loved curling up on for a good read. Through the upstairs window, she could see the same dark wood bed that she and Lucan had slept on and made love in for decades. The same bed in which she'd drifted off and...

Anka stumbled back, shaking. She hadn't been here since the terrible night Matthias had ripped her from the coziness of the almost perfect life she'd shared with Lucan. Mathias had abducted her, thrown her in his dungeon, and used her for his perverse pleasure for five hellish days that she could barely think of now without retching. He'd torn her from her mate. He'd robbed her of her sense of safety, self, of her shelter from the cruelties of the world. He'd left her a brittle shell.

But she couldn't look at this beautiful house without the other memories crashing in. Lucan leading her inside for the first time, smiling nervously, wondering if she'd like it as much as he did. Lucan serving her breakfast in bed wearing nothing more than a grin. Lucan across the table as they shared roast beef and Yorkshire pudding while he listened to her talk about her day. Lucan reaching for her in the dead of night because he couldn't wait another second to touch her.

Gone. All of that…just gone.

"Anka?"

Her head snapped around to one side as a figure emerged from the back garden. Her heart stopped, and she felt frozen. "Caden."

"Anka, you're home. You look pale. Is something wrong?" her former brother-by-mating asked, coming closer. "Why don't you come in?"

Horror and longing washed over her at once. A part of her would have loved to be inside the space she'd once shared with Lucan to soak in the memories of him. And what would Lucan say if he found her inside, especially if he brought his surrogate here for the night?

She shook her head furiously. "No. Thank you."

"It will always be your home, too. Sydney and I can go…"

"Stay." The word fell numbly from her lips.

Lucan needed his brother. Sabelle had told her about his mate mourning and the stabilizing influence Caden had been after Lucan almost lost his soul and sanity. Anka hated that she'd been the cause of so much of her former mate's pain. She hated even more that she'd added to it by being with Shock.

But now, it was too late.

"Come in and let Sydney make you some tea," Caden insisted. "You really do look pale."

"I-I'll be fine. Thank you. I'm sorry. I didn't mean to intrude…

" She felt the magic surrounding the house. Lucan hadn't blocked her from going inside. Caden had added his magic, also recognizing her as mistress here. Why? They couldn't possibly want her here now.

She backed away. "Please don't tell him I was here. He's healing finally. Moving on."

"Anka, don't go." Caden's face hardened. "Lucan isn't over you. He never will be."

The man she'd seen smiling at the pub? He looked more than a bit happy. She couldn't disrupt that. His anger earlier that day? Well, Shock had always brought out his worst. Besides, what did she have to offer him now? Scars, secrets, nightmares, a whole new need he wouldn't be able to comprehend. He'd been fond of the china doll he'd married. Perfectly feminine, always sweet, playing just the right role in his life. Genteel and mannered, never raising her voice. Never angry. She couldn't be that girl anymore.

The woman in her knew better now.

"I have to go. This was a mistake. I'm sorry." Anka swallowed and darted outside the little picket fence surrounding the yard, ready to teleport to Shock's.

As she dipped into the shadows under a huge elm tree, Lucan and his surrogate suddenly appeared on the front steps, his arm slung around her small waist, hand curled around the woman's hip. Anka couldn't breathe again. God, that sight hurt so badly, like everything inside of her was bleeding out. She wrapped her arms around herself to stop the hemorrhaging, but nothing could curb the steady flow of anguish.

Caden flicked a glance over his brother's shoulder at her, then whispered in Lucan's ear. Quickly, Lucan spun around. For an electric moment, their eyes met. Then he shoved away from the brunette, running down the stairs toward Anka.

Why? Probably because she'd ruined his evening. Even if he thought he wanted her back, she could never again be what he needed. He was better off with the lovely surrogate. And maybe… someday he'd find love again. It hurt deeply to think of him content and mated to another. But she would always love him. She wanted his happiness above all else.

As he made his way through the little gate and headed for the tree under which she'd taken shelter, she wrenched her gaze from his and teleported back to Shock's house.

Anka held in a sob as she stumbled inside. She couldn't keep torturing herself with thoughts of how Lucan would spend his night. How he probably spent most nights. She had to move past the heartache, let him live in peace so she could be the woman who rose from the ashes of her own tragedy to fight for what she wanted more than anything—Mathias's destruction.

To start that, she had to find Shock.

Now inside the little house, she felt his presence immediately. She prowled down the pokey hallway, to the bedroom they shared. The mattress squatting on the floor took up most of the room, white rumpled sheets contrasting with the dark hardwood floors. He stood just outside the wardrobe, leather jacket in hand, which told her he'd been here mere seconds. He wore no shirt, leaving every bulge and ridge of his heavily-muscled torso on display. He took up all the space and air in the room.

When Shock caught sight of her, he flipped off his sunglasses and tossed them on a little bedside table and pinned her with a probing stare. As she did whenever she saw his unusual eyes, she steeled herself.

He marched across the room. "I know you left Bram's over an hour ago. Where the fuck have you been?"

Anka didn't answer. He'd discover for himself. When he was sober and wanted to know, she had zero means of hiding from him. His psychic abilities were stronger than any she'd ever encountered.

Shock gripped her arm. Barely a moment later, thunder overtook his face. He snatched his grip back with a hiss and shook his head. "You saw that wanker kissing another woman and still went to his house? Are you trying to torture yourself?"

He yanked her against his body, plastering her against the searing heat of his chest. Instinctively, Anka grabbed onto him, her fingers at his lean waist, brushing the ridges of his abdomen.

"I-I didn't mean…" *To go there*. But Shock wouldn't care.

"To chase that prick to his house? That barmy fuck who couldn't save you from Mathias? The one who didn't fight to bring you back to the home you'd known for over a century? Anka…" He fisted her curls gently in his hands and eased her head back until she looked into his eyes. "You know you can't be what he wants anymore. You are no longer that woman."

God, she knew. Did he have to throw it in her face?

"If that's what it takes to bring you some peace with your life now, yes. I accept you as you are. I won't make you pretend to be someone you're not. What would the high and mighty Lucan MacTavish do with you now? Dress you again in fine silks for his pointless Privileged parties, then take you home for polite sex?"

She wanted to push Shock's words back at him. But too much of what he'd said was true.

"What then? Will he look the other way when Mathias knocks on your door again?" He thrust his fingers deeper into her hair and clung. "You can't let Lucan hurt you again, little one."

She hadn't grown up Deprived, the lower rank of magickind's society, as Shock had. She had grown up a member of the supposed Privileged class, but she hung onto that classification by her fingernails. Her family had lost all connections, power, and influence in the past few centuries. No member of their family had ever been influential enough to sit on the magical Council. Regardless, her parents hadn't approved of her childhood friendship with the elder Denzell boy, Shock. But that had been okay. They understood one another after she'd discovered his secret. To gain his trust and make him feel safe, she'd told him hers. They'd been nearly inseparable for decades, and she hadn't been surprised when he Called to her.

Then Lucan MacTavish had looked her way, pinning her with his hot blue gaze that had seared all the way down to her soul. In that moment, the air had stopped. Her heart stuttered. He was the most beautiful man she'd ever met. And *he*, the nephew of a

Council member, wanted her. A man so privileged, the scent of it oozed from his pores. With his deep voice and wry smile, he'd quickly charmed her out of a kiss.

She'd fallen in love the second his lips hungrily covered hers.

"Oh, stop mooning," Shock grumbled. "Or get to the part of your memories where the fucker leaves you alone in your house without special protection so Mathias can abduct and violate you. Get to the part where he loses his fucking mind instead of coming to your rescue. Where, when he finally sees you, he lets you go with barely a token protest, then brings a surrogate to the bed you once shared."

Anka shoved her face in her hands, wishing she could block out his words. "Shut up!"

"Fuck no. I'm not going to watch you turn yourself inside out for the prat who tried to mold you into his ideal woman, then didn't bother to be your hero when you needed him."

Anka wanted to refute him, but nothing Shock said was wrong…at least not totally. After she and Lucan had mated, she'd taken his cue on everything. How to dress, how to behave, how to socialize. She'd done everything to be the sort of mate who made him proud. She'd never wanted him to regret her less-than-perfect bloodline. One year had slipped into decades, then into a century. She barely remembered what it was like to live a life where she wasn't striving to please Lucan.

Then Mathias had taken her. Afterward, she'd felt so stricken, so dirty and guilty and tainted, she'd barely been able to face her former mate, but she'd forced herself to do it so she could perform the *helbresele* spell and heal his mate mourning. Once done, the ease with which he'd let her walk away…she had to wonder if he was secretly relieved to be rid of the barely Privileged woman he'd shared his home and life with.

"Of course he is," Shock cut in. "For fuck's sake, if I'd been in Lucan's position, I would have burned down the world until I found you. I would have killed anyone stupid enough to stand in my way."

That wasn't idle talk from Shock. He would burn down the

world for anything he believed was important, and over the last few months he'd proven over and over that he would do whatever necessary to protect and care for her.

"That's right." He wrapped his arms around her more tightly. "And what did Lucan do?"

According to Sabelle, he lost his mind.

None of it was important now. She couldn't keep glancing over her shoulder and eyeing her past. She had to look ahead.

"That's not what I want to talk about, Shock."

He peered at her with those unusual eyes, dissecting, digging into her thoughts. Anka let him. There'd be no keeping him out anyway.

"Oh, fuck no! You are *not* fighting Mathias."

She'd known that would be his reaction. "I don't need your permission. You're not my mate."

It was a low blow, and she regretted the words as soon as she spoke them. Face tight with anger, he grabbed her. Then her remorse seeped into him. His face softened. "A few words will fix that, Anka. Speak the Binding to me. I've waited over a century for you."

Anka closed her eyes as guilt slid through her. "I'm not ready to belong to anyone now, and I won't give you the power to stop me from fighting. I *need* this. Please understand."

Shock swore and pushed away. "Then why the fuck are you here?"

She hesitated, almost hating to say it. Her request sounded so selfish, but she couldn't afford to hold back. "I want you…in that way." She nodded to the restraints sticking up from all corners of the bed, waiting for her wrists and ankles. For that crop he'd tucked under the mattress. "Please."

"Why?" he challenged.

Anka knew his expectation. If she wanted him to force her to accept pleasure without the crushing guilt, then she had to play his game. Quickly, she stripped off her skirt, blouse, knickers, and bra. She left on her thigh highs and shoes, then dropped to her knees, staring at him with big, pleading eyes, tears pooling in them. "I need you."

"Fuck," he swore almost under his breath. But his fingers slid into her hair, grabbing a fistful at the crown and tugging, forcing her gaze to remain on him. "You're bottled up, aren't you?"

"Yes." The word trembled from her lips. "I'm on my knees. I'm begging."

He stared down at her, and she trembled with the jumble of anticipation, sadness, shame, and anger all roiling inside her. No doubt, he could feel every one of her emotions. So many were attached to Lucan, and she pushed thoughts of him aside. Tonight had nothing to do with him. He had his surrogate now. She needed this for her, to unravel her feelings, to scrub herself raw of the disgrace. For the energy.

"That's right. He has nothing to do with this, Anka. It's fucking rubbish, me shoving my cock inside you, pounding at you, yet hearing your thoughts revolve around how much you miss that wanker and how guilty you feel for fucking me. Not tonight. One thought of him, and it all stops. Are we clear?"

"Yes, Shock," she said softly, squirming with need.

He paused, sending her a long, considering glance, making her wait.

Finally, he nodded. "Hold still. You move when I tell you to move. Not before."

Relief poured through her. "Yes, Shock."

Her voice had softened again, dropped and turned husky. He responded immediately, his cock growing in his leathers.

He bent to cup her face in his big hands. "Are you sure?"

God, the softness of his voice pried under her brittle surface and began worming its way into her head. She could take his anger all day long, but his kindness killed. She knew well that she couldn't be the mate he wanted. Not to him, and not to— She didn't dare finish that thought. She didn't even deserve Shock's help. But she needed it.

Anka barely held in a sob. "Yes, Shock."

He sent her a sharp nod. "On the bed. On your back. Spread

your arms and legs."

She hurried to comply, her heart racing and lifting, knowing that by the time he finished, she would feel a bit lighter. The bed felt firm at her back, sheets soft as she breathed hard.

Shock nodded his approval, then dropped his leathers, revealing strong thighs and calves, bunched with muscles, big feet, long toes. "Look at me."

Anka's gaze traveled up his body, pausing over his heavy testicles and thick cock standing hard, tall, impatient. His flat, strong abs moved with every breath. The bulges of his pectorals, shoulders, and arms all screamed out his power. His relentless gaze penetrated her. Her nipples beaded. An ache settled behind her clit. Knowing exactly how he affected her, Shock sent her a chilly smile.

Dropping between her spread legs, he grabbed her waist and flipped her over to her stomach, then secured her ankles and wrists with the nylon restraints. The fastenings were simple Velcro. She could escape if she truly wished to…but that was the last thing she wanted.

She looked over her shoulder at him with pleading eyes, her whole body trembling. His face tightened, and he moved his hand over the corners of the bed, sealing her restraints with his formidable magic.

Now there was no escape.

Shock covered her body with his, every hard angle crushing her soft curves. She cushioned him, arching to him as he settled between her thighs. He growled in her ear. "You take what I give you. You come when I tell you."

Her breathing hitched. "Yes, Shock."

He rose up on his hands and knees, hovering over her, his breath hot across her neck. He reached for the crop. Anka barely had time to steel herself before she felt the sting of the crop's stiff leather across the cheek of her bum. She cried out.

"You can do better than that," Shock admonished.

"So can you," she tossed back at him.

"Itching for a sore arse, little one?"

She didn't get a second to answer before he thwacked her again, this time across the other cheek, then across each thigh, up her back, across her shoulders, then down again, dangerously close to her moistening folds. She sucked in a breath, trying to assimilate the pain covering her skin quickly, like a blanket. Shock gave it to her hard and fast, and she'd probably be gently bruised tomorrow. The thought gave her an odd sense of peace she still didn't understand.

It didn't take long before her thoughts were spiraling and spinning. The pain overcame her defenses, and her fragile shell splintered. Her body began shuddering. The dry sobs came, but no tears fell. Shock knew better than to let up. He merely slowed.

"Give me more. Let it out," he growled in her ear. It was nothing less than a command.

The sweet permission flowed through her brain and her body. And there was no way to keep the pain in any longer. Tears poured out in big, heaving sobs, scalding her cheeks, soaking the sheet beneath her.

Shock threw down the crop and rubbed his rough hand across the flaming cheeks of her backside, both soothing and deepening the heat, further unraveling her. The tenderness in that touch hurt almost as much as the crop.

"Shock..."

With a whispered curse, he blanketed her body with his own, trapping the heat searing over her skin between them. His lips swept across her neck as he wedged a hand under her body until his fingers found her sex and settled over her needy clit. She was so wet it almost embarrassed her.

Why did she need release this way now? Whatever Mathias had done to her had rewired her brain, forced her to only accept pleasure when commanded. She'd always been good at bottling up her feelings, but now pain and growled demands not only gave her pleasure, but released everything pent up inside her. She hated it, hated Mathias. Hated that she was powerless to stop this need. *What would Luc—* Anka didn't finish that thought.

"Shh. Focus on me, Anka. Take me now," Shock demanded as

he used his huge thighs to spread hers wider, then slid his cock home in one powerful surge.

His size always made her catch her breath, and he gave her very little opportunity to adjust. Her body bowed. She gripped the restraints with a cry. His fingers across her needy bundle of nerves and his lips brushing her skin slowly relaxed her. Finally, Shock worked completely inside her body and began a slow, ruthless pace that nudged her up the mattress more with each thrust. He'd occasionally bring her back down with a savage grip on her hips, fitting her against him until there wasn't a breath between them. The restraints scraped her wrists. The sheet chafed her nipples. Shock's goatee abraded her shoulder. And it all put her on the razor's edge of ecstasy.

His teeth dragged over the spot between her neck and shoulders. "You make me hungry."

He was going to send her beyond insanity. When he took her this way, the pleasure was always so intense, she screamed her throat raw, then blacked out for long minutes. The loss of control was complete, and it almost terrified her. But Shock had seen to so many of her needs, even spending long hours with her in the beginning to learn what she responded to, what would make her let go of all the rage, pain, and desire trapped inside her. She owed him her all.

"Do you want me?"

"Always," she promised.

"I'll hold you to it." Then he bit down.

And Anka shattered with a sharp, keening scream that carried through the entire house and echoed back. Pleasure bulldozed her, bringing every corner of her body to tingling life with a rich swirl of pleasure that made her dizzy and sent her soaring. Behind her, Shock sucked at her neck and pumped into her harder until he cursed, groaned, then emptied inside her. She flew, floated, to a place with no pain, no regret, no feeling…just blessed silence. And dark. She closed her eyes.

When she came to, he'd withdrawn from the bed and dressed,

shoved his sunglasses in place, and now prowled the room, a bottle of Scotch in hand.

"All right, little one?"

She stretched, sighed, stared at Shock. The usual guilt thwacked her in the stomach. The emotion was useless and would only brass him off, so she stifled it and rose. "Of course. Thank you."

A sudden pounding on the wall had her jumping. His glower filled her vision. "I don't want your fucking gratitude."

He'd never asked for it, would never say it out loud, but he wanted the one thing she could never give him. Her heart. It hadn't been hers in a century.

"That's shit, Anka. You never tried." He grabbed her by the arms, gripping so tightly, she gasped.

"Don't do this. We've been over and over this. It serves no purpose."

"What more do you fucking need from me?"

He rarely discussed anything in such straightforward terms. That he was now made her pause. Guilt crashed through her. "Nothing. You've done everything I could ever want and more."

Shock scowled under his shades, his dark brows a *V* that disappeared under the black plastic. "Except be that pussy Lucan."

That was the Shock she knew. The one who lashed out when he felt threatened, worried, or afraid.

"Boo fucking hoo. Cry me a river," he sneered. "I'm not afraid."

Anka let the remark pass without calling him a liar. It was enough that he flinched as she thought it. His status quo was changing, and he didn't like it. She understood.

"Glad to hear it." She smiled. "Starting tomorrow, I'll be spending my days training to fight Mathias. I appreciate everything you've done for me, Shock. Truly. But I need to do this."

His stance changed, his stare dissecting her. "I can teach you more than those wankers."

"Maybe, but it's rubbish. You won't. You can't protect me forever."

Shock certainly looked like he wanted to try. He crossed his leather-clad arms over his massive chest. "Lucan can't protect you at all. You better avoid him while you're learning to fight. Or he will crawl inside your head and take a shit again, Anka."

She closed her eyes, trying to empty her head. But he was right. Lucan didn't understand. He never would. "I doubt I'll see him that much. Marrok will probably instruct me on human fighting, and I'm sure Bram will work with me to improve my magic skills. I doubt I'll see Lucan at all."

"Good." Steel rang in his voice. "If the fucker touches you, I will kill him."

Chapter Three

Dressed in faded jeans that had somehow gotten too big over the last few months and a long-sleeved cotton shirt that allowed for free movement, Anka walked into what had once been the ballroom on Bram's recently rebuilt estate. In this iteration of the mansion, he hadn't bothered to make it posh or elegant. The wood floors and the mirrors covering one whole wall existed purely for training purposes, and weapons lined the other walls. Punching bags hung from the ceiling. Windows overlooked the shooting range and archery target. There wasn't a stick of furniture anywhere in the room.

She tiptoed into the quiet, taking everything in. After appearing at dawn as instructed, Bram had sent her to the ballroom and told her to wait. Pacing, she fidgeted, and each minute that ticked by chafed. She'd been waiting for weeks. Months. Revenge was a red haze in her head. The next drink she craved. The drug she needed to keep living. She had no patience for waiting.

But like everything since the night she'd been ripped from her former life, she didn't have a choice.

Gnawing delicately on her lower lip, she fingered the handle of a wicked-looking knife hanging on the wall, ran her palm down the length of the bright red punching bag hanging nearby, recoiled at the sight of a very menacing gun gleaming in a rack full of weapons.

God, was she in over her head? The room reeked of sweat and testosterone. They practiced violence here every day of their lives. She'd never killed anything, not even an insect. But she'd make an exception for Mathias. That meant starting here and learning every one of these weapons proficiently. No matter how much it terrified her, how much it wrung from her body or heart—even if it cost her very life—she would take that bastard down.

Suddenly, she felt heat at her back. An arm wrapped around her neck and dragged her against a hard body. The man's other arm hooked around her waist with a growl. Panic descended and she screamed, fighting and thrashing with her body. But her attacker's height, weight, and strength was superior, his hold unyielding.

Anka tried to teleport away, but something blocked her magic. When it didn't work, she bent her head, bit him, dug her nails into his forearm. Shoved, pushed, screamed. Nothing. He didn't budge or move even a fraction of an inch…except to press a growing erection into the small of her back.

The feel of his silent demand made her freeze. A sob caught in her throat. "Don't. No! Please."

Instantly, he released his grip on her and stepped back. Breaths heaving, heart pounding in a frightening rhythm, adrenaline flushed through her system as she whirled and backed away, wide-eyed.

"Lucan?" She pressed a hand to her chest, stunned.

He merely nodded at her. "I see we'll be starting at square one."

"What are you talking about? What the devil are you doing here?" She frowned. "We're not starting anything. Where's Marrok?"

He shrugged, his black T-shirt clinging to his lean frame and broad shoulders, outlining every ripple of his pectorals and abdomen. Her mouth went dry. He'd always looked fit and masculine when they'd been mated. Now he looked so incredibly male. Virile, formidable. Like the warrior he'd become.

"With Caden, presumably whipping Duke's arse back into

shape. A few days away with the humans to try to contain the Morganna situation and…" He shook his head with faint regret. "No one here gets a break for any reason. That should probably be your first lesson."

She wrapped her arms around herself, thoughts flying. It wasn't as if she'd asked for a break; she'd begged to be here. But Anka refused to start an argument with Lucan, even if he seemed to want it. "Lesson? I'm waiting for Marrok or Bram, so we can start my training. I certainly wasn't expecting you to sneak up on me and attack. Don't do that again!"

A grim smile lifted his mouth—one she'd seen curl up in joy, turn down in sadness, open to her with passion before he seized her lips in a tender kiss. This caustic expression was one she'd rarely found him wearing. "You'll be waiting forever on them. I'm it, love. I'm your trainer. Over the next weeks and months, I'll come at you at any way I damn well wish to make you learn, and you don't get to tell me no." He raised a sharp brow. "Still want to be here?"

Anger pricked her, followed by horror. What the devil was going on? Anka shoved her confusion aside and focused instead on quelling the hurt that Lucan didn't seem excited about being here with her. "*You're* my trainer?"

Lucan simply smiled. The expression wasn't nice.

The ground fell out beneath her. "But Bram said—"

"What you wanted to hear. I drew the short stick. If you're determined to fight Mathias, I'm the one who's going to teach you how. Unless you'd like to quit."

His tone told her that he'd ten times rather she gave up. That's what the old her would have done, whatever he wanted her to do. Now? She crossed her arms over her chest and glared at him, one brow raised.

"Bram has a sick sense of humor."

"I won't argue with that," Lucan quipped.

"I'm not quitting."

Impatience crossed his familiar, dear face. Being this close to him filled her with a longing that almost made her knees give way beneath her. Anka drew in a deep breath. This weakness wouldn't help her fight Mathias. She had to focus.

"Pity, but as you pointed out earlier, it's your choice. That's your only choice, though. Everything else is my call. Remember that. Do as I say or quit. Are we clear?"

"You're being a bastard." And somehow his hard attitude was arousing.

"Is that a yes or a no?"

She gritted her teeth. He'd always had a frustrating stubborn streak. Apparently, it had grown during their parting.

"Yes," she hissed.

Lucan smiled smugly, and she fought to stifle her anger. He wanted her to get mad, goad her into losing her temper, so he'd have a valid reason to refuse to train her. Figuratively speaking, he'd shoved her to her knees and forced her to heel. It annoyed the piss out of her.

She shifted her weight from one foot to the other, painfully aware of the fact that his commanding attitude also made her wet.

Damn it.

"Good to hear. The next thing we're going to talk about is your attire. It won't do."

Anka looked down at herself, then at his jog pants and trainers. "What's wrong with what I'm wearing, then?"

"It's too baggy. It will inhibit your movement. It will give anyone wanting to attack you something to grab onto. It doesn't allow me to see your technique as I teach you. I can't feel where you're putting your punches and kicks."

"*Feel*?" The stunned question slipped out. "I've asked you not to touch me."

"Sorry, love." A satisfied smile slipped across his face. "Remember, training my way." He shrugged and gestured to the far side of the room. "Or there's the door."

"You're going to throw that in my face again?" She blinked at him. Where had the patient man and tender lover she'd known for a century gone? In his place stood a man who challenged, pushed, and baited. Both controlled and controlling. Anka shifted her weight again. No way could she lie. She was wetter than the last time she'd moved.

She closed her eyes.

"Every chance I get," he assured. "You can only be here if you're truly committed. I'll test you hard and often. Still with me?"

"Yes." How many times was he going to ask her? "Yes. Yes! Yes! Damn it, yes!"

He quirked a brow. "Good. Get angry. You're going to need it."

Anka could feel her temper bubbling up inside her. She'd never gotten really, truly angry around Lucan. A well-bred, Privileged mate wouldn't. So she'd always swallowed any rising ire and deferred to him. That she didn't have to now was both terrifying and freeing. But she was done taking the path of least resistance. If anger would help her train better, she'd let it out.

"I'll come dressed more appropriately tomorrow. Now stop being a horse's arse and show me what to do."

Lucan drew in a deep breath, watching her with those blue eyes that never failed to lure her in and make her ache to be close to him. He shrugged and sidled up to her. "I want to start with self-defense. I don't know if it would have saved you the night the Anarki came to our door, but it couldn't have hurt." He stared into her eyes, all sincerity and sadness. "I've wished a thousand times since that day that I'd shown you how to defend yourself. I never thought you'd need it in our own home. For that, I'm deeply sorry."

His speech caught her off guard, and so soon after Shock had popped the cork off her emotions, she was having a hard time bottling them back up. The sting of forming tears assaulted her eyes, and she blinked them away. "I don't know if it would have helped, but that sounds worth learning."

He sent her a nod, then prowled closer, circling behind her. She tensed.

"It's just me," he whispered as he hooked his arm around her neck and dragged her against his body again. His wide shoulders cradled her, hard chest and abdomen supporting her. His hard cock nestled at the small of her back. Almost as soon as she felt it, he eased the lower half of his body away. She ached, knowing that he was every bit as aroused by this close-quarters touching as she was. But their relationship was over, the chasm so wide between them that nothing would fix it. Sex would satisfy her deep longing to touch and soothe him—and it would be the biggest mistake of her life.

Bracing his other hand at her hip, he held the lower half of her body just slightly away from his, but he bent his head right to her ear and murmured, "I've come up behind you with the intent to attack you. What's your first instinct? Do it now."

His low voice in her ear, demanding of her, made her shiver. She *really* shouldn't respond to it or him. Then his words sank in. First instinct?

For a moment, she froze. Then his grip tightened, and actual panic started to creep in as her fight or flight instinct took over. She tried desperately to thrash and shove his arm away, anything to get free from his unyielding hold. Lucan wasn't budging. She tried to push harder, getting her whole body into the struggle, jostling against him, kicking back with her feet, moving her entire torso so she'd be harder to hold onto.

Lucan wrapped his arm around her neck tighter, then moved the hand at her hip across her waist, yanking her right against him, trapping her arm against her body. Then he hooked one calf around her legs and hauled her up on her tiptoes. She had one arm free to fight back, but though she shoved, yelled, and thrashed, Lucan's hold on her was absolute. Her frantic movements slowed. Each of her blows was harder, more calculated, but nothing she did had any effect on his grip. He squeezed her against him and began dragging her away.

Panicked, Anka tried to drag her feet. "No…" Tears stabbed at her eyes. "No, Lucan, don't! Please…"

Immediately, he released her and turned her toward him, cradling her face. "Look at me. Just me." Slowly, she focused her wild gaze, and he stared back, face heavy with concern. "I don't think you're ready for this, Anka. You haven't worked through everything that's happened to you."

"Consider this my therapy." She sniffled, determined to hold her tears back.

"Training isn't the place to work out your inner demons. You need a clear head and a single purpose. Every time I come up behind you, you're panicking, love." He closed his eyes, regret carving itself deeper into his expression. "I wasn't there that terrible night. For that, I will always be sorrier than you'll ever know. I don't know the details of your attack, but I can guess that Mathias grabbed you from behind. I'm not doing anything to intentionally frighten you. It's all right if you're not able to fight or face this kind of violence. There's nothing wrong with leaving the fight to the other wizards and me."

His words washed over her, gentle, almost pitying. Shame filled her. And anger. Lucan didn't understand. She couldn't outrun herself anymore. She'd tried. There was no peace in being a bystander, especially not in her own life. As frightening as this was, doing nothing terrified her far more. "I'm not giving up. I'm not quitting. And no, you weren't there, but it's not relevant. Mathias needs to be brought down, and I'm going to help. Tell me what I should have done and we'll try again."

"All right." Lucan cocked his head and stared. Clearly, her answer surprised him. A little smile played over his mouth.

She knew that look; he was up to something. She narrowed her eyes at him. "Is your goal to train me or try to figure out how to make me quit? Seems you're doing a lot more of the latter than the former."

He shrugged with a guilty smirk. "I confess. That was my first plan. I don't think you belong shoulder to shoulder with a group of men fighting to the death."

Anka stepped closer, shoving her face right under his. "I'm not the china doll you married. I've already been broken. There's very little that can hurt me now. I'll get better. I'll adjust. I'll earn the right to fight."

Regret overtook his face again, this time with confusion. "Anka, you were a lovely, beautiful mate to me, not a china doll. You—"

"Did everything the way you asked of me. Dressed, spoke, walked, socialized. Even fucked. You'd be surprised if you knew the real me."

He reared back. "The witch I knew never would have used that language. Further proof of Shock's bad influence."

"It's not as if he taught me the word, Lucan. I never said it because I didn't want to displease you. Just like I never wore pants or fixed my hair in any style except loose curls down my back. Now I'm doing things that feel right to me." She shook her head. This anger directed at him was neither his fault nor well timed. "Forget it. I'm here to learn, not discuss ancient history. Tell me what I need to know, then attack me from behind again."

For a long moment, Lucan studied her like he wasn't entirely sure what to make of her outburst or the information she'd given him. Anka wondered furiously if he'd ever had any idea how much of her true self she'd repressed to please him. But that didn't matter, did it? She'd come here to be worthy of this fight. Everything else was shit.

"All right. I won't argue, for now." Silently prowling forward, he grabbed her arm and spun her, bracing his palm at her elbow. "If I sneak up behind you, your best weapon will be here." He patted the pointed bend in her arm. "Try to work it past my defenses and jam it into my abdomen as hard as you can. If you're not getting the opening you want, don't forget that, for women especially, legs contain some of your strongest muscles."

"I could try to kick someone in the…balls who's behind me?"

At her stumble over the word, he quirked a smile, then shook his head. "No. You'll reach fuck all in that position and put your attacker on guard. His foot, love." He gently whirled her in front and slightly to his side, leaning around her so that she could see his face. He demonstrated what he wanted with one foot, raising it and stomping it down on the ballroom floor with shaking force. "If someone's foot had been under mine, that would have hurt like hell, yes?"

"Absolutely." She blinked at him, only now aware that his body cradled hers, and his arm curled around her waist, fingers caressing her upper arm.

The heat of his touch seeped into her, warming places that had been so dark and cold inside her for months. As he stepped up behind her, his palm brushed up her arm. He hugged her against him again, settling his chin on her shoulder. She heard his exhalation, rougher than normal, in her ear. His other arm wrapped around her waist again, and he held her tenderly, as if the past few months had never happened. She closed her eyes, her breath trapped in her chest, wondering if she'd feel his lips on her neck and his suggestive murmur against her skin the way she had for a century. Her entire body ached with the thought of Lucan holding her again. But he'd bloody moved on. His appearance with the surrogate yesterday was painful proof of that. Everything that had passed between her and Shock yesterday only underscored the fact that she wasn't living that old life anymore.

Problem was, Anka still wasn't completely clear how to live this life.

She stiffened in his hold. "Are you ready?"

He sighed in frustration. "Anka, truly. You don't have to—"

"Are you ready?" she demanded, her voice lower and more purposeful.

"Ready."

Impatience laced his voice, but she shoved it aside and kept on. "Attack me."

Behind her, after a split second of hesitation, he tightened both arms and moved to wrap his legs in hers. Once he did that she'd lose a big advantage. She had to act now.

Curling her hand into a fist, she braced it with her other hand and used the force of both arms to drive her elbow into his stomach. His grunt accompanied his whoosh of air, and his hold on her eased. Using the opportunity, she raised her foot, glanced down at the placement of his black boots, then stomped down on his toes as hard as she could.

He howled and hopped away immediately, clutching his foot. “Bloody hell!”

Anka winced. She hadn’t meant to actually hurt him, just to see if she could perform the maneuver. Still hopping on one foot, he looked up and shot her a sharp glower that dared her to apologize and hinted it wouldn’t go well for her.

She stifled a smile. “I did that right, then?”

Lucan let go of his foot and limped her way again. “You did. We’ll go again. Stand with your back to me.”

She did, shoulders tense, breath shallow. Her senses felt heightened, her nerves dancing with electricity as anticipation slid through her. Long seconds passed without incident. She couldn’t hear Lucan, merely feel him in the room, watching, thinking.

Having his eyes on her was doing something to her composure. Had he noticed the changes in her? What would he think if he saw her scars? She frowned, shoving the thought away. He’d be every bit as horrified as she was, no doubt. Lucan liked beauty, perfection. He prized feminine loveliness, perfectly dressed and perfectly docile. All the things she couldn’t be anymore, so standing here anticipating the feel of his hands on her again, even as a training exercise was—

Lucan grabbed her from behind suddenly, his arms encircling her fast as lightning, clamping her against him like steel bands. She cursed herself for drifting away mentally.

Her first instinct, to struggle, kicked in. She tried to breathe, to remember this was Lucan, not Mathias, not a member of the Anarki. He wouldn’t actually hurt her. But panic bled into her thoughts and started crowding out all else. She thrashed and screamed. He only held her tighter and started crossing that leg over hers to trap her entirely.

“Think,” he growled in her ear.

The lessons of the morning whipped through her head and, almost without conscious thought, she rammed her elbow into his stomach. His grunt of pain filled her with grim satisfaction. She kicked away the leg about to wrap around hers, which put him off balance. Before he could compensate, she lifted her knee, then stomped down toward his foot. He dodged her, and she cursed. He tightened his arms again to make his hold unyielding.

"C'mon, Anka. Fight me."

What the hell did he think she was doing? Anger surged, burning through her veins. If he wanted a bloody hellion, he was going to get one. She twisted her body from left to right, driving her other elbow into his ribs.

"Fuck," he growled, backing away.

She took the opportunity to shadow him back, waiting until he planted his foot, then smashed it with her own. He growled at her, then shook his pained foot, his sides heaving. Was he trying to get his anger under control?

He turned and shot her a killing glare. She'd seen him truly angry so few times in their mated life. But her recollection was that he looked much like this. His nostrils flared, and he righted himself to his full height, towering over her.

"Good," he barked. "Now let's talk about a frontal attack. If someone is coming toward you, get your knees and hands ready."

"To kick and punch them?"

"Not exactly. I'll teach you to punch eventually, but until you get good at it, you're going to be easily blocked, and you're not likely to get enough power behind the blow to stop anyone. You'll only hurt the hell out of your knuckles. And if you're not careful, you'll break one of your fingers or your thumb. Raiden did it with the first punch he threw."

She couldn't help but smile. "Did Ronan laugh at him?"

"His twin brother gave him one long ribbing. We had to call Conrad, the healer, and try to explain. He doesn't quite understand, of course. Always wants to know why we're simply not using our magic. You know the answer to that, don't you?"

"I remember you saying that Mathias had some human Anarki, that he'd ripped out their souls and used them as soldiers. Magic doesn't work on them?"

Lucan nodded. "They're like zombies. Terrible creatures with rotting flesh and the body temperature of an ice cube. They're impervious to magic. Don't waste your energy hitting their rotting flesh with a spell. You'll have to fight human and nasty with these creatures. First thing you can do is to take the heel of your palm," he said, tapping the pad of flesh, "and drive it into the creature's nose. Shove hard. You'll only get that chance once. Then they'll definitely fight to kill. They don't seem to feel pain the way we do, so you have to disable the body or brain entirely to keep them from coming after you."

Anka looked at the heel of her palm and simulated the movement in Lucan's vague direction with a frown. "I can see how this would hurt, but if they don't feel it, why do this?"

"Drives the bone in their nose into their brain, killing them instantly. But you have to shove as hard as you can. Hesitating or not putting your all into it can get you dead."

She nodded, understanding. She'd seen the undead that made up a chunk of Mathias's army, the Anarki. They made her shudder and want to shrink away. Now she'd have to stand and fight. *Palm to the nose, hit hard.* "Got it."

"The next maneuver is one you likely know. The problem is, it's your last line of defense physically. By the time your attacker is close enough to you to use this move, you've lost a lot of options in terms of self-defense. Running, unless you're successful here, is unlikely. He's probably either reaching for you or got his hands on you. You can't panic. You'll have to look him dead in the eye and get closer." Lucan sidled up to her, his body nearly brushing hers. "As he's reaching out to grab you, you'll have to latch onto his arms." He put his arms around her and dragged her body close, fitting her exactly against him, where she'd been thousands of times, cuddled in his protective embrace.

Her knees almost gave way, and she had to remind herself that the days in which she could throw herself against him and ask prettily for his affection were long gone. Instead, she sucked in a determined breath, grabbed his flexing biceps, marveling at how hard his body had become, then nodded. "Got it."

"Use your arms to propel you forward as you lift your knee to his groin." He raised a brow. "Gently for training purposes."

Carefully, she gripped his arms, bringing her body even closer, then raised her knee between his legs, barely touching the cushion of his sensitive balls. When he gave a little grimace, she pulled away, stepping back.

"If these zombie-like Anarki can't feel pain, why do this?"

"I didn't say they couldn't feel pain at all. You've got to give them a whole lot before they do. Usually they fall apart, literally. The older the formerly-human Anarki get, the more brittle their bodies. Go for the neck, chest, or knees. And watch out for the black blood. Awful stuff." He grimaced. "Gets everywhere and smells terrible."

"So I've heard. I'll keep their vulnerabilities in mind. What else should I learn today, then? Knives? Guns?"

"Not yet, little girl. We master self-defense before we move on. No learning offense until I know you can protect yourself."

She frowned. "What about new magic? You've all practiced something more advanced, right? Weaving complicated spells together and—"

"In good time. Master one skill first. Then we'll move on."

"At this rate, it will be weeks before I learn even the minimum necessary to fight Mathias."

"Likely." His stare dared her to object.

The old Anka never would have argued. Now she refused to stay silent. "All of you need me in this fight. You're a force stretched thin and exhausted. I can help if you'll take the damn nappies off me. You didn't wait to fight. You jumped in and got dirty."

He arched a brow at her and crossed his arms over his chest. "And we almost got our arses killed regularly. We jumped in because no one else could or would. That's not the same situation now. Let's give you time to learn properly."

"While others die? While you risk yourself unnecessarily?"

"If you're not ready, and we're in battle, you're nothing but a liability to us. Then we have to protect you before we can fight anyone. Do you think you're even prepared to defend yourself against an attack? Really?"

Before Anka could object or reason with Lucan, he snapped his fingers. Every light in the room went dark. The doors shut. The loud click of the locks reverberated in the silence.

Anka gasped, startled. "Your magic worked."

"And yours is locked down in this room while we train," he said in the pitch black. "Now you'll have to fight me off physically."

That sent her heart into overdrive. She backed away a step. "Lucan, what the devil are you up to? What do you mean, fight you off?"

"Prove that you've mastered self-defense. I'll give you a ten-second head start. Go!"

"I don't want to play this game."

"You're wasting time. I'm going to come after you, Anka. And if I'm pretending to be Anarki, I'm not going to play nice. Five seconds."

He meant it; she heard the serious tenor of his voice. Instinct kicked in. She turned and fled. Seconds later, she heard him charge after her. Her heart rattled and pounded madly in her chest. She couldn't see anything in the pitch black, and tried to picture where she was running, but knew there was nowhere to hide. The impulse to flee a dangerous predator breathed hot down her neck. Her brain kicked in, and she knew the worst strategy she could employ was to hide in a corner where she'd be utterly trapped.

Mathias had taught her that.

Instead, she stopped running, crept closer to the center of the room, listening for any hint of Lucan, alert for the sound of a footstep or a breath. She forced herself to relax and beat back her panic as she mentally reviewed what he'd taught her.

Crouched, ready, Anka waited. Long moments passed in complete black silence. Nerve endings sizzled. The hair on the back of her arms stood up. Lucan was near.

The thought had barely cleared her brain when she felt a warm steel band around her waist. Another hand snaked into her hair and pulled hard. Lucan panted in her ear. Along with a dose of fear, a dangerous thrill rippled inside Anka. Her stomach cramped. She screamed, twisted in his embrace, clawed at him, but he wasn't letting go.

"Fight me," he demanded in her ear.

Pushing aside memories of another wizard and another time, she sucked in a breath and scrambled for her next move. Wriggling her arm free, she shoved it forward, then reared back with all her might. Her elbow split nothing but air. In her ear, he chuckled, and she realized that he had leaned far to the other side, clamping her pinned arm to her waist—where she could never touch him.

She stomped the ground, looking for his feet, finding only the hardwood floor. Frustration and anxiety played with her head, and she stomped faster, frantically seeking to defend herself.

"You're panicking. Focus. Think," he snarled in her ear.

Anka had no idea what to do next to fight him off, and she supposed that he had proved his point. She hadn't yet mastered self-defense. But she couldn't quit and show him that she didn't have any business fighting. She had to work herself free.

Ceasing the pointless stomping of her foot, she shifted her weight and kicked back, right into Lucan's shin.

"Shit!"

Triumph swelled at his curse. But he didn't let go. The short-lived victory died. She couldn't ram the elbow he'd pinned down into his stomach, so she fought dirty, digging her fingernails into his thigh.

He hissed, then let go of her waist to grab her arm in a viselike grip. With her torso free, she reared back, using her whole body, hoping to catch him off guard and knock him onto his arse. He merely tightened his grip in her hair and pulled harder, sending a flash of pain across her scalp. Her eyes watered. With that one tug, he immobilized her body.

No. Bloody hell, no. She wasn't going to roll over and play dead. She was taking the word "quit" out of her vocabulary starting now, right along with "defeat." Mathias had hurt her more deeply than she'd known it possible to survive, but now that she had, she'd be damned if she let herself be defeated.

Anka had no doubt that her next and only move was going to hurt. But she'd rather take the physical pain than the dent to her pride.

She lunged forward with all her might, trying to wrest herself from his grip. Instead of letting go, that stubborn bastard Lucan released her hair and wrapped both arms around her waist. As they tumbled down, a moment of pure accomplishment roared through her. She'd brought him to the ground! That was a victory in itself. Now she could fight, tooth and nail. Scratch and claw and battle until he knew she was serious about beating back the Anarki and killing Mathias.

Before they landed, he jerked, twisting his body until he cushioned her fall. The impact still hurt. As he grunted in pain, her shoulder rammed into his unforgiving chest. Her head bounced against his hard shoulder.

As she tried to roll away and continue the fight, he tightened his hold on her and murmured, "Are you hurt?"

She paused, taking mental inventory. "Just shaken."

Before she could draw in another breath, Lucan rolled them over, positioning her on her back. He slid between her legs, and he used his thighs to part hers wider, settling his hips in the cradle of hers. He was as hard as she'd ever felt him. Fire and need sizzled through her.

"What the fuck were you thinking?" he barked, breathing hard.

"Of breaking your hold. Fighting back."

But all she could feel now was his body against hers, hard in all the right places, sliding across her skin. Everything inside her lit up. Yearning bubbled in her veins.

"Instead of being upright with some mobility to keep fighting, you're under me, pinned, gravity working against you. Regret that decision?"

Yes. No. She closed her eyes, no longer interested in fighting him. God, she'd never imagined being this close to Lucan again. Pain mixed with longing until it became a terrible ache in her chest. She had to gather every bit of her control not to lift her hips to him and pretend the last three months had never happened, especially when he pressed his erection right against her moistening, softening folds. He wanted her, too—or at least his body did. She bit her lip to hold in a moan.

"How will you get free now?" His voice had dropped to the rough murmur she knew he only used when aroused.

The longing in her chest spread crushing fingers through her.

"I-I…don't know."

His breathing was jagged as he braced himself slightly above her, on his elbows. Anka could feel him staring down at her.

"You won't until I release you." The words were like a vow, and her heart stuttered. "Why did you come home last night?"

The question came from nowhere, blindsiding her. "It was a mistake. I'm sorry. I should have guessed that you'd have… company. I didn't mean to ruin your evening."

"I don't give a shit about my evening or my company. I sent her away and went looking for you. You came home for a reason. Why?"

Anka's heart started galloping, out of control. He'd sent the surrogate away? He hadn't taken her to their bed last night and… She squeezed her eyes shut tightly, unable to bloody think of him with the witch.

But all night, as Shock slept beside her, she'd been unable to imagine anything else.

"This does nothing to help my training."

"Damn it, Anka! This is the first time in months I've had the opportunity to get a straight answer from you. I'm not letting you up until I've heard the truth. Tell me why you never came home before last night. Tell me why you left me to wonder for weeks if you were even alive. Tell me why you didn't love me enough to come back."

Tears threatened. He totally misunderstood. She'd loved him so much that she'd cut her heart out to spare him what Mathias had made her. She had loved him enough to leave him with the fantasy they'd shared for a century. She alone bore the crushing weight of reality now.

"Unless the Anarki are going to pin me to the ground and ask me pointless questions, let me up."

Above her, Lucan tensed. His harsh breaths fanned across her lips, and she shivered. He was close. So close that if she just lifted her head a fraction, their lips would touch… She wanted his kiss with a guilty need that thrummed heavily through her, with a crushing weight of need pressing in on her chest.

Suddenly, he sniffed, then ripped away from her with a long string of foul curses she'd never heard fall from his mouth before. The second his body no longer covered hers, she felt a bone-deep chill that made her wonder if she'd ever feel warm again.

"The Anarki won't say anything, just kill you. I've promised Bram that I'll teach you everything you need to know to defend yourself and fight back. But goddamnit, you'd better take a shower before you come back for training. The stench is killing me."

Lucan snapped his fingers, and the lights slowly flicked on, gradually getting brighter until she saw the angry brilliance of his blue eyes, his stiff stance, the fists clenched at his sides.

She frowned and shrank away from his contempt. "I did shower."

"Not good enough," he growled. "You smell like that horse's arse."

Shock. Knowing she intended to train today, he'd covered her in his scent, blanketing her body, rubbing all over her. Fresh shame sliced her open. "Sorry."

Lucan's stare outlined her body, studying her magical signature with a curse. More shame and guilt slithered through her. No doubt, he'd taken note of the change in her energy level from yesterday—and knew exactly who had provided for her.

Suddenly, his stare zeroed in on her wrist. His eyes narrowed with question, then fury. Anka looked down. Her long sleeves had ridden up in their scuffle. Her breath caught. *Oh, no*!

She tugged at the sleeve, to cover the red chafing and faint blue bruising circling her wrist, but it was too late. Lucan grabbed her arm, pushed the sleeve up, and inspected the markings. With a growl, he tore at her clothes, batting away her ineffectual hands, until she stood shivering in her bra and knickers.

Incredulous fury rolled off of him as he walked a circle around her, taking particular note of a bruise at her hip. Then he ripped her knickers off and cursed in a long, vile streak unlike anything she'd ever heard Lucan say. Anka tensed, flinched, feeling the stunned rage coming off him in pounding waves. She tugged to get free, but his grip was far stronger.

"Did that motherfucker do this to you?" he growled. "Did he hurt you?

The explanation stuck in her throat. Lucan had always been a tender lover. He would never have restrained her, mounted her like an animal, used her. He would have been horrified if she'd asked him to—and if she'd liked it. Fresh guilt surged. Damn, she felt… dirty. What could she say?

"Yes."

"That's it!" he shouted, his contempt echoing all over the room. "I'm done, Anka. Whatever he's holding over your head, whatever he's using to force you to endure this." He held her wrist right under her eyes. "It ends now. I'm going to kill him."

"Lucan…wait! Don't. I-I asked him to."

Chapter Four

As gray clouds hung low in the afternoon sky, hovering over the small, somber gathering of magickind, Lucan bowed his head out of respect for Tynan's passing into the next life—and because if anyone saw his face, they'd realize he was a breath away from homicidal.

At the O'Shea estate somewhere much farther north than he'd ever ventured, he glanced up to see his friend and fellow warrior laid out on a cold stone slab, his battered body naked except for the ceremonial burial cloth spread over his hips and groin.

In his mind, all Lucan could see was Anka, her wrists chafed and bruised, her backside black and blue, her expression guilty. All he could hear was his former mate's hesitant, stuttering confession that she'd *asked* the fucking wanker Shock to hurt her.

"This day, we send a great wizard and a brave warrior into his nextlife. Go in peace," a stooped old priestess in a red cloak droned to the group of a couple dozen witches and wizards.

Lucan sure as hell hoped Tynan had finally found some peace. And beheld his true love, Auropha, in this nextlife. As long as Lucan had known him, Tynan had never had either.

The fallen wizard's brother, Asher, was nearly a replica of

Tynan. Dark hair, gray eyes, but without the "storm cloud ready to drench" mien. Instead, Asher gave off a tightly reined anger. Not surprising, Lucan thought. The wizard's older brother, who should have had hundreds of years ahead of him, was dead—largely because of the people assembled here to pay their respects today.

Beside Asher, Bram stood, head bowed, his golden hair ruffling slightly in the chilly breeze. Beside him, Sabelle stood looking painfully beautiful, holding hands with her mate, Isdernus. Big, burly Ice didn't bow, not out of disrespect. He watched the gathering protectively with narrowed green eyes, ready to defend his mate and friends at any sign of danger. Arthurian warrior Marrok and his mate Olivia made a perfect picture of grief, clinging together for comfort. Kari sobbed quietly on Ronan's shoulder, her blonde hair whipping in the wind. The big twin looped an arm around his dainty mate's waist, consoling her as best he could, but Kari had been perhaps Tynan's closest friend. The pretty human barmaid wouldn't easily recover from this loss. Beside her, Tabitha squeezed Kari's hand. Ronan's twin, Raiden, stood behind his redheaded mate and stroked Tabitha's belly, growing with her coming youngling. Fiery Sydney cast worried glances down to Kari. Syd's mate, Caden, watched with a frown. Their friend Felicia had remained behind since the service required magic, and the sweet Untouchable negated it. Undoubtedly, her mate and fellow warrior Duke hovered nearby, watching over her.

A terrible truth struck Lucan in that moment: Everyone here had someone to rely on, to adore, to turn to in crisis, someone with whom to unburden themselves, to share laughter, to make love, to grow old. Everyone but him. Even Bram had Emma. Though they'd been apart since the morning after their mating, Lucan knew Bram would find the errant human again someday. It was only a matter of time.

Lucan's own mate—former mate, damn it—had given herself to a Mathias supporter. She lived under Shock's roof and slept in his bed voluntarily. And she had asked him to hurt her.

Anka had been saying for months that she wasn't the same

witch he'd mated a century ago. Maybe she told the truth. The woman he'd known would have been horrified if he'd been rough enough to leave marks on her body. He would have been horrified with himself. And now…he didn't understand at all.

"What is the matter with you?" Caden murmured in his ear.

He cut a glance at his younger brother. "Nothing."

Caden raised a dark brow. "You're growling. Honest to fuck growling. What happened during your training session with Anka this morning?"

"Later." This was hardly the time or place.

At the head of the slab, Asher took a sacred vial of water and cast a protection spell over it. "Peace, brother. Go with my love."

The grieving man looked like he wanted to crack open and break down. He swallowed back his pain and gave the jewel-encrusted decanter to Bram, who murmured words over it for well wishes and a happy nextlife. Everyone else did the same, including the few distant relatives of Tynan's who'd chosen to attend. Across the slab, in the back, Lucan spotted the sophisticated Sebastian Blackbourne, apparently the Magical Council's representative here. His father, Carlisle, headed up the Council. A more sniveling, backhanded bastard Lucan had rarely met. The son didn't *seem* like the father. But Lucan well knew that appearances could be deceiving. That calculating expression on Sebastian's face told Lucan the dodgy git was up to something.

But that wasn't the only thing on his mind. This morning when Anka had first arrived at Bram's estate, he'd thought she looked well, far more like the Anka he'd shared a century with. An hour in her presence had shattered that illusion. This Anka argued, stood her ground, was determined to do things her way. This one was a fighter.

Damn if that hadn't made him hard.

The vial of water came his way, and Lucan bowed over it, adding a spell of protection. He couldn't wish upon his departed friend a happiness he didn't feel. Inside the vessel, he sensed Sabelle's siren magic granting him calm and joy. Bram's addition to the magical concoction was the most potent. No way Tynan would dare to have a miserable nextlife, and Lucan knew his best friend had put that amount of energy into the spell because of his crushing guilt. Tynan's death wasn't Bram's fault...but as leader of the Doomsday Brethren, Bram disagreed. He should have saved Tynan somehow. Lucan made a mental note to punch some sense into his friend later.

As the rest of the gathering added their magical enchantments, Caden leaned over to him again. "Spill it now."

The stubborn arse never let up. Caden had given up his prosperous job and a perfectly comfortable life in Dallas to care for him after Anka's abduction. No matter how many times he told Caden it was all right to take Sydney and return to that life, his younger brother insisted that his future was here, entwined with the Doomsday Brethren.

With a heavy sigh, he whispered to Caden, "It went badly. She lacks even the most basic skills."

"You had none when Marrok started training you."

Lucan couldn't deny that. "It's not the same. I'm in the fight to protect, not to have revenge."

Caden shrugged. "Ice wants revenge for his sister's murder. How is that different?"

He tried to wrap his head around a hundred possible answers. That she was female, and therefore to be treasured and coddled, sat on the tip of his tongue. If Sydney heard that, she'd beat him silly. And it wasn't exactly the truth. Anka was smart, capable of learning, had the drive to excel, but he couldn't bear the thought of her in harm's way. Or being hurt.

After this morning, he knew she wanted the pain. That bothered him most of all.

"Something isn't right with her, brother. She's unhinged or unbalanced. She's..." *Changed.*

The decanter of blessed water made its way back to the priestess, who smiled beneath her long crimson hood. "Very many blessings here, for one cut down in his prime. He will be well cared for in the nextlife. To this wizard, we give the element of blessed water."

The gnarled old woman poured the contents of the vial over Tynan's beaten body. His deathly pallor sparkled for a moment in the weak sunlight. Lucan watched Sabelle huddle deeper into Ice's arms as Kari looked away, whispering to Tabitha, whose hair glinted fire-red in the sun. Something stabbed the backs of Lucan's eyes. Tears. Fucking useless. He'd shed too many of them in the last three months. He knew too well that crying changed nothing. He could still feel every bit as hollow inside after the storm, and he always felt weaker for it.

But as the priestess held her hands over Tynan's chest, Asher raised up a bejeweled box, complete with the O'Shea crest, and lifted the decorative lid. The wizard looked as if his jaw was going to break, he clenched it so hard. The priestess closed her eyes, and seemed to find some place within herself, focusing her magic. Tynan's heart pushed up from his chest, lifted from his ribcage by the powerful woman's spell, then filled the box in Asher's hands. But that was all for show. Tynan had buried his heart with Auropha four months ago.

Asher slammed the lid on the box and set it at the head of the slab. The gathering turned with the priestess to a lonely patch of soil with a freshly-dug hole in the center. She said a few more blessings over the box, then slid it into the consecrated soil on their lands, the center of their family energy. "For this wizard, we provide the blessed element of earth."

Bram, Asher, Ronan, and Ice all stepped forward on cue to light a ceremonial torch. This part would take the longest and horrify the human mates, Kari and Sydney. But this part of the service was sacred and required.

Lucan stared through aching eyes as the torch bearers lit Tynan on fire as the priestess intoned, "Of this wizard, we create the blessed element of fire."

The sacred water had been spelled to act as accelerant, and Tynan quickly started to char, burn, melt. Kari gasped and turned away, grief all over her face. Sydney grabbed the woman's hand, closing her eyes.

He forced himself to watch, wondering if Tynan wasn't better off. He'd never again have to think about this magical war. He'd never again have to imagine his love at the hands of Mathias. And he'd absolutely never again have to endure living with the crushing guilt of not saving her and wondering what the fuck he was going to do with the remaining centuries of his life now that the one woman who completed him was lost to him forever.

Lucan sighed. Granted, Anka wasn't dead, but for him, she might as well be. The woman who had inhabited her body was sure as hell gone.

The crackling of the flames roared over the pall of silence. Caden chose that moment to break it. "What do you mean Anka is unhinged?"

He didn't want to answer. He'd fucking rather forget what he'd seen, what she'd told him, and live in a state of wretched ignorance. But he couldn't undo this morning. Caden had been one of the few bright spots in Lucan's last three months. Having Caden and Sydney live with him had kept the worst of the loneliness at bay. His brother's mate was particularly insightful about his moods, and always seemed to know when he needed cheering up. But a video game or a good joke wasn't going to solve this. Nor was a cupcake or a spot of tea. But maybe logic would. Caden could often offer objective advice. Maybe Anka's behavior would make sense to him.

"She's bruised—wrists, ankles, shoulders, neck." He closed his eyes, remembering his rage as he'd torn off Anka's clothes and revealed contusions in nearly every color of the rainbow. "Hips, thighs, arse."

"Like he beat her? That sadistic fucker!" Caden snarled in his ear. "Why doesn't she leave and come home—"

"I asked her the same thing. She told me that she asked Shock to bind her down and use her this way. She says she needs it." Lucan turned pained eyes to his brother. "Anka is the gentlest soul, and she *begs* him to hurt her. Why?"

Caden paused, pressed his lips together grimly. "He restrains her, you say?"

"Yes." Admitting that was a stab to the chest. "By her own choice."

"Does he spank, flog, or whip her?"

Lucan glared hard at his brother. "Fuck, Caden! It's not like I handed her a goddamn quiz. Does it bloody matter?"

"Not really." Caden shifted his weight, looking reluctant to open his mouth, as if it would be as dangerous as opening Pandora's box. "Did Anka try very hard during your mating to please you?"

A thousand soft, sweet memories tugged at him, bringing as much pain now as they once had pleasure. "Yes. Her thoughtfulness, her desire to make others happy, was one of her sweetest qualities."

"Listen carefully," Caden instructed, voice low. "That woman is still inside her. She's simply started expressing her submissive nature sexually, and Shock is acting as her Dom."

"*What*?" The words were so foreign, Lucan couldn't process them. "No! She always liked to be touched tenderly, stroked, petted, coddled. Bound and beaten? Never."

Raiden leaned in with a bit of a wince. "I think Caden is right. For what it's worth, so does Ronan."

Lucan's gaze snapped up to the rest of the crowd. The twins were watching with matching expressions of compassion that labeled him a poor sap. Bram smiled tightly. Ice sent him a firm nod. He didn't dare look at any of the women. Mortification and fury plowed through him, and Caden dragged him away from most of the crowd, toward the back of the gathering.

"I don't understand." He gaped at his brother, feeling as if some foundation of his world had fallen out from under him.

"You said yourself that she'd changed. I'd say this is one of the changes, but it sounds like the tendency has always been there. Maybe this is how she lets out her pain now. Maybe what happened with Mathias made her recognize her needs. I don't know."

"Her needs? To have the shit beaten out of her?"

"Keep your voice down," Caden growled.

His brother was right. He had to get a hold of his rage. Now wasn't the time, and this wasn't the place. They were here to bury one of their own, and he was so mired in his own shit that he'd forgotten the terrible meaning of this ceremony.

"You're right. We'll talk when this is over." Lucan forced himself to take a deep breath and let it out slowly.

"Bram will be busy with Council business. Because you know it's impolite to talk to Asher about taking Tynan's seat and trying to save magickind before the service is complete," Caden drawled.

Lucan nodded, glad he wasn't necessary to that process. "I suppose that's why Sebastian Blackbourne is here, to convince Asher to go to the dark side and support Mathias."

"I fear that sums it up."

Lucan scanned the crowd. "Uncle Sterling isn't here."

"Our uncle, despite his tenure on the Council, isn't going to argue our cause better than Bram. Relax."

"Right."

They stepped back in with the rest of the crowd as the priestess extinguished the fire with her magic and collected the ash of Tynan's body. Nothing more remained of the strong, tormented warrior now.

At the head of the stone slab, Asher's face tightened. The man's eyes were glossy with tears he refused to shed.

The priestess sent him a soft expression of sympathy as she handed him the urn with Tynan's ashes. "With this wizard, we free him to the blessed element of air."

"Go well, my brother," Asher whispered as he waved his hand and released the ashes to the wind whistling across the dusky sky.

Moments later, the sun set. Tynan's ashes scattered, and a peaceful hush settled over the crowd. He was carried away—his troubles, his grief, his impotent rage, his terrible loss. Gone.

Lucan closed his eyes and envied the fallen warrior.

"This is why Bram hasn't let you back into battle," Caden murmured in his ear.

Because Lucan had contemplated suicide by Anarki? "I know."

There were painful days and nights he'd considered begging Bram to let him fight. Or going in search of Mathias all alone in his lair and throwing caution to the devil. But in his heart, Anka was still his responsibility, despite their broken bond. She might need him to protect her someday. He'd failed her miserably once. He would not falter again.

"I wouldn't let him," Caden admitted.

Lucan smiled wryly. "I know."

His brother's love and support had been one of the few joys that had kept Lucan putting one foot in front of the other so that he could continue to exist each day.

Shortly thereafter, the crowd began to break up. Everyone lined up to pay their respects to Asher, offer their help and condolences. They did, one by one, then teleported away. Lucan stepped forward and looked Asher O'Shea in the eye. The poor bastard looked like he'd been gutted. It wasn't only Tynan who'd suffered. The living left behind to cope and grapple and try to move forward perhaps suffered more, with no end in sight. He cursed the Anarki and Mathias. He cursed Shock's younger brother, Zain, for bringing the terrible wizard back so he could be evil's right hand or whatever creepy aspiration he had. And as long as he was cursing one Denzell brother, he might as well curse both. Shock certainly deserved every bit of his rage and contempt.

"I'm beyond sorry, O'Shea."

Asher's face closed up even tighter. "Thank you. Besides Bram, you two are the last of the Doomsday Brethren here. I want you all off my property. Don't ever come back."

Lucan wasn't offended by Asher's anger. Fury had become his old friend since losing Anka, so he well understood how the grieving man felt. He debated the wisdom of his next words, but figured that he and his fellow warriors had already been dismissed. He couldn't do more damage.

"In your shoes, I'd hate us, too. We allowed a grieving wizard to fight. He was reckless and let himself be taken in the hopes of killing Mathias. You have every reason to despise us. I can only tell you that I lost my mate in this war. I understand bitterness and grief. Your brother was a good warrior. A good man. He will be avenged. The Doomsday Brethren will make certain of it."

Asher stared, his face stony, looking as if he held in a string of heated curses for the sake of decorum, but his hold was wearing thin.

"Ultimately," Lucan continued, "Mathias killed your brother to have one less wizard to oppose him and upset the balance of the Council. Keep that in mind when you weigh your Council decisions."

"As much as I hate all of you, I hate Mathias more. Now get the hell out of here." Asher sent Lucan a sharp nod of dismissal.

Caden only patted Asher on the shoulder. "I'm very sorry."

Then he grabbed Sydney's hand and teleported out. Lucan followed suit, watching Bram and Sebastian Blackbourne hover around Asher as he said the last of his good-byes. With a shake of his head, Lucan popped home, not envying either of the wizards left behind. The responsibility of steering magickind in times of civil war was an awesome one.

Back at his house, Sydney kissed his cheek, followed by a soft peck on Caden's lips, then excused herself upstairs. His brother watched her sassy sway all the way up the stairs, and Lucan envied him the happiness and solace Caden could take from Sydney in good times and bad. Fuck, he sounded like a morose wanker, crying in his whiskey or whatever. Right now, he'd love a drink. But Caden would disapprove, and he refused to stoop to Shock's level by being a full-time drunk.

Speaking of stooping to the arsehole's level… "What do you mean by Anka being sexually submissive to Shock?"

Caden slanted him an impatient glance. "C'mon. You've been around a lot longer than I have. Certainly you've heard of these things."

"Of course. But I can't picture it. I know almost nothing about it. I…I'd hoped that you meant something else." God, he could use that drink now. "For fuck's sake, I don't understand why she would want that prick to give her pain. And how would you know about this?"

His brother had the good grace to flush and pretend interest in the wall. "When I lived in Dallas and worked for the paper, I was called out to photograph a murder near a kink club. The guy who owned it was a witness, and we started talking about the crime. Then eventually about other things. I went a time or two until Sabelle brought me here to help you. I was…interested." He grinned. "There's something really nice about seeing your red handprint on your mate's pristine white bum."

Having never tried such a thing, Lucan had no idea. Sex had been for fun and energy before he met Anka. After her, every other female on the planet had ceased to exist. Lately, it had been a chore necessary to stay alive. Surrogates helped, being either as professional or as romantic as the client wished. He'd tried both approaches. They both made him feel like a sorry shitbag afterward. Like a wizard in his prime whose mate was fucking someone else.

He was ready to do whatever it took to change that.

"I think I need to hear more."

Caden's eyes nearly popped with surprise. "You're sure?"

Lucan sighed. "I can either lose Anka forever to the prick able to give her what she says she needs or I can try to be that man. I love her still. I want to love her always. I may not understand this, but I'd rather be the bastard leaving a handprint on her bum."

His brother nodded as if impressed. "That's how I'd look at it, too. I wasn't sure if you were ready to be that logical."

"I don't think I have a choice. Being near her today…" He sucked in a breath, trying to calm himself. Even thoughts of being close to Anka made him hard, almost rabid to have her under him, his cock buried deep inside her, making her his again. "I haven't felt that alive in three months. I'm not letting her slip away again. How do I learn what I need to know?"

Caden retrieved his mobile phone from his pocket, punched a few buttons, then tucked it away again. A second later, Lucan's beeped with a text. He fished out the device and stared at the phone number, the country code for America first.

"His name is Mitchell Thorpe. He runs a club named Dominion in Dallas. The smartest, most patient bastard in the world when it comes to BDSM education. When you talk to him, tell him I'm interested in resuming when I can." He grinned.

Lucan saved the number with a grim expression. Everything was happening so fast, and today had been a complete clusterfuck from start to finish. This morning, he'd all but dry-humped Anka like a dog in heat until he'd smelled Shock all over her and seen the marks he'd left behind. Then Lucan had just been an angry bastard. Tynan's funeral had completed the buzzkill. And now he needed to talk to this kink master. He shook his head tiredly.

"What time is it there?"

"Dallas is six hours behind us." Caden glanced at his watch. "So…it's about noon. Thorpe should be in."

Indeed. "Thank you. Now go spend time with your mate. I've got a phone call to make."

Anka watched Sabelle pace the floor of Bram's office, staring at the witch she'd once considered her closest friend. They'd barely spoken in three months. She'd missed her friend's mating to Isdernus Rykard. Sabelle choosing Ice certainly would have been a surprise to all of magickind, who regarded Sabelle somewhat like their princess because of the prominence of her bloodline. Those same people would have considered her mate far beneath her, somewhere between a madman and a punch line. But the more Anka watched her friend with Ice, the more she knew Sabelle had made the right choice for her.

"Your brother will be fine," Anka said quietly to the other witch.

Ice pressed a cup of tea into Sabelle's hands. "She's right, love. It's a meeting, not a battle."

Sabelle toyed with one of her long, blond curls and frowned. "I get the feeling it's both. But I'm glad you didn't go."

Sabelle smiled at Ice, and his answering look of devotion stabbed Anka like a knife to the heart. Lucan had once looked at her like that. Now that she'd told him about the way she begged Shock to take control of their sex and give her pain, he'd never look at her that way again. That was why she'd confessed. He couldn't go on pining for what would never be. But it hurt so badly to know he would feel something between contempt and loathing for her for the rest of their centuries.

"I was better off not going," Ice said. "Apparently, my underdeveloped ability to keep my mouth shut when my overdeveloped bullshit meter goes off is a liability in politics."

Sabelle grinned absently while staring at Anka. Bloody hell, she'd forgotten to mask her thoughts.

"Exactly," Sabelle seemed to say to both of them. "Can you excuse us, Ice?"

Ice glanced between the two of them, green eyes narrowed. "Girl talk, is it? I'm definitely not staying for that, especially if you're going to talk about Lucan MacTavish. Wanker."

Anka blinked, stunned, as Ice turned away and left the office, shoulders barely squeezing through the doorway. Despite his huge boots and his even larger frame, he barely made a sound as he trekked across the tile and disappeared up the stairs.

"Why does Ice dislike Lucan?" Anka asked.

"What do you mean you told Lucan that you beg Shock to take control and give you pain?"

Damn Sabelle for reading her thoughts. Anka wanted to tell the other witch that she didn't have the energy to explain twice in one day, and that it was deeply personal. Would magickind's sweet princess even understand? Under all that, the truth embarrassed her. Not that Sabelle hadn't just read every one of her thoughts. "I asked you first."

Anka sighed. Yes, that sounded very mature.

Sabelle smiled, but the happiness in her expression abruptly died. "Lucan almost died after Mathias broke your mate bond. His mate mourning was like nothing I've ever seen. Even Aunt Millie said it was more severe than she'd ever encountered. If you hadn't healed him when you did, I don't think he could have lived much longer. He'd nearly gone feral."

Her heart caught. Anka wanted to believe Lucan grieved her loss that much because he'd genuinely loved her. But he hadn't known her, not really. He'd missed the façade, the comfort object. The abrupt nature of their torn bond would have added to his distress.

"No," Sabelle insisted. "He loved *you*. He still does."

Not anymore. Anka folded her hands in her lap. "Go on."

The witch paused, gathering her thoughts, then shook her head. "You must understand… Mourning to that extent depleted his energy very rapidly. All of the Brethren had trained hard the day you were taken. Their tanks were empty, Lucan's included. After your disappearance, we tried surrogates, but he was so violent that he scared them all away."

Her breath hitched, and Anka feared where this was going next. She forced herself to ask, "And?"

Sabelle pressed her lips together. "And…I finally stepped in. Of course, this was before I became mated to Ice. We had no idea where you'd gone or even if you were alive. He was slipping away from us. He'd been reduced to something near an animal, with no rational thought left. Only his sense of smell and taste remained. I washed with your soap and shampoo. I wore your clothes. I did everything I could to make him believe that I was you. Eventually, he accepted me."

Eventually, Lucan had covered Sabelle with his body, sunk his cock inside her, and taken her with the same passion he would his mate. On the one hand, Anka knew she had her friend to thank for Lucan being alive. Sabelle was the kind of selfless person who would put herself at risk to save another.

On the other hand, she had a vivid image of Lucan and Sabelle entwined in bed, Lucan's fingers in her hair, his body between her long, spread legs, taking her with force and need until she cried out in ecstasy beneath him and took every bit of his seed inside her womb. God, she was going to vomit.

"It wasn't like that." Sabelle reached for Anka's hand in reassurance.

She pulled away. "Are you going to tell me that you never found pleasure with him?"

The other woman hesitated, looked down. "No."

"Or that he never found pleasure in you?"

"No." Sabelle looked at her, desperate to explain and helpless. "But Lucan finding pleasure—and more importantly, energy—was the point. If he hadn't, I would have failed him."

And heaven forbid the perfect Sabelle Rion Rykard ever fail at anything.

"He would have died!" the beautiful blonde almost pleaded.

Anka felt immediately small and petty for her thought. It might be wrong of her, given her relationship with Shock and that she continued to live with the wizard and share his bed, but she couldn't help the feelings of impotent upset and jealousy plaguing her. Then her logic kicked in. Lucan was alive because Sabelle had given of herself to help him. She would be mourning her former mate in a completely different way if her friend hadn't sacrificed to save him.

"I understand." Anka dragged in a shaky breath. "I'm sure Ice does, too. He'll eventually let go of his anger."

"If that were the extent of the situation, perhaps." Sabelle rose and paced. "You haven't been here and so much has happened… You're aware that several members of the Council were murdered?"

Anka frowned, wondering what that had to do with Ice and Lucan. "Of course. Even if I haven't been here with you, I haven't been living under a rock, Belle. I know Clifden O'Shea and Thomas MacKinnett were killed."

"Carlisle Blackbourne knows Mathias was responsible."

"And he's done nothing about it?"

Sabelle shrugged. "Well, I suspect he knows that Mathias had them killed. I can't prove it. And no, Blackbourne did nothing. In fact, he tried to help Mathias win a seat on the Council."

The idea of a madman making rules that govern magickind sent fear tearing through her bloodstream. "So Blackbourne is either crooked, afraid of Mathias, or both. Bram and Ice have their work cut out for them."

"They do, but Ice's election to the Council was by no means easy."

"I'm sure not, being Deprived and…whatnot." Anka didn't mean it as an insult, and hoped that Sabelle wouldn't take it that way.

"And being considered a lunatic? Of course I know you're not insulting Ice, dear. He's a good man and he earned that spot. Tynan, God rest him, slipped into his grandfather's seat at the time, so Clifden's vacancy was no issue. MacKinnett had no heirs, however. Bram and the others plotted to fill the seat with someone who would vote with the Doomsday Brethren and give them more sway over the Council decisions."

"How *did* Ice get elected? The Council hasn't seated any member of the Deprived in forever. Bram would have had to sponsor him, and I'm sure your brother would have preferred to get behind someone easier to elect. Someone from a good family. Someone he knows well and can trust. Someone the Council would look favorably upon. Why not Lucan? Because his uncle already sits on the Council?"

"That's one reason, yes. But for a time, Bram insisted Lucan could still win the others over."

"So Ice dislikes Lucan because Bram preferred his friend over his sister's suitor?"

"No." Sabelle looked decidedly nervous now, hovering near the arm of the sofa, wringing her hands. "Bram insisted that the best way to get Lucan on the Council was to show his good connections and stability."

"Everything with the Council is about appearances." Anka rolled her eyes.

"Exactly. Bram insisted that if Lucan became mated to someone of good family who could bolster him, someone whose bloodline was above reproach…"

Everything Anka wasn't. Someone like… "You?"

Anka choked the question out. But as soon as it left her lips, she knew the answer. Sabelle mating with Lucan would have made him not only an obvious contender for a Council seat, but virtually unbeatable, despite the fact that his uncle occupied another seat.

The pretty witch nodded. "Lucan and I stood ready to speak the words. But I came to him fresh from a night in Ice's bed, tears covering my face. Lucan called it off before the words were spoken."

To spare Sabelle, who had been obviously in love with her mate. Lucan had a big heart; he wouldn't want anyone hurting, least of all the woman who had saved his life. And he had never nursed political aspirations. He would have accepted a Council seat to help Bram, not for any ambition of his own. But the very fact that he'd been willing to Call to Sabelle and have her speak the Binding to join their lives for the rest of their centuries ripped every one of Anka's insecurities open and filled them with crushing pain.

She blinked once, twice. She saw Sabelle's pitying expression. Her heart thudded dully in her chest. Tears scraped the backs of her eyes like a thousand little claws scratching in evil glee.

"Anka." Sabelle knelt at her feet. "Lucan never loved me, except as a friend. You have his heart still, I swear."

Did his heart matter now? If she held it, he'd certainly been willing to cast it aside and mate with a witch whose family and stature were far above her own. He'd been ready to embrace a proper mating with someone far better than her. For a century, he'd sworn her family didn't matter to him. Every time he'd uttered those words, she'd been sure he'd lied gently to spare her. And now she knew the truth. All this time, Anka had been drowning in guilt for shacking up with Shock, heartbroken that she was hurting Lucan with her refusal to come back and her inability to explain… But Lucan had been moving on, ready to take another into his home, bed, and life.

He might as well have stuck a knife in her chest and carved out her heart, leaving her hollow and bleeding, foolishly pining for a man who'd hidden the ugly truth from her with lies.

She supposed that made them even.

Anka jumped to her feet. "I must go."

"Don't. You're misunderstanding totally. Lucan loves you, dearest. He is incomplete without you. I know he'd give anything to have you back."

"No, he'd give anything to have the meek weakling who hung on his every word and did exactly as he bid. He didn't want a real woman, Belle. He wanted one who fit into his world. He certainly never wanted one to *be* his world."

As she stumbled for the door, Sabelle at her heels, Ice blocked her. "She's telling you the truth, Anka."

"Were you eavesdropping, my caveman?" Sabelle sounded somewhere between cross and amused.

"Maybe just a bit." A smile tugged at Ice's face, which disappeared as he looked Anka's way again. "I know Bram and Caden are quite worried about Lucan. He's not bouncing back from losing you. He seems to lack will. I think his heart is broken."

Or he had missed out on having the sort of mate he deserved with Sabelle and now regretted the moment of weakness that allowed such a prize to slip through his fingers.

"You both think he loves me?" Anka raised her challenging gaze to Ice. "Would you have *ever* stopped looking for Sabelle if she had been taken from you? Would you *ever* have stopped pursuing her again once you found her?"

Ice gritted his teeth, and cursed in a soft whisper, looking away.

Anka had her answer. "Of course you wouldn't. Because Sabelle is your heart, your soul, your other half. You know her. You know that you love and need her. No matter what she said or did, you would never rest until she was yours again. Lucan let me go with barely a protest. Think on what that means, Ice."

As she inched between him and the portal, Ice stepped aside and let her go. He'd only done so because he knew she was right and had no argument against her logic. Lucan had thrown in the mental towel on her months ago. Her revelation this morning would only pound the final nail in their coffin deeper. Though Lucan had never said a word on this score, Anka knew her bloodline and family hadn't been good enough for him. And now that he knew what she needed in bed, what she craved…well, he'd write her off entirely as damaged goods, take his energy from surrogates, and someday take a well Privileged witch as his new mate.

Perhaps Lucan wasn't wrong. Maybe there was something wrong with her, and she deserved this toxic relationship she shared with Shock. Whatever the case, she was locking Lucan away with the rest of her past and moving on with her future. She was now free to become *exactly* who and what she wanted to be, his expectations be damned. As soon as these training sessions ended, she'd do everything in her power to cut him from her life—and her heart—forever.

Chapter Five

Lucan walked into the training room, his head full. Information he'd gleaned from Mitchell Thorpe yesterday tripped over things he wanted to say to his former mate. He understood Anka's needs now—in theory, anyway. Everything the fetish club owner had explained cast a glaring floodlight into her psyche. And he was stunned. All those decades he'd lived with and loved Anka, never realizing that she was submitting her will to him, while he'd never met—or even sensed—her needs. Guilt crushed him. Why hadn't she ever told him that she craved something different?

Flipping on the lights, he paced to the boxing gloves, absently unknotting the laces. A door slammed behind him, and he zipped around to welcome Anka, a perfectly prepared speech on the tip of his tongue.

But it wasn't his Anka who walked toward him. Instead, a razor-sharp goddess swayed in his direction. She wore her pale hair pulled away from her face in a severe braid that obliterated all the outrageously feminine curls he'd once loved running his fingers through. The thick rope of tresses hung over one shoulder, its tail swinging lazily against the bottom curve of her breast. Those luscious orbs he'd once caressed and suckled tenderly were now hugged by a tight black tank top. The garment dipped over the flat of her abdomen, nipping in to cinch her tiny waist. A pair of black leather pants cupped her lean hips and slender thighs before tucking into black boots that laced up to her knees, complete with heels that lent her an extra few inches of height. All in all, she looked like a cross between a kick-ass female warrior and a wet dream.

Lucan gaped mutely at her, aware that his jaw had hit his chest some time ago. He knew this woman intimately, still loved her with every beat of his hollow, broken heart. But the Anka he'd known preferred to blend into the background. The one standing before him now with a raised brow demanded his full attention without a word. She made his blood pump. Her presence grabbed him by the cock and squeezed unmercifully.

"Anka?"

The curve of her little smile mocked him. She meant that expression to be a barricade. His demure Anka had been replaced by a spitfire who would scratch and claw and fight for what she believed in. He needed her to believe in him again.

"You told me that my clothes yesterday weren't appropriate for lessons. Too baggy and the like, you said. No such problem today, I trust?"

It wasn't a question, but a dare. Clearly, something besides her wardrobe had changed in the last twenty-four hours. Something deeper. This external transformation mirrored a change inside her, and Lucan wanted details. In the past, he might have cuddled her on his lap and simply asked what troubled her. One look at her fiery amber eyes told him she'd thrown a silent gauntlet at his feet, daring him to live with her defiance or rein it in. The barricades around her heart and mind stood strong and thick. Until he earned her trust again, scaling them would be a snarling battle.

Lucan smiled back. *Guess what, love? I understand now. Let the battle begin...*

If she wanted to challenge him to win her back, heart, body, and soul, he gladly accepted. At least he was in the game again, no longer shut out by the pain she'd wielded like a shield and his own regret.

Snippets of his enlightening conversation with Thorpe echoed in his head. *Her trauma didn't create this submissive need in her, Lucan. Turning herself over to another allows her to give the most tender parts of her soul and let go of her pain, yet retain the power to stop the scene at any time she wishes—something she didn't have when she was raped. Shock simply tapped into the need to please she's likely always had, waiting for the right man to understand.*

The right man, Shock? Not for Anka.

But now Lucan understood what had driven her to seek his guidance during their mating about how best she could please him in dress and manner. He'd merely assumed that she wanted to fit in and gain acceptance from his very traditional parents, despite her less than sterling family. Perhaps that had been true to a point, but he now saw that hadn't been her only motive. He'd been so bloody damn stupid these last three months, letting his hurt, confusion, and guilt for all she'd suffered rule him. Never again. The worst thing he could do now was continue to allow the distance between them. In fact, he suspected that his worst mistake had been licking the wounds of her rejection, rather than demanding she come home months ago. She hadn't needed the time to heal; she could have done that at home. What she'd really needed was to know he still cared.

Water under the bridge now. She was here in front of him, and blast it all if he wasn't going to make every goddamn second count.

"Your clothes are perfect. Thank you." Lucan glanced at his mobile phone. "But you're late."

She shifted her balance, sticking one hip out as she crossed her arms over her chest. "You're not my keeper. Are you here to train me to fight, or do you just want to chastise me for not being good enough, Prince Lucan?"

Prince Lucan? He raised a brow. Where was this venom coming from? The fact that he'd left her with Shock instead of staking his claim again or something more? Whatever the case, she was purposely pushing him. To see his reaction? Likely. Wouldn't she be surprised when she got one…and probably not what she expected from the man who'd once been her tender, solicitous mate.

Because for the first time in months, he had focus and a goal firmly in mind.

He walked toward her slowly and snapped his fingers, conjuring up a pair of chairs from the dining room. "Before we get started, sit. I'd like to talk to you."

Anka bristled. "What's there to talk about? I'm here to learn to fight, and I can't do that sitting on my arse. If you don't like my attitude, I'm sorry. But I don't live to please you anymore."

He couldn't miss the bitter hurt in her voice now. He'd been mistaking it all these months for contempt. But she was challenging him, testing him to see if he gave a shit. Because *she* did. If she didn't care, her words wouldn't bleed anger and accusation. His responsibility now was to pinpoint the hurt so he could begin to heal her. He must find what she needed and give it to her.

"I told you yesterday, Anka, that isn't how this works. You may stay or go. Unless I say otherwise, everything else is up to me. Sit," he repeated gently but firmly.

He watched her need to please war with the pain battering her heart. The battle raged across her delicate face. Patiently, he stood nearby and waited.

Finally, she exhaled a breath that shuddered with impatience and plopped in the chair, lean legs crossed. "What do you want? Because I'll tell you something. You can annoy the piss out of me and make my life difficult, but I will not give up."

"I didn't ask you to quit."

"Not in so many words, no. But you'd rather I did. It would make your life simpler."

"In some ways, it would," he admitted. "While I like the idea that you'll be ready for any trouble that might come your way, I would be greatly relieved if you decided to stop training to fight a terrible battle that I fear will only end with you being hurt."

"Hurt again, you mean?" She arched a brow at him. "Mathias has already hurt me. And one lesson I learned quickly was that I was ill prepared to deal with him. You coddled me and protected me from the real world. For that, it kicked me mercilessly until it nearly killed me. I can't be that fragile bauble. I won't be helpless again. Besides, it's not as if I matter to you anymore."

Her impassioned speech slammed him back in his seat. God, so many things to address with her, so many stones unturned, so many unspoken promises broken. He was going to have to step back even more, start at square one with trust, before he ever started digging in her heart.

"You matter very much. It's why I coddled you perhaps more than I should have. I wanted to take the responsibility of your welfare off your shoulders. I never considered you helpless, just someone very dear to me. The fault for every terrible thing Mathias did to you is mine, love. I left you defenseless, and he used you to weaken me. I am sorrier than you will ever know that I wasn't there for you when he came. I deeply regret that I slipped into such severe mate mourning that I lacked the sanity to find you. Every day, I curse the fact that I didn't save you before he broke our bond and ravaged you. I am in despair if you think you didn't matter then and don't matter now. I realize you have no reason to trust me at the moment, but you have my most sincere promise that I will do whatever it takes to fix that. I will never again let you down."

Anka blinked, stared. Clearly, she'd expected a rude comeback, an argument. He'd disarmed her with his sincerity and honesty. He could see some of the fight leaving her in the way her face softened and her shoulders rounded.

"I don't fault you for what Mathias did to me. When it happened, neither of us fathomed that he would stoop to that level."

"*I* should have. I knew he was attacking families and taking women. I should have realized that he would bring the fight to those who opposed him. I was so absorbed in gearing up for battle that I didn't realize how vulnerable I'd left you."

And that fact still pained him as nothing could. He'd been so busy trying to protect magickind that he'd left his own mate alone to fight one of the worst evils their people had ever seen.

"It's over and done. Leave it."

She sounded ready to forgive the unforgivable, and he couldn't. Nor did he understand. Where did her anger come from, if it wasn't over his failure? "I can't. I should have seen to your safety before anything else. I should have kept myself together when Mathias broke our bond so I could save you. I failed you, and it eats me alive every day."

"You had no control over your mental state, any more than I did. Witches lose their memories. Wizards pine, sometimes to insanity. I don't blame you for that."

"What do you blame me for, then? Don't say nothing. I hear it in your voice."

"Are we going to chat all day or get some bloody work done?"

"Your attempt to avoid the question isn't going to work. We have quite a bit of training to cover. So the sooner you tell me what I've done to anger you, the sooner we can move forward."

"Who says you have? Why is it about you? Maybe living with Shock, his attitude has rubbed off, and it's made me a bloody bitch."

He shook his head. "I know your dirty little secrets, love. And one of them is that you like to please those around you." When she blanched, he dropped his elbows to his knees and stooped a bit to look directly into her eyes. "It's all right. Except you don't always tell the people in your life what you need in return. I won't let that happen with me again."

Lucan's heart pounded furiously, and he wondered if she heard his unspoken message. If she needed a best friend, confidante, or lover, he would fill the role. If she required a firmer hand, well… he would take care of her there, as well. She would get his undying devotion. If anyone left marks on Anka in the future, it wouldn't be Shock. He'd kill the dodgy fuck first. He wouldn't push Anka too hard—yet. Despite her appearance and attitude, she was still fragile. She needed his reassurance. But he'd soon test the theory that she also needed so much more. Anything sexual now would have to wait until they established more trust. Otherwise, she would run to Bram, who would put someone else in charge of her training. He must be careful.

For now.

Anka's face closed up. "What the devil does any of this have to do with teaching me to fight Anarki?"

"You can't learn from a trainer you don't trust. And I can't teach a pupil who won't open up to me and tell me what's in her head. This is hard, physical work. Doing things halfway or not telling me what you require from me can get you killed. We have to be a team, rely on one another without question. I won't tell Bram that you're ready to fight until I know it's absolutely true."

"Fine. I trust that you will not allow me to be hurt in training."

Her answer was just a breath shy of petulant. Whatever hurt plagued her, she held it tenaciously.

"That's a start, but there's a certain mental and emotional trust that comes with placing your life in another warrior's hands, love."

"Stop calling me that."

"Stop telling the trainer how to train." He raised a disapproving brow at her.

She dropped her gaze to her lap. Her unconscious show of deference was both a confirmation of Thorpe's words and an affirmation of his own new understanding. He liked it, too, which took him a bit by surprise. Perhaps that made him something of a caveman, but her vulnerability touched him. Her sad air of fragility under the leather and fighting attitude made him vow to do whatever necessary to make her whole. He grabbed the edges of his chair to stop himself from rushing her, covering her pretty red bow mouth, and devouring her.

Drawing in a breath for self-control, he thought through his options. If he had more time on his side, he'd draw her out slowly, making sure she felt cared for and secure every step of the way. But with Morganna on the loose and Mathias plotting who knew what, not to mention Shock digging his meaty fists into her heart, time wasn't his friend.

"Before we proceed, I think it's important that we work on building our trust again. I'm going to ask you a question, and it won't be an easy one to answer. When I'm satisfied that you've answered it completely and honestly, I will reward you in return."

She raised a brow. "Did you sit about playing 'Truth or Dare' with the other boys and offer them a lolly, too?"

"One more burst of sarcasm, Anka, and I'll tack on a five-kilometer run." He'd rather not threaten her when she seemed so fragile, but she continued to needle him, testing him just enough to make it clear that she sought his attention. "Do you understand?"

"Yes, Lucan."

God, he loved the way she said that. Her voice was low and angry, but carried a hint of softness that made him even harder.

"Good, love. Either tell me why you're angry with me—"

"What good will that do? You're here to train me. I'm here to learn. End of story."

"Thank you for your summation, but I disagree. We are here to build our trust. That includes honesty, even if it's brutal. Even if you think I won't give a shit, I want your sincere answer. If I don't wish to hear something you have to say, I'll tell you. Otherwise, you don't make those decisions for me."

Her eyes flashed defiantly. "Stop talking to me like a three-year-old, you sodding bastard."

"Perhaps I am a sodding bastard, but I'm one who's ready to run five kilometers. Are you? If not, I suggest you answer my question or hear the other, then decide."

Her lips pursed with annoyance. Anka might not like this, but she needed it. It was working. This was the most productive conversation they'd engaged in since her disappearance. The woman who'd walked in here ten minutes ago was far stronger-willed than the Anka he'd lived with. This one was fighting…but hurting. If he was clever and firm enough, she would eventually begin to trust and lean on him again. He simply had to keep his wits about him, exercise his patience, and let her work it out in her head, giving her a nudge here and there when she required it.

"What else do you want to know?" She gritted her teeth.

"If you won't tell me what I've done to make you angry, then I want to hear exactly what Mathias did to you."

Horror flared her amber eyes wide. She shot up, scrambling back, knocking her chair over. It clattered against the hardwood floors. "Absolutely not."

Lucan couldn't mistake the trembling in her voice. He longed to take her in his arms and assure her that she could trust him with her story, that nothing she said could make him care less. He must know the details of her trauma eventually. She couldn't truly begin to heal until she let out the truth.

Frustrated at her reticence, he fixed a gentle but resolved expression on his face. "Anka, I've given you a choice. Several, in fact. Pick from two questions, choose a five-kilometer run, or quit. I've been more than fair."

She swallowed, paced around her chair. Lucan nearly bit his tongue at the gentle flare of her hips and the delicate curve of her arse, that thick silken rope of hair hanging to the small of her back, begging him to tug on it and bend her back until her lips trembled just under his. How long had it been since he kissed her, smelled her. Tasted her. A mere three months…and yet, forever. Bloody hell, he'd missed her.

Anka whirled around to face him, her expression sharp and decisive. "All right, then. I'll run. Let me pop out and get my trainers. I'll be back—"

"No. You must run now. In those shoes. Or that option is off the table."

"I can't, and you bloody well know it."

"I told you to come prepared to train. If you're not…" He shrugged and couldn't help but grin. "The boots look stunning on you, I admit. But I'm fairly certain you thought you'd wear those nasty heels in case we practiced self-defense again and you got to pound your dainty little foot down on mine." She flushed guiltily, and he broadened his smile. "Sorry, love. If you're not prepared to run, you'll have to answer me or quit altogether."

She thrust her hands on her hips. "When did you become a manipulative arse?"

"Are you resorting to name-calling because I'm determined to train you properly?" He stood and righted her chair, brushing dangerously close to her.

Blast it all, she smelled so achingly familiar. He'd missed that scent, spent entire nights in their closet breathing in her clothes, trying to catch even the faintest whiff of her flowers and musk. Thankfully, today she smelled nothing like Shock. He prayed his baggy jog pants and long T-shirt covered up the erection desperately seeking her attention. Of course he knew she'd had sex since her rape—and wasn't that a stab in the heart?—but he had no notion how afraid she might be of him. Of real intimacy. Perhaps one reason she asked Shock to hold her down was to force her past her fears so that she could accept energy without thought or guilt. He'd find out for certain soon.

"I'm calling you a manipulative arse because you're forcing me to tell you things that don't concern you."

Her anger didn't concern him? Her *rape* didn't? Oh, she was so very wrong. Everything about her had been his business once and it would be again.

"Sit." He voiced his demand in soft tones, but put steel behind it.

Anka glared at him for a long, silent minute. She actually contemplated walking out, he could tell. Lucan both wanted and feared it. She would be safer if she quit, but he might never be this close to her again. He waited, watching her small fists clench, her mouth purse mutinously, then she dropped into the chair.

"I'm not quitting."

The old Anka would have at his first hint of displeasure. This one? Well, if they were going to repair their relationship, it would require honesty and better communication. Besides, seducing the surrender of this strong-willed creature would be a delight. "Which question will you answer, then?"

She drew in a fortifying breath. "I'm angry with you because you're being a bloody pillock."

"That's a five-kilometer run tomorrow, Anka, for sarcasm and lying to me. You came in wearing an attitude like armor. I'm not the enemy. I'm here to help you. If you can't drop your shields and trust me, we'll never make it out of these chairs so that you can train. If I'm going to get nothing but attitude from you, we're done for today."

Her nose flattened. She bit her lip, and her eyes welled up. A moment later, she shook her head, shaking off the expression. But he'd seen the worry and fear. "All right, then! I'm angry with you because you nearly mated with Sabelle. Are you happy to know it hurts me? Does that give you some sort of thrill?"

He *was* happy. Not that that he'd caused her pain, of course. The acknowledgement, however unwilling, that she still cared tingled through every last nerve in his body. "I'm sorry if that hurt you. Let me explain."

"It doesn't matter."

"It does. No, don't look away from me." He waited for a pregnant moment, until she complied. "I see you readying an argument. Don't. Just listen," he insisted. "It. Matters. At the time Sabelle and I discussed mating, I believed you forever beyond my reach. I'd thrown myself entirely into saving magickind to have a damned purpose in life. Sabelle and I would never truly be more than friends, but there are worse things to base a mating on." He shrugged. "Ultimately, I stopped the proceedings. She was clearly in love with Ice. After the way you and I had been cruelly parted, I refused to wish either of them that sort of pain. And because you were honest with me just now, I will be honest with you." He grabbed her hand and stared directly into her eyes. "I ultimately couldn't take Sabelle as my mate because she wasn't you and my heart refused any other."

Anka reared back as if he'd punched her in the stomach. She shot to her feet once more and turned away furiously. "You can't say that. Shock will read my thoughts."

"I don't give a piss about Shock, only you."

Anka looked torn, and Lucan wanted to stop her internal debate. They couldn't heal until they hashed everything out. He gently brought her around to face him and cupped her cheek in his hand.

She was still so soft, still looked so pure and small and lost. His chest buckled. "Anka, whatever is running through that pretty head of yours, tell me. Trust me to help you."

She jerked away, tapped her toe, obviously thinking. Finally, she squared her shoulders and drew in a sharp breath. "Sabelle is my best friend, and you two…"

When her eyes teared up again, Lucan had endured enough of the distance between them. He reached across the empty space, locked his hands around her waist, and pulled her into his lap. "She kept me alive."

Anka closed her eyes, hiding her pain from him. "I know."

And she still didn't like it. That was a very good sign. "Look at me, love."

"Don't call me that."

"Anka?" He dropped his voice, giving it tender authority.

Her eyes flew open, and she focused on him. "Good. Love, I would have died without her. I'm sure she told you that."

She nodded, dropping her gaze. Her dark lashes brushed her cheeks, and Lucan could see her fighting the hurt. "I have no right to care."

"Logic doesn't always ease the pain. You went to Shock when you didn't remember me, yes? You left the safety of your cousin's flat, desperate for energy to power your magic, weren't you?"

Anka hesitated, then nodded.

Lucan tucked a finger under her chin and lifted her gaze to him. "Logically, I know you would likely have died without him. I should be grateful to him for keeping you well, giving you a roof, just like you should be appreciative of Sabelle's efforts. But logic doesn't always erase what our heart tells us. Can you forgive me?"

He held his breath. This answer was important, vitally so. He would find a way to move past everything that had happened between her and Shock if she could forgive him Sabelle's well-meaning efforts. Even if she didn't, he would climb that mountain somehow, too.

Anka drew in a shuddering breath, clearly thinking when the

door to the training room burst open. Lucan shoved Anka's smaller body behind him, ready to meet the intrusive threat head-on. Instead, he found his brother standing in the doorway, brow raised.

"Bram is calling everyone together. The ladies have found something in their research that he wants us all to hear."

He shot Caden a glare that protested his brother's terrible timing. "Five minutes, and we'll be there."

Caden shook his head. "Now. I think it has something to do with putting down Morganna for good."

And if they could eliminate Morganna, the Doomsday Brethren and magickind would have one less worry on their plates. Perhaps then he could afford to focus more on Anka. And they might not need her to fight quite so soon.

Lucan sighed with regret. "We'll be there in a tick."

With a nod, his brother turned away. As Caden ducked out the door, Anka edged around him and tried to waltz past. Lucan grabbed her arm in a steely grip and turned her to face him.

"We're not finished with this conversation."

"We have to be." She jerked her arm free. "I will extend you trust as my trainer. I know you will never hurt me and will do everything in your power to teach me what I need to know to stay alive. In return, I swear I will learn whatever you wish, practice in whatever way you desire, and do my utmost to be an asset to the Doomsday Brethren. But it doesn't matter if you forgive me for Shock or I forgive you for Sabelle. That would only matter if we intended to mate again. And that will never happen."

Lucan stared at her retreating back, mentally pulling out the figurative knife she'd just stabbed into his heart. The terrible words were part of her armor, the way she meant to keep distance between them so she could protect herself. But from what? Him? He knew she didn't love Shock. When forced to choose between him and that Denzell wanker just over a century ago, Anka had chosen him. She'd been ready to leave the bloody berk a few days ago, from what Sabelle said.

Yet she'd gone back, surrendered her body and will to him

again. Maybe she had more feelings for Shock than she had a century ago. Maybe she thought she needed him because Shock met her secret desires as no one had.

Lucan clenched a fist.

"What the devil are you doing?" Bram barreled toward him with a scowl. "We're waiting for you two."

When Anka disappeared into Bram's office, Lucan snarled at his best friend. "There is no way I can train Anka without getting personal. I'm going to touch her."

A smile creased the stressed lines of Bram's face, making him look more like the carefree playboy Lucan had known for centuries. "You think you're surprising me?"

Sly bastard. "She'll complain."

Bram shrugged. "I'm not coming between two former mates. Nor will I tell you how to train her."

Finally, Lucan had something to smile about. "I'm going to wrest her away from Shock and make her mine again."

"I hope so." Bram slapped him on the back. "I'm bloody tired of seeing two people I care about so much being so sodding stubborn and walking around with long faces. Now let's go."

They walked into Bram's office to find the rest of the warriors assembled, along with some of the mates. He spotted Anka by the window, alone, the morning sun glinting off her severe braid, staring straight ahead at some unknown point on the wall—and avoiding eye contact. Sabelle stood on the far side of the room, anchored to Ice's massive body by his strong arm. Belle's face broke his heart as she looked at Anka with hurt swimming in her eyes. Normally, the best friends would have gravitated together, and a hot flare of frustration rushed through him. Damn it, Anka was determined to close herself off from everything and everyone to shut out any possible hurt. That simply wasn't like her. He was going to have to open her up and fill her heart with love once more.

With a determined sigh, he sauntered over to Anka and planted himself beside her. "You're hurting Belle's feelings."

Anka looked away, focusing her attention on Bram, who now

stood behind his ornate wooden desk at the front of the room, books spread out before him. "She has Ice."

"She is your best friend."

"She is from an impeccable family. She is the sort of mate you deserve." Anka pushed away from the window to find an empty chair in the back corner of the room.

Where the devil had *that* come from? There were so many damn things wrong with Anka's statement that Lucan didn't know where to start. Definitely, they were going to sort this out. If she thought she could end the discussion by moving to a corner, she was sorely mistaken. But here and now wasn't the time to make that clear.

"Thank you all for coming on short notice. Special thanks to Olivia, Sabelle, Sydney, and Felicia for tirelessly prowling through Merlin's rambling tomes to find something—"

Duke burst through the door a moment later, interrupting Bram's speech. He looked as if he'd like to tear off more than a few heads and ask questions later. Lucan frowned. Simon rarely lost his cool. His visible frustration didn't bode well.

"Good of you to join us. Where the bloody hell have you been?" Bram asked.

"Dealing with some of the worst sort of scum. Television producers." Simon shuddered. "The long and the short of it? All the murmurs I heard about exposing Morganna are true. We must act now!" He raked a hand through his hair, and Felicia came to his side with a concerned frown knitting her brow. "The BBC has planned an in-depth look at the tragedy at Stonehenge. They intended to publicly surmise that supernatural forces could be at work and even found people to interview about *magickind* specifically. Yes, us. They're still airing the exposé, but after our 'conversation,' they are omitting the speculation. For now. As if that isn't bad enough, an American cable show called *Ghost Hunters* is planning an episode about the spirit of Morganna le Fay haunting England and killing innocents. Not precisely true, since it's the witch herself and not her spirit, but too close for comfort. I'm still seeing articles pop up in various newspapers and tabloids. Sydney, I'm going to buy up the paper and fire your former editor if *Out of This Realm* doesn't stop speculating about the Stonehenge attack."

Sydney sighed. "I've told Holly to shut it. She's not exactly listening."

"At all." Displeasure made Simon growl, and Felicia tried to soothe him with a gentle brush to the shoulder.

"For fuck's sake." Bram paced. "Not what I wanted to hear. Can't you stop them?"

"I have—for now. But I can't hold them at bay forever. Money will only buy so much, and then…well, won't they be asking why I'm willing to pay hundreds of thousands of pounds to silence them? Coupled with all the speculation about why I seemingly haven't aged a day in the last decade, there are bound to be difficult questions. I don't want to put too much spotlight on myself or any of us. But we're running out of options."

Lucan held in a curse. Duke had been raised human, but he understood magickind's current problems perfectly.

"Before the humans look too deeply at you, before Morganna brings another inquisition down on magickind, before the death toll skyrockets, yes. Damn it all! We must rid ourselves of Morganna. Whilst you were gone this morning, we've found some new information that might help. Ladies?"

They all looked at one another, then Felicia nudged Olivia forward, who rolled her eyes and trudged over to Bram. Marrok looked on proudly.

"This morning, we stumbled across something that I believe will help us, but we need a bit more interpretation. I know some Arthurian folklore and legend, and I've asked Marrok what he knows from that period since he lived it. Anyway, we've managed to piece together a few facts. We've always known that Merlin created some way to ultimately destroy Morganna. He exiled her previously so that she would suffer the sorts of trials she forced on others, but he knew she was scary-strong and ultimately left a way to kill her for good. According to this passage, it's a potion. The eyewitnesses of the Stonehenge attack said that she seemed to be frantically searching the relic bit by bit and killing anyone who got in her way. I can only guess this potion is what she sought."

"How did she know about it?" Ice snarled.

Olivia frowned. "I don't think Merlin made much secret that it existed."

"Knowing my grandfather, he would have taunted Morganna with the knowledge," Bram drawled.

"You'd do the same," Lucan pointed out, and Bram nodded with a grin. "Even if we find this potion, she won't drink it. She's too happy being out of exile and terrorizing others again."

"Precisely. I'm sure she wants to destroy it, which is why she's hunting for it. That would make her almost invincible. Old age might get her eventually…but somehow she's already lasted far beyond a normal magical lifespan, so I have to believe that she's gathered dark forces to work for her and somehow keep her alive."

"That's possible?" Duke asked, wrapping his hand around his mate's delicate fingers, as if he wanted to keep her closer.

Bram shrugged. "That's the power of magic. It's not as if the laws of nature and physics always apply. If you're strong and crafty enough, you can even cheat death."

"Looks like she's learned. Fuck," Ice grumbled on the other side of the room.

For once, Lucan perfectly agreed with Sabelle's gruff mate.

"Where might we find this devil's potion?" Marrok asked. "Does Merlin say? I've a yen to force it down her evil throat."

Everyone turned to Olivia, who sighed, shoulders slumped. "We don't know exactly where it is. You know Merlin would never have organized the information outlining *where* to find the potion with the instructions for actually retrieving it from its hiding spot. And that's all we found, details about how to get our hands physically on the potion once it's discovered. And it's not going to be easy."

Bram jumped in. "Indeed. The potion, wherever it is, is caged by a spell. Merlin wouldn't have wanted to make it simple for

Morganna to obtain and destroy it. The good news is that we know now what we need to snatch it up. The bad news? The order is a tall one."

"Well, spit it out, then," Lucan demanded. After his session with Anka had been cut short, he found his patience running thin.

Bram raised a brow at him, then his stare skidded over to Anka. She sat, back straight, chin raised, shoulders squared, staring straight ahead.

Her bravado was utter shit. Lucan saw it. *Felt* it. Wanted to get underneath it to reach the fragile woman underneath who seemed to think she was somehow too damaged for him or somehow not good enough. Impatience chafed him, but he swallowed it down. She needed time to heal, his attention, and the certainty he would be there, no matter what. No way could he convince her of all that in a day or two.

"The first component to undoing Merlin's spell is someone from his bloodline." As Ice stood to his full height, wrapped his arm more tightly around his mate, and glared across the room, Bram calmed the big warrior immediately. "I'll take that. There's no need for Sabelle to be involved." As Ice relaxed back at his mate's side, the lovely blonde witch nudged his shoulder with a scowl.

Olivia grabbed Merlin's book. "The next component is trickier. The blood of someone from Nimue's line."

"Nimue? Who is that?" Duke asked. "Sometimes, I bloody hate that I didn't grow up magical. Sorry I'm so far behind."

Bram sent him a grim smile. "Nimue is otherwise known as Viviene. Most commonly known as The Lady of the Lake, the witch who was Merlin's student and lover, who eventually tricked him into his tomb. Finding someone of her ancient bloodline will be difficult."

Tabitha shoved herself up from the sofa, her swelling belly more pronounced every day as Raiden's youngling grew within her. "I think I can help there. My father, before he was killed, updated a document filled with magickind's most sacred bloodlines, including Nimue's. He didn't publish it, so we have an advantage there. Morganna won't know where to look." She gestured to a thick, yellowing book her mate currently held on his lap. "I'm glad you told me to bring this, Olivia. Keep talking. I'll continue looking. My father handwrote most of this, but I think I've nearly figured it out."

The Doomsday Brethren's leader smiled her way, then Raiden helped her back to her seat. Before anyone could even resume speaking, the crafty redhead was flipping pages again, the paper occasionally scraping against her protruding belly.

"While she looks for that, I'll tell you about the last requirement of Merlin's to release the potion," Olivia continued. "There's a reference here to the second washerwoman. Whatever that is, we must have one of those."

Lucan frowned. "What does that mean?"

"A banshee," Anka whispered fearfully from the back of the room. And no wonder, the nomadic women who roamed the earth washing the bloody clothes of those about to die, singing the death wail, were feared by all.

He spun his head around to stare at his former mate. She hadn't spoken a word since this meeting began. Why give voice to her thoughts now? And how did she know the answer?

"Anka is right," Bram said. "But not just any banshee. I remember Merlin telling me that there are three types: the maiden, the mother, and the crone. This is where the spell gets difficult. In addition to the blood of someone from Merlin and Nimue's lines, we need the second generation in a banshee line, so one who is also a mother. She wards off the spirits guarding the potion."

"What?" Lucan completely lost his patience. "Is that even possible? Weren't the banshees obliterated hundreds of years ago? The few who weren't killed by the paranoid Council idiots ended their own lives, rather than endure public execution. I've heard rumors that a few still exist...but I would never have stopped Anka's training for this meeting if I'd known you were basically looking for the impossible."

"Sounds like the equivalent of an Elvis sighting to us humans,"

Sydney piped up.

Bram shot her a disapproving glare. "It's improbable, Lucan, but not impossible. We must keep looking or we'll never be rid of Morganna."

Into the momentary silence, Tabitha gasped, going utterly white. "I found Nimue's bloodline!"

"Well?" Bram prompted impatiently.

"Lucan's right. This isn't possible."

"Supposedly opening Morganna's tomb and resurrecting her was impossible, too, but here we are dealing with the bitch. So tell us. Who do we know that's a descendant of Nimue?"

"There is only one living member of the line." She placed a trembling hand over her belly, Raiden wrapped his fingers around hers, giving a soft squeeze of comfort. "It's Mathias. To end Morganna, we're going to have to undertake a dangerous hunt for a banshee…and make a deal with the devil."

Chapter Six

Anka fidgeted. Lucan's watchful gaze never strayed. She schooled her face impassively as talk of teaming up with Mathias and capturing a banshee continued. Her heart froze up, failing to beat for long minutes. Oh, God. She didn't want to dance with the devil. Facing him again would be hard enough, but being his partner would be impossible. But Mathias wasn't her only worry.

For Anka's entire childhood, her mother had harangued her daily about keeping their deadly bloodline a secret. *Don't trust anyone, girl. And definitely don't ever sing.*

If people knew the truth, she could be hunted, incarcerated, killed. Every day, she thanked their Creator that being a blend of other species didn't reflect on a magical signature. Banshee camps weren't that distant a memory, historically speaking. Hunted by paranoid witches and wizards in their remote banshee villages, the women had been captured en masse for centuries and dragged away from all civilization. Their mouths were always magically sewn shut forever. Often, they were slaughtered. Entire generations of banshees perished together. Her grandmother had given her life so that her mother could escape such a camp. Eventually, her mother had mated with a wizard, kept her secret to the grave, and made

Anka promise to do the same. And in the century she'd been mated to Lucan, she had never once given him any reason to suspect just what blood ran in her veins.

But now…she hesitated. Would telling her friends her secret help them end Morganna, so they could ultimately turn their focus on Mathias again? She wanted that bastard gone so badly, would give *anything* to see the scum who'd torn apart her life defeated and dead. She'd risk exposing herself, seeing horror and pity on the faces of all she'd called friends for centuries. She'd even risk being ostracized for the rest of her life. But if she spoke now, Lucan would forever know that she was as inferior as she felt. He'd never touch her again. And maybe that was better for him.

No. That was definitely better for him.

Anka opened her mouth. Then she closed it. After keeping a secret like this from Lucan for over a century, if she revealed it now, he would feel completely betrayed. The thought of hurting him more stabbed her like a physical ache. And ultimately, revealing her tainted bloodline could do nothing to help them retrieve Morganna's potion simply because, while banshee blood ran through her veins, she wasn't a second washerwoman. She wasn't a mother. Not that she and Lucan hadn't tried in all their years together to conceive. It hurt to, once again, be useless.

"Do you have something to add, Anka?" Bram asked from across the room.

"No." She avoided looking at anyone.

Unless she could be helpful to the cause, this shame was hers—and hers alone—to bear.

From the corner of her eye, she saw Lucan. He watched her with a slight frown wrinkling his brow, as if trying to figure her out. He wanted inside her head. She didn't dare let him. Later, she'd worry about how much she'd inadvertently revealed today or why he'd changed from the tender mate she'd known to the delicious alpha male who'd made her knees go weak with nothing more than a firm tone. He hadn't mentioned her bruises again, but she'd wondered what he must be thinking. Was he revolted…or curious?

Did he want to try *that* with her?

The thought rattled her. She could take the pain from Shock. It released her anguish, scrubbed her soul raw and clean so she could go on, less burdened by the past. But it didn't touch her heart. Lucan taking control of her, pulling her hair in his fist as he plunged inside her with one merciless thrust after another, murmuring in her ear how much he wanted her… The fantasy alone completely undid her.

She could never let him that close again.

"Are we truly sure Mathias is the last of Nimue's line?" Ice asked, slanting a dubious glance at Tabitha. "Maybe your father got it wrong. Wasn't Mathias a Chillingham?"

"On his father's side, yes," the pregnant redhead said. "On his mother's side, the origins were shrouded in mystery. My father made notes that her magical signature was unlike any he'd ever seen. But being one of Nimue's descendants would do that *and* explain all the power he wields. It's not simple magic."

"Indeed," Bram cut in. "The only more accomplished witch of Arthur's time was Morganna."

Ice shook his head. "Then I want to know why the barmy fuck thinks he's more powerful than Morganna herself. Why would he resurrect her, assuming he could bring her to heel?"

"Male ego?" Sabelle smirked beside him.

Ice whispered something in her ear that made her blush. Anka looked away, unable to watch the blatant show of affection. The envy stinging her brought on a terrible, guilty pain.

Lucan's gaze cornered her again, sharp with awareness. She raised her chin and a challenging brow before directing her attention to Bram and the matter at hand. "I'm against this idea. Are you actually suggesting that we make an alliance with Mathias? We don't have a banshee, and he'll only use us."

"Just as we'll use him," Bram quipped. "She must have done or planned something beyond frightening to force Mathias to seek us out."

"Or he's hoping we'll all get ourselves killed trying to stop her."

Anka frowned.

"And he might not be wrong," Bram conceded. "By all accounts, she is one dangerous bitch."

"Aye," Marrok cut in. "'Tis far more than the marks of her fingernails she leaves on a man's back. An expert in baiting traps, she is. No man will easily outsmart her, and mayhap not at all. Each of us should be ever wary."

"Indeed," Bram seconded. "This might be a trap, as you point out. But our resident Yank, Olivia, has a quaint saying. What is that?"

The violet-eyed beauty smiled. "You have to play the hand you've been dealt."

"Precisely. This is our hand. Sadly, Mathias seems to be dealing the cards, but nevertheless, we will play. Send Shock a text, Anka, will you?" Bram asked, strolling closer.

She sighed, grateful for something else to focus on. As soon as she had, she received an immediate reply. "He said he'd be here to discuss Mathias's proposition. But you know Shock. With him, that could be two minutes or two days."

It wasn't as if Shock ever answered to anyone. Not Bram. Not even Mathias. Certainly not the woman he lived with and slaked his lust on, fooling himself all the while that he loved her. She knew better. Someday, he would, too.

Lucan's eyes narrowed, and he opened his mouth. Before he could get a word out, Shock's audible calling card rang out. Bram charged toward the door.

"Stay here," Lucan demanded before leaving, hot on Bram's heels.

Anka had to reach Shock first, make sure he gave away no hint of her secret. She bounded up and followed the wizards.

Lucan turned on her as they raced to the door. "Bloody hell, woman. Don't you listen?"

"Shock isn't going to hurt me."

He snarled, his blue eyes flat and hard. "Bollocks! If you give him enough time, he will."

"He's had plenty of time. He's kept me alive and protected me." *He's kept my secret for nearly two hundred years, just as I've kept his.*

"The things I haven't done. Right, then." With a curse, he turned his back on her, his long-legged strides carrying him to the door.

"That wasn't meant to be a commentary about you," she argued softly.

"But that's what I know to be true."

"Don't act as if it matters anymore," she called after him. "Let's forget it and stop hurting one another, shall we?"

"Enough!" Bram snapped. "Stop bickering and focus. Or isn't Morganna being on the loose, exposing magickind to potential slaughter from the humans, while we have to make nice with Mathias because of it real enough for you?"

Guilt stung Anka. "Sorry."

Lucan looked away, closed-mouthed and closed off.

Bram flung the door open to see Shock leaning against the portal. He visually bypassed Bram, gave Lucan the universal glare for "fuck you," then fastened his gaze on Anka.

"You need something?"

A part of her wondered if he'd really come simply because she'd said she needed him. In the past, he might just as often have flipped her the bird and disappeared back into a bottle. She winced. She couldn't take the thought back. He'd already read it.

Thunder crossed his face. "Don't fucking think that. I've been here for you in all the ways that count."

Anka couldn't argue with that, so she just nodded and silently pleaded with him not to breathe a word about the banshee in the room. "We need to talk to you."

He gave her a slight nod. "We?"

"You know I've thrown my lot in with the Doomsday Brethren."

"You're bloody serious?" Shock pushed his way past Bram and entered the house.

"Come in, then. Don't wait for me to invite you," Bram snarked. "We're willing to negotiate with Mathias about ending Morganna."

No emotion crossed Shock's face. "I'll get word to him."

"Of course you will," Lucan sneered.

Even behind the sunglasses, Anka knew Shock's eyes narrowed. She felt the anger radiating from him. Lucan wasn't any less seething. The need for violence shimmered off of him. She turned, frowned, wondering what had gotten into him. Could he be…jealous? Did he still care? She didn't want to hope so. Hope hurt too much when reality crushed it. But the truth was, she was jealous of Sabelle and every other woman Lucan had touched. Maybe—

Very aware of Shock's growl and his charge toward her, she broke off the thought and tiptoed back.

Lucan stepped between them, as if he meant to buffer her from Shock's anger. "She is a grown witch who can make her own decisions."

"I can also speak for myself." She gently pushed Lucan aside. "I'm sorry, Shock." And she was. He'd done so much for her, yet she repaid him by pining for her former mate every single day. "Yes, I'm serious. For my sanity, I need to be a part of sending Mathias to hell, of stripping him of his sense of power and personal safety the way he stripped me of mine."

Shock stared at her for an uncomfortable minute, probing, penetrating her thoughts. She winced as he intruded. He wasn't subtle or careful, and it hurt more than a little. But she allowed it. She allowed him to know that she wasn't here, intending to dangle herself in front of Lucan with the hope that he would take her back. She gave him the peace of mind of knowing that, no matter how badly she wished otherwise, she intended to be nothing more to her former mate than a trainee.

Finally, Shock turned to Lucan, brows narrowing into a vee as he thrust his way into Lucan's face. "Hell, no. This bleeding arsehole isn't training you. He isn't touching you. I know exactly what he's thinking. What the fuck could he teach you except to neglect your responsibilities and turn rabid when danger strikes?"

Fury rumbled across Lucan's face. "You know nothing about mate mourning or the lengths I would go to in order to see Anka protected. So fuck off. You manage to be conveniently absent whenever there's a battle. What do you think you can do for Anka? Ignore her for a bottle of scotch, then beat her arse blue for the hell of it? You've kept her in that ramshackle place you call home. It's falling down around your ears, and have you taken proper care of her? Do you know that she's allergic to shellfish and coconut? Do you care that she prefers a very particular brand of silk knickers? Did you bother to find out that she likes to be held when she's sleeping and that she'll have nightmares and wake crying, needing to feel that you care?"

Anka closed her eyes. With every word, Lucan was reminding her of so many of the reasons she'd loved him. Yes, she had given herself to him—heart, body, soul, and free will—but he'd given her so very much in return, particularly the kind of understanding she wasn't certain she could ever find with another man. But that yearning made her weak. She could no longer afford the deepest wishes of her heart, not with Mathias still on the loose.

"Oh, boo hoo," Shock spat. "Anka doesn't need that anymore."

Lucan turned a glare full of burning anger on her. "Is that really true? Have Mathias and Shock really gutted your heart so much that you no longer seek the love and reassurance you once craved? Or do you simply keep telling yourself that's the case?"

"I don't need any of that anymore." *And I can't afford to need you.* The words sat on the tip of her tongue, but she couldn't make herself say them. They burned every inch of her flesh, all the way to the deepest part of her soul. "I was a stupid, fragile princess who knew nothing about protecting myself. Mathias taught me that in the most vicious way possible."

Lucan looked like he wanted to argue, but Bram cut in. "We are here to discuss Mathias and negotiate an agreement under which we will all hunt Morganna jointly. Anything else now is petty and pointless. I won't have you wasting my time whilst you two squabble like children. Are we going to save magickind or not?"

Lucan completely ignored his best friend's pretty speech. "You're going with the china doll excuse again, Anka? Can you stand here and tell me you don't need anything we once shared?"

She swallowed down a searing lump of need, struggling against the lonely, hungry part of her that still yearned for him. "I've said I don't need any of it."

Defeat crossed Lucan's face, slumped his shoulders. A surge of blistering fury followed. "Then it's a damn good thing I don't want them, either."

He lied. Because she'd hurt him. Anka didn't dare blanch, but his words gouged her, emptying out a hole in her heart and pouring pain inside.

"When did your period start, then?" Shock challenged Lucan before turning to Bram. "Got a tampon for him, mate?"

Lucan stiffened, blistering hatred seizing him in a single lunge, complete with a look that could kill. "You've changed her. Ruined her. You're going to pay. I will kill you if it's the last thing I do."

Shock smiled like a shark, all teeth and bad attitude. "Not if I kill you first."

"Shut up!" Bram yelled.

Beside her, Shock raised a hand, looking like he intended to hurl a lethal dose of magic right at Lucan's chest. He let it fly with a snarling battle cry.

Nothing happened.

With a curse, he looked up to find Felicia standing there, wearing a Mona Lisa smile. "Simon suggested that you might be having a bit of difficulty finding your way back to the office. Shall we?"

Shock flung his hand down and grabbed her by the elbow, dragging her toward Bram's lair. Behind her, Lucan followed, a carrot Fate dangled in her face, offering her everything she still wanted—but kept just out of reach.

She no longer wants me. She no longer wants me. She no longer wants me.

The mantra resounded in Lucan's head over and over, a clanging echo, jarring him each and every time the ugly truth raced through his brain again. She didn't want him. How many times and in how many bloody ways did she have to tell him before his stupid heart finally understood and gave up?

As Shock dragged Anka away, clutching her in his meaty fist, he tried not to look. Tried not to plot murder. Maybe she preferred an emotionally stunted wankstain to a wizard who would do anything, even lay down his life, for her.

"She didn't mean it."

The soft, feminine whisper curled into his ear from somewhere just behind him. With a scowl, he turned to find Felicia standing there with a hopeful little grin.

"What do you mean?" he demanded.

"Anka, saying she no longer wanted any of the things you mentioned. She was lying. I could tell all the way from the next room. The stench was terrible. She wants them badly. She wants you."

That was good news, the best he'd had all day. But…why lie? Why rip his heart out—again—in front of an audience? Why make a spectacle of his feelings and his memories of their mating?

"I see the questions on your face. I have no answers. I can only say that she lied."

His gaze swerved back to Anka. Did Shock have something he held over her head that forced her compliance?

Before Lucan could ask anything more, Felicia departed upstairs. He entered Bram's office, which had been cleared of the rest of the Brethren and their mates. Bram would make sure that Shock could read none of their minds. That parlor trick shouldn't work with Felicia in the manor, but somehow, for some confounding reason, Shock's ability to read minds could be dampened by nothing.

Putting as much distance as possible between Shock and himself, Lucan resumed his spot on the far side of the room, by the window, where no one—especially Shock—could get behind him. He didn't need to be stabbed in the back again.

Anka settled into the corner and tried to make herself small. Felicia had sworn that her refusal of him was a lie, and her body language certainly bore that out. His former mate scooted as far away from Shock as he could. The leather-clad wizard was having none of it, sitting on a nearby ottoman and dragging her onto his lap. She opened her mouth to protest. One of Shock's brows rose above those bloody stupid sunglasses. Anka closed her mouth, lips pursed grimly. Lucan looked away.

She didn't love Shock, and for that, he had to be grateful. Of course, that didn't mean she loved him either, but he wasn't giving up on her again.

"Thank you for coming, Shock." Bram stood behind his desk, using it like a podium. He opened the negotiation with precision and purpose.

"Now that I'm here, what do you want?"

"It's not that simple. First, you're a dodgy sort. You happen to know a banshee?"

Anka stiffened. Lucan supposed that she might not appreciate her current lover being maligned. A little smile lifted the corners of his mouth. Anka might not like it, but he surely did.

"Dodgy? Fuck you. You called me here to ask about banshees?" He cocked his head and released a long-suffering sigh. "Name me one person who knows one. Why the fuck do you ask?"

Bram smiled tightly. "Just curious. Before we join Mathias in any effort to destroy Morganna, we need a few assurances."

Shock settled back, leaning against the wall, his arm still snugly around Anka's tiny waist. She relaxed a bit against him. "People are dying, and you want to negotiate?"

"When did you become a fucking humanitarian?" The words

were out of Lucan's mouth before he could stop himself.

God, why couldn't he just shut up?

Bram pinned him with a warning glare. "Are you helping this effort?"

He shook his head. "Sorry."

"Excellent." Bram turned back to Shock. "Yes, I want to negotiate. If Mathias is so concerned about magickind, too, he can agree to the terms quickly, and we'll get started. First, he must give us full and complete information about Morganna. Everything he knows, we'd bloody better know as well. If I find out he's hidden anything at all from us, no matter how minor, I'll cut him off cold, and he can find some way to put Morganna down by himself."

Shock shrugged. "I'll tell him. Doubt he'll have a problem. I'm sure, however, that he'll want similar assurances. You have to puke up everything you know about killing Morganna."

Lucan looked up and found Bram staring, those blue eyes of his speculating about how little they could trust Mathias. Very little, Lucan was sure. But what choice did they have? And not for anything would he think about— No. He would not risk tipping Shock off. Instead, he pictured a fantasy. He started with one he'd had many times: Shock sliced wide open, his blood spilling all around as he lay on a street every bit as dirty as his soul and watched his life force leaving him as the birds swooped down, one by one, to eat away at his entrails in a slow, painful death.

"You wish," Shock growled.

"Indeed, I do." Lucan simply smiled.

"Focus, damn it!" Bram pounded a fist on the table and waited with seething impatience until everyone did as he demanded.

"Bossy wanker," Shock muttered under his breath.

Anka elbowed him through his leather coat. He grunted, looking mighty displeased, but said nothing.

"If I agree to share my information with Mathias, he must agree that he cannot attempt to use it without my knowledge or consent. He must also not act alone. We will be a team, which means he will abide by the same rules that govern everyone else in this effort. I lead it. That's non-negotiable."

Shock wore a smile that snarled "you must fucking be kidding," but he merely said, "I'll pass it on."

"Anyone he wishes to talk to about Morganna or the information we have must be someone I approve. He cannot share what we know with whomever the hell he wants."

"Yes, yes. We're all on the same team, playing by the same rules, blah, blah, blah. Is that it?"

Bram looked ready to spit nails, but managed a halfway cordial nod. "I suppose I don't need to tell you that he should decide quickly."

"He came to you, wanker. I think he understands quite well."

"The moment she's captured or put down, all hint of being bosom buddies is over. No more of this 'enemy of my enemy is my friend' tripe."

"Precisely." Shock looked as if the negotiation amused him.

"I still say this idea is barking mad." Anka couldn't hold her silence any longer. "Mathias will stab you in the back."

"Not if we stab him first." Bram smiled, then directed his attention back to Shock. "So, once he's agreed to all the terms, have him contact me for a meeting. We'll swap information and make a plan."

Shock gently nudged Anka off his lap and rose to his considerable height, scraping huge palms down his leather-clad thighs. "Am I done being your errand boy for the day?"

"I think so, yes."

"Good. Then fuck off. Anka?"

He held out a hand, as if he expected her to go with him. Lucan looked away. He couldn't stand to see Shock touch her in any way.

And because he'd been stupid enough to think it, Shock smirked and wrapped a meaty arm around Anka's tiny waist, dragging her body against his, then lowering his head for a noisy kiss. She struggled, pushed, but Lucan closed his eyes. Every muscle in his body tensed with the need to save her, but the fucking image of Shock's mouth on hers had burned into his brain. How could he help a woman who refused to be saved?

Suddenly, Shock growled, then turned an accusing stare down on her. "Not happening, Anka."

"You might control my body, but you will never control my wants," she said softly.

Then she cast a gaze in Lucan's direction. In that split second, he saw a lifetime of longing before she looked away. Lucan's heart sped up. A sweet flush reddened Anka's cheeks, and he'd give anything to know what she'd thought about him that had shoved Shock away.

With a growl, the big wizard in leather pushed away from the wall and headed for the door, leaving Anka behind. Lucan knew he should leave well enough alone. He and Shock would never be friends. Even the thought made him laugh. But he wouldn't let a golden opportunity to needle the bastard go by.

He followed Shock out of the room, holding Bram at bay with a raised palm. Reluctantly, Bram backed away with a roll of his eyes.

"What is it?" Shock turned and confronted him. "You're itching to say something and even trying to mask your thoughts. If you weren't as inconsequential as the stains on your knickers and you were actually worth the effort, I'd dig into your head, but I'm fucking tired of your delusions about taking Anka from me—as if you can even begin to give her what she needs. So spill out whatever you're dying to tell me."

"I'll give her *everything* she needs."

Shock threw back his head and laughed, the sound cutting and caustic. "You're going to tie her down? Take a flogger to that perfect little arse? Leave welts where there was only smooth skin? Never. Your delusional rubbish otherwise is only a joke. If you care about her, you'll see that you can't help her now and shove off."

When Shock turned to leave the house and teleport away, Lucan grabbed his arm, fingers gripping harshly. "I'm man enough to give her what she craves, as well as the love she deserves. You're too emotionally stunted to help her there. I'm putting you on notice. I had her for over a century. I'll have her again."

When Lucan returned to Bram's office, the sight before him made him stop dead in the doorway. His best friend gripped his former mate by the shoulders, looking deeply into her eyes as he talked softly to her. Bram was mated himself. Though his little human Emma had left hours after he'd taken her, that made her no less Bram's. And he was no less hers. So Lucan wondered what the hell was this touchy-feely conversation with his former mate about?

Shoving down his jealousy, he cleared his throat. "Am I interrupting?"

Anka jumped guiltily, then spun to face him. "No. Bram had a question. I'd planned to return to the training room and wait for you."

Maybe, but when Lucan looked over her head to Bram's face, he saw something different. Not lust or any romantic interest. Speculation. Something was up here.

"No more today," Bram said. "Lucan and I have unfinished business. Return tomorrow."

She whirled back to the Doomsday Brethren's leader. "I need this training time. I won't be any good to you if I can't be ready for the next battle and I—"

"And all of this will be absolutely worthless if we're not ready for what's to come."

Bram wanted to talk to him. Lucan got it now. He nodded to Anka. "Tomorrow morning early, love. I'll set aside the entire day so we can continue working."

Anka's lips pressed together mutinously, and she looked ready to argue. Damn, he'd rather gather her against him, make those lips soften under his, take her home and lay her down in the bed they'd shared for a century…

"Lucan?" Bram snapped.

He returned to the here and now. "Yes?"

"We're leaving now. Let's go."

"Of course." But Anka stood close, looking at him like she wanted to stay, confide in him… Then her expression closed up, and she nodded. "Tomorrow, then."

Before he could say another word, she exited the room and teleported away from the manor.

"What is the matter with you?" he demanded of Bram.

"You two will have time to make eyes at one another tomorrow. Today…something is wrong with her. Did you notice?"

No way to miss her tense, defensive behavior earlier. "The moment Shock arrived—"

"She froze up before then. When we started talking about the requirements to get our hands on Morganna's killing potion."

Lucan swallowed, feeling like a heel. God, she'd been completely traumatized, and he'd been too jealous and angry to see how badly she needed comfort. "The talk of Mathias, of working with him… That must terrify her."

Bram winced. "And no wonder why. I don't know precisely what he did to Anka, but we can all guess."

Indeed. And Lucan had lain awake night after night for months, castigating himself for failing to recognize the danger to her, for allowing her to be brutalized, for not coming to her rescue when she needed him. "We must shelter her from him. Whatever it takes."

Bram's face tightened. "She wants to be a warrior. I don't like that any of us have to deal with the violent scum, but it comes with the territory."

Lucan wanted to refute him, but couldn't. "So you were… comforting her?"

"You can't think I'm looking to shag her?"

"Not exactly, no. But you two looked far cozier than I've ever seen."

Bram nodded. "Trying to read her mind. You know I have to touch her to do that."

Of course. He'd forgotten. "Anything?"

Regretfully, he shook his head. "Such a thick layer of ice. An even thicker one of fear. She knew what I was about and blocked me at every turn. Living with Shock has taught her more than a few tricks about shielding her thoughts."

Naturally. But that didn't make the stab in his heart easier to take. "I've got to figure out how to read her in my way, dissolve her barriers, persuade her to tell me what she fears and how I can help."

"Good luck. Shall we go banshee hunting?"

The question surprised Lucan. "Now?"

"I'd rather find the washerwoman and have her in my back pocket before Mathias does. We must control as much of this equation as possible if we want to banish Morganna and be alive at the end."

"You're right." And he had to get his head out of his longing for Anka and back into the war if he wanted to remain standing at the end and keep his former mate safe. "Any idea where to find one?"

"None at all. They like remote villages by bodies of water. We'll scout a few and hope we find something. But we must get our hands on a banshee fast or we're fucked."

Chapter Seven

Anka entered the manor the next morning, dressed again in her leathers, boots, and figure-hugging tank, hoping her severe braid and severe expression hid her utter nervousness. Another day alone with Lucan loomed, smelling his scent, longing for him—and desperately trying to hide it. Another day of wondering what would happen next in her quest to repay Mathias for all he'd taken from her.

Rolling over to find Shock blessedly gone, she'd showered alone and arrived under Bram's roof early. To her surprise, Lucan already waited.

Their gazes connected the second she entered the room, and she felt the jolt all the way through her, a tug on her body, a ping in her brain, a squeeze on her heart.

"Good morning." Somehow she managed to sound calm and collected.

"Morning. I'd planned training today, but the larger issue of the war calls again. Bram wants to see everyone in his office now." He crossed the room, looking more hesitant than she could ever remember. And concerned. "I argued against this. I want you to know that. Lean on me, if you need. I'm here for you."

The gravity in his tone set alarm bells ringing in her head. "What the devil is going on?"

Lucan's face tightened. "The devil is an apt way to put it. Mathias has come to negotiate."

"Here?" At Lucan's nod, she backed away, eyes widening with panic. "Now?"

Of course she knew that Bram planned to talk with the bastard, use him as a temporary ally, but she never imagined actually sharing the same roof with him again. God, she wasn't ready for that. Bloody hell, she couldn't breathe.

Lucan closed the distance between them and grabbed her in his arms, pressing her face to his solid chest and kissing the top of her head. The cold terror that had iced her veins just moments ago began to thaw with him so near.

"Whatever's passed between us, whatever you believe, I may have failed you before, but I will never let him hurt you again, I swear." Lucan grabbed her face and stared deep into her eyes.

Helplessly, she stared back, wishing she could just lose herself here. But that was impossible. She had to stand on her own two feet from now on.

Gently, she eased away. Lucan's speech was mere words. Mathias had not only hurt her, he had *changed* her. Irrevocably. Knowing that only a few closed doors separated them, panic became an icy fire under her skin, urging her to run. The months fell away, and she was in the home she'd shared with Lucan again, in their bedroom, eating a bowl of soup and curled up with a book when she felt a disturbance in the protections around the house. Instead of teleporting out, she'd climbed from bed to investigate… and been surrounded immediately, Mathias leading the pack with his fingers digging painfully into her arm as he smiled widely into her frightened face. He'd taken great delight as he'd torn her robe away with his hands and described in detail every way he planned to desecrate her. It hadn't taken him long to do exactly as promised.

"Anka." Lucan's concerned voice crashed through her memories. "Come back here, love."

She blinked up into his beloved face. His strong grasp, the tender command in his expression. He meant to keep her safe.

"W-why?"

"He claims he's agreed to Bram's terms and is here to talk. Shock came with him."

And again, Lucan's very tone asked how the hell she could live with a man who consorted with her tormentor. She didn't have an answer except to say that Shock had always protected her, from the time she'd been a child. After she'd been freed from Mathias's grasp, she'd gravitated to Shock in her stunned, terrorized state. He was the one person she knew could help. By the time she'd remembered Lucan and their love…well, knowing that she'd run to Shock, given him her trust and her body, how could she expect her former mate to forgive that? To take damaged goods? To understand who she'd become after forcing herself to rise from the ashes of her mental funeral pyre?

And now, she could never expect him to accept the glaring omissions she'd kept to herself during their century together. If the truth about her bloodline ever came out, God how he would loathe her.

"Why do I have to be in the same room with him?" Her stomach knotted so tightly at the thought of looking into Mathias's icy eyes again and remembering all the horror.

Lucan paused a very long time. "At any point, we might all be going into battle together to dispense with Morganna. We have to put the war against Mathias on hold to protect magickind from exposure. We need him for now."

She gasped, then bit her lip. None of this should surprise her, and she was reacting too emotionally. They shared a common goal for the moment. Her own personal vendetta would have to wait until they'd ridded magickind of the evil witch's threat. Besides, she might learn something about Mathias's weaknesses if she fought beside him now.

"If I refuse to be in the same room with him now, I look weak. Afraid."

He nodded. "I wish I could tell you otherwise, but yes."

Anka drew in a deep breath, telling herself that she could handle it. She *would* handle it. "Right, then. I won't be a coward. Will he be training with us, as well?"

"No. As Bram told me earlier, we're not letting the wanker in on all our secrets."

A small relief, but she'd take it. "Are they waiting now?"

"Everyone has been arriving over the last few minutes. Bram let me break the news to you privately."

Because everyone thought she was fragile. And wasn't that the truth, really? Shock knew that she cried in the shower. No way to hide anything from him. But Lucan? She stared up into those so-blue eyes of his. He couldn't read her mind, but he knew her so very well in some ways. In other ways, not at all. Perhaps that was because for the last hundred years she hadn't really been herself.

"I'll be all right. Let's go." She turned for the exit and headed to Bram's office.

Lucan grabbed her arm and pulled her around to face him again. "Hold up, love. You don't have to pretend with me. I'm your trainer here. Your protector. I want you to take part in the meeting because it sends a signal of strength. The Doomsday Brethren will look completely united. But if you're not ready—"

"Don't. I said I'm all right." She jerked her arm free.

Hurt crossed Lucan's face, and she ached to soothe him. Nothing good could come from that. The urge to lean on him was strong, and she hated that he felt as if he'd failed her. If he had been there the night she'd been abducted, Mathias and the Anarki would have vastly outnumbered them. They only would have killed him.

They left the ballroom that had been converted to a training center and headed through the manor toward Bram's office. Just outside the door, Lucan stopped her again, tucked her behind him. "I'll go in first."

She grabbed his arm, and he leveled a questioning glance at her over his shoulder. Anka simply shook her head and released him. "Go. I'll follow in a moment. Alone. I can't appear as if I need you to hold my hand. Because then he's won, really."

Lucan pressed his lips together, looking as if he bit back a pile of words. "You don't have to be this brave. I'm proud of you for trying, but—"

"Yes, I do. Go."

He sighed and shook his head, his glance lingering on her. Finally, he yanked the door open and disappeared inside the office. Drawing in a deep breath and clenching her fists, she watched the door close behind him and stood against the nearby wall so no one saw her lingering outside like a coward. Mathias had already won one battle, shattering her mating and her soul all in one day. But she'd be bloody damned if she would let him crush her pride for good.

Shaking out her nerves, she reached for the handle and whipped the door open, standing tall, chin upthrust, in the portal. She focused on the wall just beyond Bram's head as she entered. A cursory glance around the room told her that Shock and Mathias had settled somewhere off to the right. She headed left, grateful to have Lucan nearby. He leaned against a bookcase, the move seemingly casual, but it brought him even closer. Helpful, but she didn't dare look at Mathias.

"We're all here now," Bram said from behind his desk. "This meeting is a sad necessity, and if anyone doesn't like it, they're welcome to fuck off. We've a few new rules to cover. Everyone rings for admittance now, no exceptions. Everyone must play well with others, or when the big fun comes, you won't be allowed to participate. I'll handle all suggestions or inquiries now."

The room remained dead silent.

"Lovely. No magic in meetings," Bram went on, then gestured to Felicia. "Our resident Untouchable will make certain of that."

"Her mate can work magic in her presence," Mathias objected with a tight smile.

Anka found herself shrinking against the wall. God, just his voice. The sound of those familiar, silky tones that haunted her nightmares... He'd cajoled her response with it even as he hurt her.

Hearing him speak now opened up a big black hole and started to suck her down into those hellish days all over again.

"Anka," Lucan whispered. "Stay with me."

She blinked, her gaze zipping up to his. He met her stare, solemn, sure, knowing that she needed his strength. They connected for only a moment, but the gesture was important and hopefully gave her the courage to go on.

"Yes, but Simon won't do magic," Bram argued. "He's given me his word, and I trust him. If he breaks his word, he will be removed. Anything else?"

"When did females become standard issue warriors?" Mathias cut his gaze directly to her.

Anka choked back her horror. *Say something*! The demand flew through her brain, but she couldn't make herself open her mouth and speak.

"The members of our ranks are none of your concern," Bram drawled.

"She's terribly soft." Mathias stabbed her with a knowing smile. "All over, as I recall. She takes pain far better than she gives it. A beautiful witch, but how much backbone do you really have, dear?"

Lucan tensed, straightened away from the bookcase, and charged toward Mathias with murder on his face.

Anka grabbed his arm and held Lucan back. "Don't."

He zipped around to face her, jaw tight. His eyes were a blue riot of fury, a walking harbinger of death. His entire body was taut. For long moments, she didn't think she could hold him back. Even Bram started to head their way. But finally, Lucan cursed under his breath and backed away.

Mathias had taken everything dear from her in a matter of minutes. The bastard wasn't taking her dignity, too. Shoving down her fear, she ignored her hammering heart and pushed away from the wall, forcing herself to glare right into his glowing eyes. "I'm more than willing to dish out pain and see how well you take it."

Mathias smiled as if amused. Shock stood impassively, while Bram raised a brow at her. "That won't be necessary, Anka. Let's stay on topic."

"Let's," Mathias agreed, then began crossing the room to her, his gait a slow, hip-rolling swagger full of aggressive intent. She froze. His careful restraint terrified her because it was only temporary. And then…

Lucan shoved her behind him with a glare at Mathias. "Back off."

"What? Anka and I are old…friends. Have you missed me, poppet? I've missed you."

"If you've come to play head games with one of my fighters, get the fuck out now." Bram's tone rang with pure steel.

"I haven't given her time to miss you," Shock growled at Mathias. "Are we here to talk about killing Morganna or flap our jaws?"

"Thanks for the segue," Bram drawled as he watched Mathias. "What do you know about her plans?"

Mathias stared at her for a long moment, looking like a predator ready to play with its food, before finally giving Bram his attention. "Precious little. Since she isn't known for her restraint or control of her temper, that troubles me. I have no idea what she will do, but I know what she's capable of. That should trouble us all."

Bram's expression took a grim turn. "She said nothing about her intentions?"

"She's definitely got revenge on her agenda. You and your sister will be at the top of her list. Marrok…" Mathias sent him an apologetic smile. "She still hasn't forgotten. And Olivia, she's willing to forgive her flesh and blood for betraying her, but I'm certain she'll want you to help her destroy all her enemies in exchange. If not, I suspect you'll find your name on her hit list, as well. So unless you want to kill your mate, be prepared."

Olivia grabbed Marrok's beefy arm. He wriggled it free and slipped it around his little mate, looking down at her with rapt concern. "We will not bow to her. 'Tis naught but a bitch and a bully, she is."

"What he said." Olivia nodded.

"What else?" Bram barked.

Mathias shrugged. "She knows that Merlin left behind a potion to kill her for good. She's determined to get her hands on that and destroy it."

"Naturally. My question is, how do we know for certain you're not in league with her?"

"You don't, I suppose. But she's brassed me off completely. Three sweet little witches in my dungeon ready for play, and she freed them all. And made them her mental slaves, of course. Together, they managed to kill some of my most trusted associates. I barely got Zain free before they gutted him."

"Shame," Caden said. "The world would have been a better place without him."

"I happen to think the same of you all, but that's not productive now, is it?"

"Indeed not." Bram paced. "So she's annoyed you. Why should I believe you're not aligned with her?"

"I refused her…charms. Given that she tried to kill me in my sleep afterward and very nearly decimated the Anarki in her violent rage, I think it's safe to say we'll never be aligned." Mathias frowned at Marrok. "I can't decide if you're brave or stupid since you shared her bed. Lovely, but no."

Olivia elbowed Marrok. Ruddy color flooded the big warrior's cheeks. "Aye, 'tis a lesson I learned hard."

"Most assuredly. Then there's exposure to the humans. I may have flirted with the idea, but I've never actually done it, especially not the way she's gone about it. I have no other assurances to offer you, Rion, except my vow that it's in my best interest as well as yours to see Morganna gone. I can't have her ruining my plans, after all."

"Of course, you'd want all the evil spotlight on your own ugly arse," Ice groused.

"Isdernus. You've been so quiet." Mathias turned a winning smile on him. "I hope it pleases you to know that I think of your delectable sister often. Gailene was a treat. Tragic that she died so quickly."

Ice lunged toward Mathias with a growl. "I'm going to kill you, you sodding fucker."

"Bram." The evil wizard had the temerity to look both shocked and afraid.

Everyone knew better, and Anka seethed. The bastard was using their own rules against them and enjoying every second of it.

With a curse, Bram rounded his desk to intercept Ice. "Play nicely or there's no war for you."

"That's fucking rubbish! He can't fling the fact that he killed my sister in my face—"

As Bram pushed at Ice to keep him at bay, he turned to Mathias. "Not another taunt about the violence you've done or would like to do to any member of the Doomsday Brethren or their loved ones. That falls under the 'playing nice' rule."

Mathias's smile glittered as he sat in one of the chairs. "Oh, did I upset someone? So sorry. I'll do my best to refrain."

No, the bastard would do his best to needle everyone's soft spots, Anka knew. He was merely testing them now, but in a few minutes he'd already learned that she feared him, Lucan would do his best to protect her, fury still rode Ice about his sister's terrible murder, and that Bram would step in and act as the impassive third party when necessary. Mathias was definitely up to no good. But she did believe that Morganna wasn't on his side, damn it.

"I've spilled everything I know about Morganna. What do you know?" the evil wizard asked Bram.

"We're still investigating. Merlin left behind a potion. Even a drop of it will kill her. But we have no idea where it's hidden."

"Ah, so that's what she's been seeking." Mathias laced his fingers over his flat abdomen and crossed his ankles as he leaned back in his chair. "She's been scouring all things old, hence the attack on Stonehenge. I also know she's kicked around a bit in Glastonbury."

"I've no idea where Merlin would have stowed the potion."

"You'll find it. And when you have it, I'll find Morganna."

"Even if we find it, I'm afraid obtaining it isn't that simple. Merlin put requirements on it, which is why you're here." Bram quickly explained about needing the blood from both Merlin's and Nimue's lines.

"Interesting, but I'm not certain how I can help."

"We know you're Nimue's last living descendant."

Mathias frowned, then looked to Tabitha, his gaze lingering on her swelling belly. "Your father is still helping you from beyond the grave. That must be of some comfort, then."

But not as much as actually having her father here, and Anka was struck mute with horror to realize how many lives had been altered forever by Mathias's greed for power and violence while she'd been separated from this group of people. Marrok had nearly died, while Caden and Sydney had barely escaped with their lives. Her own cousin, Aquarius, had nearly perished at Zain's hands simply because Mathias willed it. Ice's sister had been his victim a few hundred years ago, almost followed by Ice himself just before he and Sabelle mated. Simon's brother had been in Mathias's grip. Raiden's mate, Tabitha, had lost her entire family. Tynan had suffered the brutal killing of the witch he'd yearned to mate with, then allowed Mathias to take his life months later just to stop the anguish. So much tragedy, and why? So the bastard could be the king of evil?

Lucan stepped forward and withdrew a terrible, serrated knife dangling from a strap around his hips that she hadn't previously noticed. "Why don't we grab his sewer-shit blood now and leave the carcass?"

Bram stood between him and Mathias with a raised brow. "The blood has to be from a *living* descendent of Nimue. Back off."

Anka stared. Lucan had never been one for aggression or violence. He'd also never been anything less than solicitous and tender with her. But this other side of him… She watched him with open confusion. Sabelle had told her that mate mourning had changed him. Had the sudden severing of a century old bond been somewhat like losing a limb? Or more like losing a heart?

Shock lifted his head to glare at her in a stern warning. Yes, she supposed there would be punishment in her future, but if this day kept getting harder to bear, she'd need it.

Mathias merely smiled at Lucan. "So you need the blood of a living relative of Nimue and of Merlin. Sounds simple enough."

"Not quite. Unfortunately, we also need a banshee. Know one?"

Those pale blue orbs fell on her, aglow with malicious glee, and Anka's heart froze. "Most think they've been exterminated, but there must be one nearby. I'm sure of it."

It was all Anka could do to remain still, not fidget, not leave. Not give herself away. She swallowed and stared at a bare spot on the wall across the room, willing her churning stomach to settle, her pounding heart to slow.

Bram looked to Felicia for confirmation, who nodded. Frustration crawled across the Doomsday Brethren leader's face. "Do you know one or not?"

Anka resisted the urge to wring her hands. Mathias couldn't lie with Felicia in the room. Would he give her away? Would Lucan look at her in horror?

Shock stood and shot her a furious stare before getting in Bram's face. "We've already covered this. Banshees are in hiding, aren't they? We could all know one and have no fucking idea."

Bram's expression said that he didn't believe either one of them, and with good cause. Again, she wondered if she should confess. She tapped her toe nervously and reviewed all the reasons she'd already considered, then came to the same conclusion. She could be risking everything when she couldn't make a difference. Unless she became a mother, her bloodline was useless to this cause.

"If you run across a banshee on the next street corner, send her this way, yes?" Bram smiled tightly, then turned back to Mathias. "No ideas where Morganna's fatal potion might be hidden?"

Mathias shook his head. "Unlike Merlin, Nimue didn't like to hear herself pontificate. She left almost nothing behind in the way of writings. I'll check what I have, but I expect there's nothing."

Another dead end. How long would she have to endure

Mathias's presence at Brethren gatherings under this pretext of killing Morganna when no one had all the right tools? Bloody farce. And for what? So he could taunt them all? Get closer? Earn the trust of someone foolish and maybe break them apart from the inside? Was anyone in this room that gullible?

"You look at your records. I'll keep searching through what I've got. You let me know if you find anything of use. I've shown you mine, as the saying goes, so you can show me yours. If I discover that you've left me with my pants down and my cock twisting in the wind, there will be hell to pay."

Mathias laughed, so damn smug. He was using the Doomsday Brethren to help him do his dirty work while getting an up close and personal view of everyone involved. They all knew it. That they had to let the terrible scum employ them to help with a joint cause that benefited them all only made Anka angrier.

"Of course. I'll keep tabs on Morganna so the slippery witch doesn't get too far from us while looking for the potion's hiding place. In the meantime, keep seeking out that banshee. She can't be too far." Mathias stood, his grin a bit too chipper and amused to be anything but grating. "This has been fascinating. Stay in touch."

Bram gave him a sharp nod, then dismissed him without a word. No love lost there. Everyone else watched him leave with rage in their eyes. Shock followed, and Anka mentally screamed at him: *If you care for me at all, how can you pal around with the wizard who nearly killed me*? Shock turned his head sharply in her direction. Behind those shades she knew so well, she sensed him narrow his eyes. But he said nothing as he followed Mathias out the door. Once outside the manor, they teleported away. The place felt instantly lighter once they were gone, and everyone breathed an audible sigh of relief.

Except Anka.

She stormed out of the office and ran into the training room. She didn't bother to grab boxing gloves, and it didn't matter that she didn't know precisely how to use the punching bag, she simply hauled back and made to punch it with all her might.

A strong hand clamped around her bicep, holding her back. Heat slithered through her body, mingling with the anger pumping through her blood and jacking up her heartbeat. Anka wanted to scream.

She turned to glare at Lucan over her shoulder. "Don't try to stop me."

"You could hurt yourself if you do that without gloves."

"I don't bloody care! I can't hurt myself any more than he hurt me. Sitting in that room with him today, being forced to look at his smarmy face and remember everything…" She choked back a sob, then caught herself. No weakness now. When she was here, she was a warrior and she had to act like one.

She tried to punch the bag again, but Lucan threw himself in front of it.

"Hit me instead," he demanded.

Anka reared back, staring like he'd lost his mind. "What? No!"

"You're angry, and you have every right to be."

Pressing trembling lips together, she tried to contain her roiling emotions. She could not fall apart, could not cry, could not scream. Drawing in a shuddering breath, she fought to bring herself under control again.

"Hit. Me."

The snap in his voice whipped her with demand. She would never want to hurt him, but he stood there and offered his body so that she would have the means to release her anger.

"Anka, now."

An absolute command, and she unconsciously heeded it. He might not find her ladylike and genteel anymore, but wasn't she done lying about that? She was a witch from a shady family, a secret banshee, a victim of Mathias's evil thirst to destroy magickind as they knew it. Damn right she was furious and bitter and terrified out of her mind. And if Lucan wanted to be her punching bag, she would accept it.

Tentatively, she curled her hand into a fist and connected with his stomach. It was hard under her knuckles. No give at all. He didn't grunt. His breath didn't whoosh out. Instead, Lucan raised a brow at her, silently asking where she was hiding the rest of her anger.

Throwing him a defiant gaze, she hit him harder this time, again in the abdomen. His body swayed a fraction, but he gave no other outward appearance that she'd impacted him at all.

"Hit me like you'd planned to hit that bag. No," he corrected himself, "hit me like you want to hit Mathias."

Her gaze zipped up to his, fearing she'd see pity there. Understanding met her at first, then encouragement. He wanted her to do this. Why? She frowned, and he quickly understood her confusion. His face softened for a moment.

"Let it out, love. All that rage has been trapped inside you, right? Give it to me. Let me help you. If you hurt me, I'll tell you."

"But—"

"I wasn't there for you when you needed me most. I need to be here for you now. Not another word, Anka. Do it."

She gave him a shaky nod, unable to speak the appreciation she had for him in that moment. This wasn't for him, and he wasn't making her beg to release her pent-up emotion, like Shock did. He was giving her the *opportunity* to let it loose. From the moment they'd met, he had shown her his giving heart. For just a few moments, he was willing to be the rock she leaned on. God, even if that made her weak, she desperately needed it.

Pulling her fist back, she let it fly with a shout. The primal anger screeching for release burst as she connected with his abdomen.

"Again!"

Anka complied, even though her knuckles smarted. Roaring, she reeled back the other fist and connected with his hard middle, almost mindlessly gratified when he grunted. So she switched hands and repeated the process again. Again. Again.

"He hurt you, Anka."

"Yes." *Whoosh*. Punch. *Whoosh*. Punch. A river of rage fueled each blow.

"He took you from your home."

"I hate him!" *Thud. Crash. Smack.* She simply hit now. She no longer cared where or how hard.

"He took your dignity."

Eyes squeezed shut, she responded with more short, angry jabs as tears streamed down her cheeks. She screamed.

"He took your pride."

And he relished crushing it! She pummeled Lucan continuously, imagining that she could give Mathias all the pain bottled up inside her. "He took everything. My home, my dignity, my pride, my body, my security. Every fucking thing!" She gasped, panted, punched. "He took you from me!"

In that moment, speaking the words aloud slammed the reality home. Mathias had not only stolen her life and her dignity, but the one person she relied on most. The foundation of her life. The lover who made the beating of her heart worthwhile.

"No. I'm right here, Anka. I'm always here for you."

How desperately she wanted to believe that. But so much had happened, and if he knew all the secrets she'd kept from him… "No, it's gone. You're gone. Everything is just gone!"

He grabbed her shoulders. "That's not true, love." Lucan gripped her shoulders tighter. "Feel me here. I haven't left. What do you need to believe that?"

Anka tore herself away from his grip. Every time he touched her, he was like the sun. Hot, bright, filling her with warmth after three months of arctic ice slogging through her veins. She paced away, rolling her shoulders back, strides eating up the floor. The anger kept unraveling her composure. The need for things she could no longer have frustrated her more than she could contain. And at the top of the list of the things she couldn't have anymore? Lucan.

She whirled to face him. He stared across the distance between them. Only a few feet apart, really. They might as well be a world away. How could she heal the breach she'd unwittingly created after Mathias's torment? She didn't know how.

Reality crammed that fact down her throat until she choked. Yet…Lucan never looked away from her, his eyes heating up as his fists clenched and unclenched. His jaw tightened. His nostrils flared. He wanted her. God, just being in the same room with him got her wet.

"Touch me." The words were out before she could stop them.

His eyes flared as she stormed toward him. Lucan met her halfway, and suddenly she was wrapped in his arms, pressed tightly to his wide chest where she could feel the mad rush of his heartbeat. His lips crashed down on hers frantically, lacking finesse. But she *knew* that scent, his flavor, deep down. It swirled around her like a drug, and she lost herself in it, letting it drown her fear and good sense. Passion roared as he pressed her lips open and plunged deep into her mouth. The kiss was urgent, more frantic than they'd ever shared. Her desperation for him reeled through her, and she stood up on her tiptoes, mashing her lips even tighter to his, caressing his tongue with her own as she inhaled him. It wasn't enough. It never would be.

The voice of reason in the back of her mind protested her surrender with a squeak, then blessedly shut up. Joy and need took over.

Anka clutched Lucan's shoulders, dragging him even closer for a sweet moment before she pushed him away and tore off his shirt, shoving the tight black tee over his head. Then she sucked in a breath. His body showed the rigors of training and the hardship of war. He'd always been well formed, but now he was sculpted, thick muscles bulging everywhere, prominent veins raised with effort and tension. His wide chest rose and fell with harsh breaths as he watched her. His erection bulged through his jeans, hard and jutting and hungry.

Everything about Lucan called to her senses and her heart. She'd been so damn miserable for weeks and months. He had suffered, too. He had mourned beyond what most could imagine. They couldn't have forever anymore, but could they have right now?

She pushed aside worries about Shock and training for the war. She refused to think about her scars. And it was far too late to worry over the lies she'd told Lucan for a century, about the river of betrayal between them.

"Whatever you're thinking, it isn't more important than right now," Lucan murmured. "Than this. Than us."

Her breathing accelerated, and she inhaled his musky, familiar scent, now edged with something different, something more potent. Wild.

"Come here." The demand in his two words shivered down her spine. She wanted to heed them. So badly. Every muscle in her body tensed with need. Desire flooded between her legs. Her arms itched to wrap around him and accept the pleasure and shelter he offered.

Bloody hell, why was she fighting herself? No more. She refused to keep on. Consequences be damned.

Anka took those last two steps, peeling the tank top off her body and throwing it across the room. Lucan took in her lacy bra and all her pale skin with hot eyes. He sucked in a breath, then wrapped an arm around her, yanking her against him. She hissed as their bare skin met with an electric tingle that shuddered down her spine.

Tossing her head back, she stared into those blue eyes of his, always so expressive and tender—except now. Desire pounded her from that gaze, unrelenting. An answering hunger consumed her and made everything between her legs throb.

He tugged on her braid until he positioned her face directly under his, her lips inches away. "Last chance. You want to stop?"

Did she want to let Lucan go? Did she want to keep giving Mathias power over her life?

"No."

She raised up on her toes again and slammed her lips over his. With a groan, he opened and took her mouth once more, eating at her like a starving man. He wound her braid around his fist with one hand. The other cupped her cheek. Both hands kept her exactly where he wanted her with no room to back away. As she curled her tongue around his in a frantic push, she assured him that she wasn't going anywhere.

That's all it took before he clawed her bra off, leaving her heavy breasts free, before he curled desperate fingers into the waistband of her pants and shoved. The leather was skin tight, unmoving. He growled into her mouth and snapped his fingers. Her pants were gone. So were his clothes.

He heaved her up and carried her to the thick mat across the room, then shoved her on her back, settling between her spread legs. He broke the kiss to stare into her eyes again. Checking on her? Wanting confirmation? She curled her fingers, rubbing her knuckles against his cheek. It felt good, like something she'd done a million times in her past life. But she wasn't that woman anymore, and she didn't want him gently now. She wanted him to take her. She wanted to close her eyes and pretend that she still belonged to him, that he was claiming her in the rough, primal way of a man in love, determined to possess his woman in every sense possible.

Anka gripped his shoulders and dug her nails into his skin until he stiffened. His eyes narrowed before a little smile floated across his mouth. Then he snapped again, and her arms were magically pinned to the mat above her head. She couldn't move, couldn't stop her breath from hitching as Lucan loomed closer, closer…

His lips met her neck, his tongue laving her collarbone, then his teeth nipped down to her breast. She arched up to him, and her nipple slid into his mouth. Even though he only sucked in the hard tip of her breast, it was like his hot embrace encompassed her entire body. Her breath caught, and she yanked against the invisible bonds, trying to pull her hands from the mat and slide them into his hair.

Lucan didn't heed her struggles. Instead, he merely worked the nipple deep and slow, sucking, biting gently, and sending a million tingles scattering through her body, along with her logic.

His fingertips traced a line down her ribs, over her waist, down to her hip. She stiffened. Would he notice the edges of the scars there? Would he feel them?

"What's wrong, love? You've gone tense."

"Faster," she demanded. She needed it. Her body burned for it. She didn't want to deal with what he might find on her body now, only with the pleasure he drizzled over her like warm syrup with every single touch. "More."

"It seems like I've waited a lifetime for this. I want to relish this and explore you. I don't want to hurt you."

He was going to treat her like a china doll again? Of course he was. That's what he wanted. That's what he'd always want.

"Let me up. Now!"

"Anka… Love, I simply want to be careful with you. You've been hurt."

"And I've healed. I'm a woman, not a breakable trinket."

He shook his head, jaw clenched. Was he beating himself up? Frustrated with her lack of ladylike behavior? Whatever. He released her with a sigh.

She was done trying to do and be someone she wasn't. Now he was going to see the real her.

The moment her hands were free, she shoved at his shoulders, pushed him to his back, and straddled him, her thighs around his abdomen. She gripped his wrists and held them to the mat, then slid her hips down. Her wet folds spread down his abdomen until the thick jut of his cock speared her. Then his wide, blunt tip pierced her. His eyes widened as she shifted lower, lower, lower until she seated him completely inside her. She threw back her head and moaned at the blinding ecstasy of feeling Lucan filling her again.

He raised his hips to her with a deep groan. "Anka… God, yes!" His eyes drifted shut for a long moment, then flashed open as he gripped her tight. "Just like this. I've wanted you so badly."

"I *need* this. Give it to me."

With wild, almost frantic gyrations, she speared his hard cock inside her over and over, no rhythm, no technique, just feeling him as deep inside her as she could. He held back, passively allowing her this feral mating. He stretched her so perfectly. She'd been made for him. Having him deep inside her was like being home again. Sun and warmth and the sense of belonging she'd missed stole over her, and if she closed her eyes, she could almost believe that nothing terrible had ever happened between them.

As Lucan wrenched his hands free and wrapped them around

her hips, he took control of her thrusts, his fingers pressing again over the scars that hadn't been there before. The truth all came flooding back to her. But he didn't stop or question or pause. Lucan simply spread his legs apart and pressed his hips up, pounding into her with sure, deep thrusts. His fingers bit into her skin as he controlled her body. She might have started this and she might be on top, but he took over so effortlessly and gave her every bit of his passion.

"You look incredible." His gaze caressed her mouth, her tingling hard nipples, the long line of her torso and her bare folds. "Like every dream I've had for months."

And with words like that, he was going to work his way back into her heart. If he'd ever left it. She couldn't stand to be near him and yet sometimes she simply wanted to hear his voice so badly she wept… Nothing made sense anymore. The hurricane her emotions had become swept away her logic altogether.

Now, Lucan was her only anchor.

"Stop. Don't say anything more." Because if he did, she would only cry.

Lucan pulled her down until her chest rested against his and held her tight as he filled her in deep, sure strokes, slowly taking her apart as pleasure filled her with a glorious, tight tingle.

"I can't keep this to myself, Anka. I've never made any secret of the fact that I miss you."

Impossible not to sink into him after that. Everything about him was so dear, and now she could only remember all the reasons she'd fallen for him. She'd adored his tenderness once. Now she ached for it with every nerve in her body—even as she knew it would unravel her completely.

Then he wrapped his arms around her, his hands splayed across her back. She went completely tense, her eyes widening with panic. She tried to stifle it, but wasn't fast enough.

Up and down her back his hands trailed, tracing the raised lines that hadn't been there before her abduction. Now he knew. God, he knew. Yet another imperfection revealed to him, and everything inside her clenched. She wanted him so badly, but couldn't stand being less than perfect in his eyes. Hell, she really didn't make any sense.

Thrashing madly, she shoved away from him, forcing his hands off her back. She got to her knees and stood, dislodging his hard length from inside her clinging flesh. Heaving deep breaths, she stood over him and shook her head, then searched frantically for her clothes. This was a mistake, letting him get this close.

As she backed away, he rose and stalked toward her, hard cock glistening with her juices, an angry red that demanded her attention. "Come back here now."

She shook her head insistently. "Forget it. We're done."

"You don't want sex, fine. We don't have sex. But I want to look at your back."

"Fuck you."

His eyes narrowed. "You've never said that word before. That's twice in one day."

"Why the fuck do you care?" Maybe if she could misdirect him, he'd be so annoyed by her behavior, he'd forget the scars.

"I never stopped caring," he said softly.

While she blinked at him, took those words in, he lunged at her, grabbed her wrist, then pulled her closer. A moment of hesitation, that's all it had taken. But the cost was fatal, she knew that as soon as he grabbed her shoulders, turned her, and shoved her to her knees on the mat. With a snap, the lights in the room flared so bright they were nearly blinding white. She blinked away the tears burning her eyes. She could struggle now, but why? The damage was done. She couldn't hide anymore.

"Dear God." His voice shook.

And she knew what he was looking at, the mass of pink lines crisscrossing her back, each representing an angry flay that Mathias had taken out of her skin with his favorite whip. He'd enjoyed her blood, her pain, her begging. Eventually, she'd learned to shut up, but not quickly enough to avoid the scars. He'd drained her energy completely for days so her body couldn't heal properly. Then he'd forced so much energy into her with every ravaging thrust that she'd feared she'd go mad.

She bowed her head and sobbed.

"Stay with me, Anka," Lucan commanded softly. "Come back to the here and now. Don't let your thoughts leave me, love."

"My back is ugly."

"It's you, and you could never be ugly." He knelt behind her, and his lips touched her mangled skin.

Surprised shuddered through her. Was he insane? Anka flinched and struggled in his grasp, but Lucan wasn't letting her up.

"Damn it. Stop!" she protested. "You can't do this. There is no us anymore. I'm no longer your responsibility. Let me go!"

He brushed a soft hand down her back. His lips followed, then his soft tongue traced the same path. "I'm so sorry you went through this. I'm so sorry I wasn't there for you. I'm here now."

"It doesn't matter!" she screamed. "Everything has changed. I can't be that perfect girl anymore. And now you know. So what the fuck ever. Where are my clothes?" She looked around for them.

She needed to get out of here, away from him. Before she completely broke down and sobbed for all the love she would never have again and didn't deserve, for never being what he wanted and needed. That was never truer than now.

Lucan clutched a hand around her nape and forced her back to her knees on the mat. "Stay right there. Do not move, Anka." The deep timbre in his voice, the hint of sensual threat, made her gasp. He meant business. "Do you hear me?"

Chapter Eight

Lucan waited, holding his breath. Anka was finally talking to him, opening up about what was in her head, her heart. That could only be good for both of them. He knew at least some of what had befallen her at Mathias's hands. But the knowledge made him want to kneel beside her and weep.

For her sake, he couldn't. She needed his strength. He'd already let her down in so many ways. He couldn't fail her again. Though he wanted to think about everything he'd just learned so he could decide how to cope with the guilt of her pain, she *needed* him now. That was far more important.

With one hand clamped down on her neck, the other pushing her hair away from her face, he lowered himself to her side, then tucked a finger under her chin to raise it. Her amber eyes pleaded. Her lips trembled. His heart burst into a million pieces. God, he'd do anything for this woman.

"Talk to me, Anka."

"No. Let me go."

She sounded so damn defeated that it broke his heart. He shook his head. "No. I've done that once. I won't do it again."

"I'm not your problem."

Anka, regardless of what she thought, was *his* mate. One kiss, and that certainty had roared through him. He'd wanted nothing more than to put his mouth all over her and drink her in before reciting the words that would bind him to her once more.

He bit his tongue and held back the words. She wasn't ready for that. Anka had a great deal of emotional healing to do. They had to repair the trust between them. Lucan vowed to do whatever it took and be there with her every step of the way.

"You're right. You aren't my problem because you're not a problem at all. You're a tender woman who had the misfortune to be attacked by someone terrible, bent on hurting you to destroy me. You endured and survived. I'm proud of you for that. The fact that you're here with me warms my heart. You're the most beautiful thing I've seen in months. Your scars aren't you." He lowered his hand to cover her heart. "This is. What's in here makes you the special woman you are. Trust me to help you."

Anka swallowed, froze. Her fingers tightened. She looked as if she desperately wanted to believe him…but didn't. Couldn't? Lucan bit back his frustration.

"Stop. Just stop!" she shouted. "I don't need pity. I'm doing just fine without you feeling sorry for me. Or did you want to fuck me for pity, as well?"

Was that what she thought? Or was she simply attempting to push him away? In either case, Lucan was having none of it. Her anguish choked him. Had Shock done anything to help heal her mental scars? Or had she been like this for months, a knotted ball of pain, pushing away anyone who tried to help her? Now that she was talking to him, there was no way he'd let her go now, especially not when she needed to purge this toxic agony inside her.

Some of Mitchell Thorpe's words came back to him. The dungeon owner had predicted that Anka would push him to see how committed he was to her needs. She was about to find out that she couldn't dislodge him with a crowbar or all the magic in the world.

"Pity has nothing to do with how I feel, love," he growled.

Then he pushed her back to the mat. Lucan didn't give her a

second to wonder what he planned before he settled her under him, spread her legs with his knees, and speared his cock deep inside her again. Under him, she bucked, jolted, gasped.

"What the hell are you doing? Let me up! I don't want your pity." The tears streaming down her face broke his heart.

He retracted almost to withdrawal, then began plunging into her one sure, slow stroke after another, angling her hips so that he hit that sensitive spot inside her that never failed to send her straight to climax. "Does this feel like I pity you? I want you, love. I want to hold you, heal you. In your words, I want to fuck you. You lost everything that horrible night, but so did I. And now you're here with me again. Unless I'm hurting you, stop assuming you know how I feel and take everything I want to give you. Let go of all the hurt inside you."

She dug her fingernails into his shoulders and threw back her head in pleasure with a high-pitched gasp. "Lucan!"

"That's it, love. You're so wet, and the way you cling to me… God, I've fantasized about being with you again. Endless nights of imagining just this."

Their lovemaking blistered him in a way no surrogate could, even more than the tender caresses they'd shared during mating. Being with Anka had always moved him, brought him closer to her, strengthened their bond. But pinning her down with his body weight and ravaging her, teeth bared, hips pistoning, was unraveling something inside him he'd kept tightly under wraps for a century. Anka had always been a bit reserved and prim, delicate. He'd treated her accordingly in every aspect of their lives. But now… She spread her legs wider under him, bit the lobe of his ear hotly, and writhed under him, her folds even slicker, swelling up, tightening around him until the pleasure bottled up inside him. Ruthlessly, Lucan tamped it down. Anka first.

Sliding a hand between them, he circled her clit with his thumb and smiled when she cried out and tightened on him even more. Energy started to swirl between them. Pinpoints of dancing light and invisible strands of power wrapped themselves around them both. Her skin flushed, and her breathing all but stopped. Yes, she was about to tumble over into the abyss of pleasure, and the way tingles gathered at the base of his spine and his sac tightened, Lucan knew he couldn't hold out long against this massive roar of pleasure.

He dug his free hand into her hair and forced her face under his. "Look at me."

She blinked open, her eyes glassy and unfocused. Slowly, she fixed her stare on him and whimpered as he shoved his thick staff even deeper than before. "Lucan..."

"Yes, love. Let go for me. Let it happen. I'll be here to catch you."

As she stared into his eyes, her entire body tensed, and he felt her sex clamp down on him in a vice-like squeeze. She screamed his name, and the sound ripped away the last of his restraint. He braced himself against the mat, using the floor as leverage to push deeper into her, forcing his way in again and again, even as her slick walls milked him, coaxing him to follow her over into climax. Bloody hell, that brewing euphoria at the base of his spine ballooned. Nothing was going to stop this whirling bliss from exploding his body into a million pieces.

As her nails dug deeper into his shoulders and she looked at him with her heart in her eyes, Lucan lost the last of his composure.

"Aww, love." He panted, feeling the mountainous swell of pleasure grow and surge, reaching its inevitable conclusion. "That's it. You feel so... *Yes*!"

His body combusted as the colossal sensations rolled through him. He thrust and plunged into her until he lost the ability to coordinate his body, until he could no longer breathe. His hot seed bathed her walls, and he felt her contract around him again with a cry, creating another starburst of feelings. Heart chugging, breath sawing, pleasure storming, he nearly blacked out.

He dragged a huge draught of air back into his lungs as the thick, bright mass of energy slammed into his body. His sweat-slicked chest covered hers as he wrapped his arms around Anka and forced his buzzing head to clear so he could focus on her.

"You all right?"

She froze for a long moment, and Lucan feared that he'd hurt her in some terrible way. Had she bled? Felt pain because of his rough touch?

Finally, she nodded. "I'm all right."

But her breathing was shallow, her gaze furtive. Discreetly, she pushed at his shoulders.

"What's the matter?"

"Can't breathe."

Lucan frowned. She lied. Beneath him, her chest rose and fell. But he lifted to his elbows to give her a bit of space. "Better?"

Her face tightened up more. "Let me up."

"What's the problem, Anka? We've done nothing wrong. We were mates. We can be again. I love—"

"Off! Off now!" She shoved at him frantically, her breathing fast and frantic and uneven. "Get off!"

Panic made her movements frenzied. Her behavior made no sense, unless… "Are you afraid of Shock?"

The fresh flare of her eyes, as if her lover's reaction had just occurred to her, stabbed her with more upset. "I can't do this now. Please let me up. I-I can't have you on top. The weight." She squeezed her eyes shut. "Mathias…"

Fuck! Lucan withdrew from the clinging depths of her body, still hard, still hungry for more, and rolled to his feet. Mathias had pinned Anka down, mounted her, made her afraid of remaining face-to-face-with the man who loved her still. The thought crushed something inside his chest. That fucking arsehole would pay with his bloody life if it was the last thing he did.

Lucan helped Anka to her feet. Her entire body trembled as she jumped around, seeking her clothes—looking anywhere but at him.

"Anka." He grabbed her arm gently and tried to bring her into the circle of his arms.

"Don't." She shoved away from him. "Please, don't. I have to go."

"Let me hold you, love. You're upended, afraid. Don't leave

like this. I can make it better."

"No." She finally looked at him with those big amber eyes, tears swimming. "You can't. You'll only make this more difficult. Please…don't."

"More difficult how?"

She jerked around the room, collecting her clothes. "You don't understand."

"Then explain it, because you're right. I bloody don't understand."

"It's…done."

She wriggled into her pants, yanked on her bra and shirt, struggled into her boots. Lucan watched the surreal scene, confusion clawing through him. "It doesn't have to be."

Anka finished dressing and turned on him. "Yes, it does! More than the skin on my back has changed. I can't begin to explain. And if you knew…" More tears of hopelessness fell down her face, and she shook her head. "Honestly, Lucan, you deserve so much better. Fall in love with someone else, someone whole. This can't mean anything to me. Neither can you."

She backed out the door to the ballroom, and Lucan watched her, trying to process her words. Why wouldn't she at least stay and talk to him? What didn't he know? Why the hell would she think for a moment there was anyone better for him than his destined mate? How could she take all the love he sought to give her and simply refuse it, especially when he suspected she wanted it badly?

"Keep telling yourself that I don't mean anything to you, but I was just inside you, love. I know otherwise. I don't want someone better. I want *you*."

Another tear ran down her face as she shook her head. "Good-bye."

Anka dashed out and teleported away. With an aching heart, Lucan let her go—for now. Until he could figure out how to reach and reassure her, forcing her to accept his comfort or the outpouring of his heart would be pointless. One thing he knew about Anka, when something troubled her, she withdrew into herself. And if he pushed her now, she would only close herself off even more tightly. Which meant that he had to figure out how to take away all the pain inside her quickly and act, or he might truly lose her forever.

But this wasn't one of her simple worries, like she'd worn the wrong shoes for a dress, or invited the wrong people to an All Hallows' Eve festival. The pain he'd witnessed today came from deep inside a bubbling well of it, and he'd never seen such anguish on her beautiful face. She hadn't really dealt with her attack and the scars Mathias had left behind yet. But he sensed that more troubled her.

With a curse, he magically pulled on his clothes, stretching his taut shoulders, still stinging from the bite of her sharp little nails into his skin. He didn't know exactly what caused her woes, but he wasn't giving up on her until he'd discovered them all. He'd stand beside her until she faced each and every one. Then maybe she could be ready to take his hand and come home.

Energy burned inside him like a giant fireball, and Lucan paced, raking a hand through his hair as thoughts pinged through his head. He clenched his fists to keep from bouncing off the walls. The buzz jolting him only reaffirmed what he knew: Anka belonged with him. Surrogates were visually attractive and their energy sustained him, but every time he visited one he died a bit more inside because the woman he touched wasn't the one he craved. He never felt more alive or ready to conquer the world than he did after holding Anka.

Her signature when she'd backed out the door radiated pure vigor in all his colors. No way Shock would miss seeing that telltale sign. One look at Anka and the fuckwit would know what they'd done. In the past, Lucan might have gloated about infuriating Shock. Today, he refused to waste a moment caring what Shock thought. The arse would read Anka's mind and see every touch they'd shared today. And then what? Were Anka's tears guilt? Or did Shock scare her? Did the bloody git have some hold over her?

Lucan didn't know. Was that what Anka meant when she said that he didn't understand?

Tearing out of the ballroom, he stalked across the manor to Bram's office door. He didn't bother knocking, but pushed his way in to find the other wizard sitting alone, scanning a human newspaper.

"No, really. Come right in and interrupt me." Bram punctuated his sarcasm with a raised brow as he lifted his head. Immediately, his tight expression went lax with surprise. "For fuck's sake, your signature! You and Anka…"

"Not another word," he grumbled. It was none of Bram's bloody business. "What do you know about Anka's situation?"

"Situation?"

"With Shock," he bit out impatiently. "I don't understand why she continues to go back to the prat when I think she might be afraid of him. Does he have some hold over her?"

Bram hesitated, opening his mouth, then closing it again.

Lucan frowned. Bram was never at a loss for words.

"What do you mean?" he asked finally.

Tossing up his hands in frustration, Lucan glared. "Why does she continue to live with him if he frightens her? How is he holding her against her will?"

Rising to his feet, Bram paced across the room. "Why would you think it's against her will? She's lived with him for months."

Wasn't that a fucking stab in the heart? Every time he lay in their lonely, cold bed, remembering every other winter for the past century that they'd cuddled up together and kept warm, now he lay awake, staring at the ceiling with cold feet, tormenting himself with the thought that Shock wrapped her silken body in his embrace and held her through the night.

Lucan shook his head. "She has, but something's wrong now. She acts as if she's torn up and terrified. She said that I wouldn't love her anymore if I knew the truth. What bloody truth?"

Bram shrugged. "How would I know, man? Do you think she means the truth about her torture at Mathias's hands?"

Lucan scrubbed a hand across his face. Closing his eyes only brought the picture of her scars glaring into his head, and he swallowed hard. "He hurt her so badly. I…saw. God, she must have suffered. My tender little Anka wasn't prepared to deal with such a monster. It's no wonder her mind is as tortured as her body. And I didn't do a fucking thing to save her."

That bitter reality stabbed him over and over.

"We've talked about this." Bram clapped him on the back. "You tried, man."

"I went into mate mourning, nearly turned feral, and almost killed your sister for helping me. I did nothing useful while my treasured mate endured the unspeakable. And now she's under Shock's thumb, carrying some…secret. I can't be useless this time. Surely you know something helpful. Anything."

Bram dragged in a deep breath. "Nothing. I'm sorry. She's told me nothing about her captivity, only that she wants revenge. She didn't talk to me about Shock at all. I only know what you do, they've been…friends forever." He grimaced. "Maybe she thinks she owes him."

"For rescuing her from the hell I didn't do a damn thing to save her from?"

"That guilt isn't helping you, mate."

Lucan heaved a deep sigh. "I know. But she's hurting, and I don't know a single thing I can do to help her except to love her. And she acts as if my devotion terrifies her. I can only think that she's worried about Shock's retaliation. Those bruises on her body…maybe the wanker has done more than act dominant."

"Did he ever beat Anka before you mated with her, do you know?"

No. He never had. Shock, back in those days, had been a sarcastic, fuck-off sort of prat. Not much had changed there. But he'd always been willing to do *anything* to coax one of those bright smiles out of shy Anka. So, as much as Lucan hated to admit it, he didn't have difficulty believing that Shock genuinely played power games in the bedroom with Anka because she wished it. Lucan cursed. Wondering why the hell she hadn't ever asked him for something she needed was only going to eat him up inside.

He shook his head as he made his way over to the decanters of alcohol and poured himself a straight whiskey. "There's some reason she's trapped with Shock."

"I hate to suggest this, mate, but maybe she loves him."

Lucan snapped around. "No. If she loved Shock, she never would have opened herself to me today. She never would have kissed me like her very happiness depended on feeling me close to her. There's something going on with Anka. If she's never talked to you about Shock or her captivity, can you think of anything else that might be troubling her?"

Bram approached, clapping him on the shoulder. "You know she's never been one to talk about her problems. She's never said a word to me about Mathias or her relationship with Shock. I wish I could be more help. But with my own mate abandoning me after a single night and disappearing into thin air, I don't think I'm the best person to talk to about your romantic troubles."

Lucan nodded wryly. "You have a good point. But I'm not letting her go again. Today proved that she still cares for me. Somewhere under all that pain and uncertainty, under Shock pressing her beneath his thumb, the feeling is there."

The smile fell from Bram's face. "That may be, and as your friend, I want you to be happy, whatever that takes. As the leader of this small army? I need to make certain you're focused on war and getting another soldier ready. Do whatever you need to win her back, but woo her on your own time."

Lucan's anger spiked. "My feelings aren't interfering with your bloody fucking war."

Bram raised a superior brow. "Really? So besides making love to Anka today, you two got in a full day's worth of training by noon?"

With a curse, Lucan looked away, clenching his teeth. Bram knew well that he and Anka hadn't managed any training. The morning had been eaten up by the impromptu meeting and the unbelievable sex that had shoved every reason he'd ever loved her back into his face. Now, it made him really look at his life and the rift between them.

"You forcing her to meet with Mathias this morning rattled her."

"She may have to fight beside him someday. If a chat in a crowded room bothers her, then she's never going to be ready."

As a protector, Lucan wanted Anka nowhere near the cruel bastard who had torn their lives in two and rended the very fabric of their bond. But as the warrior who'd seen the scarred, determined witch struggling to become a soldier in her own right, he understood that she needed to defend herself and fight. That she needed the opportunity to repay Mathias for what he'd done to her.

"We've only just started. Give me more time with her."

"As long as you understand that sweet nothings and footsie can't appear on our packed agenda."

Gnashing his teeth, Lucan bit back the urge to tell his best friend to fuck off. "Understood. I've promised you that my first priority is to make her ready for the war. I'll hold myself to that. I'm asking you as a friend to tell me whatever you know about her relationship with Shock. If I had information about Emma, I'd tell you."

Bram stared and said nothing for a long moment, then nodded. "I won't gossip or speculate, but if she comes to me directly to talk, I'll pass it on."

It wasn't what Lucan wanted, and he realized that he'd be better off if he talked to Sabelle. Bram's younger sister had a gift for mind reading, so she might have picked up on something. But if not, he'd muster on. He hadn't wrested Anka from Shock, held her as his treasured mate for a century, then had her ripped from him tragically just to lose her to Shock forever simply because she was too afraid to overcome whatever fears and hurts stood between them.

A familiar chime rang through the air, and with a simple lift of his hand, Bram eased the magical security around the manor. Predictably, Duke rushed into Bram's office in an impeccable charcoal gray designer suit with his hair ruffled, looking impatient and a little afraid.

"We've got a massive problem."

From behind him, Simon's half brother, Mason, emerged. The human barrister nodded emphatically. "I have friends at Scotland Yard willing to call me when anything…unusual happens, no questions asked. I received a call fifteen minutes ago that a stunning blonde with a terrible laugh is at Hadrian's Wall holding an entire group of people hostage. She refuses to let them go until she sees you."

Chapter Nine

Anka teleported to a remote corner of the little park not far from her cousin Aquarius's house. She walked in the anemic afternoon sunshine, a tweed coat wrapped around her shivering body. What had she done? Opened her body to Lucan completely, in a way she didn't think she'd ever accept a man inside her again. Yes, but she'd also opened her heart. Bloody hell, that man got under her skin, sometimes with just a look. A touch. One of his soft whispers. He'd always known exactly how to reach her heart. And still did.

A very bad sign, indeed.

For her transgression this morning, she would have to give up the home she had considered her safe haven these past two and a half months, at least temporarily. No way would she hurt Shock with the visible evidence of her desire for Lucan. He had every right to be hurt and furious. After all, he'd stood by her through the worst of her recovery following Mathias's assault. He'd waited on the fringe of her life for over a hundred years while she'd been mated to and loved Lucan. Sadly, she would have to risk going it alone for a few days. But it would be all right. She was stronger now, more able to protect herself.

As Anka wandered the crowded London streets, her mobile

dinged, alerting her to a text message. She pulled the mobile from her pocket, stomach rippling with tension. If it was Shock wondering where she was… Anka winced as she slid the little bar across and read the message.

Back to manor now. Emergency. Bram

With a frown, Anka turned and ran down the street, making her way to the little park again, finding a dark corner behind a few trees and evergreens in which to teleport away. Moments later, she was back at Bram's, arriving as the others did. Caden shouldered up to her, eyeing her signature with a raised brow and a little smile. Of course he could see that she'd obtained a whole lot of energy from Lucan. No avoiding that.

"Not a bloody word," she warned.

"So, I shouldn't speculate that when I see my big brother next, he'll be wearing a smile?" Her brother-by-mating teased her, of course.

She couldn't stop her own embarrassed grin.

Directly in front of her, Isdernus, Sabelle's mate, thundered up the steps to the manor. After a *whoosh*, Raiden and Ronan Wolvesey arrived, ribbing one another about some prank. Lucan pulled the heavy portal open and admitted them all.

Before she could file in, another loud rush of wind alerted her to a newcomer. The hair on the back of her neck stood up, and she tensed, turning slowly. She bit her lip as her worst fear was confirmed.

"What the fuck?" Shock shouted. "Anka!"

Lucan shouldered his way through the door and lunged for her, sliding his arm around her shoulders protectively. "I won't let him hurt you."

She looked up into his resolute blue eyes, sending him an almost apologetic glance. "He won't."

"Get your fucking arse over here right now," Shock demanded.

"Don't listen to him," Lucan urged.

But she didn't really have a choice. Because Shock had protected her when Lucan couldn't. Because they'd long been friends. Because Bram had insisted that she remain with Shock and take her energy from him. Because she owed him her life.

"I must," she said softly. "I'm sorry."

Lucan clutched her tightly. "No. Damn it, Anka. Come home with me. You don't need him. I'll take care of you."

God, how sweet but naive of him to think they could make love once and resume any semblance of their past relationship. That's what he wanted; it was all visible in his searching gaze. If he only knew… But she didn't have the courage to tell him all her dirty little secrets and drive him away for good. She ached to cling to the fantasy that he could still love her forever.

"Lucan..." She caressed his stunned face with her apologetic gaze, wishing so badly that he could understand, yet knowing that he never would, before she slipped out of his embrace.

"Anka!"

The yearning in his voice hurt her, but she steeled her backbone and made her way to Shock.

He stood on the lawn, all leather and badness, fists on his hips, drilling holes into her psyche. His probe into her head was neither painless nor subtle. Anka allowed him in, endured his thrashing through her memories. He quickly found what he sought and replayed her encounter with Lucan this morning. Teeth clenched and lips a thin line of displeasure, he closed the distance between them and grabbed her arm.

"You let him fuck you."

Maybe she could have argued that the sex hadn't been premeditated or that he'd simply caught her in a weak moment. She might even have convinced Shock that she'd been running low on energy and needed more in order to continue training. In the end, she gave him her thoughts. She refused to lie to him.

"Yes. As you can see." She raised her eyes up to the signature surrounding her, blaring Lucan's bright colors in his face.

"You want to explain?" he growled.

The others were watching now, stopped dead and staring at the scene unfolding on the lawn. She could feel their gazes stuck in her back like little blades, none sharper than Lucan's. "Not really. And definitely not now. There's an emergency."

"This is pretty fucking important, wouldn't you say?" Shock dragged her against him, then winced. "Bloody hell, you still smell like him!"

A growl resounded behind her, and she didn't have to turn around to know Lucan charged toward her, trying to rescue her from the big bad Shock. Instead, she pulled her arm from his grasp, refusing to be in either man's clutch. Revenge came first.

"We'll talk later."

She turned and stepped into Lucan's path as he bore down on Shock, looking ready to tear the leather-clad wizard limb from limb. She planted her hands on his chest and shoved him back with a push. "This isn't important now."

"The hell it isn't." The anger that rolled over Lucan was palpable, so thick it was nearly tangible. His nostrils flared and his brows thundered down into a dark vee as he looked over her shoulder, directly into Shock's face.

She could almost feel his smile mocking Lucan and wanted to slap sense into both of them. "Bram declared an emergency. We can't afford this petty fighting amongst ourselves. Neither of you have ever been jealous of the time you spent with another warrior training."

Shock opened his mouth to protest, and she knew what he meant to say, that she and Lucan hadn't exactly been working on the rigors of sword play unless his "sword" inside her counted. She snapped her fingers, unwilling to let a single syllable about that fall out of his mouth.

"Shut it. Later. It was a mistake. It won't happen again."

"The bloody hell it won't!" Lucan shouted and tried to charge past her to attack Shock.

She threw up a force field between the two of them, thanking her lucky stars that Felicia must not be near. This was one trick she'd forced herself to learn and learn well after her abduction. She put it to good use now. Because energy brimmed through her, she could keep it up, concrete thick and impenetrable for hours upon hours. It might take that long for either of them to see reason. She sighed impatiently.

"Stop it now, both of you! Bram brought us here to deal with a problem, not for you to tear one another's heads off because…why, Shock? I generated energy with someone else?"

"It was far more than that, damn it," Lucan insisted.

Yes, it had been. And the moment the thought crossed her mind, Anka felt Shock's formidable magic ripping at her shields. Wincing, focusing to hold it together, she did her utmost to keep Shock and Lucan apart. Her mind whirled, trying to find a peaceful end to this dilemma.

"Stop being wankers," Bram barked from the manor's front door. "Inside. Now!"

Lucan and Shock continued to stare at one another as if murder was in their near future. Bram's directive didn't faze either in the least.

"Morganna is attacking an SUV full of humans at Hadrian's Wall."

Neither wizard backed down an inch. Bram cursed and made his way onto the lawn.

"So unless you want all those humans to die and for the event to be plastered all over the telly and the rags again, you two need to stop arguing over the pretty witch and fight the bad one."

Shock twitched. Lucan pressed some of the tension out of his shoulders. Still, neither backed down.

Anka frowned, pain streaking between her temples. Holding up the force field between these two brutes was sapping her strength and making her head ache. She closed her eyes, brow furrowing, and tried to focus on keeping the wall in place. If she didn't…well, each had threatened to kill the other. She believed they meant it.

"What the hell is the matter with you two?" Bram shouted. "You're hurting her!"

Both their stares latched onto her. Lucan's gaze seared her face as she felt the blood leaving it. Shock shoved his way into her head, thrashing around.

Almost at once, they both backed away. Shock's fingers curled into fists. Lucan's chest heaved, his face contorting with rage. But they held themselves back. For her. She might not deserve their consideration, but at the end of the day, she was grateful for it.

Tentatively, she began to drop her shields. Neither charged past them, as she had feared. They simply stared, both willing her to sidle closer, choose one over the other. They behaved like bloody children with a favored toy.

Shock growled at the thought, and she resolutely ignored him, turning away from both of them and marching toward Bram. One by one, everyone filed into the house, into Bram's office, where he paced restlessly. Mason stood in the corner with Duke, both on mobile phones wearing strikingly similar frowns.

"For the past half an hour, Morganna has been holding hostages. The news outlets are racing furiously to the scene. We need to reach Morganna before they do, save the humans, and do it quietly. She's likely looking for Merlin's potion, scouring landmarks old enough to contain a vial my grandfather would have hid over a millennium ago. When Stonehenge didn't pan out…I suppose she thought to try this next. I've no idea how we approach her without dying. Ideas?"

Duke snapped his mobile shut. "She's already killed one man. Time is of the essence. The minute the BBC arrives, this goes beyond our ability to control it."

The tension sucked the air out of the room instantly. Everyone looked around for a too-silent moment. Bram broke it by tapping his fingers on his desk.

"Marrok, do you still have the weakening bracelet Merlin made for Morganna? The one with the amethysts I gave you when you were convinced that Olivia was Morganna reincarnated?"

The big warrior shook his head with a silent apology. "'Twas destroyed along with my little cottage. We've since searched the rubble and found naught. Sorry."

Bram nodded, a gesture of acceptance. But no one thought for a moment that he was happy about it. "Duke, did you discover anything useful when you and Felicia went back to the cave Morganna had been imprisoned in?"

"Nothing, unless you count a knee-deep layer of rocks and dust. Anything that had been in there was likely forever crushed when the ceiling caved in."

Bram bit back a curse. "And no sign of the Doomsday Diary. Damn."

Duke shook his head. "None."

Anka listened with sinking dread.

"Bloody hell. So we have to confront her without having any means to slow her down or placate her?"

"It looks that way," Lucan piped up suddenly. "I think you should stay behind."

Instantly, Bram shook his head. "We'll need every warrior we've got to handle her."

"She's out for your blood," Lucan reminded him.

"Exactly. If she'll trade me for the tourists, maybe we'll get somewhere."

"Why hold the tourists hostage at all? None of them can possibly know where Merlin would have hidden her killing potion," Anka pointed out.

"Good question." Bram frowned, looking for an answer, then turned to Duke and Mason. "Has she made any demands that you're aware of?"

The brothers looked at one another, reluctance all over their faces. Finally, Duke sighed. "Sabelle or you."

"Bram," Ice growled from across the room.

"Agreed. My sister stays far away from this bitch. In fact, where is she now?"

"With all the wives, including Felicia, at our caves," Ice answered.

"Sabelle and Tabitha are trying to relax Felicia enough to allow them to use magic in her presence. They've been working on the exercise for a week now. They're making progress. But I won't send any of them there to face Morganna, even my Fe," Duke murmured.

"They're safe in Swansea," Ice reassured everyone especially himself. "Even if Morganna plotted to nab the women, Felicia will stop the ancient bitch from getting anywhere close."

Anka didn't ask aloud if it was possible that Morganna's magic could cancel out an Untouchable's dampening abilities. Likely not, and no sense in worrying every warrior here about the safety of his mate. Morganna had her human hostages. That would occupy her for a bit, surely.

"I agree with Lucan, Bram," Anka spoke up. "I think you should stay here. In fact, I think all of you should stay here and let me go instead."

Every male head in the room turned to her as if she'd grown a set of horns and suddenly sported a third eye.

"No!" Lucan and Shock barked in tandem.

Bram wasn't any less subtle. "Have you gone mad? When you don't have the information Morganna wants, she'll only grow impatient and kill you."

Though the lot of them was generally brilliant, they were still male and could be a bit thick at times. "But I'm female. We're all familiar with her well-documented distrust of men. She might not like that I can't help her right away, but I can pretend to befriend her. I can promise her that I'll help trap you, Bram. I can win her trust long enough to release the hostages. Because, let's be realistic, we're not going to capture her without a plan. We're not going to entrap or keep her until we know her weaknesses. We're not going to kill her without that potion. Your time would all be better spent finding the location of that elixir. If I can placate her for now..." Anka shrugged. "Why wouldn't I?"

"I don't like it," Lucan snapped, looking like he wanted to cross the room and take her into his arms.

She sent him a sad smile. "I didn't ask you to do anything but see the logic in it."

Everyone else stayed mute. Except Shock.

"Fuck no!"

"I wasn't asking your permission, either. It makes sense. She won't see me as a threat. I'll make up some crazy story about Bram double-crossing me and this being my opportunity to get revenge. Maybe I can find out what she knows. Maybe not, but if I can persuade her to release the hostages, then we've achieved some small victory."

The dead silence in the room that followed actually gave her hope.

Bram cleared his throat. "You have some valid points. I won't disagree with them."

Lucan whipped his head around to glare at his best friend as if he'd lost his mind. "Are you mad? You wouldn't send Emma to talk to Morganna. Why Anka?"

"Emma is his mate," she corrected softly. "I don't belong to anyone but myself."

Her words were like a bomb in the room. Shock growled. Lucan shot her a furious stare, clearly ready to argue. But no one else objected.

"I don't like it, Anka," Ice finally admitted. "Though the idea has merit."

"I wanted to fight. I admit that I'm not yet ready for battle, but mingling with witches who thought themselves above me for over a hundred years taught me to wield my tongue like a sword. I can do this."

"As much as I hate to admit it, I don't see a better plan," Duke grumbled. "But she's damn dangerous, Anka."

Duke didn't need to state the obvious. "I'll play up the girl power angle or figure out what she wants to hear and tell her that. But the worst thing we could do is send a group of male warriors in to do battle with her. She'll come out fighting. There won't *be* any talking. The incident at Stonehenge proves that she has no regard for human life, and the longer we debate, the more likely she's killing off humans even now. Or that the BBC will reach her before we do. What's it going to be, an infiltrator or a war before we're ready?"

"Bugger," Caden groused. "I'm afraid she's right."

Lucan turned to his younger brother with an expression of disbelief. "Have you lost your bloody mind?"

"We've been around and around this," Anka insisted. "Unless you have a better idea, let me go."

Shock grabbed her wrist. "Fuck, no. I told you that."

"You're not my mate." She spit out the cutting words, instantly regretting the hurt that skittered across his sharp, craggy face. Anka softened her expression and pressed against him for a hug. "Thank you for caring now, as you always have. But time is running out. If I'm to keep magickind out of the news, I must go now." She squirmed out of Shock's embrace, looking past the betrayal on Lucan's face, and flashed Caden an inquiring glance. "Have your mate call that rag she used to work for. Fish around for what they know. Tell her to float some other story about Morganna, if necessary. Magickind doesn't need more attention. I'll…" Be back? She couldn't promise that. If Morganna turned that legendary petulance on her, she might die with all the humans. Best not to even mention that. "I'll do my best."

Then, with a last glance at Lucan, his desperate, alarmed stare willing her to stay, she smiled regretfully and let herself out.

The wind whipped across the hilly plains along the length of Hadrian's Wall. After she'd left Bram's, Anka realized that she should have asked more questions about Morganna's location, at least for show. The reality was, someone had died here recently, and her banshee senses could pick up on death. Despite the wall being over a hundred kilometers long, it took her less than two minutes to find the right location, near Carlisle. Morganna leaned against the shiny white Land Rover, picking at her nails. Her froth of platinum hair, almost like a cloud, cascaded down her back. Five people in the vehicle pressed their terrified faces against the glass, eyes pleading. The sixth was already dead. Morganna looked absolutely bored.

As Anka approached, her heart hammered viciously. On the outside, Morganna le Fay might look wee and delicate. On the inside, she was one terrible bitch who took great pleasure in forcing others to her will. By all accounts, she was also much like a two-year-old, determined to have her way.

Morganna's head popped up at her approach, and her violet eyes narrowed. They looked so much like Olivia's that Anka nearly faltered as Morganna took in her signature. "Who are you, witch?"

"I'm Anka. I've come to help."

She raised her brow to a disdainful arch. "Why would I need help? I assure you, I can kill this lumbering transport full of silly humans with nary a problem. One flick of my hand and—"

"I've no doubt," Anka broke in, speaking the truth. "But I understand that you're interested in finding people of a certain bloodline who can help you with a quest. I know where to find one of them."

Not for anything would she give over Sabelle's location. Yes, she might envy the beautiful witch, her perfect mating and her past intimacies with Lucan. Sabelle might be from a better bloodline and her magic might be more unique than her own—but Anka wasn't about to let her envy change the fact that Bram's sister was still her dearest friend.

"Do you?" Morganna didn't bother to walk away from the Land Rover, but merely teleported across the distance until she leaned into Anka's face, nearly nose to nose. "How would you know whose bloodline is of interest to me?"

"I live with Mathias's second-in-command, Shock. I hear things."

"The big, dodgy one with those dark contraptions covering his eyes?"

Anka nodded. "The very one."

"Whatever they've sent you to say is of no interest to me. I don't trust either of them," she drawled.

"Of course you don't," Anka assured the pale witch. "They're men. Why should you?"

Morganna's gaze sharpened. "Who is it you think I wish to find? And why, pray tell, should I trust you?"

"Well, it made sense that you would want to have a bit of a… chat with Bram Rion. But if not, I'll take myself away. It was an honor meeting such a legend." Anka backed away, praying the other witch would take her bait. If not, she'd have to find some way to free those hostages.

Not two steps later, Morganna grabbed her wrist. The witch's power, sizzling like an electrical current under her skin, nearly knocked Anka on her arse. She struggled to stay upright and not shudder from all the might coursing under the other female's skin.

"I want Bram Rion," Morganna hissed. "He alone can tell me where I can find something..." The witch weighed her words carefully. "Of value."

"After he tells you, will you let him go then?" Anka tested the waters.

"Of course." Morganna smiled.

Anka didn't believe her for a moment. "Pity. I rather think someone needs to finish the prat off and put the rest of us out of our misery."

A slow, devious smile crossed Morganna's face. "'Tis something I can arrange with minimal effort, little witch. Can you bring him to me?"

If she promised to deliver Bram to Morganna on a silver platter, the bitch would surely suspect a trap. No one got anything for free, and Morganna knew she had made many enemies over the centuries. This parody of politeness was a façade, and if Anka failed to play the game correctly, Morganna would rip her throat out magically and pull the heart from her chest while it still beat. And it would mean nothing to her. It would certainly cost her very little effort. No, Anka knew she had to be coy.

"Maybe. Eventually. But the way I hear it, you don't want to just kill him immediately. Eventually, yes. But you need information first."

Morganna looked just a bit impressed, despite herself. "You are quite well informed. Been eavesdropping? Or does that big brute tell you things when he's between your thighs? Men are, after all, so often led by their cocks."

Anka forced a conspiratorial smile. "They are, but in this case, I've been digging for information myself. You see, I'm with him somewhat against my will."

The half-truth fell out, and she had to stop herself from wincing. Anka wasn't exactly sure where this conversation was going, but now that the die had been cast, she had to play her part to the end.

Sidling closer, Morganna examined her carefully. "Really? You can't leave him?"

"I could," she corrected. Something in Morganna's tone told her the other witch would lose all respect for her if she sounded helpless before a mere man. "Let's say he has something I need, and I've purposely ingrained myself in his life until I get it. Then I'll have no problem whatsoever cutting him loose."

That made her smile. "Excellent. So, 'tis been your idea to find information to help me because…?"

"Because I'd hoped that in exchange you could help me as well."

Morganna would be suspicious of anyone simply offering to help, but the reluctant respect dawning in her slow smile said that she understood a good barter. "Indeed? What have you to offer?"

"I will find all the information pertaining to that item you seek and—"

"Item?" she asked sharply, dragging a long white claw across Anka's cheek. "What do you know about it?"

Time to lay her cards on the table. "I know it's a potion that will kill you. I know that Merlin made it and hid it. I know a few things about extracting it that you probably don't."

Bram was probably going to kill her for this, but since he wasn't here to consult, she had to play this her own way and repair any damage later.

"Such as?"

"Not so fast. I need something in return for helping you."

"Step carefully. I can kill you instantly."

"You can," Anka agreed readily. "But then my information dies with me."

Petulance crossed Morganna's smooth face. Anka had no trouble understanding why Marrok once found her desirable enough to bed. Despite the centuries of life and exile, she was beyond beautiful. Her violet eyes looked so much like Olivia's but lacked all the warmth and compassion her friend's possessed. Instead, they gleamed with cunning and conceit.

"Perhaps 'tis a deal we can strike. You will tell me where to find the potion and how to extract it, and I will grant whatever little request you have."

"Shouldn't you hear my request first before you decide you can, in fact, grant it?"

"Are you questioning my ability, girl?"

Dangerous line of conversation. Anka quickly shook her head. "My question was rather meant to ask whether you'd wish to help. I know well that you'll be able to conjure any magic you wish."

That bit of ego stroking seemed to mollify the ancient witch. "Exactly. If you give me all I've asked for, granting your wish should be of no consequence. Tell me what you know about the potion. I'll decide if the bargain is worthwhile."

Anka nodded and pretended to pace, her head whirling. What to say? She had to give over something… Saying anything false could backfire. The point of this conversation was to begin to build trust. She couldn't do that with a lie. Eventually, she'd have to use Morganna's trust against her, but she couldn't do that until she'd built it.

"I know the potion is held by one of Merlin's spells."

"Of course it is." Morganna sighed. "Tell me not the obvious, silly witch. 'Tis something useful I expect to receive in exchange for helping you."

Gnawing on her lip, Anka came to a decision. Bram would probably be furious, but if he wanted to play this role, she'd be happy to put him in a bloody dress and let him mentally fence with someone who'd had centuries upon centuries to perfect her skills. "There are three requirements to dislodge the potion."

"Where is it hidden?" Morganna barked impatiently.

"I'm still searching for that information. Merlin's notes are not always helpful, you know."

"Pompous lout," Morganna grumbled, then narrowed her eyes suspiciously. "Three things, you say? What are they?"

She must play this very carefully. Talking to Morganna was a bit like fencing on landmines. One misstep and… "Well, I can't tell you *everything* now, can I? I must keep something to barter with." Anka pretended to pace and think, giving Morganna's impatience time to grow and hopefully overcome a bit of her better sense. A long shot, but the witch had never been known for her restraint.

"You must tell me something, else I'll be hard pressed to believe you know anything of use."

"I understand." Anka couldn't give up the information about Bram's or Mathias's bloodlines. She would likely hunt them both down and imprison them for her purposes. They needed Bram for this war. And Mathias… No one was taking that revenge away from her, least of all a witch who should have been dead long ago. "One of the things you'll need to retrieve the potion is a banshee."

"'Tis simple enough." Morganna shrugged as if that presented no problem at all.

"Perhaps you're not aware that finding one these days is somewhere between incredibly difficult and impossible."

Morganna's thundering frown almost set Anka back on her heels. "'Tis clearly a lie, as I am now looking at one."

Anka couldn't stop her eyes from widening with horror. "How did…"

The words slipped out before she could stop them. She clapped her hand over her mouth, knowing there was no way to undo the damage she'd already done. Dread slid sickly through her stomach.

Had she already ruined this entire ruse?

"How did I know?" Morganna rolled her violet eyes. "Silly girl, back in my era, banshees were well known. Certain bloodlines left telltale signs. If none of the useless younglings now know what to look for, 'tis their stupidity at fault. But I knew what you were the moment you approached."

Anka's head spun with ways to save this plot before it fell down around her. She leaned in as if to confide in Morganna. "It's my secret. No one knows."

The witch shrugged, as if her confidences were of no consequence. "Your signature says you were once mated. He knew not of your banshee ancestors?"

Anka shook her head, having no idea how to answer without digging a deeper hole. This ploy had become desperate and dangerous. Her heart drummed, and she wondered how she could have been so careless as to give Morganna any information to use against her. But it was too late now.

"No one knows. Being a banshee now will likely get a woman killed."

"Foolish men, always desperate to make war with what they fail to understand. Your secret is safe. After all, I need you. Perhaps you should just come with me, sweet girl."

Morganna reached out for her. Anka barely managed to dance out of her grip, but she knew absolutely that she escaped only because the other witch allowed it.

"Well, there is one problem if you wish to use me to help you unlock the potion."

"What is that, pray tell?"

"Of the maiden, mother, and crone, the banshee you require must be a mother. I am not."

"Aye, 'tis clear from your signature that you have no children. Can you bring me a banshee who does? In return, I can grant you a wish or two."

"I know of no other banshees. Most have been killed or entrapped forever."

Morganna sent her a considering stare. "They were not terribly popular back in my age. Idiots. 'Tis creative I will have to be. No matter."

With a shrug, she grabbed Anka's arm. That surge of power burst through her body, making her shiver once more. The blast jolted her body. She lost sight and the ability to breathe. Her thoughts raced preternaturally fast. Her heart nearly pounded out of her chest. The charge tensed every muscle and nearly made her hair stand on end.

Suddenly, Morganna released her. "That should do the trick."

Anka flopped to her knees and forced her eyes open so she could look up at Morganna. In the Land Rover behind her, she heard the screams of the hostages, all terrified that the blonde witch would hurt them as she'd been hurt. In truth, her body felt devoid of most energy, each limb limp, her bones as fluid as water. She fought to find her breath enough to ask, "What happened?"

"I like to think we've just done one another a favor, dear. This shan't take long, so I suggest you make your way to your man quickly."

"What…do you…mean?" She could barely gasp the words out.

Morganna laughed, a light, tinkling sound that rang with mischief. "And spoil the surprise? Nay. Run now. I will send for you when I am ready. You can give me the rest of the information I want and thank me then. Off you go."

Anka shifted one foot to the flat grass beneath her and braced both hands on her knee, forcing herself to her feet. Unsteady, she wavered for a moment. A wave of dizziness nearly sent her onto her backside, but she parted her feet and held out her arms to steady herself.

"The hostages…they play no role here. You'll only expose magickind to the humans."

Morganna gave a disapproving frown. "Aye, 'tis worried you all are about that. In my age, magic was common knowledge, and the inferior ones feared us. But that battle is of no interest to me. I merely want that potion."

Just then a van rolled up with the BBC logo emblazoned on the side. Anka stiffened. Failure pummeled her. She was too late. Hadn't saved anyone. Done everything wrong again.

"Horn-swined louts, these human insects. But I will release the screaming annoyances in the contraption and wash away their memories of this, if you do my bidding."

Hope percolated inside her, a slow bubble among the scattered mess of her thoughts. "What do you require of me?"

"Go to your man." Morganna grinned widely. "I have seen to the rest. Do what comes naturally, sweet girl. Good-bye."

Chapter Ten

Stunned, Anka watched with wide eyes as Morganna made a sweeping gesture with one hand. The people in the SUV seemed to shake their heads, blink, then stammer in confusion. The driver peered about suspiciously, then blustered at the passengers before starting the Land Rover again and rolling over the grassy landscape, growing smaller and smaller until they disappeared into the gray sky. Morganna had wiped their memories clean, and without even looking at them. Who knew what she'd done with the dead? That kind of power made Anka quake.

The potent witch disappeared a moment later, leaving Anka alone on the windswept landscape with a BBC reporter scrambling from her van and grabbing her cameraman's arm, urging him to run straight for her.

Bad, bad idea, talking to the reporters. And the urge to go home—her real home with Lucan—struck her with more force than lightning. But fear could do that to a person, make them want the gentle comforts of the familiar. Now wasn't the time. That time might never come again.

She climbed over the low row of stones remaining from the Roman wall once meant to keep the Scots from invading Roman

Britain, then quickly ducked behind it. Once crouched behind the ancient stone, she teleported back to Bram's manor—and, disoriented, she promptly tumbled onto the hardwood floor in a heap.

The whole group of warriors closed in on her, each wearing concerned expressions. Their worry pressed in on her like a vise, squeezing from every direction. Having so many people crowd around her rubbed her wrong. No, it was having so many males close. Uncomfortable. Frightening.

A dizzy wave threatened to take her down. She shook her head, but it wouldn't clear. When she moved to her feet and stumbled, Lucan reached out to her. Shock got there faster and dragged her against his massive, leather-clad chest.

"What happened?" Bram demanded of her. "Did you see Morganna?"

"Are you all right?" Lucan looked desperate to get his hands on her, reassure himself that she was unscathed.

"Why the fuck did you go to Morganna?" Shock squeezed her tighter. "Bloody barmy."

Yes, probably.

"'Tis hardly a witch with whom you should toy." Marrok's face thundered with both disbelief and disapproval.

But she didn't really hear him. Someone here smelled good. Scrumptious. Her mouth watered. She moaned softly as blood rushed to her sex with a pleasant tingle. She swelled instantly as she dragged that musky male scent into her nose again. Her folds moistened quickly, pulsing with need. The compulsion to feel *his* mouth over hers made her want to crawl along each and every one of these warriors until she found the one currently making her senses sing.

She licked her lips and tried to clear her head. Answers. They wanted answers about her encounter with Morganna. Whatever this wave of longing was, to feel the heavy press of *his* body shoving her to a mattress, driving between her legs, and feeding the inferno suddenly raging there…yes. Please. Who was he? Which male? She whimpered, then stopped herself. No. Morganna and the war and everything that had happened was far more important today. She must focus.

"I saw Morganna." She couldn't help herself; she sniffed at Shock. Hmm, that was nice. Her nipples perked up. But was he the man lighting her body aflame? She ran her tongue up a sliver of his chest, bared between the leather jacket, and he shuddered against her. Maybe.

Behind her, Lucan cursed, something low and dirty. Something her body very much wanted to do with him again. Something that made everything feminine in her pulse with need.

Bram wrapped his fingers around her arm in a gentle squeeze and tugged her around. His touch sent pain searing down every one of her nerve endings. She cried out with agony and nearly fell to her knees. "Don't!"

He released her instantly. "Anka? Are you all right?"

Lucan steadied her, brushing stray hair from her flushed cheeks. "Is your arm hurt, love?"

That delicious scent wafted into her nose again, and she leaned closer to Lucan. She blinked up into his blue eyes, feeling so very hungry. Her vision wasn't quite working. Everything looked out of focus. But all of her senses urged her to tear off her clothes, strip him down to the skin, and rub against him until she enticed him to cover her with his body and—

"Back the fuck off, MacTavish," Shock growled and jerked her back against his hard chest, cradling her head against him with a big, rough hand. The zip of his jacket pressed uncomfortably into her ear. But it didn't hurt nearly as much as her own clothes.

She squirmed, trying to remove the rasp of the fabric from her oversensitive skin, but that only chafed more, like wearing head-to-toe coarse wool. She squeezed her eyes closed and tried to endure the pain of the harsh material scraping her hypersensitive skin over and over.

"Please…" She spoke the words to anyone who would listen. "Hurts."

"Let go, Shock," Bram ordered. "I fear Morganna has done something to her. She's flushed, as if she's feverish. She's not—Anka?" He shouted her name as Shock eased up on his hold.

She grimaced. Bram didn't smell right to her at all. When he tried to take her cheeks in a gentle grip, she cried out and tried to turn her face away. His light touch shouldn't hurt…but it caused her untold pain. She shuddered and curled into herself.

"Don't!" Tears welled in her eyes.

"Anka? Love…" Concern rang in Lucan's deep voice, and she wanted to tell him that she was going to be all right. But it didn't feel that way.

"That's it," Bram said. "She's burning up. Ice, pop back to your cave and bring Sabelle here. I'll call for Aunt Millie. We may need them both."

Why would Sabelle and Millie come? The thought confused Anka, but the need to get away from Bram and closer to whomever smelled so luscious wracked her. Sabelle and Millie… insignificant concerns now.

Moments later, Anka was vaguely aware of Ice disappearing, of Shock cursing, of Lucan peering at her with concern marring his brow. And of that musky, male scent teasing her nose and slowly driving her mad. It shoved all else aside.

"What do you mean, Morganna's done something to her?" Lucan demanded as the need inside her began blazing so hot, it burned away her senses.

"*Hmm.*" She tried to sniff him. Was he the one she desired? Too many competing scents. Too much searing desire for logic. "Come closer."

Instead, Bram pushed him away and forced everyone else out of her space. "Anka, how are you feeling?"

"Don't touch me." She flinched. "It hurts."

Bram held up his hands where she could see them both. "What are you feeling?"

"Ache." Stringing two thoughts together hurt terribly, too. "Need help."

"Of course." Bram raised his hands to cup her shoulders. She lurched back before he could touch her, and he lowered them without any contact. "What sort of help do you need?"

"Please…" To her own ears, desperation laced her pleading voice. "Now."

"Of course, love. What do you need?" Lucan murmured softly.

She trembled, the fever raging in her body. Only one thing could ease her now. "Sex."

Her response impacted his chest like a boxer's blow. The air left his lungs in a *whoosh.* That one word made his heart stutter. And his jaw drop.

Beside him, Marrok coughed to smother his own laugh. Damn if that didn't rub Lucan the wrong way.

"This bloody isn't funny!"

"I know, mate. Sorry." Ice tried to keep a straight face. "Her response was so, um…bloody unexpected."

That was an understatement. In the century he'd been Anka's mate, Lucan had always known when she wanted his attention. She had little ploys, like wearing a shorter skirt to dinner, or letting the strap of her negligee fall off her shoulder as she sent him a coy glance from their bed. Sometimes she'd simply kissed him until he'd lost all thought. But never had she verbalized her desire, let alone blurted it like that.

Shock growled at him, and Lucan ceased that thought. Bugger, he hated the bastard for being able to read his mind and promptly resumed thinking about another one of his favorite fantasies: Shock chained and gagged, being boiled in acid, his skin falling off slowly, layer by layer, as he screamed in horrific agony.

"Fuck off." Shock shook his head, and Lucan was fairly sure if he could see behind those ridiculous sunglasses, there would be some eye rolling as well.

"None of this is helping her," Bram snapped at them. "Go now,

Ice."

With a nod, Ice ducked out of the room. A pop and a jolt in the next moment told Lucan that the wizard had gone to collect his mate.

Caden sidled closer, staring at Anka. "What the devil do you suppose is wrong with her?"

"No idea."

But there had to be something Morganna had done to make her nearly mindless with this need. He swallowed. No way to deny how badly he wanted to be the one to fill it. And her.

With a meaty, outstretched hand, Shock reached for Lucan's throat. He ducked out of the way at the last moment, mentally replaying a vision of Shock being decapitated over and over. He rather liked that fantasy, too.

"Stupid fuckwit," Shock grumbled, then turned his attention to Anka.

"'Tis much like what Olivia endured, which led to our mating," Marrok said. "The fever, the need."

Bram shook his head. "But quite different, I suspect. Rather than magic forcing the hand of an untransitioned witch trying to glean power from her mate, this is something more sinister. I doubt it's a coincidence that she's fallen into this state so shortly after seeing that ancient bitch." He leaned down, putting himself eye level with Anka. "Talk to me. You saw Morganna, and then what happened?"

She reared back, her face wrinkled with distaste. "You smell… wrong. Go."

Bram cast Shock a confused stare. The lumbering git clearly had no idea what to think either and shook his head.

"We've got to help her," Lucan insisted.

"Is she your responsibility anymore?" Shock bit out. "Last time I looked, she was your *former* mate."

"We're going to argue about this now, when she's been hit by something we don't understand that's hurting her? Maybe we should waste the time to whip out our cocks and compare sizes, too."

"Fuck you twice! I don't need this shit. I don't need you—any of you. I'm taking Anka home." Shock scooped her up in his arms, and she looked so delicate against the hulk of leather striding across the room.

"Wait," Bram called. "What if she's not strong enough to make the trip? Sabelle and Millie will better know how to care for her, but we must figure out what's wrong first. I've never bloody seen this. It can't be a human ailment; we know that. But I'm at a loss—"

"There's a first," Shock sneered. "You're often clueless. Sabelle and your dotty aunt can't tell me anything I can't bloody figure out for myself." The big wanker turned and looked Lucan in the face. "If she needs sex, *I'll* give it to her. All she can handle and more."

Lucan reined back his thoughts on that topic, including the murderous urges making fury spread like fire in his veins. He forced himself to send Shock a placid smile. "She's a warrior of the Doomsday Brethren, not your mate, either. Not your responsibility. Bram, what do you think is best now?"

In Shock's embrace, she keened in sharp, howling tones and started pulling at her clothes, scratching and rubbing at her skin.

"We'll let Sabelle and Millie look at her when they arrive. Then we'll decide. For now, Lucan is right. Anka stays here."

"You think you're going to fucking make me leave her in your care?"

Bram cocked his head and looked at Shock like he was a barmy nutter. Then again, he was. "I can restrict your ability to teleport Anka away and kick your stupid arse out of here. Or you can stay and play nicely with the others. What's it going to be?"

"Cock-sucking twit." Shock stiffened, as if he were ready to set Anka down to free his hands up to throw punches. But he didn't. "She needs me."

"That's very possible," Bram conceded.

Did that mean Bram meant for Shock to take Anka upstairs, remove her clothes, and— Lucan shut off the thought immediately.

The stab of pain that went with it hurt too much to continue that contemplation. Yes, he knew Anka warmed Shock's bed, but being so near, *hearing* it, would devastate him.

"Yes, that's exactly what I mean, you pathetic fuck," Shock clarified.

Anka cried out again, the sound rife with frustration. She kicked and flailed, grabbing at the buttons on her pants and shoving at her black tank. "Help!"

As she grabbed a handful of her shirt, she scratched her way up her abdomen. Blood seeped up from the open wound, a little pool of crimson against her pale skin. She shoved at one of the straps of her top and ended up scratching a deep path down her arm. Blood quickly ran to her elbow. He was done asking questions or permission. Instead, Lucan lunged forward and grabbed Anka by the wrists.

"Stop." He commanded her in a voice that brooked no disagreement.

She stilled instantly, before heartbreaking tears leaked from her eyes, wetting her cheeks. "Help!"

"I want to, love. What can I do?"

She began panting and twisting her arms, her body flailing helplessly. "Touch. Me."

Fuck, he wanted to. So badly. He felt Shock's stare on him, and their gazes connected. As Anka cried more, Shock looked willing to defend his right to Anka, like a dog pissing on a fire hydrant. Lucan swallowed back his bile. Anka came first. The argument could last longer than Anka had, given the severity of the spell affecting her. He would concede to Shock ten times over so that she could live. They could fight another day. A world without Anka? Unthinkable.

He leaned up in Shock's face. "Take her upstairs. If she needs sex, give it to her. Fix her, whatever it takes."

"Damn straight," Shock snarled, then spun away with a still squirming, screeching Anka, pleading for him. For help. For sex. After his exit, an eerie hush settled over the room.

Bram clapped him on the back. "As hard as that must have been, you made the right choice, mate."

Absently, he nodded. Logically, yes. Inside, he felt as if he'd signed away his right to Anka forever. Like he'd permanently shoved the sun behind thick gray clouds with his own two hands. Like he'd never know warmth or light or happiness again. But if that's what it took to keep her alive, he'd endure it. If she died, though… He'd make it his mission in life to hunt Morganna le Fay down and murder the bitch in the most horrific way possible.

Duke and Mason excused themselves under the pretext of following up with the BBC and any local news authorities to see if any word of Morganna's attack had leaked out. The Wolvesey twins were, for once, somber. They promised to teleport themselves to Swansea and keep watch over the rest of the females. A few had expressed interest in learning to fight physically, in case the Anarki came calling. All the wizards had agreed, and the twins had already spent a bit of time working with the ladies to start them on the basics. Marrok said he would tag along to help.

Caden threw an arm around Lucan's shoulders. "How about I take you to The Witch's Brew and get you sloppy drunk for a few hours?"

"No."

His brother looked over to Bram, silently begging for a little help. Bram shrugged.

"Come on, brother," Caden tried to coax. "You don't need to stay for this. After a pint or ten, you'll no longer give a shit about anything."

"I'm not leaving her until I know she's all right." He swallowed, knowing it would rip him open and tear out what was left of his heart to listen to her give her body to that bastard, to hear her cries of pleasure as Shock took her. But if he gave Anka what she needed to be well again, Lucan was willing to endure any agony, hear every one of her torturous sounds, just to know she'd come back whole.

Bram sighed, then nodded. "Let's sit. Get comfortable."

"And drink." Caden shoved him to a sofa in Bram's office then poured a bit of liquid into a crystal glass. It was amber, dark and aglow as the light hit it, like the color of Anka's eyes when passion overtook her.

And Shock would be seeing that soon. He would be pulling away her clothes, taking her mouth under his, covering her body with his own, then shoving his cock— He couldn't finish that thought.

Lucan slammed back the alcohol. "Another?"

Caden glanced at Bram, who nodded. Then his brother brought the decanter over and poured another glass full of the booze. Hell, he hadn't taken the time to taste it. Didn't know what it was. Didn't care. Didn't pause before he swallowed the rest of the glass again without another thought.

The warmth of the alcohol started to coat his bloodstream. It wended through his system quickly. Damn, it should be relaxing him. He should feel looser, be able to breathe without wanting to punch a wall or rip someone's head off. Instead, it only made him realize how agitated—no, furious—he felt. Goddamn the motherfucking bastard. If Shock let Anka hurt herself again, if he harmed a single hair on her head…

Caden eased the glass from his hand with a tsking sound. "Brother, if you crush the glass, you're only going to hurt your hand. Less time training with Anka, then."

"True. Thank you." He had to get his head screwed on straight, but he couldn't do that sitting here like a fucking idiot, waiting for her first scream of pleasure to erupt. He leapt to his feet and prowled to the window, staring out at the dead grass browning the lawn. The gray sky hid every ray of sunlight, smothered the warmth. Wasn't that a metaphor for his life? The last three months had been bleak in every way. Lost, without any way to reach Anka emotionally, he'd used every bit of his will to hold himself together. But now… God, how could he endure this?

For her, he had to.

Bram stepped out of the room, and a moment later a gong and a chime announced that Ice and Sabelle had arrived. The trio filed in quickly. No one said a word. The silence slowly killed, and all Lucan wanted to do was crawl into that fucking bottle and lose himself until this ordeal was over.

"Where are they, mate?" Ice asked Bram.

Bram's reply was quiet. "Upstairs."

Inside, Lucan shoved down his rage. He wanted Shock dead and would do whatever necessary to make that happen. In fact, the sooner the better. Like now.

He rose to his feet. Caden pushed him back down. "There's nothing you can do, brother. Sit in silent support. Drink, if you must. But you cannot go up there. You've conceded to Shock, and your presence will only start a fight. Anka doesn't need that."

Lucan wanted to ask how Caden would feel if he had to give Sydney back to Jamie, the wanker, or any of the human men his mate once dated. But it was a pointless argument, and Caden wasn't the enemy.

"You're right." He poured another glass with a shaking hand. He'd lifted it halfway to his lips before Anka's scream pierced the air, a high-pitched screech. Pain? Terror? "What the hell?" He charged for the door. Bram and Ice held him back with a mighty shove. He struggled and shouldered, trying to work past them. Caden yanked on the back of his shirt, tossing him to the sofa with a shove.

"Stop it! We have to let them be, at least for a bit. See if Shock can help her."

"What if the dumb wanker won't admit that he's hurting her? What if he causes her more harm?"

Or, Lucan wondered, what if he ran to Anka's rescue, only to find that she didn't want rescuing? That she no longer wanted him?

He surged to his feet and paced, feeling too tightly wound. He was going to break apart if he didn't find some way to channel this energy. Shock was taking care of her, and he had to let it happen. Her needs were more important. His…his were all in his head now. He had to get it together.

"Then we'll intervene," Bram assured. "Sabelle, does what I've told you about Anka's condition ring any bells?"

She shook her head, and Lucan's heart sank. Not only was Anka upstairs with the biggest arsehole he'd ever met, but she suffered from some ailment none of them had ever seen or could even understand.

He sucked in a breath. "Is Millie coming?"

If anyone could shed light on Anka's sufferings, it would be the older witch.

"On her way. Finishing up with the birth of a youngling. She said to give her a few minutes."

Lucan raked a hand through his hair, wanting to pull it out. What if they didn't have a few minutes? Above stairs, Anka screamed again, a shrill sound that bespoke terror. He darted for the door again. Once more, his brother and best friend held him back.

"He's hurting her! God, can't you hear that?"

"We heard a scream," Caden said. "We don't know what caused it, pain, pleasure, fright… Nothing terrible is going to happen to her up there. We have to let this play out."

"Seriously? Shock is Mathias's second in command. For all we know, he's using some of his boss's terror techniques on her and..." He couldn't bear to contemplate all the ways Shock could hurt her. Or she could hurt herself if the frenzy continued untreated and unabated. Fuck, he should have told his own nobility to pack a lunch and take a hike, then grabbed Anka for himself.

A light tinkle of a chime and what sounded like the shake of a tambourine later, and Bram left to admit his Aunt Millie. The spry little woman sported a mountain of graying hair piled onto her head in a heavy bun. She looked like anyone's dotty grandmother. Sharp as a blade, she had thankfully been around magickind forever and knew all kinds of magic none of them had ever seen.

Lucan ran to greet the woman at the door, standing beside Bram anxiously. The second she crossed the threshold, he held her hands. "Please tell me you can help her. I'm desperate."

Bram slanted him a frustrated glance. "Let the poor woman breathe."

He wanted to bite Bram's head off. He wanted to tell Bram to go to hell and stay there. Instead, he backed off. Clearly, this wasn't helping.

"Thank you." Bram smiled tightly and explained the situation to Millie.

The little witch frowned. "If Morganna did something to her, I'm sorry to say it might be anything."

"Can you sedate her or make her more comfortable—"

Another one of Anka's sharp screams of terror cut its way down his spine. Fuck, he was going to crawl out of his skin if he had to hear that sound one more time. It hurt all the way to his soul every time he imagined her in the kind of agony that could produce that sound.

Bram grabbed him, holding him back again. Lucan hadn't even been aware that he'd darted out the doorway and was making his way to the stairs. "If I have to hold you back again, I'm putting you into a deep sleep," Bram told him. "And I'll make sure you wake with one hell of a headache, mate."

Was he the only one who heard Anka's clawing pain and terror?

"I'll need to look in on her," Millie said. "Only then will I have any idea how or even if I can help."

"I'll take you." Bram shot Lucan a warning glare that strongly advised him to stay put.

Caden wrapped an arm around his shoulders with a hearty slap. "No worries. I've got him. Go on."

Watching Millie and Bram disappear up the stairs seemed to take forever. Sabelle followed. Wondering what Anka was suffering while the older woman took her time with every step she ascended gnawed away at his composure. Finally, the trio disappeared onto the landing, down the hall, and into a bedroom. Ice appeared a moment later, thrusting a full drink into his hands.

For a moment, he stared at the whiskey or scotch or whatever it was. Then he nodded his thanks at Ice, lifting the glass to his lips and tossing the liquid to the back of his throat. It burned a path all the way to his stomach, but it didn't take away the anxiety gnawing at him.

He paced in the foyer. It was either that or bound up the stairs, brain Shock until he couldn't move, and take Anka into his arms and give her whatever she needed. Sex? Love? Hell, he'd take her shopping for a year if that's what she needed to snap out of this mystery ailment.

Minutes slid by, one turning into another, then another. The screams still sliced through the air now and then, punctuated by more than occasional whimpers. Each sounded more pitiful than the last. Fuck, he couldn't take it anymore.

Asking Ice to refill his drink, he pretended to pace past Caden, then darted up the stairs. His brother was close behind him, but Lucan quickly found the door Anka lay behind by following her screams.

He burst inside the bedroom and found Shock, sans jacket. His leathers hung half open. He held Anka's wrists to the mattress. Bram clasped her ankles. Between them, Anka thrashed and howled, her face contorted into a mask of agony. Millie stood above her, checking her glazed eyes, tsking at her feverish skin, trying to pet and soothe her while performing an exam.

Shoving Bram aside, he grabbed Anka's ankles himself. She hesitated and opened her eyes to fix her gaze on him.

"Lucan…"

"I'm here, love."

She whimpered, trying to curl into a ball. The sound was so pitiful, it tore at Lucan.

"Tell me how to help her," he pleaded with Millie.

The older woman hesitated, wringing her little hands. "I don't know this for sure, mind you, but I've seen spells like this, usually given by an unscrupulous wizard." She shook her head, the bun that looked as if it weighed almost as much as she did unmoving on her head. "But in this case, another witch unleashed this on her, then left her alone… Oh, dear."

"What is it?"

"I believe it's a fertility spell. They're quite dangerous and require a great deal of power. They've been banned for centuries. Witches inflicted have died."

Died? His heart revved up, pounding in his ears. He wasn't going to lose Anka, not after finally having her back in his arms again. "What can we do? Whatever it is, I'll do it."

"I'm afraid it's not that simple. The fertility spell is one that first acts on the inflicted like an aphrodisiac. She will usually choose the first male her body accepts and demand repeated exchanges of sexual energy. Usually in a few days, the spell wanes. The spell automatically makes her repel all mated wizards. Their smell is putrid, their touch painful."

Which explained a lot of Anka's behavior. He zipped his gaze over to Bram. "Go. Now."

The wizard backed away. "Leaving. I'll keep the others occupied and see what else we can find out about this spell. I'll send Ice out to scout for Morganna. Or a banshee."

With that, Bram left.

Anka immediately calmed a bit, her body only occasionally jerking and twitching now. Lucan sat on the bed at her feet and tried to massage her ankles and shins in soothing strokes. "You're going to be all right, love." Then he focused on Millie again. "What else?"

"As I said, she usually takes the first wizard her body will accept. There is one exception, however. If a witch's true mate is in the vicinity, she will reject all others until he comes to um…service her, I'm afraid." The little witch winced.

"What?" Shock barked.

"She will only have her true mate if he's nearby." She tried to smile as she looked between the two of them. "The way she responds to both of you… I think she's a bit torn. She may accept either of you."

That was hardly news. Shock growled at his thought.

"The good news is, since Bram left the room, she's calmed considerably," Millie pointed out, voice chipper.

That was thankfully true. Anka's breathing had evened out. She no longer cried or screamed or acted as if pain tore her apart.

Experimentally, Lucan let go of her ankles. Shock did the same to her wrists. Anka shifted restlessly, eyes closed, arching in invitation and spreading her leather-clad legs. Her body searched for a lover.

"Get the hell out!" Shock snarled at him.

"Why do you think you're her true mate?" Lucan challenged. He had to be it. No man would ever love her as he did. He hadn't shown it well after she'd been abducted. He hadn't been there. By God, he planned to be here for her now—and every day thereafter.

"She came to me after Mathias's torture, and *I* saved her. I've protected her. I've lived with her. I've waited for her for over a hundred years. You..." Shock sneered. "You only fucked around, lost your bloody mind, then retreated to lick your wounds like a beaten dog."

The truth stung like a bitch, and he would have loved to pound Shock into a wall, but Anka needed one of them now. He blocked the other wizard out and addressed Millie. "How can we know who her true mate is if she can't decide?"

"She will. It's been hundreds of years since I've seen this spell, mind you, but my recollection is that if any man tries to touch her once her true mate has, he will be roundly rejected."

"You called it a fertility spell. Does that mean that the man she accepts...?"

"Becomes the father of the child she will likely conceive? Yes. It doesn't always work, of course. It depends on the power of the person casting the spell."

Since Morganna had cast it, it ought to be potent as hell. Chances were, if Anka accepted him now, he'd not only be her lover again, he might also be her mate once more. *And* the father of the youngling they would probably conceive.

"Great. Thank you, Millie. Is it too dangerous for Anka if we ask you to leave us?"

The older witch shook her head. "Honestly, there's nothing more I can do for her now. I suspect that only one of you two can help. Good luck."

The door opened, closed. A sliver of air and light passed into the room, breezing over Anka's face. She cried out, a tiny little mewl he could barely hear. The scratches she'd given herself earlier had nearly healed, but she was clearly still in some pain. And her nipples stabbed her tank top, a sign that her desperate body still needed attention.

But from who?

Lucan swallowed. The plan rolling through his head was a calculated risk, but could also eliminate Shock from Anka's life and bed forever. Everything depended on Anka. "All right. If she accepts you now, Shock, I'll concede. I'll go away, leave her alone, and never try to win her back again."

"About bloody fucking time. Get out."

"You have ten minutes with her. If you can't prove that you're her true mate, you will leave her to me and not ever try to win her back."

Shock's head whipped around. "You think you're dictating to me?"

"Would you prefer me to go first, then? I don't mind at all."

"Fuck no!"

Lucan shrugged, trying to hide the worry that he might be making the biggest mistake of his life. "It would seem as if those are our two choices. Pick one and let's get on with helping Anka."

Shock lowered his head, looking down at the woman they'd both give their lives to save. He could say a lot of awful things about the wankstain, but he had to admit that Shock cared very much for Anka and always had.

Lumbering to his feet, Shock rolled his shoulders and looked toward the window. The shutters had been drawn. Between that and his ever-present sunglasses, Shock shouldn't be able to see a damn thing. But he stared for a long moment as if the wooden slats closed to the afternoon sun could provide any answers.

"Get the fuck out of here."

Lucan shot Shock a smile, feigning a confidence he didn't feel. "That's great. Enjoy it. I have no doubt I'll see you in ten minutes."

Chapter Eleven

Lucan emerged from the bedroom. Shaking, he closed his eyes and braced himself against the wall. Leaving Anka to Shock's dubiously tender mercies once had been the bloody hardest thing he'd ever done. The second time around, knowing that Anka might accept the prat as her true mate forever, was much harder. His only consolation now? Anka and the strength of the love they'd shared for over a century. His mate mourning had been deep because she had been everything to him. If he'd ever given her any cause to doubt that, he'd castigate himself eternally. As it was, he felt plenty of guilt for not being there when Mathias abducted her. And for not understanding her needs before their mating had been cut brutally short.

If Shock emerged, defeated, any time in the next ten minutes, Lucan swore with everything inside him that he would embrace and honor Anka's yearnings. He would take care of her, no matter what.

"You look green," Bram drawled from a leather wingback chair just outside the door.

Lucan quickly explained everything Millie said after his departure. After Bram picked his jaw up off his chest, he sent Lucan a solemn stare. "So now you wait?"

"Now I wait." He fucking hated it and didn't know how the hell he'd stand it.

"Drink?"

"No. If the few I've already had haven't relaxed me, nothing will. But I am her true mate. I have to be."

"Perhaps that's the reason neither you nor Anka have truly let go. Sabelle told me that even when Anka appeared indifferent, her thoughts were often wrapped entirely around you. I don't know what's driven her to make half the decisions she has."

"Fear? Maybe she thinks that too much has happened and that she can't come home again. She's scarred. That bastard flayed her flesh wide open and drained her so that she couldn't heal. She feels less than perfect, though in my eyes, there's no one more so. But I've got eight minutes more to find out if I'll have the opportunity to convince her of that."

Bram nodded and didn't try to fill the silence.

Anka screamed into the soundless void a moment later, making the hair on the back of his neck stand up. Her suffering ripped at his composure. Lucan paced nervously, wanting to rip down that door and hold her. He would slay dragons for her, damn it, if she would let him.

Shock growled something low and short. A demand. A crash followed, then another horrific scream. A bump very much like someone hitting the wall resounded next. Shock cursed. All the while, Lucan held his breath, hoping Anka would come to her senses and realize that he was the only man for her.

"It doesn't sound as if Shock is having an easy time of it," Bram observed.

"No." *Thank God.*

Then all fell quiet again. Lucan tried not to take that as a bad sign and fought to erase the frown creasing his face.

"Why do you suppose Morganna hit Anka with a fertility spell?" Bram asked to distract him.

Lucan was grateful.

"That's the question, really." It had circled in his own head once or twice. "I can't imagine why. If Morganna merely wanted to reduce the numbers of the Doomsday Brethren, she wouldn't bother to make Anka fertile. She'd simply kill her. There's nothing in it for Morganna to make the next generation of Doomsday Brethren. She doesn't know Anka at all, so why do her a 'favor'?"

"Agreed. Even if Morganna read Anka's deepest desires, why expend the energy to make a stranger's wish come true?"

"Exactly."

"Not that Morganna is terribly logical. From everything we know, she's impulsive and wretchedly temperamental."

"Do you think Anka angered her?"

Bram shrugged. "Maybe, but again, if she did, why not simply kill her?"

"You're right. Not logical at all."

Before he could reply, another of Anka's blood-curdling cries split the air. Shock's low voice echoed off the walls, the tone coaxing. Then frantic footsteps pounded across the floor, a frenzied fumbling with the doorknob. Lucan snapped to attention, inching closer to the door, digging his fingers into his thighs to stop himself from wrenching it open.

"Anka!" Shock barked on the other side.

She cried out in answer, a fearful sound of denial. Scuffling filled the air, then a thud. Unnerving silence followed. It dragged on. Lucan waited, paced, wondering what the hell was happening behind that door.

Then a sound he'd dreaded hearing: the rhythmic squeaking of bed springs.

Low moans bounced off the walls next, hers, Shock's. It didn't take long before the tempo of the bed springs picked up pace, and Anka gave an impatient little huff, throaty and sexy. Shock moaned long and low, a sound that dripped pleasure and shriveled Lucan's gut. Fuck if he didn't want to crumple into a heap of misery.

So that was it; Anka had accepted Shock over him. Even now, the shitty bastard was sating her need and would soon fill her with seed. With his youngling.

So much for being her true mate.

The sympathy on Bram's face was more than he could bear. "I'm sorry."

Lucan squeezed his eyes shut. Defeat slid like a thick sludge through his veins. He felt the last of his breakfast chug in his stomach as it threatened to come up. The rest of his fucking life would be spent with surrogates having polite exchanges of energy, never knowing affection or tenderness. Certainly not devotion. And never love.

Anka had chosen Shock. Would they mate now? What would her life be like? Could the git really make her happy? Would he watch her favorite movies with her, despite having seen them a million times? Would he rub her cold feet in winter? Or run her a steaming tub and pour her a glass of wine when stress worked her into a cute little tizzy? Would he know how tenderly she needed to be loved when she looked lost after talking about the death of her mother?

Before now, he had bet his very heart that the answers to all those questions were no. Apparently, he'd been wrong.

Swallowing the rising bile, Lucan forced himself to shove away from the door. He had to get the fuck out of here. One foot in front of the other. Only a few more to the stairs. Bram leapt to his feet and fell into step beside him.

"You'll understand that I can't train her anymore," Lucan murmured.

His life had shattered permanently. Once, he'd believed that he and Anka would somehow reunite. Now, he knew better. He felt… stunned. Broken. Soon, the anger and grief, the abject despair he'd known recently, would hit him. He would drink heavily, rail at anyone who would listen, then bury himself at home in a life of total solitude. How could he have been so bloody wrong about what was in Anka's heart?

Bram hesitated, then nodded. "I'll ask one of the others to assume her training. If she conceives, I'll restrict her or eliminate her altogether. I know she wants revenge against Mathias, but if

Shock gets her with…" Bram sighed, as if realizing he'd said the one thing designed to turn Lucan somewhere between miserable and murderous. "If she does conceive, I'll remind her to focus on the life in front of her, not the one she's left behind."

Lucan would do well to remember that himself. As he stomped onto the first step, descended to the second, he resisted the urge to look back. He'd want to tear into the room, and for what? Did he really want to see Anka naked under Shock while he strained to fill her fertile body with energy, pleasure, and seed?

With a grimace, Lucan whipped around and began running down the stairs before a scream unlike any other ripped the air in two with a shrill wail. Stomping feet came next, a curse, and the jiggling of a doorknob drew him back around. Finally, Shock wrenched the door open and stood in the portal looking disheveled, his hair askew, his jacket hanging off one shoulder. He sported a series of angry red gashes down one cheek. Marks from Anka's fingernails. He zipped his leathers up, shrugged on his coat, and squared those concealing black shades on his face. Then he charged toward the stairs, stopping just beside Lucan. Menace rolled off him in an angry wave.

"I fucking hate you. You're a pussy and you don't deserve her. If you don't give her what she needs now and always, there won't be a hole deep enough for you to hide in. I will hunt you down and kill you as slowly and painfully as possible."

Shock was…leaving? Conceding defeat? Hadn't he and Anka just been having sex? Hadn't Shock been feeding her need created by the spell?

Lucan didn't plan to stay here and ask the bloody lout, not when Anka was alone and hurting.

He zipped past Shock and ran for the open bedroom door, searching out the desperate little whimpers coming from inside.

A sudden crash had Lucan spinning back, one fist raised, his wand ready in the other. But the noise hadn't come from an invading foe. Instead, Shock had punched the wall, knocking a hole through the plaster and paint, leaving a gash and bleeding knuckles behind. He glared at Bram, daring the wizard to say something. Bram merely rolled his eyes.

"Bugger." Shock shot Lucan a disdainful snarl. "What are you looking at? Why are you standing there when she's waiting? Do you need me to draw you a fucking picture?"

Anka had really rejected Shock, given the bastard the heave-ho?

"Yes, for fuck's sake! Go!" Shock shouted, then stomped down the stairs, slamming his way out the front door. With a heavy bang, he teleported away.

Anka had rejected Shock…and now she waited for him.

Shaking, his heart flipping madly in his chest, Lucan rushed into the shadowed bedroom, shutting the door behind him. It took a moment to adjust to the dimness, but he found her huddled in the corner with frightened eyes, clutching the spread from the bed up to her chin. She trembled so hard, her teeth shook.

His heart broke.

Lucan forced himself to take slow steps into the room and kneel in front of her. One thought circled his brain over and over: Shock wasn't the true mate of her heart.

But what if he wasn't either? That question haunted Lucan as he reached for her, giving her plenty of time to reject his touch if she needed.

"Love?" He reached out for her, his hand closing the distance between them until he cupped her cheek.

She gasped, trembled harder. "Lucan."

"Am I hurting you?"

"No. The pain of Shock… I couldn't bear to have him touch me. That hurt brought me out of the frenzy, but your hand…that's nice."

He could touch her and not cause her pain, as Shock had. Hope crashed in, thrashed around inside him, making mayhem of his logic. Did that mean he *was* the mate of her heart? Shoving aside the question, he forced himself to focus on her and her alone. "Tell me how I can help you, Anka. Or can I at all?"

She closed her eyes and her body started to shudder with sobs. God, he wished someone would simply take a knife to his soul and cut him wide open to bleed out. It couldn't hurt less than seeing her suffer, than this misery making her delicate shoulders shake.

Then she nuzzled her cheek into his hand. "Tell me what's wrong with me."

"Morganna put a spell on you, love. You'll be all right in a few days. You're not dying. There's no need to worry. I'll stay by your side, if you need me."

"Shock…" She opened her eyes and looked away. "He tried to…" She swallowed another sob, not letting it loose. "But it hurt. I couldn't stand it, no matter how patient or coaxing he was. It was bloody agony. Something I'd closed my eyes a hundred times and endured for the sake of energy and friendship, but I couldn't tolerate him—or the sudden pain—today. I'm sure you would rather not discuss him, but I've no one else to talk to."

His heart stopped. Hope surged. She'd only ever *endured* Shock's touch? "You didn't want him?"

"In my head, yes. He's safe. But in my heart, I couldn't. I just couldn't."

Relief let loose some of the stranglehold wrapped around his lungs and evened out the careening between hope and fear. Breathing came easier, thoughts quicker. He nodded as he gathered her into his arms. "We only want what's best for you, so he left. I'm here. You'll tell me if I hurt you."

"I already hurt," she whimpered.

He released her instantly, despair spiking inside him. "Is that my doing?"

"No." She leaned in and nuzzled her face in his neck. "You feel good."

There was a wealth of meaning in that sentence. He soothed her and made her feel protected. But when she nipped at his earlobe and kissed a little spot just beneath, he shivered. Comfort and safety obviously weren't the only things on her mind.

"It's coming back, the frenzy." She sounded slightly panicked.

"You needing, love?" He gently pulled the bedspread away from her tight grip and set it aside where she couldn't reach it and hide from him again.

Beneath it all, she sat naked, a flushed tangle of soft skin and shaking legs. She closed her eyes and turned her face away, looking embarrassed and torn. "Yes. I'm sorry."

He hooked his finger under her chin. "Look at me." He waited until she complied, blinking those amber eyes up at him, now swimming in tears. "Never apologize to me for what you need. Just tell me so I can help."

"It's not very… proper."

A slow grin stretched across his face. "Even better."

With a tremulous smile dawning, she looked into his eyes. "I've missed you."

"Love, I've died every day without you."

Her smile fell. "You're better off without me."

He dropped the smile instantly and gripped her chin more firmly. "You let me make that decision. Don't think you're going to make it for me, especially without talking to me. I want you. I want to be here for you. I want to give you what you need. All you have to do is tell me what that is."

Anka hesitated, drew in a shaky breath. Then she launched herself at him, throwing her arms around his neck and seizing his mouth in a demanding kiss that made him instantly hard. A million questions still buzzed through his mind, but he shut them all off. Later, he'd get answers.

As he stood with her wrapped in his arms, he carried her to the bed and tore his mouth away for a moment. "Tell me if I'm hurting you."

She nodded solemnly, her dark lashes wet with tears. Then she pressed her lips to his again, her tongue probing hungrily, asking, seeking, pleading. It went straight to his cock. He was touching her, tasting her.

He was the mate of her heart.

Joy soared inside him as he laid her back and covered her body with his own. Under him, all her soft, exposed skin beckoned, silk and perfume intoxicating him. Longing tightened him like a bowstring. He swallowed against impatience. After today, she would be his again. She'd never go back to Shock. Lucan smiled before he took her lips again. She might even have his youngling.

"Did you hear what Millie said about the spell?"

Anka closed her eyes, cheeks flushing. "Yes."

"You understand what this means, then?"

"Can we just…not talk now?"

Something inside him softened. She might not be ready to face all this, and as much as he wanted to unleash the pent-up need screaming inside him, he had to be sure she could cope.

"No, love. I won't do this without your full cooperation."

She sighed. "I understand. My heart has chosen you. I might conceive. Yes, I still want this and you. Please…" Under him, her lithe little body began to undulate, her hips lifting and seeking.

All the desire he'd held at bay through sheer will broke through his good intentions. They should probably continue this conversation, decide what happened next for them. God knew he wanted to Call to her again so fucking badly.

Right now, he couldn't spare any more words.

Toeing off his trainers and pushing his sweat pants down to his hips, he captured Anka's mouth in a desperate kiss, forcing her to take every hungry sweep of his tongue, every conquering press of his lips. Anka murmured nonsensical words of encouragement between each kiss, guiding his hand to her peaked nipple. He groaned into the next kiss, pinching and pulling at the tender little nub, satisfied when it hardened even more.

He bent and took her nipple in his mouth, holding it gently between his teeth so he could lash it with his tongue. He did the same with the other, panting. Desire roared inside him like a freight train, charging at him full speed. It was going to run him over utterly, leave nothing behind. He gripped the mattress, struggling to subdue his impatience. But her little mewls only drove him higher.

Squeezing the corner of the bed with all his might, he unleashed his aggression on the mattress beneath her. He couldn't bear to hurt her. The springs bent with a sickly metallic clink. He released the mattress, mentally cursing. But it was too late. The bed collapsed at the edges, sagging sadly.

She cried out with approval, gripping her hands in his hair. "More. Harder."

"Be careful what you wish for, love."

"Now!"

Back to monosyllables. Interesting… Maybe the more he fed her need the more the spell gripped her? Who the hell bloody cared? She wanted something. He'd be damn sure to give it to her.

He kissed her ruthlessly again, pinching her nipple harder. She gasped into his mouth, her hips rising up. His bare cock slid between those sweet, slick folds. He swallowed against the rising flood of lust threatening to overtake his senses.

Soon, so soon, he'd be buried deep inside her, and he hoped to fuck he didn't emerge for days. Right now, he craved one thing so badly, had dreamed of the moment he had the right to do this again.

Shimmying down her body, he stopped to lap and nip at her swollen nipples, relishing her hands in his hair. The little beads hardened even more, and she arched up for him, setting her breast deeper into his mouth. With a moan, he seized them, ate at them. Damn, he'd missed her.

Finally, the lure of her scent became too strong, and he worked his way down her body.

"Spread your legs, love."

Her little cry went straight to his cock. She knew what he wanted, what he craved. Slowly, she complied, parting those pretty pale thighs for him in welcome. Her delicate folds, slick with need, opened to him so beautifully. When they'd been mated, he'd often had to sneak this in, always had to coax and persuade her that he wanted her this way, that it wasn't unladylike. Now, she pushed his head closer to her tempting flesh.

The tangy scent of her sweet spice made his entire body seize up. Hunger belted him in the gut. Impossibly, he got even harder

"Lucan!"

God, he loved the sound of her desperation. "You want something?"

"Now. Please. I need it. Right now."

"Are you asking me to lick your pussy?" His gruff whisper barely sounded over her rough, sawing breaths.

She'd always hated that word, been shy about the act itself. And he was pushing her, some devil inside him wanting to know if she was really, truly ready for him again, even the more demanding side of him that he used to restrain. It strained against his mental chains, and unless he put it away entirely, the need to have his every way with her was going to emerge.

"Yes! With your tongue. And lips. Please. Deep…"

Hell, she not only assented, she begged. That pleased the feral animal he'd caged deep inside him. "Can you lie still for me and take it, love?"

"No!" Her hips bucked and gyrated, urgently seeking relief.

He gripped her, held her down. He liked the thought of her at his mercy, especially when she needed it so badly. Eventually, he'd give her all she needed and more. But for now, her beseeching released that primal part of him and he didn't think he could shut it back off. He didn't want to.

"Try, Anka. Try very hard."

With a whimper, she gave him a shaky nod, then stilled her body. Under his palms, her thighs trembled. He could *feel* her want. Harnessing and holding it lent him another level of power he could use to pleasure her. She was giving him permission to undo her in every way he wished. It was the sweetest gift ever. He planned to savor it, just like he savored her.

Hungrily, he lowered his mouth and gorged on her, kissing her slick folds as he would her mouth, tongue darting and probing, lips brushing, nibbling at her, attacking with a passionate fervor that had her crying out loudly and clutching his hair in her fists as she dragged him deeper into her flesh. Her flavor exploded a kaleidoscope of sensations inside him, the strongest insisting one thing he'd never stopped believing: Anka belonged to *him*.

As he had the first time he'd tasted her, Lucan got utterly drunk on her flavor. Dizzy, head-buzzingly intoxicated. Her wild flavor seeping onto his tongue clawed him with hunger, made him relentless for more of her sugary tang. And her surrender.

Voraciously, he ate her. She fought to stay still for him. But with every lash of his tongue on the little bud of her nerves, every pluck with his lips, she fell deeper into the abyss of desire. He did everything possible to shove her deeper still. The same desire sucked him under. Lucan didn't give a bloody damn if he ever found his way out.

Beneath him, her thighs trembled. Her body tensed. Her uneven breaths melted into a litany of pleading little cries, all in the sound of his name.

Her urgency drove him to possess her even more. He drew his tongue over her flesh again, an unhurried torture that had her fisting the sheet and screaming even louder. Her legs fell open wider. She jerked her hands in his hair mercilessly and brought him deeper still into her flesh with a cry. The way she completely opened herself humbled him—and it aroused the hell out of him.

He spared a moment to lift his head and growl, "Look at me."

A keening cry fell from her mouth, protesting that he'd abandoned the achiest part of her body. But she complied, opening her glassy eyes to stare at him. Without a word, she pleaded.

Smiling now, he rubbed a slow circle around her little bundle of nerves with this thumb.

"Do you want me to keep licking your pussy, love?"

Frantically, she nodded, lifting her hips and crying out an unintelligible sound.

"Beg me."

"Please… More. So close. Need it." She dug her fingers into his hair again and tugged. He kind of liked the little bite of pain. "Need you."

"Good. I'm going to remind you of that for the next few days.

You'll give me everything, yes? So I can help you past this spell?" He swirled his thumb around the hard little knot again. "Don't hold back."

"I won't. No. Don't stop. Please, Lucan."

He might be twenty kinds of bastard for pushing her, but now he knew what she needed. It was as if demanding that she verbalize her desires had given her permission to unleash them. Or maybe he'd never pushed her hard enough before to work through her reserve. Whatever the case, he wasn't settling for the silent, sweet trysts they'd once shared. She had a raw need throbbing inside her, too. He was going to keep that part of her needing and desperate. God knew that's precisely how he felt.

"I've got you, love." He pressed his thumb in on her. "I want you to fly apart now. Can you do that, come for me?"

She gasped and clutched the sheet with one hand, scraping her nails into his scalp with the other. "Can't…stop…it."

Excellent. He didn't wait for her response before he fitted his mouth over her wet feminine folds again and consumed her. He curled his tongue around her clitoris, feeling her body thrash, freeze, then shudder as she screamed incoherently, a cry of pleasure that went on forever.

It was the sweetest sound, almost as sweet as her tangy flavor flooding his tongue and the pulses of energy darting around him.

Perfect. He felt like a giant, twenty feet tall and invincible. His cock throbbed against the slightly starchy sheet below them, angrily demanding a place in her soft, wet well. He peered at her as her breathing slowly regulated. A fine sheen of perspiration covered her chest. Her cheeks were flushed. She'd never been more beautiful to him.

"Perfect, love. Feel good?"

"No!" She arched and pulled on his hair ruthlessly. "Inside me. Now!"

Well, who knew under all those demure skirts and pretty curls that she could be so demanding? He liked this raw side of her.

"You didn't ask me."

Yes, he toyed with her. He couldn't seem to help it. Having her desperate for his touch did something for him, and not just his ego, though that didn't hurt. But it torqued up his own need. With her pleading desire ringing in his ears, there was no way he couldn't grab her and take her relentlessly until exhaustion claimed them both.

"Lucan…begging you. Can't wait."

"Neither can I."

He wriggled his way up her body, his arms curling under her knees to take her legs up with him, spreading her wide. As soon as they lay face to face, he stilled, wondering if this position would bring back terrible memories for her.

"Now!" she screamed at him.

He couldn't quite stop the smile crawling across his face as he probed her hungry opening with his seeking cock and shoved deep in one thrust.

Instant nirvana.

Her flesh clung, so bloody tight. He shuddered as a tingle swept down his spine and settled into his balls. His eyes rolled to the back of his head. Bloody hell, he wanted her. He couldn't restrain or contain his craving to incinerate her with his touch, with their need. Yes, in some ways she was familiar and beloved. Home. But this Anka was like a new sun dawning across his horizon, ushering in not just a new day, but a revelation. She'd always been lovely, but this Anka oozed sensuality, owned her femininity. The way she cried out for him, undulated under him, nipping hungry kisses across his shoulder to urge him deeper and faster, this passionate Anka unraveled him like never before.

Once inside her, he couldn't stop to savor her. He couldn't be gentle. In rapid strokes, he slammed into her, the wild cadence of his thrusts pinning her to the mattress. In some ways, he felt as if he'd never left her. His heart certainly never had.

Anka clung to him with her arms and her sex, as if she never intended to let him go. That suited Lucan. After today, he didn't plan to ever release her again. She would never spend a night in any man's bed besides his own.

"Lucan!"

"Take it, love." His thrusts picked up speed, punctuating every word he spoke. "Take. Me. Deep."

With every plunge inside Anka, her eyes widened with pleasure. Her body softened. Her nipples engorged with more blood. Bloody hell, her berry sweet lips called to him, and he couldn't keep from tasting them. He slanted his mouth over hers feverishly, filling her with his tongue as he stretched her sweet, clenching folds with his cock. Every instinct screamed at him to seize her, inhale her, never let her go.

As she dug her nails into his shoulders, an electric jolt zapped through his body. He threw back his head with a moan. "Yes, Anka! I'm never going to stop touching you. Mine." He bared his teeth and growled at her. "Mine!"

She opened her mouth, an obvious apology on her lips. He stopped her with a brutal kiss, drinking her in as he sank deeper and deeper into her, losing himself in her utterly. When he finally lifted his head, a heartbreaking frown overtook her face, mixed with denial, sharp desire, and finally resignation. He wasn't sure what she intended to say, but he couldn't let those words out.

"Not a word. Now that you've chosen me, I won't let you leave me again. Take me. All of me. Yes. God, yes. Love, oh… Just. Like. That."

Again, he picked up the pace, hearing Anka's breathing race, watching her skin flush, her eyes glaze over. As her defenses fell and she surrendered, he could see her heart, bare and honest, reflected in her shimmering eyes.

"You love me." His heart soared when he saw hers in her eyes, begging him to love her back. "You do, but you're scared. Don't be. I never stopped loving you."

"But…" She cried out, part pleasure, part sorrow.

"No! I'm not letting anything come between us again. Ever. Mine. Mine. Mine!" He ground deeper inside her with every word.

Her back arched as her legs spread even wider for him. Head

thrashing, mouth gaping, she began to pulse around him. Lucan changed the angle of his stroke to hit that one perfect spot inside her designed to give her total bliss. Anka felt the change, gasped when the head of his cock scraped those sensitive tissues.

"Lucan, oh my… I…yes!"

Her face said that her head wanted to cease all yielding to him. But it was too late. Whatever ran through her brain made absolutely no difference now as her climax rushed to a peak. To Lucan, there was nothing they wouldn't and couldn't work out, given enough time. "Yes! Beautiful, love. Perfect. We belong together. Look at me, Anka." She blinked up at him, her gaze fastening on his. "Give it all to me."

He refused to let her look away as her mouth opened with a helpless scream of ecstasy. Hovering directly above her, he fused their gazes together and fell into her, deeper under her spell. "Oh… yes. That's it, love. That's right. Give me everything."

She came apart for him, her eyes wide and beseeching, as if so much pleasure scared her. As many times as they'd made love before, it had never been this profound, so directly from the heart. The thought that he might have finally won back the woman of his dreams *and* planted his seed in her womb made Lucan lose the last thread of his composure. Gripping her hips in his hands as she continued to shatter around him, he growled out her name in an agonized breath and emptied himself utterly inside her clasping body until he felt boneless and replete.

His strokes slowed, as did his heartbeats and his breathing. Peace covered him like a blanket, and he sighed in contentment as he looked down at the witch he loved more than his life.

Anka closed her eyes against him, crossing her thin arms over her chest and curling into herself as tears leaked from her eyes.

Gently, he grabbed her wrists and firmly eased them to the sides of her body. She might feel as if he'd scraped her raw to the soul. God knew that's how he felt. But no more hiding. No more evading feelings, conversations they needed to have, emotions they needed to share. Whatever they had to face now, they'd do it together.

Lucan brushed damp curls away from her cheeks and smiled down at her. The gesture squeezed her heart until it bled love for him. "Anka, don't cry, love. What we shared was stunning."

She nodded, unable to disagree—even as more tears fell and regret rolled through her. Their lovemaking had been urgent, primal…and yet soul-soaringly beautiful. But if he could see the ugliness of what she was and what she'd done lurking underneath her pretty surface, all the way down to the lies she'd kept hidden, he'd be horrified. Eventually, he would hate her.

With a thumb, he wiped away her tears again. "I see you trying to crawl back into your shell, and I won't have it. I love you. I believe you love me, too. Do you want to deny that?"

She hesitated. Hurting him more wasn't an option, but if she opened herself up totally, she'd only fall deeper in love. Still, it wasn't fair to him to give him nothing but lies. She'd done it for a century, swearing to herself that she'd do everything else possible to make him happy. But in the end, all her dirty little secrets had pulled them apart—and always would.

"I don't deny it," she whispered. "But please believe me. I can't be what you need."

"What I need?" He rolled to his side and propped himself up on his elbow. "Love, I don't think I've been what *you've* needed until right now. I will search for the rest of our lives to find ways to atone for that. But don't you dare shut me out. I won't allow it."

His voice rang with a note of steel she'd never once heard from him during their mating. She wasn't sure where that deep, shiver-worthy voice came from, but she found not heeding it nearly impossible. Still, for his sake, she had to try. "Lucan, listen…"

"No, you listen." His eyes narrowed. The passion-dark blue that had lured her in moments ago now turned flinty and hard. "You *chose* me over Shock. I am the mate of your heart. We both know it. And I want that heart, along with your devotion and your soul because I'm going to give you mine in return."

"But you don't know what sort of soul you're getting anymore. Mathias…changed me. He tainted me. He used me in ways you can't fathom." She bit her lip, realizing that Lucan would take that to mean sexually. Mathias had, but that didn't disturb Anka as much as the rest of the ugly truth did. "There are things you don't understand."

"Then tell me. We will work together to repair the damage he's done to your psyche," Lucan vowed. "But neither your heart nor soul are black, love. Don't paint yourself that way and settle for loneliness. Don't let him defeat you or us." He caressed her cheek." I'm not perfect, either. Far from it. But the one thing I know without a doubt is that my love for you is true. I believe yours is, as well. If we start with that, if we begin with the knowledge that we belong together, then the only thing that can keep us from our happiness is our own foolishness."

Damn it, his words were beautiful but wrong. He didn't understand because he didn't have the wretched knowledge she lived with each day. She refused to burden him…or risk the censure she feared seeing in his eyes. "What you've said, it's very romantic, but too simple. There are so many things… My family wasn't good enough for yours."

He frowned. "That never mattered to me, and my parents came to love you."

"But they, along with everyone else, wondered why you chose me as your mate."

"Because I love you, and whatever you imagine their opinions are don't matter in the least to me. Why do they matter to you? And what does this have to do with Mathias? You're grasping at straws, trying to keep us apart."

Anka's heart stopped at his keen insight. Of course she was grasping at straws. How else could she put him at arm's length without confessing that she'd neglected to mention for over a hundred years that she'd been born a banshee? Or the horrifying things she'd done with her "gift"? Telling and releasing him might be the most humane thing. Sadly, she was too much of a coward to risk his horror and condemnation.

"I see your mind turning. Mathias raped you, I know that. I've seen that he abused you terribly. How can you think for a moment that it's your fault?"

Yes, that was another black stain on her soul. "I begged him," she sobbed, "for more. Always for more."

"*Terriforz*, love. He forced you to crave him. You know that."

Regardless, the truth hurt like hell. "When I close my eyes at night, I hear my pitiful pleading for that monster! It haunts me, and it plays again over and over in my head."

"Is that why you asked Shock to dominate you? To replace Mathias's touch with something else?"

Bloody hell, he would bring that up. Her needs would be another rift between them eventually. She couldn't imagine Lucan throwing her onto his bed, forcing her face-down while he smacked her backside red with a crop, sometimes until she bruised. It would pain his compassionate heart to hurt anyone. And she understood completely. Self-loathing ate at her for her urges.

"Not…exactly." She did her best to be honest. "After I came to stay with Shock, I'd bottled up all my anguish and misery. I refused food or comfort. And as long as I was coherent, I refused energy. He forced me to take it and found a multitude of ways to make me release my emotions so I could cope."

"You wanted to lie down and die?" He sounded aghast, his question almost an accusation. But didn't he see?

"Of course I did. I'd lost everything. And as my memories returned…"

She tried to cover her face with her hands, but Lucan grabbed them, pressing them into the mattress. "Whatever it is, we face it together. No hiding. I'm here for you."

Anka struggled to free her hands, but Lucan wasn't budging. "Let go! You wouldn't say that if I told you everything."

"So tell me everything, every dirty little issue that you think I won't be able to deal with. Mathias made you beg him to fuck you.

He whipped and used you. What else is it you think I can't handle?"

"He made me kill!" She flung the furious words at him. Then bit her lip to stop herself from confessing the rest of the awful truth. If she had a spine or she could scrape together some courage, she would tell Lucan everything—and release him once and for all.

But even in that, she failed. She lacked the bravery or will to drive them apart forever. For that, she hated herself even more.

"Kill who?" His voice had gone soft, like he finally understood the gravity.

"I don't know. I don't remember very much. I blocked that night out. But Mathias teleported me to someone's home and forced me..." She shook her head. "Dead, all of them. Wizards, witches… younglings."

Horror dawned over his face. Anka couldn't look. She turned away, eyes closed, as fresh tears streamed down her cheeks. "I've done something despicable and repulsive that I can never take back! I stole lives." She drew in a shuddering breath of regret. "And it hardly matters whether I was compelled to kill or that I would never have had any hand in their deaths ordinarily. The fact is, I *did*. And there's no taking it back. I am haunted by the screams of the little ones crying for parents who already lay dead…" Their ears bleeding with her banshee song. But she still continued to wail because the consequences of stopping were too terrible to contemplate. So the nightmares of little younglings frantically covering their own ears as they sought cover, only to fall, screaming and writhing, until she'd sang them to sleep forever, continued to haunt her. She would spare Lucan that pain.

And now he might have planted a youngling of his in her womb. *No! Oh God, no.* She had no business being a mother after what she'd done, or consigning an innocent babe to be hunted and hated for her blood.

She shoved him off of her, frantically scrambling out of the bed. Grabbing her clothes, she began untangling them, trying to don them—even as the feverish need from Morganna's spell possessed her again, filling and tightening her nipples, throbbing through her sex. Even her lips ached to kiss away the frown on Lucan's face until he wanted only to thrust his way into her body and make love to her again.

Impossible. She could never give him another opportunity to plant a seed in her womb.

Lucan sat up, grabbed her wrists, and hauled her into his lap. "Stop, Anka. Stop! You can't run from what happened. It's tragic. You're a gentle soul, and I can only imagine how deeply that scarred you. But I don't love you less for being forced to hurt others. I love you more for enduring. Don't let Mathias win."

Had Lucan gone utterly mad? She met his stare, her mouth gaping open. Then she closed it. He would assume that Mathias had put some terrible spell on her to compel her to kill others, that she hadn't chosen that fate of her own free will. The alternative had been unthinkable.

"You might think you love me still, and that proves what a giving, kind person you are, but I can't stand myself anymore, Lucan. I hate looking in a mirror. I loathe what I've become. You can't save me or be my hero. You can't convince me that nothing is my fault. You can't persuade me that my 'good heart' absolves me of all my wrongdoing. But you can let me go and believe me when I tell you that you'll be so much better off without me."

Chapter Twelve

Anka stumbled back from the bed, watching in miserable resignation as Lucan softly slumbered. When he woke, he would be
furious that she'd hit him with a light sleeping spell. It would last no more than fifteen minutes. He would awake refreshed and alert. And thoroughly angry.

She swallowed, staring. *You've made your decision*! She could stand here and review all the reasons she'd come to this conclusion, or she could stop second-guessing herself and do what needed to be done. The time for making excuses and leaning on others had passed. If she intended to emerge from her own ashes, she needed to start rebirthing herself now.

No fear. No leaning on others. No hesitation. No regrets.

After stepping into her clothes, she approached Lucan and pressed a soft kiss on his lips, savoring him for a long moment. Most likely, she would never have this opportunity again, probably never be this close to him. Would he see her upcoming actions as a betrayal? Would she create the sort of chasm between them that could never be bridged?

Likely so. As much as it hurt, it was better for him.

Once she'd donned the clothes, they chafed immediately. Her sensitive skin protested, but she forced herself to dart out the bedroom door and run for the stairs.

"Where are you going?"

Anka whipped her head around to find Bram in a wingback chair tilted back on two legs, propped against the wall. He raised a brow and sent her a cutting glance.

"Why does it matter? Before you agreed to let me join the Doomsday Brethren, you made me promise to whore myself out to your double agent. Don't worry. I'll uphold my end of the bargain."

"What about Lucan?"

Her conscience stabbed her. "What about him?"

"Your heart chose him."

She crossed her arms over her chest. "My head is overruling that decision. Why is that a problem for you?"

"It will be a problem for Lucan."

"I'm sorry, but as you've said more than once, war isn't pretty."

Bram nodded curtly. "Quite true. So you're just going to break his heart?"

"I'm going to let him get on with his life." She sent him a tight smile and changed the subject. "Are you expecting Millie back soon?"

"Yes. She'll want to check on you. I don't imagine that she'll be happy to hear you're leaving already. Morganna's spell probably has hours, maybe even days, left."

She shrugged with a confidence she didn't feel, gritting her teeth against the flush suffusing her skin and the cramping in her womb. All too soon, the symptoms were going to overwhelm her again. She couldn't let Bram know that every step she put between her and Lucan was excruciating, like she'd cut open her chest with her fingernails and pulled out her own heart. He'd only put on his noble hat and try to force her to stay.

"It's my problem. I'll deal with it." She nodded toward the bedroom where she'd left Lucan. "You deal with him."

Without another word, she jogged down the stairs and

disappeared outside. Dusk was coming, and the wind was whistling a howling tune through the barren trees when she made her way back to the park near Aquarius's flat. She conjured up her coat from Shock's house. It protected her from the winter chill, but added to the discomfort crawling over her skin. Forcing one foot in front of the other, she breathed in the fresh air, hoping it would soothe her, and headed to her cousin's little place.

Anka let herself in with a wave of her hand, hoping to find her quirky little cousin brewing green tea, making some wretched health food that no one—magic or humankind—would ever eat. Instead, the place stood still, uninhabited and silent. The explosion of color Aquarius left in her wake was everywhere, but her cousin wasn't home.

With a grimace, Anka eased inside and flopped down on the little blue sofa, a hand-me-down relic from another century. Ghastly uncomfortable and stained, the furniture still brought comfort. It was every bit as oddball and familiar as her cousin.

And she'd arrived not a moment too soon.

A shudder washed over her. Anka drew in a deep breath to steady herself, but another wave hit her almost immediately, more fierce than the last. Her nipples ached for a touch, a warm mouth. And the flesh between her thighs burned as if someone had torched her with a dancing flame against her swollen folds. Damn bloody spell! She needed a man to ease the debilitating ache.

No, she needed Lucan.

Curling her arms into her empty abdomen, she doubled over, biting her lip to hold in a cry. Aquarius had very human neighbors, and Anka knew that if she was too loud, one of them could call 999 to "save" her. She'd have a devil of a time explaining that she simply had to wait out Morganna's spell. And hope it didn't kill her.

The emptiness of her sex was a seeping, empty gash. She fell back on the couch, her breathing labored, her entire body throbbing for what she would never have again: Lucan's touch.

Her clothes scratched and chafed beyond anything she could endure now. She tore them off until she was blessedly naked. With a lot of cramping and seizing up, she managed to divest herself of everything. But that didn't do anything to diminish the frightful ache slicing her in two.

She curled into a ball and tried to rock herself. Sweat poured off of her, and all she could think of was Lucan. By now, he was probably wondering why she'd left him. He was probably worried about her.

Little wonder Bram believed she could die if she went unsatisfied for the duration of this spell. The way her over-sensitized skin rasped against itself and the coarse fabric of the sofa made every nerve in her body sizzle with acute pain. Her taste buds bulged and throbbed without his kiss. Her breasts swelled and peaked, and she could feel blood still rushing into the tips, overwhelming her with too much sensation. Not having Lucan's hands on her was a torture all its own. She reached between her legs to ease the debilitating need that dragged her closer and closer to mindlessness. But touching herself only hurt more.

Thoughts of Lucan made her sex clench and spasm. She needed him, had to have him. If she died without him… wouldn't that be what she deserved?

Sweat rolled over her skin, and she closed her eyes, trying to close out everything but the fantasy in her head where Lucan found her, led her to his bed, crawled between her legs, and tongued his way up her slick flesh until she cried out in…

"No!" Anka sat upright, expecting to be huddled on the sofa. Instead, Shock knelt between her legs, holding her thighs wide, his lips slick with her juices.

"Still hurt?" he asked.

She nodded. "Don't."

He drew his hands away immediately.

Anka wanted to apologize for her rebuff, caress his cheek. She wished she could let him know that, whatever their respective shortfalls as people that didn't allow them to be a real couple, a part of her would always love him, despite the fact that her heart had chosen another.

He sat back on his heels with a sigh. "Aquarius came home and found you delirious and writhing on her sofa. She called me. Why did you leave MacTavish? You love him. He wants you. Are you afraid to be happy?"

Shock made happiness sound so simple. Order it from the value menu and *poof*! Someone served it up immediately, steaming and tasty, in a cardboard takeaway container.

"Doesn't matter." She curled her knees into her chest as another cramp overtook her. She cried out and bit her lip. Had to be mindful of the neighbors.

"It fucking does." He picked her up in his arms.

Even that small touch sent every nerve in her body hurtling headfirst into an acute pain that had her screaming, neighbors be damned. Shock dropped her like a hot potato and cursed.

"You need him, little one, especially now. I think he's worthless, but…"

"Can't have him."

He sighed. "You've grown stubborn, Anka."

"Living with you." She grimaced, bracing for another wave of pain.

"You're in agony and you're making jokes?"

She forced a small smile. "Working?"

"For fuck's sake. Where is your mobile?"

So he could call Lucan to come and care for her? Yes, that's what he would do. Under all his bad attitude and bluster, he cared for her deeply. She had hurt him…yet he was willing to put her needs above his own.

"Not telling."

Shock didn't waste time chastising her, just rummaged through the pockets of her discarded clothes, finally pulling the device free. "Where is the wanker's number?"

As he scrolled through her menus, she forced her mind away from the pain and the pending wave of ruthless desire threatening to choke her. "Make me sleep."

"I already tried."

She frowned, blinked up at his scowling face. "When?"

"The second I walked in and saw you thrashing about in total misery. Believe me, calling the do-good fucker isn't my first choice."

So, in the absence of any other plan, Shock would give her back to his enemy and sacrifice his own happiness to save her. His innate goodness and loyalty to those he cared for had endeared him to her from day one. She wished it could be enough.

"I found it." He started pressing buttons.

In a moment, that call would connect. Lucan would be awake and probably come running. He would insist on giving her whatever she needed to feel better. And they would create the next generation of banshee. Lucan would draw ever closer to finding the truth she sought to protect him from.

She had run out of options and out of time.

With only a vague plan in mind, she'd come to Aquarius's. The moment to set it in motion had arrived. Once these words were spoken, even Lucan couldn't touch her.

Anka licked her dry lips, trying to form all the words coherently. "As I become a part of you, you become a part of me. I will be honest, good, and true—"

"What the fuck are you doing?" Shock threw the phone aside and knelt to her. "Don't."

Saying the words he'd waited over a century to hear. Binding to him. It had to be done eventually if either he or Lucan were ever going to really be free. This was manipulative and terrible—and the only way she could help both of the men she loved. "I heed your Call. 'Tis you I seek."

"You don't mean any of those words. Shut it! Bloody shut it right now!"

He needed this. He might really hate her timing, but someday he would thank her. The fact that it gave Lucan an easy reason to turn his back on her forever didn't hurt, either.

Gathering her strength, she drew in a shuddering breath and finished her vow. "From this moment on, there is no other for me but you."

An explosion rocked her, splintering her with an agony a hundred times worse than what she'd endured before. She only thought she'd known pain, but she'd been wrong. Apparently Binding to the wizard her heart hadn't chosen while craving another made her pain more terrible.

She yelped and cried, curling into a tight ball on the sofa. Death had to be coming soon.

"Why the fuck did you do that?" he asked softly, his hand hovering over her as if he wanted to touch and comfort her but didn't dare.

"I am…" She swallowed. "Your mate now."

"Do you think I want you now, when I know your heart belongs to that wanker? I couldn't escape to the bottom of a bottle fast enough every bloody time I fucked you and you were pining for him. I don't want to do that for the rest of my life. I don't want to be your second choice, Anka."

"Agreed." She clenched her fists, trying to breathe past the pain buzzing through her system. "Did this…for you."

"So I can remember every fucking time I come near you that you didn't want me first? No. Hell no."

She shook her head and tried to focus on the words, not the suffering. "Take me to Millie."

Shock hesitated before understanding dawned on his dark face. He ripped off his sunglasses, and she had no doubt he'd done it so that she would see how deeply her gesture had disturbed him. Eventually, he would thank her. Maybe in a century or two. Now, he was simply furious.

"Are you fucking kidding me? You did this for me, to free me. No. Absolutely not. A mate breaking right now will kill you."

"Not…worst thing."

"Is that what you think? That's shit. Do you hear me? Shit! I'm already going to lose you and—"

"You don't love me."

"Oh, now you think you know my heart?"

Despite the torture of her raw pain and empty sex, she smiled. Shock was always confrontational when someone touched his emotions. "Yes."

"You know fuck all."

"Take me to Millie."

He sighed and moved to curl his arm under her shoulders, then another under her knees.

The second he did, the torment of the touch became unbearable. "No! God, don't. No…"

Shock jerked away immediately.

Sobs came. She needed to see this through. Let Shock loose to finally live the rest of his life so that he was completely free to fall in love with the mate destined to complete him, not the trophy he wanted to spit-polish shiny and show off to Lucan and every other Privileged bastard when the occasion arose. If Lucan believed that she'd chosen Shock to share her life with, at least temporarily… Well, that would make his decision to find a better woman even easier. And Bram might have insisted that she live with Shock, but he would have to get over it if she chose to put her head on another pillow.

"Fuck this." Shock shoved his glasses back on and grabbed her phone again. "I'm not letting you die over this."

"Lucan can't touch me now."

He paused. "He can't fuck you. But I'm guessing he's the only man who can touch you. He'll get you to Millie. Once she douses this spell of Morganna's, we'll talk about what happens next."

She opened her mouth to argue, and Shock shook his head, nudging her with his knee. Predictably, a whole new hurt ravaged her, reducing her to a panting, whimpering mass.

He completed the call, barking into the mobile. "Get to Aquarius's. Anka needs you."

Shock had barely disconnected the call before Lucan banged on the door.

"Don't tell him," she cried out.

"That you're going to break our happy little mate bond? I'll say whatever the fuck I want."

With heavy, booted steps he stomped to the door and wrenched it open. Lucan charged in and took one look at her magical signature which now proclaimed her Shock's mate.

The betrayal on his face broke her heart into a million pieces.

"Why?" He choked the word out.

She didn't have to pretend agony this time. Anka lowered her head to her knees, still curled up to her chest, and let the sorrow pour out. She'd wanted to free Shock for all he'd done to help her. She'd wanted to drive Lucan away and spare him all the ugliness he couldn't and shouldn't have to handle.

But God, it hurt far worse than she'd ever imagined. Far worse than any side effect of Morganna's spell ever could.

"Millie," she gasped out.

"I can't touch her," Shock barked. "Binding to me only increased her pain."

Lucan turned on him. "Then why did you let her? You had to know… Her heart made a different choice. Of course this was going to cause her untold anguish."

"It's not as if I encouraged her. I'd Called to her over a century ago. How was I to know that she'd pick this special fucking moment to finally accept?"

"You couldn't read her bloody mind?"

"Not without feeling her pain, douchebag. So I stayed out of her head. Are you really going to blame me for this now?"

Anka listened to them argue, grimacing as the next wave of need dismantled her coping mechanisms and decimated her energy reserve. She screeched in agony. Both men lunged to her side.

"Stubborn witch," Shock grumbled. "If I could touch you, I'd paddle your arse."

She tried to smile. "Can't."

"But I can," Lucan growled. "If you were any stronger…"

The worry on his face eclipsed any menace he might have been trying to convey. She reached out to touch him, then thought better of it. "Millie?"

Confusion twisted Lucan's face, and Shock rolled his eyes. "Take her back to Bram's, wankstain. She wants his aunt."

Lucan looked ready to pound Shock's skull into little pieces, and Shock's raised brow certainly invited him to try. But they both backed down—for now. For her sake.

"This isn't over. We'll be talking about this. He might be your… *mate*—" Lucan spit the word at her. "—but once you're better, we're going to talk about everything, you and I."

She nodded weakly, aware of another heated rush flushing her body as Lucan drew near. Her womb spasmed. Her sex gaped and clenched. Her nipples throbbed. And the raw craving for him sapped her energy so very quickly.

God, was Morganna's spell going to kill her?

Finally, Lucan cursed and brought her into his arms, against his chest. The pain eased a bit, and she sighed with the momentary relief. "Thank you."

"Don't thank me yet," Lucan snarled. "I'm not nearly done with you."

They teleported back to Bram's house, and the moment their leader opened the door to admit them, his eyes widened as if he'd just seen flying pigs. Thankfully, Anka had passed out during the teleportation. The overload of pain making her scream had been more than Lucan could bear.

What had she been thinking, running away and Binding to Shock, especially while enduring Morganna's spell?

"I don't know," Shock admitted.

"But bloody hell…" Bram's accusing stare zipped up to Shock. "You let her Bind to you *now*?"

"I've already covered this shit with bachelor number one." Shock hooked a thumb in Lucan's direction. "Ease up, you git."

"Where's Millie?" Lucan demanded. "I want her to tell me more about whatever enchantment Morganna put on Anka. It's sapping her energy too fast."

And at this rate, it would likely kill her before it waned.

"I'll summon her." Bram looked Anka over with grim eyes. "And tell her it's an emergency. Put Anka back in the bedroom."

Lucan charged up the stairs, aware of Shock a half-step behind. He wanted to tell the bastard to go away, that Anka wasn't any of his business. But she'd chosen him to be her mate, though she knew her heart had decided otherwise. Why?

As he set her on the bed, he looked up to find Shock rubbing a hand over his tired face. "She's doing this to free me."

"From your existence without sex? I'm fairly certain you've been having your fair share since she came to live under your roof." He couldn't keep the bitterness out of his voice.

"Yeah, and if that bugs the hell out of you, well, so sorry, Sir Galahad. But she spoke the Binding to me because she intends to let me go. Forever. Like you said, her heart chose, and it wasn't me."

Shock believed that Anka intended to break their bond?

"Someone get the guy an award," Shock quipped. "Exactly. How else am I ever going to be free to love someone else or whatever crap is running through her head?"

"But why now? It might kill her."

Meaty hands curled into fists. "I don't think that idea bothers her the way it does you or me."

Bloody hell! "She didn't fucking talk to me."

"Join the club. She's really not the same woman anymore. Her independent streak is a mile wide now."

"Clearly."

Lucan paced, trying to take it all in and understand the ramifications. "So Anka spoke the Binding and…hoped I would see your bond?"

He nodded. "Then lose your bloody temper and denounce her eternally so that once my bond with her was broken, you'd no longer give a shit. That's my guess."

He snorted. "That isn't going to happen."

"Do you truly love her?"

Turning to Shock as if he'd lost his mind, Lucan frowned. "How can you doubt it?"

Shock looked at him as if he'd lost every shred of sanity. "You hardly demanded that she come back to you after she healed you from your mate mourning. You left her with me and didn't fight for her. What was anyone supposed to think, except that your pride was more important than your love for her?"

Shock's speech stung like a bitch. Worse, Lucan realized there might be a kernel of truth to it. He'd been so broken and angry when he realized that Anka hadn't come home to him, and had assumed she'd rejected him for a prick he couldn't stand. She'd broken his heart. And he'd been too proud to ask why.

"Seeing the picture now? She cried herself sick when she teleported to your house by accident a few days ago and found you'd brought a surrogate there."

She'd seen him leading someone else into their house while he'd been gearing up to close his eyes and pretend that he was no longer alone. Knowing that he'd hurt her badly stabbed bitter fury into his chest. That day, he'd been desperate to prove that he could hold someone else within those four walls that Anka still haunted with her presence. And he'd failed miserably. One look at Anka and all thoughts of another female had fled.

Now only regret remained.

"I see you're beginning to understand. You left me to pick up the pieces and blamed her for staying with me when you gave almost no indication that she mattered."

"That's crap." Lucan pushed him in the chest. "I begged her to come home."

"Once or twice. But she was hurting and terrified. She needed reassurance. When her spirit was bruised and her self-confidence battered, you took her refusals far too easily. After that, how the hell was she supposed to believe that you really cared?"

When the hell had Shock become Dr. Phil?

"It's not hard, you stupid prat, when I can read her fucking mind."

There was that. "Why give me so many helpful hints when she's your mate now? Morganna's spell will wear off, and you could keep her for yourself then."

Shock tossed his hands in the air. "It's not me she wants. And I won't take her free will. Is it such a stretch for you to believe that I'd do anything for her?"

At this point? "No, but isn't there a part of you that wonders if, perhaps, over time, you could make her love you?"

"She already loves me," Shock assured him, totally confident in that assessment. "But not as much as she loves you. It fucking pains me to say that, but for her sake, I did. Don't make me regret it."

Lucan nodded, stunned. Shock wasn't exactly who or what he'd believed or expected. His feelings for Anka had peeled back the layers and revealed someone more human, more sensitive—

"Oh, blast it. You did *not* just think that I'm sensitive." A scowl thundered across Shock's face.

"Not at all," Lucan lied.

"Spectacular. Now fuck off."

After everything Shock had told him? "Sure. Happy to. Feel free to do the same."

"Once she's well, absolutely."

They both stared at Anka, who sighed softly, tossing and turning on the soft sheets of the bed. She needed his touch. Lucan realized it innately. It pained him to put a hand on her naked skin while her signature blared with the proof of her bond to Shock. But this wasn't about him, and Shock had put him in his place.

Falling to his knees beside the bed, he cupped Anka's cheeks. "I'm here, love. Stay with us. You're going to be all right."

At least he hoped that would be true.

"Millie will be around in a tick!" Bram called up the stairs. "Sabelle will be back, too, to see if she can impart any calm to Anka with her siren ability."

Perfect. Why the bloody hell hadn't he thought of that sooner?

Maybe Sabelle could ease Anka and help her survive the mate breaking. He prayed. A world without Anka… He shook his head and tried to quiet the terror in his belly. Knowing that she was under Shock's roof had been gut-wrenching and terrible, but at least he'd always known deep down that he would have the chance to talk to her again. If she didn't survive now, Lucan didn't think he would either.

"We have to believe that she'll make it," Shock grumbled, looking at her with a frown. "Fucking hate it when she goes pale like this."

Yes, Lucan hated it, too.

"Listen…the mate mourning." Shock swallowed. "Is it really bloody awful?"

Lucan lifted his head, realizing that Shock would soon endure what he had after Mathias had destroyed his bond with Anka. Any other day, he would have rejoiced at the thought of the big, leather-wearing arse feeling pain. Today, it all just felt petty.

"Beyond awful. I don't remember more than constant agony, an emptiness inside me that nothing could fill, wrenching grief, and a fury that wouldn't die."

"That does sound bloody fucking awful." And Shock looked nervous as hell about it.

"I don't have any reassuring words."

"Then give me something, man. If I lose my fucking sanity, do me one favor?

At this point, as much as Lucan hated to admit it, he owed Shock a debt of gratitude.

"All right. What do you need?"

"When the bond is severed, if my mind snaps, just kill me."

Chapter Thirteen

"We're nearly finished," Sabelle advised as she stuck her head out the bedroom door.

Stuck in the hallway waiting, Lucan wanted to pace, but sat fidgeting and restless. In the wingback chair beside him, Shock looked ready to crawl out of his skin.

"This is bloody awkward." He tried to make light of the situation. "Isn't it? You sitting next to your current mate's ex, waiting to become her ex, as well."

Shock flipped him a glare. Lucan could see nothing behind the sunglasses, but he felt the heat of the wizard's annoyance all the same. "Thank you, Captain Obvious."

So much for that line of conversation. Lucan tapped his toe, straining to hear any sound coming from the room, any indication of whether Anka was going to be all right. They all knew that Shock wouldn't be once this was over.

"That's right," Shock snarled. "You promised to end me."

Lucan wasn't exactly certain how he would do that, but he owed Shock. On any other day, having a free invitation to kill the bastard would have been cause for throwing confetti and donning a party hat. Not today. Damn it.

"I'll keep my end of the bargain," Lucan promised.

Then he couldn't take the waiting anymore. He hopped to his feet and paced the hallway. "What's taking so long? Mathias ripped us apart in what seemed like a matter of moments. I barely felt an inkling of Anka's panic and fear before it was done."

"I expect Millie and Sabelle have to be careful. Her energy is waning, isn't it? She's already in pain. I don't bloody know."

Perhaps not, but those sounded like good guesses. "She might die trying to free you, and I'd really love to hate you for it. But she made a choice. In her place, I would have done the same."

But Lucan didn't know if he could live with it.

"You think I'm fucking thrilled? When she's well—not if, but *when*—my pissed off is going to blow like an illegal Guy Fawkes tribute right in her face," Shock grumbled, then sighed. "Will you Call to her again?"

Anka had left Lucan once more—a clear indication that she had no intention of spending the rest of her centuries by his side. But as Shock had aptly pointed out mere hours ago, Anka needed reassurance. She needed someone to fight for her. He planned to be that man. No way was he letting her go now.

"We'll get there."

Shock snorted. "Even if you have to pull her by the hair? She likes that, you know."

The visual made him ill. "Not another damn word or I'll lose all the Zen and 'Kumbaya' I've got going now and punch your face."

"I'd actually prefer that."

Lucan couldn't help it; he laughed. He never could have guessed when he awoke in his cold bed alone this morning that by nightfall everything would have changed. He was the mate of Anka's heart, and he was going to hold her to that. The rest? Window dressing that didn't matter. Whatever roadblocks they'd faced previously, he would work to put those behind them and rebuild Anka's delicate sense of self-worth until she understood that whatever Mathias had done to her didn't matter to him in the least.

She mattered.

"Good. She needs a firm, guiding hand now. I won't give her back to a pussy. I'd fight for her tooth and nail if you weren't strong enough to give her what she needs."

Give her what she needs. A phrase Mitchell Thorpe had been very fond of using. Lucan understood that his first responsibility to Anka was to ensure her emotional wellbeing. And he would. Then they would have a serious tête-à-tête about why she hadn't returned home to him after breaking free from Mathias. Trust issues lurked there. Lucan wasn't sure why, but he'd get to the bottom of that posthaste.

Sabelle popped her head out the door again. "Lucan?"

He sprinted for the door. "What is it?"

"She needs energy desperately. Now." Sabelle stepped back to admit him.

Lucan hesitated. "I can't exchange energy with her until the bond is broken. You know that."

"It will be too late then. She'll be…gone."

"What the fuck?" Shock cursed from behind him.

Lucan raked a hand through his hair. "How do you know I won't be hurting her more?"

"I don't. But at least she will have the energy to endure."

Right, then. Another ugly truth. Another goddamn conundrum with no simple solution.

He glanced over his shoulder. Shock looked exhausted, like he wouldn't give a shit now if a train ran him over. Hollow cheeks, black stubble dusting his jaw, clothes rumpled, demeanor prickly. But he wasn't budging from this vigil. In an odd way, Lucan admired the other wizard's resolution. He didn't trust Shock a whole lot—except when it came to Anka. Today, the git had proven that he would always do what was best for her, no matter what.

"What do you think?" he asked Shock. "I don't want to hurt her, but failing to intervene doesn't sound like an option."

Shock nodded. "When she screams, it will fuck with my mood. But you don't have a choice. Go."

Indeed. Lucan swallowed down his jangled nerves. Anka needed him…but he couldn't, in good conscience, leave Shock alone now. He'd promised.

Lucan whipped out his mobile and sent a quick text to Caden.

"Bloody hell, no!" Shock bristled. "I don't need your little brother babysitting me."

But the badass wizard's time to protest was over nearly before it began. Bram was letting Caden in the front door. Ice followed him up the stairs. Together, they flanked Shock with identical mocking smiles. Clearly, they both hoped that Shock lost his mind.

"Too bad, Denzell," Ice quipped. "Be a good boy or you won't get any ice cream later."

"Fuck off." Shock glared at them both, then stalked off to the wingback chair against the wall again. He looked up at Lucan. "Go."

Nodding, Lucan addressed his brother. "You know what to do. If the worst happens, wait for me."

No way would he turn his back on his promise or shirk his responsibility. If Shock snapped, Lucan vowed he would see the grim duty through.

Shock read his thoughts, and his head popped up. A stare passed between them, an understanding. He nodded. "Thanks."

"I owe you." The three hardest words for Lucan to admit aloud, but they were true. Then he ducked into the bedroom.

Millie fussed in the shadowed room, lit only by a circle of candles. The older woman hovered over Anka's deathly pale form as she thrashed and moaned on the mangled bed, her eyes closed to the world. Sabelle gripped Anka's hand tightly and closed her eyes, obviously trying to impart healing, soothing emotions.

"Is it working, Belle?" Lucan asked softly.

Her apologetic glance spoke volumes. "Not really."

"Damn it." He turned to Millie. "What can I do to help her?"

"Wrap her in your embrace. Let her feel your love. She may not hear you, but tell her what's in your heart, anything that may entice her to come back. She's not fighting as hard as I would like.

She's letting herself…drift away."

Panic crashed Lucan's system. Sabelle lifted her head to chastise him. "You can't let her feel that from you. You'll scare her. Give her your love. Deep down, that's what she wants."

"And when I'm done and I think she's free of danger, we'll leave you to energize her." If Anka lived long enough. Millie didn't say that, but he heard the caveat just the same.

Grimly, he nodded and stripped off his shirt. Sabelle glanced at him in question. Millie's eyes widened, her expression a bit scandalized.

"She likes skin-to-skin contact," Lucan mumbled. "In case she can't hear me, I want her to feel me and know that I'm here for her."

He didn't wait for commentary or permission, just folded himself onto the bed and wrapped his arms around Anka, gathering her against his bare chest.

Bloody hell, she was positively glacial. The slight shivering of her body sent a shaft of dread through him. He did his best to rub her arms, press his cheek to hers—anything to give her his body heat.

"Keep her as still and warm as you can. Her dropping body temperature is forcing her to shiver and thrash to stay warm, but that's depleting her energy faster," Millie explained.

As he suspected. "On it. How much longer until you're done?"

"Somewhere between ten and thirty minutes. I'm nearly at the critical point. I'll have to work slowly or…"

Millie didn't finish that sentence. Lucan didn't want her to, either.

"Go ahead. I've got her."

He sounded so damn calm. Panic wasn't an option. But inside, he quaked all the way down to his foundation. Everything he loved in life— his family, his Doomsday Brethren mates, the sun, the first snow of the winter, great Indian food—none of it mattered without this woman in his arms. The last three months had taught him that unequivocally.

"Anka?" he whispered in her ear. "Love?"

She stilled. Gasped. Then she burrowed deeper against him, as if seeking his heat. He wrapped his arms around her tighter.

"It's Lucan, love. I'm here for you. I'll always be here for you, no matter what. Don't you dare leave me. We've got too much left unsaid between us. You've got too much life left."

Sabelle poked his arm. "I can sense her feelings a bit. She's given off this huge internal sigh of relief that you're here. Keep talking to her."

"She can hear me?"

"It seems so."

Thank you, he mouthed to Sabelle, then turned his attention back to Anka. "You feel good in my arms. I've spent so many days and nights believing that I would never hold you like this again. To have you here is a miracle. Don't leave me to suffer without you, love."

She stirred in his arms and shifted closer. Everything about this moment choked him up. Anka's sweet female scent filled his nose. Her familiar curves pressed to his with barely a sheet over them. He shoved it down to press their chests and abdomens together. Her heart beat against his, lethargic and faint.

"Fight! Come back to me, love. You've survived too much to give up now. Just a bit more, then we will work everything out, you and I. Whatever kept us apart before, whatever you think I can't accept or forgive, I promise you, there's no mountain between us so high that I won't scale it to be with you."

Lucan heard a sniffle and glanced up to find tears streaking down Sabelle's cheeks. "She definitely hears you now. She wants so badly to believe you."

It was a first step. Hope brushed gentle fingers across his heart. "Anka? I'm telling you the truth, love. Whatever is preventing you from leaning on me, share it with me. We can do anything together."

Behind him, Millie drew in a shuddering breath. "Kiss her. Then you'll have to let her go so I can finish this."

He zipped his stare up to the old witch. Let her go? Already? "Why can't I hold her through the rest? She needs—"

"You. I know that. But no, you can't. She must exit a mate bond alone." Millie gave him a pitying glance with sad blue eyes. "Say your good-byes, just in case, lad."

Good-bye? *No. Fuck no*! Lucan drew Anka in even tighter and felt his own tears scald his cheeks. "Anka, listen to me, love. Please fight for yourself. For us. I can't lose you. It will kill me." He clutched her as if his life depended on her. Because it did. Why the fuck couldn't he keep her wrapped up, his arms and legs surrounding her? Why were they even risking this?

"Stop!" He rolled to his back, splaying Anka across his chest, and glared at Millie. "Don't finish this. She can stay Shock's mate if it means she stays alive."

"You would give her to him?" Sabelle asked with her mouth hanging open.

"I'd rather have her alive and with Shock than have to surrender her to the four elements for her nextlife."

The pity on Millie's face deepened. "I'm sorry, lad. I can't stop now. If I do, she will die. Anka must have energy before Morganna's spell wears off. She can't take it from Shock, only you. But the mating ensures that she can't make love with anyone except her mate."

What a twisted fucking tangle.

"Why did you do this, Anka?" He gripped her against him. "God, love. I…I would do *anything* to keep you alive." An idea seized him, and he glanced up at Millie. "Transfer my life to her."

"What?" Sabelle yelled. "You can't—"

Lucan ignored her. "Do it."

The old witch hesitated, wringing her hands. "I can transfer life. You know that means you'll…go to your nextlife."

"Of course. Don't waste time! Just do it."

Still, Millie paused. "Even if you gave your life, she might not accept it. Sabelle?"

Bram's sister shook her blonde curls, her beautiful face mottled red with tears. They all knew how desperate this situation had become. But no one could stop the train from barreling down the tracks, headed for the collision course straightaway.

"She won't take it," Sabelle choked. "She's adamant. In her head, she's screaming. To her way of thinking, whatever happens… happens."

"And losing you might kill her," Millie pointed out.

Lucan swallowed, holding Anka's beloved form against him, frantically searching for any option. But he kept coming up empty.

Losing her for good might kill him.

Fuck, this couldn't be the last time he held her. He refused to believe that she would never smile at him again, that he would never see her lashes flutter open, that he would never have the opportunity to bring her back to their home so he could finally be the mate she needed. That they would never see a youngling of theirs birthed into the world. They would never get to grow old together over the centuries. That Anka would simply be gone, the space she'd once occupied a void, empty—as his arms would be forever.

He sobbed into her neck, his grip on her desperate. The soft strands of her hair spilled over his fingers. Her faint exhalations feathered across his cheek. Her heart beat against his. In moments, they could all be still…gone forever.

"Aren't there any other options?" Hell, he sounded like he was pleading. In a way, he was.

Millie's frown was apologetic. "I'm sorry."

This was it. He had to let her go now or he *would* lose her forever. Lucan hugged her against his body, grief clawing its way through his chest. Helplessness wracked him. It made him so fucking angry. Anka had always been a gentle soul, kind and giving to others. She'd listened, soothed, made people laugh. Despite her leather pants of late, that woman still resided in Anka's body. He wanted her back, along with the warrior-in-training who had shown so much moxie. He wanted that heroine who had come to him with towering resolution.

That was the answer. She'd wanted to fight. He needed to make that desire for justice burn in her once more.

Lucan rolled Anka beneath him. Her eyes remained closed to

him, her lips slightly parted and slack. He caressed her cheek. Bloody hell, she was so beautiful, inside and out. If he couldn't appeal to her with love, he would appeal to her the only other way he had left.

"Stay strong, love." He pressed his lips to hers softly, willing as much energy into her body as he could. "As soon as Millie is done, I'll be back for you. Then I'll do whatever it takes to help you get your revenge against Mathias. It's what you want, isn't it? You're not going to let him beat you now. You won't give up until you repay him for everything, will you?"

In the little chair beside the bed, Sabelle sat up straight and opened her eyes wide, mouth gaping. "She's fighting now."

Lucan sent her a shaky smile of relief and kissed Anka gently again. "That's right. You're a survivor. Come back to me so we can continue training. We'll make you a champion worthy of putting down Mathias for good. I'll pledge you everything I have, all that I am, all that you need. Just come back to me."

Sabelle stared at Anka, then frowned. The expression deepened with each moment. Alarm raced through Lucan.

"What is it?"

Suddenly, Sabelle clapped her hand across her mouth, looking completely stunned. "She's thinking that she can't be one of the Doomsday Brethren anymore. Something about my brother refusing her because she'll no longer be going back to Shock every night."

Lucan frowned. Anka's concern hardly made sense, but now wasn't the time to sort it out. He had to focus on Anka, on persuading her to fight for her life and her retribution. "Don't worry about Bram, love. I'll talk to him. Smooth it over. You'll still be able to train. We'll fight Mathias. I will do everything in my power to make sure you get revenge."

Sabelle peered at Anka for a long moment, then nodded. "She's relieved. Anka wanted to leave Shock before she began training. Had, in fact. Apparently, my brother was quite insistent that she return to him. She was only allowed to join the Doomsday Brethren because she agreed to stay with Shock."

Anka had tried to leave Shock nearly a week ago, and Bram had refused her? Fury rose in a wave, joining with betrayal to create a tsunami that threatened to drag him under. He reined it in for now. "It's fine, love. Kiss me now. I'll be back when you're free."

For what he prayed wasn't the last time, Lucan swept his lips over hers. Beneath him, she lay lax and still, her breathing shallow…except for one little moment. Her lips puckered, parted. She gave a little moan. He savored her—her little exhalations against his skin, her scent wrapping around him, her sweet flavor, the goodness he could taste on her. Somewhere in there, she loved him still. She needed to deal with her yearning for retribution, and they needed to talk about trust. Then, he would make goddamn sure they were happy for the rest of their centuries together.

Restraining the urge to clasp her to him and never let go took every bit of his strength and mental fortitude. But he finally backed away, staring at her, burning the image of her beloved face into his memory forever.

Millie gently touched his shoulder. "It's time. Her energy won't last much longer. My opportunity to finish this is shrinking."

"Fight, love," he whispered to Anka. "For yourself. For us. So we can fight together and defeat Mathias. I love you."

Squeezing her hand for the last time, he forced himself to let go of her limp fingers, then slammed out the door. He'd done all he could, and it wasn't enough. Not nearly enough. The rest was up to Millie, Anka, and Fate.

He wanted to curl up with a bottle, get stinking pissed, and bawl his eyes out. He couldn't afford to do that. One thing he could control? His "friend."

In the hall outside the bedroom, Shock stood. "Well?"

With a single glance, he sent Ice and Caden away. They left down the stairs silently, Ice looking more than a little disappointed that he wouldn't get to help kill Shock today.

"There's nothing new," Lucan told Shock. "She's weak but fighting, so now we wait. Did you know that Anka was only allowed to join the Doomsday Brethren if she agreed to continue living with you?"

"Yes. That woman can't have a single thought in my presence that I can't read." He smiled crookedly. "She's really terrible at mental evasion. I knew she tried to leave, just as I knew Bram forced her back."

Son of a bitch! "Why?"

Shock cocked his head. "Bram's excuse was that she needed energy and protection."

"But you don't buy it?"

"Bram could have given her protection. Energy would have been trickier, but if Bram was going to dictate who gave it to her, he could have picked you, his best mate, just as easily. As it was, she thought of you constantly. Given all that, why do you suppose Bram ordered her to shack up with me?"

Betrayal burned Lucan all over again. "Because he wanted a spy."

"That's my guess. I don't know for certain. He's skilled enough to wipe his thoughts clean when I'm with him. He's slick about hiding. There's a wall there I can't often get past…but I don't need to be Einstein to know he doesn't trust me. It stands to reason that he assumed that while she trained here, he could discreetly pump her for information about my actions. As long as he didn't plant that ugly 'spy' word in her brain, I would be none the wiser."

Lucan cocked his head. "You've known the whole time?"

"Of course."

"And you played along?"

"It worked both ways. I could protect Anka and give her energy—or whatever she needed. But I could also read her thoughts about whatever Bram was up to."

"To pass on to Mathias?"

Shock shot him a cutting glare that wasn't hard to recognize even behind the sunglasses. "Fuck off."

Right, then. Shock's ultimate allegiance wasn't the question of the hour. Bram's was. And they were going to have it out. "Wait here for Anka. I'll be back in less than five minutes."

Lucan hated leaving Anka at all, but if she pulled through this mate breaking, he wanted her coming back to a world as perfect as he could make it for her. And he wanted to fix it for her right now.

Striding down the stairs two at a time, he walked through the foyer, down the hall, then to Bram's office. He pushed the door open, sending it bouncing off the wall. "You low-down, wretched, motherfucking scumbag."

Surprise twisted Bram's face. "Pardon me? What the bloody hell is your problem?"

"You forced Anka to live with Shock when she no longer wanted to. So she could *spy* for you. You sent a damaged woman who needed love and rebuilding back to a man who isn't her mate so she could do your fucking dirty work? You left me mateless—"

"I left her with someone who could protect and power her. Someone who had proven he could do it because he had for months."

"I could have done that for her!" Lucan growled.

"Is that right? I was supposed to believe that based on what facts? She was your mate when she was taken. You didn't recover her. You weren't mentally stable for months. I'm still not sure you are now."

"Oh, I know I wasn't there for her as I should have been. I know the fault lies with me. But while she trained, she could have stayed here with you, if you were so concerned about her safety. She would have been out of harm's way in one of your fifty bedrooms or whatever. I could have energized her here whenever she wished."

"She didn't want you."

That might have been true, at least at the time, and it hurt. "But she didn't want Shock either, you bloody bastard."

Bram stood and crossed the room, shut the doors. All hint of affability was gone. "Shock provided her with a…method to release her pain that, frankly, I didn't think you had the backbone for. Can you really give her pain if she needs it to let go of her own?"

"Yes."

After his conversation with Thorpe, he understood Anka in a way he never had. He'd seen her needs from another perspective. The most important thing now was that he fulfill her however he could.

"All right, I'll believe you." But Bram's tone said he didn't. "Listen to me, Lucan. When she asked to join us, she wasn't ready to live with you or be in love with you again. I gave you the opportunity to train her so that she could spend time with you. I suspected it would be the bridge you both needed to work through your issues so you could be together again. In the meantime, I saw no reason not to leave her in her current situation, where she seemed free of Mathias's reach and relatively happy."

"Even though you knew she wanted to leave Shock, you thought she was happy?" Lucan asked incredulously.

"All right. Maybe the word 'happy' is too strong. It is fair to say that she wasn't any unhappier than you. But if having a warrior of the Doomsday Brethren under Shock's roof made him more loyal or us better informed, then where's the harm?" When Lucan's jaw dropped, Bram crossed his arms over his chest. "All right, then. Since logic isn't denting that look of betrayal on your face, let me try again. You undoubtedly assume that I value my machinations more than our friendship. You have the luxury of worrying mostly about your life and your heart and the lonely centuries in front of you. I'm not so fortunate. I've got magickind's entire existence balanced on my back. One wrong step…" He shrugged, but clearly he found nothing trivial about it. "Before today, you questioned Shock's motives every bit as much as I did. If Anka could stay safe, if he could force her to take the energy she'd been so dangerously refusing, and if he could unwittingly provide information, then so much the better."

Lucan took in Bram's little speech. Yes, from the other wizard's point of view, that made perfectly logical sense. "You're full of shit. If Emma had come to me, desperate for energy and protection, and I had to choose between you or…Sebastian Blackbourne, for instance, I would have assumed you wanted your mate. That you could take care of her. I would have given you the benefit of the doubt, war or no. I would *never* have stabbed you in the back." He narrowed his eyes. "When Anka wakes from this mate breaking, I'm going to take her home with me, where she belongs. Tomorrow, we will return, and she will continue training. Despite no longer being able to fuck information out of Shock for you, she is still one of us. You won't tell her otherwise."

"A few days ago, you didn't want her to be one of us at all. You wanted her nowhere near the fighting."

"If anything pulls her through this mate breaking, it will be the fire of her revenge. She needs it, and I'm here to give her what she needs. Now fuck off."

Pivoting around and wrenching the double doors open, he strode out.

"Lucan, don't do this!" Bram shouted after him. "We've been friends for too long—"

"We *were* friends." Lucan didn't break stride, just headed for the stairs. "Now we just fight on the same side of the war."

If Bram had anything else to say in his defense, Lucan didn't want to hear it. Didn't care. Only Anka mattered, and he ran up the stairs to find Shock pacing.

"Impressive," the leather-clad wizard said. "'Low-down, wretched, motherfucking scumbag' has quite the ring to it."

"I wanted to add 'shitty, back-stabbing arsehole,' but I ran out of breath."

"You're really furious."

"Imagine being in my position."

Shock pondered, then nodded. "I probably would have killed him."

"Don't think it didn't cross my mind. He's obsessed with this war, so I shouldn't be surprised. Has he even put in any time looking for his own missing mate? I'm not aware that he has. I probably shouldn't be surprised."

"Actually, more than you think. He's certain that he's narrowed down her vicinity. Too bad for him he's quite wrong."

Lucan's jaw dropped. "You know where Emma is?"

"A little mission for Mathias, yes. I've kept her out of harm's way. But I've kept her under my thumb, too. Bram will never find her."

Surprise rippled again and again through Lucan. Shock was smarter—and more dangerous—than anyone suspected. Lucan had a whole new level of respect for the chap.

Shock laughed. "I'm an equal opportunity bastard. Mathias doesn't know where she is, either. I've stashed her someplace perfect. When the right moment comes…I'll tell whoever needs to know most."

That worried him. He might not consider Bram a friend anymore, but he didn't want to see a human caught in the crossfire. "Mathias will kill her."

"He might threaten to, but ending her accomplishes nothing for him. More likely that he'd use her to get to Bram."

And the wizard would give his life to spare his mate's. The instinct was innate.

"Exactly." Shock crossed his arms over his chest with a superior grin.

Which reminded him that Shock had his own agenda in this war. Not that Lucan gave a shit right now.

He ripped his mobile free from his pocket. "How much longer?"

Shock's smile fell. "I don't bloody know, but it's taking too damn long."

Yes, and waiting to hear about Anka was killing him.

The thought barely crossed his mind before the bedroom door opened. He and Shock both snapped to attention and crowded around the portal as a shaken Sabelle appeared.

Chapter Fourteen

Lucan didn't wait for Sabelle to speak. He pushed past her, ran into the bedroom, and skidded to a stop on his knees at the side of the bed. Anka looked ghostly and still as he took her icy hand in his. Her chest didn't rise and fall. Her magical signature was devoid of Shock's influence, except a tiny crack that proclaimed him her former mate. But all of her colors were fading so rapidly, his heart stopped.

Anka was slipping through his fingers. If he didn't do something, she would soon be dead. *God, no*. No way would he let her go. He hadn't come this far, discovered that he was the mate of her heart, only to lose her forever. Giving up was not an option.

He jumped on the bed beside Anka, wrapped her in his arms, and crushed her to his chest. She tumbled limply against him, a chilly, lifeless rag doll.

"What happened?" he asked Millie.

The old witch shook her head, a pained frown on her fey little face. "I tried. Once the mate bond was broken, she simply fell."

"Fell? What does that mean?" Lucan gripped Anka tighter, willing her to warm, to breathe, to open her eyes and see how much he loved her.

"I…it's a term healers use. When you're performing intricate magic, it's complicated. And it's still magic, which is imperfect and…" Millie swallowed nervously. "It doesn't always work the way you expect. I thought I'd been slow and gentle, that we'd done everything to make her warm and secure..."

"After you left and Millie began severing her mate bond to Shock, I sensed that Anka felt adrift. Cut loose," Sabelle supplied, then shook her head. "No, that's not it exactly. I felt her searching for an anchor. When she couldn't find one, she floated away."

She'd felt alone? She'd needed someone to lean on?

"I believe so," Sabelle said, obviously scanning his thoughts.

He turned to Shock, whose hulking presence Lucan could feel behind him. "Read Anka's mind. Anything?"

Shock bowed his head, paused. Finally, his head snapped up again, and he nodded. "She's still alive. Only just. She's hazardously low on energy. And she's afraid."

"Don't fear, love. You will *never* be alone again. Ever," Lucan whispered fiercely in her ear. "I've got you." He stood, draping the sheet around her naked body, then carried her out of the room, down the stairs. "Thank you, Millie, Sabelle. I'll take her."

On his heels, Shock followed. "I hear her faint thoughts. She's afraid of dragging you through the muck of her problems."

"*Our* problems," he growled to her as he headed for Bram's front door. "They aren't just yours, love. I'll be there with you. Focus on coming back to me."

"There you go, Anka," Shock bantered. "And no, I won't butt out. You don't get to die on us. You know if I have to be underhanded to keep you alive, I will. I've done it before."

Outside, Lucan gripped Anka against his chest, ready to teleport away, the urgency to get her home and plaster her naked skin against his and force energy into her little body strangling him. But he owed Shock something.

"Fuck that," Shock growled. "You owe me squat. Go."

"You're not in mate mourning."

Shock hesitated. "Maybe it's delayed?"

"Mine hit instantly. It disconnected all rational thought from my brain to the rest of my body. Instinct took over, and only my mate would do. If you're feeling none of that, she wasn't the mate of your heart, either."

Without waiting for a reply, Lucan teleported back to the house he'd shared with Anka for over a century. As he landed in the middle of the foyer, Caden and Sydney both came dashing into the room.

His sister-by-mating gasped in horror at Anka's limp form, staring with wide brown eyes.

"Dear God," his brother whispered. "Is she—"

"No. I won't let her, damn it. Sydney, start making her a bit of food. Have it ready in thirty minutes. Caden, run her a hot shower. I'll get her ready."

Both nodded. Sydney scampered off to the kitchen, and Lucan heard her rummaging through the refrigerator. Caden jogged up the stairs in record time. The water sluiced down the glass walls of the shower enclosure as Lucan strode through the door of the master suite. He passed his brother as he made for the exit. They exchanged a solemn glance before Caden clapped him on the shoulder with a bracing nod and left. In that moment, Lucan knew that his younger brother would be there for him, no matter what, in whatever way he needed.

The second the door closed, Lucan stripped himself with a snap of his fingers, then ripped away the sheet covering Anka and carried her limp form into the steamy shower, grateful for the scalding water on her frigid skin.

How the fuck to do this? How to awaken her enough to feel pleasure, to drive her body to the orgasm she would need for them to exchange a full dose of power? Or would that drain her? Did he hold her through his own release and hope that enabled her to open her eyes and accept the rest of what she needed? Time would help him figure it out, but he had none in which to dither or debate.

Bloody hell, he'd never felt less like sex in his life.

Swallowing back his panic and worry, he chose instinctually. If she'd been feeling adrift and disconnected during the mate breaking, he wouldn't leave her alone now. But she was in no shape to give him even a drop of energy.

Sitting on the tiled bench in the shower, he pulled Anka onto his lap, facing and straddling him, then braced her against his chest. The hot spray hit her back, and her skin slowly warmed. He prayed it would keep her from draining altogether. The rest was up to him—and her drive to live.

Quickly, he took his cock in hand and stroked, thumbing the sensitive head, willing himself to harden as he spoke to Anka. "Love, I'm here. *Please* take from me. Don't give up. Don't leave. I am always here for you. I'll do whatever it takes to show you."

No response—from her or his cock. *Fuck.* He had to reach her. She deserved everything he could give her.

Anka behaved courageously because she was brave. Hell, she'd gone to meet Morganna alone and was likely still suffering some effects of the spell. But beneath her barriers, Anka was fragile and scared. Revenge and independence—she'd been trying to march to those drums for months. They were providing the beat of her life now, but Anka's nature was to give. She surrendered—herself, her trust, her love. Without a mate she had no one to share herself with. Anka might have changed in some ways. In others, she was still the witch who wanted to belong, who wanted to be loved. It stood to reason that she still wanted to give her heart and her future to the man who would love her forever.

She needed to know he was that man.

Lucan took hold of her face and softly kissed her lips. "Become a part of me, as I become a part of you. And ever after, I promise myself to thee. Each day we share, I shall be honest, good, and true. If this you seek, heed my Call. From this moment on, there is no other for me but you."

In his arms, Anka shuddered and gasped.

Hope squeezed his heart. "There's never been anyone for me but you, love. Open your eyes. Let me prove it."

She whimpered, struggled to comply. Anticipation was a slick mistress, teasing him with possibilities as he held his breath. But

Anka eventually slumped against his chest in exhaustion once more.

His mood deflated...along with his cock.

Angry tears threatened. He wanted to punch something. Rail and curse. Break glass and tear down walls. Lucan contained his rage. He fucking refused to give up. She'd come back from Mathias, from Morganna. She needed him now. He wasn't letting her go.

Lucan focused on a fantasy in which Anka sat cradled on his lap, the moonlight shining on her rosy skin. In that vision, she heard his Call and opened her luminous eyes to smile at him, to Bind to him, then opened her mouth and her thighs to him. The vivid image pumped blood through his body in a rush. He got iron hard in an instant and couldn't push his way inside Anka fast enough. He needed to feel his beloved grip him in all her tight, spectacular glory.

Lucan positioned her wilting body over him, the petals of her sex opening as he breached her with the head of his cock. He hissed at the fiery line of pleasure zipping down his body while he cupped her face in his hands and swept his lips over hers. Her cool lips didn't deter him. Anka would come back to him, by God. Somehow, some way, he would restore her. If he had to exhaust and deplete himself to fill her with all his energy, reassure her with his every word and breath that he would never leave her alone again—whatever it took—he would do it.

Eating at her lips hungrily, he took possession of her body, pressing deep inside her, feeling her flesh stretch to accommodate him. *Bloody hell...* He groaned as he slid in to the hilt, and she squeezed him in welcome.

Every touch now was a revelation. Anka didn't move with him, but her quick breathing, her pliant flesh, told him that she felt their connection every bit as much as he did. She might not yet have the energy to be with him physically, but mentally? They were fused together. She *felt* everything he did.

Anka gasped into his mouth as he lifted his hips up, driving deeper into her body as he feathered his lips over hers again and again.

"You're not alone, love. Do you feel me? Take me. Together,

we'll fight."

She sighed into his kiss and leaned, grimacing until she wrenched one arm up, throwing it over his shoulder. Anka was reaching for him, wanting him! He thrust faster inside her.

"That's it, love. Move with me as much as you can. I'm here. I'm not going anywhere. Fuck, you feel so good."

The soft grip of her folds closing around him and growing slicker by the moment twisted his entire body into a seething need he knew only Anka could fulfill. Lucan shoved aside everything but the soaring pleasure, the tingles jetting up his body, the heavy ache burning in his balls. He laid her head on his shoulder gently, then gripped her backside like a man possessed and shoved his way deep into her body, grunting with every upward thrust. Damn it, he had to give to her every bit of energy he could generate so she would open her eyes and become his again.

Her lush breasts bobbed enticingly against his chest. He lifted one of the distended peaks to his mouth and sucked hard, curling his tongue around her, nipping with his teeth, as he pushed into her snug sex again.

Anka arched. More of her gorgeous flesh filled his mouth, and he suckled it all greedily before moving to the other and doing the same. White-hot need seared him. Sweat joined the warm water rolling down his face. He moaned with every rough breath as he drove deeper into her.

She managed to raise her other arm and curl it around his neck, as well, then moaned softly. "Lu…can."

"Yes, love. Be with me. Feel me. I'm going to give you everything you need."

"So…tired."

"I know. Soon, you'll feel better. Don't give up now."

"Burning up."

The residuals of Morganna's spell? "You need me?"

She murmured a sound that he took for assent as he pounded into her tight, liquid sex with a roar. Ecstasy pooled like a thick, drowning quicksand. It sucked him under, scraping down his back to gather at the base of his spine. Tingles brewed there, boiling. Everything inside him tightened, compelling him to fuck her faster. He couldn't goddamn breathe as desire stomped him flat. His heart drummed in his ears. The only other sound he heard over it was the rough sawing of his breath with every thrust in and out of her swollen pussy.

Fuck, he'd missed having her, making love to her in their house. He was bloody glad now that he'd never once managed to bring another woman into this room to try to exorcise Anka's ghost haunting his soul. This space belonged to them and the love they'd always share, no matter what happened or how much time passed. Eternity eventually eroded everything, but Lucan swore not even it could tear down this love.

After today, she would be here with him always, beside him at night, the first face he saw each day. The lips he kissed. The woman he held. They would live and love forever.

Joy erupted at the same time pleasure peaked. He held her against his chest and curled his arms around the backs of her shoulders, fingers pushing her down onto his eager cock. He growled a primal sound of possession as ecstasy detonated inside him and blew him completely away. The sensation of being suspended in the cocoon of pleasure with her went on for long, gorgeous moments. Around him, her slick walls grasped him gently. Bloody hell, he wished he could send her into this climactic bliss with him, but she couldn't afford the loss of energy. Not yet. Instead, he moaned against her mouth as he poured his seed deep inside her, vowing he'd make it up to her.

Finally, she opened her eyes, her mouth. And her soul.

She gasped as if coming awake from a dream and blinked at him, her amber eyes confused but alert. "You did it. You brought me through!"

"I wasn't giving up, love. I'm never giving up."

He kissed her, his tongue sweeping into her mouth to begin showing her again exactly how much he meant that. And how much he loved her.

Though every muscle in her body ached, despite the warm spray of water at her back, when Lucan ended the kiss, Anka lifted her lashes slowly, focusing on her surroundings. The bathroom, dimly lit by the moon and the light flooding in from the adjacent bedroom, was painfully familiar. Her eyes went wide. "You've brought me back..." *Home.*

She didn't dare breathe the word, much less believe it.

Lucan cradled her face in his hands, fusing his gaze to hers. His intent stare willed her to listen. "To *our* home, yes. You belong here."

The sweet words were nearly her undoing, just like those she remembered piercing her unconsciousness. "Y-you Called to me again?"

"I can't be any clearer about what I want, love." The blueness of his eyes was magnified by the fringe of thick, black lashes. He ripped past her defenses and looked right into her soul. "Whatever Mathias did to you, however you think that's damaged you, why ever you think you're not good enough...it's all shit. You and me and what we feel—that's all that matters."

"I'm scarred." He knew that, but still the words popped out like a confession.

Lucan shrugged. "I've picked up a few nicks in my hide these past months. The Anarki, Zain, Mathias, they've all taken chunks out of me here and there. I didn't always care enough to acquire the energy to fix it."

"But my family, they aren't..."

"I mated with *you*, not your bloodline." He frowned at her. "Love, you've always tried so hard to please me, and I adored you for it. But none of what's worrying you is your fault. If anyone should be apologizing, it's me. After you'd healed my mate mourning, I should never have let you go. I should have grabbed you, told you exactly how I felt, and refused to let you leave me.

But I didn't fight. Your rejection stunned me. I let it crush me. I took your refusals to mean that you no longer loved me."

Guilt crushed her into a million pieces. She clapped a hand over her mouth as tears sprang to her eyes. "I loved you too much to drag you into what I'd become." *And what I still am.*

God, he was stripping his soul so bare for her, how could she keep her banshee bloodline a secret? She couldn't, if she wanted him in her life. She had to be honest with him. But how could she tell him such a terrible truth—one she'd kept from him for over a century?

Lucan snapped his fingers, bringing her focus back to him immediately. "Are you hurting? Need something?"

"No."

"Then I don't know where or why your mind wandered, but it needs to stay here, on us."

Anka nodded. "Sorry. Yes."

"Good. When I'm done, you'll tell me what's on your mind, yes?"

"All right."

Softly, he kissed her lips, then withdrew reluctantly. "When I'm with you, I can breathe again. I feel whole, alive. I feel loved. No matter what else happens, I will keep pursuing you unceasingly until you either Bind to me again or look me in the eyes and tell me unequivocally that you no longer love me."

Her heart nearly burst. He was so forthright, so brave with his feelings. That made her feel even more like a coward.

"Lucan…"

"Let me finish." He held up a hand, then caressed her cheek. "I also understand that I didn't give you all the loving guidance you needed when we were previously mated. I've talked to a man…a Dominant. I've been reading up. I understand now, love. God, I wish you'd told me."

A deep flush swept up her body. Proper, perfect Lucan knew all her dark little desires? She tried to turn away, conceal her face. Lucan grabbed her chin and refused to let her hide. Still, she squeezed her eyes shut tightly.

"Stop. Look at me. Now," he demanded tenderly, waiting in silence until she complied.

When she dared to glance at him, his direct stare awaited, prying at her like a crowbar and opening up her soul. "Lucan—"

He pressed a finger over her lips. "Let me finish and don't look away. Not being completely honest is part of what led us here. I might not have been able to stop Mathias from taking you or hurting you—and it bloody pains me to say that—but maybe if I'd been everything you needed and told you how worthy you are of love more often, you would have wanted to come home to me from the first." He brushed her wet hair from her face and kissed her lips softly. "Let me assure you, there is nothing you want that I don't. I always tried to treat you so gently. You're delicate, and I often feared breaking you. I pushed down urges that I know now would have pleased you. I always wanted you desperately. I wanted to be deeper in your body and soul, but I worried about scaring or hurting you too much to do anything about it. That changes now."

She looked up, her mouth gaping open. "But what about..." Hell, she couldn't ask him for that. Could she? Anka swallowed, indecision gripping her. She hated being a fucking coward, but she cringed at the thought of his rejection.

"If it's on your mind, say it. This is the first of what I hope will be many negotiations between us, Anka. You'll have everything you need. I have needs, too." He dragged a hand down her back to cup her backside. She shifted on his lap, and his cock hardened inside her again, thick and insistent.

A bolt of desire trembled low in her belly. How easy it would be to surrender to his touch and just forget this conversation. But Lucan was right. If they were going to have any future, not clearing the air now would only come back to haunt them.

"S-spanking?"

His grin widened. He lifted Anka up his cock slowly. "Absolutely. I'm looking forward to reddening your pretty backside."

Pleasure suffused through her even as she felt another flush rush up to her cheeks, this time with a shy smile. "Will you…tie me up?"

"Can you handle it?"

Anka nodded, then moaned when Lucan eased her up his shaft again. "Yes! It's not something Mathias did to me."

"Good. Then yes." He pumped into her again, agonizingly slow. "Fuck, yes. Feel me inching my way inside you, love?" She wriggled on his lap with a whimper, and he gripped her arse tighter, keeping perfect control. "I know you do. But do you feel all the love I've kept buried in my heart? I'm giving it to you as I stretch you wide so we can join as one again. I want you to feel all my need, my tenderness, my unconditional love filling you over and over. It's all for you. Always for you."

Every slow thrust reawakened her nerves and her need. She threw back her head with a gasp.

"Oh, you feel so good, love. I'm already mulling many intriguing ideas, ways of binding you to our bed so I can do this to you for hours."

"Please…" Her voice cracked as she begged.

She didn't know where they were headed or what would happen, but she knew that nothing else mattered but him in this moment. If he truly loved her this much…maybe he could handle her terrible truth.

With a wave of his hand, he turned off the shower, then stood. "Wrap your legs around me."

His firm voice rang out in the enclosure, familiar…but deeper than ever. Sure of himself. It hadn't been a request, but a command. Complying both thrilled her heart and aroused her body. With another wave of his hand, one big bath sheet wrapped around them. The other disappeared into the bedroom.

She forgot about everything when Lucan took his first step, gravity driving him deeper inside her than he'd ever been before. She cried out, digging her nails into his shoulders, planting kisses along his neck and jaw. Though he gripped her by the arse and held her up, Anka felt herself slipping—and lacking the strength to clutch him. The energy he'd given her earlier had revived her, but it was quickly waning, drained by the heavy thrum of Morganna's spell still sucking her under.

Her suddenly heavy lids drooped, and he kissed her mouth while every step had her gasping with every deep shuttle into her body. Then the bed was at her back, the towel beneath her, and Lucan dragged her backside to the edge and stood above her.

With a leisurely withdrawal, he caressed his way down to her aching nipple. "You look exhausted, love."

Blast it all, she wanted to stay awake, stay with him, enjoy this precious moment back in her mate's arms, in the bed they had long shared. "I'm with you."

"You need more energy."

"I know. But I ache. I need."

He frowned as he pulled away almost completely, then eased the thick crest of his cock back between her shiny folds, watching himself disappear into her body with a guttural groan. "God knows I want to give you pleasure. So much that you can't stand to be away from me again. But I don't know if giving you release and you sharing your energy with me now is wise."

"Please. Please. Please!"

Lucan hesitated, then traced his fingers over her abdomen, trailing them into her plump mound and brushing his knuckles over the hard little pearl at the top.

The flare of sensation was like a sunburst all through her. Anka gasped, her eyes widening. He merely smiled as he kept up the slow torture with his fingers and his shaft, both teasing her so slowly and precisely, she had no way to fight it—or him.

"Lucan…"

"Let go, love."

She arched with a hoarse cry, grabbing the sheets in her fists and staring at him with wide eyes, panting. "Yes. Oh my—"

The scream tumbled out of her, a high wailing of her need and pleasure that shattered her all the way down to her soul while her body throbbed and pulsed with a fireball of an orgasm.

After that, she had a vague impression of Lucan's worry, his urgent driving strokes into her body over and over, slick skin sliding over her own, desperation thick in the air. Then his choked cry as he released into her again and the feel of warm seed jetting against her womb.

She reawakened later with her old silk robe wrapped gently around her body and her sister-by-mating, Sydney, rushing in with a tray of eggs and fruit, a blueberry scone nestled on the side of her plate.

Anka happily ate everything in front of her, smiling as Lucan took the fork in hand to make sure she finished every bite. He pampered her, kissed her, his face reflecting all the love she'd feared she'd never see again and wanted so desperately.

"Full, love?"

She nodded sleepily and curled up to his side, nuzzling her face into his chest, breathing in his skin and holding him close. Peace washed through her, a coveted feeling she thought she'd never know again.

"Excellent. Sleep now."

She wanted to. A full night's rest—without Shock crashing through the house during the wee hours of the morning, so intoxicated that he barely knew his own name—sounded both heavenly and restorative. But she and Lucan had unfinished business. In good conscience, she couldn't make him wait to know her secret. If, after hearing it, he still wanted her…then she would answer his Call.

"I need to tell you something—"

He placed a finger over her lips. "Is the world going to end if you don't tell me right now?"

Impatience and anxiety merely needled her, but her secret had been safe for over a hundred years. One more night shouldn't matter, except to her conscience.

"No, but—"

"No buts. You need sleep, and I'm going to make sure you get it."

Anka gave in. Yes, she wanted to enjoy one whole night of being in Lucan's arms and bed again in case he no longer loved her after she confessed. The time was stolen, but she craved these moments with him.

"You also need more energy. During the night, I'll make sure you get more of that, as well." He winked at her.

Anka hadn't believed it possible, but she fell just a little bit more in love with Lucan. For once, it felt as if her entire world was coming together again. She prayed their love was strong enough to keep them together forever.

Chapter Fifteen

In the dark bedroom, Lucan slipped from bed with a crooked smile, threw on a pair of jog pants, and padded down the stairs. Coffee, a little breakfast for the two of them, then… His smile widened. He'd given Anka plenty of energy through the night. She should be more than able to give some back to him, and he was very much looking forward to that. Having her with him all night had been the sweetest miracle. He'd barely allowed himself to sleep for fear he'd awaken and find every beautiful moment with her had been only a dream.

In the kitchen, Lucan snapped on the light and waved a hand in front of the coffee maker. As he waited for the hot brew to finish, he opened the refrigerator and contemplated the contents. He'd never mastered the art of cooking, not even magically. He could ask Sydney to help out or ring Sabelle but—

"You Called to Anka again?"

At the sound of Caden's astonished question, Lucan turned. His brother stared at his altered signature. Caden's expression wasn't condemning…but he didn't look thrilled, either.

"She's it for me, brother. My one. That can't be a surprise."

"Did she Bind to you?"

That was Lucan's only disappointment. He wanted to be certain she chose him freely, yet...if he was the mate of her heart, why was she hesitating? The waiting chafed. "Not yet."

Now Caden let his displeasure show. "She picked the enemy over you, Lucan."

"It's more complicated than that, and the enemy... Yes, Shock is a dodgy prick, but he cares for Anka. She had no memory of me after she escaped Mathias, so she took shelter from the one person she *knew* she could count on to protect her. By the time she recalled once having a mate..." He shrugged. "I'd let her down and I didn't fight to win her back. If anyone is to blame, it's me."

"That's utter shit!"

"Is it? Zain is awfully interested in your mate. If you failed to protect Sydney from him, if he ravaged her and she barely escaped with her life, would you really expect her to come running back to you with open arms?"

Shuffling into the room, Caden grabbed a coffee cup and tapped his thumb against the counter. He knew the answer; he simply didn't like it. "Probably not."

"Because every wizard knows that the unspoken part of the Call demands that you give everything, even your life, to protect your mate. I didn't. I failed her. I must earn back her trust before I can expect to earn back her devotion."

As the smell of fresh brewing coffee filled the air, Caden nodded. "So you're determined to make her your mate again."

"Yes. Anka and I will talk through whatever our problems are, but I *will* get beyond every barrier between us so we can start over. I've got her sleeping under my roof—"

"And in your bed, if the noise last night was any indication. Sydney giggled a lot."

Lucan smiled, feeling almost optimistic for the first time in three hellish months. "In the bed, on the floor, against the wall..."

"TMI, brother." Caden rolled his eyes. "You know, if it works out with you and Anka, Sydney and I are happy to move elsewhere and let you two—"

"No. You're family. I want you here, if you'd like to stay.

Besides, safety in numbers. Mathias took Anka because she was alone and unprepared. With both of us here, we'll have extra fortifications around the house. No one will catch us unprepared again."

Caden nodded, thoughtful. "That makes sense. Having extra protection for Sydney would allow me breathe a bit easier when I can't be with her. That woman has a penchant for finding trouble."

"A frightful one, yes," Lucan agreed with a grin.

"I should tell you that Sydney and I have been considering…" He sighed, rubbing the back of his neck. "She wants a youngling."

Lucan couldn't keep the surprise from his face. "You're both young. Times are dangerous."

"I don't disagree. But she refuses to put life on hold for a bully. In her head, giving into the fear Mathias makes her feel is letting him win. You know how stubborn she can be."

"You must be talking about someone else. Sydney stubborn?" Lucan teased.

Caden sent a mock punch sailing into his shoulder. The coffee maker stopped its drip, indicating that the brew was ready. They both lunged for the pot, but Lucan was faster. With a supreme smile, he poured them both cups and took a sip, moaning with deep delight.

"No more! I heard enough of that sound last night," Caden drawled.

"I'm paying you back for all the nights I was alone and had to listen to you two."

Caden's grimace said he hadn't considered that before. "We should move our bedroom down the hall."

"Good idea. You don't need to stay that close to me anymore. No more rages where I try to tear the house apart with my bare hands."

"Thank God." His brother clapped him on the back, then withdrew another cup from the cabinet, filled the kettle for tea, then waved his hand at the stove to turn it on.

"What flavor does Sydney want today?"

"She likes that PG Tips with a cinnamon stick." Caden waited for the water to boil, then fixed the cup of tea. "Good luck with Anka. You know I only want you to be happy. If she's the one, then do whatever you must to win her."

"Thanks, brother. That's precisely my plan."

As Caden left, Lucan made Anka a cup of tea. He couldn't cook well, but he could manage toast. Within seconds, he'd retrieved bread from the cupboard with a crook of his fingers and given it a magical toasting. He piled it all on a tray and conjured a flower from the garden, as well as a little vase to put it in, watching the rising sun pour into the kitchen with satisfaction. From now on, he would show Anka how much she meant to him. In big ways, in little ways… She would never doubt him again.

Rather than risk spilling the tea by jaunting up the stairs, he teleported to the landing. Faster anyway, and Lucan couldn't deny that he was damn near desperate to return to Anka's side, slip into bed with her, and wake her up in one of the thousand deliciously wicked ways bombarding his brain.

He kicked the door open. Sunlight glowed through the windows, and his gaze automatically strayed to Anka's signature to check her energy level.

At the sight of her, his mouth gaped open. The tray fell from his bloodless fingers. It crashed to the carpet with a clatter.

Anka's signature blared in a bright swirl of colors—far more than expected. Hers, yes. His, too. And colors he didn't recognize at all. A blend of their respective signatures glowing in a faint ring just inside of hers. But that only happened when…

"You're pregnant?"

Anka ceased stretching and stiffened. Her eyes flared open and she studied the edges of her own signature, her eyes growing wider and wider. She gasped, blinked, then looked at him. "H-how?" She shook her head in obvious disbelief. "Morganna's spell w-worked. Yesterday, at Bram's house…"

When she'd taken him into her body so he could plant his seed, she'd declared him the mate of her heart and given him fresh hope for their love.

And then, unbelievably…they'd created life together.

Lucan jumped over the fallen tray and leapt onto the bed, gathering her against him. "Love, this is more than I dared to hope for. I don't care if Morganna had a hand in this. Please tell me you're happy."

Anka gave him a tremulous smile and placed her trembling hands over her flat stomach. "I'm stunned. And thrilled! I've wanted a youngling for such a long time, but I never thought we'd actually be blessed."

Blessed. Yes. That was how he felt now. This was like the human version of winning the lottery. Magical couples so rarely conceived. He'd almost wanted to murder Morganna for the spell yesterday. It had nearly killed Anka, but she'd survived. And now, he was tempted to thank the ancient witch. He and Anka would hold the product of their joy and love in their arms come fall.

"Raiden and Tabitha's youngling will have a playmate. They'll no doubt be happy about that." He grinned. "Do you think we'll have a boy or a girl? It doesn't matter—"

Suddenly, her smile shifted into a dark, gaping expression of horror. "A girl. This will be a girl. Oh my…" She covered her face, but not before Lucan saw a terrible guilt rip across her face.

"I don't know why you think that, but it's all right, love. I will love a little girl. We will raise her to grow into a strong, true woman, like her mother."

Anka withdrew from him, scooting to the far side of the bed, cradling knees to her chest and bowing her head. "No! This is my worst bloody nightmare. I wanted to tell you, but not like this."

"Like what, Anka?" Confusion fused with dread in his chest. "What's going on?"

She stared at him as if her world was falling apart. "You're going to hate me!"

Alarm spiked higher. He fought to push his worry aside and keep her calm. "Tell me what you're talking about. You can tell me anything, love."

"There's another reason I didn't come back to you after my ordeal with Mathias. Do you remember when I confessed that he used me to kill a family?"

"Yes." How could he forget? Lucan willed her to spill her secret now. The feeling of standing on the edge of something terrible and looking down into an unknown chasm was ripping him to shreds.

"I killed that family with nothing more than my voice." She closed her eyes as if she could keep her shame hidden. Sobs shook her shoulders.

"Your voice?" He reached across the distance she'd put between them. "What are you saying, love?"

"I'm…" She stared at the ceiling for a long moment, looking as if she wished she could keep the words to herself forever. "I'm a banshee."

Disbelief didn't begin to cover his reaction as he drew back his hands. A ball of dread gathered in his gut, and he stared at her as she buried her face against her knees, in the circle of her arms, her pale curls spilling everywhere as she continued to sob.

Lucan didn't touch her. He opened his mouth to say something, but no words formed on his tongue. A million questions pelted his brain. Where the bloody hell should he begin? He had trouble breathing, moving. He just stared, as if that could somehow change what she'd confessed.

Her next jagged sob tore at his heart. Banshee or not, she was still the same Anka he'd always loved. She was his mate. Mathias forcing her to kill the family had clearly tormented her soul, and he had to absolve her of that now.

"You didn't mean to kill anyone."

She raised her tear-streaked face to glare at him. "I did. I took their lives willingly. Mathias told me that he would kill you if I didn't."

Her news stabbed him directly in the heart. "You did it to protect me?"

"Yes. At first he threatened to rape me, then give me to the Anarki and let them use me until I bled out, like Ice's sister. I told him I would rather die than commit murder. So he threatened the one person he knew I would do anything to save. I couldn't let him hurt you, not when I could prevent it." She scrubbed her hands across her face and sobbed again.

She had betrayed her gentle nature and slain something inside herself simply to save him? He felt sickened and humbled and confused as hell.

Lucan wrapped his arms around her tightly. "Oh, Anka. Love..."

She shook away his hold. "After it was over, Mathias returned me to his lair. That's when he broke our bond and...you know the torment he inflicted then. I only escaped alive because Shock convinced him that if you knew I lived with your enemy, it would drive you mad and inhibit your ability to fight even more."

Fury rolled through Lucan. He'd been feeling almost charitable toward Shock all day for his help with Anka. Little had he known the fucker had openly plotted to rip his heart out and kick him in the balls all at once. "It worked. For thirty-four days, I was utterly incapacitated with mate mourning. I haven't been worth a shit since. If Shock convinced Mathias to release you into his keeping, how did you come to be with Aquarius?"

"I...ran away. Shock let me. He knew where to find me, of course. He's always been able to read my every thought."

And Shock had simply let Anka go? Why?

"Eventually, I realized I'd put Aquarius in danger, so I returned to Shock. I was near death, and that was how I wanted it. He refused to let me wither away and forced energy into me that day and every day for weeks. I was revived physically, but I couldn't let go of the guilt or pain. Or the intense yearning that had me spending every night virtually sleepless. I didn't remember you, Lucan, but I *knew* I was missing the love of my life. One day, Shock had had enough of my despondent wallowing in guilt, and he spanked me. I finally cried. I finally...let go of a bit of everything that had been eating me alive. Those spankings became something of a ritual. I began to recover a bit more."

"The bruises he left on you were from more than mere

spankings." Lucan's words were a hard, low accusation.

She blushed. "They were. Sometimes, pain…frees me. I'm certain that doesn't make sense to you, but I can't feel the sting of a crop and hold in all my anguish at the same time. I have to let go of the pain on the inside to handle the pain to my backside. And knowing that someone is in control of that allows me to unchain it from that dark place in my soul and let it go."

Anka was right; he didn't completely understand. But he didn't discount her feelings, either. She believed it worked, and that was all he needed to know about Shock's discipline now.

"What made you finally remember me?

"I heard Shock on the phone one day. I don't know who he was talking with, but I heard him growl your name." She drew in a ragged breath as fresh tears fell. "Everything came back to me in an agonizing flood. I remembered you and our life together. Immediately, I came home to see you, to talk. I don't know why exactly, except that I longed to see you. But I heard your howling and your feral growls. I knew you mourned me, just as I knew I could heal you. I'd done everything I could to save you from torment. I couldn't bear the thought of your suffering, so I performed the *helbresele* spell and healed you. When you asked me to come home, I wanted to so desperately. But by then, my sins were too great. I couldn't possibly deserve you anymore."

Her explanation filled a lot of the gaps in his knowledge of the terrible events that had torn them apart. And it broke his fucking heart. How could she imagine for a second that he would think her unworthy? As much as he hated to admit it, Shock had saved her life. Finding out that she was a banshee while under Mathias's thumb must have been a dreadful jolt to Anka, and she'd had no one to comfort her. She'd done so very much to save and protect him—they would talk about the fact that she should have let him shelter her, not the other way around—and he owed her everything for her selfless giving, especially his love.

Lucan reached for her once more and drew her into his arms, against his body. She fought him, but he wrapped her in his steely embrace until the fight drained out of her. Still, she wouldn't look at him, couldn't stop sobbing.

"Love, your sins were forced on you. I would never blame you for any of them. Had you ever given a thought to leaving me before Mathias abducted you?"

"No."

"Had you ever any urge to kill before?"

She shook her head frantically. "No."

"Had you secretly been lusting for Mathias and his whip?"

"Never!" Her expression told him that the thought horrified her.

"Do you love Shock?"

Now she hesitated. "Yes."

The betrayal darkening his heart must have shown on his face. When he would have backed away, she grabbed his arm. "If I explain this to you, I must tell you everything. I have loved Shock since I was a girl. He's my best friend, my first lover, the wizard who took me through transition. For many years, he's been the keeper of my secrets and my protector."

Every word ripped into Lucan's chest and tore out his heart. "But you chose me as the mate of your heart. Do you love him more?"

She shook her head. "That would be impossible. He is my friend, yes. Always. But you are my everything."

The tight grip of his panic eased. She loved Shock as a friend. The wizard had been loyal to her. She owed him her allegiance and her affection. Lucan still didn't trust the bastard one centimeter—unless Anka's welfare was involved. Then he knew the attitude and the leather jacket meant nothing. Shock was willing to do whatever it took to save Anka and make her happy. As he was.

Lucan swallowed and dropped a kiss on the top of her head. "You are my everything, too, love. It's why I Called to you again. It's why we're going to have a youngling this fall. She will be a girl. And we will do everything to protect her. Banshee hunters still exist. This secret can't get out. *No one* can know." He frowned. "How did Mathias discover that you're a banshee?"

"When he first took me to his lair, he stripped me and started cutting me with a knife. Lots of little deep cuts, a stab here and there."

"Why didn't I feel your panic?"

"I tried to close off our bond so you couldn't. I knew if you attempted to rescue me, he would only kill you."

Even when she'd been terrified and at her most vulnerable, Anka had tried to protect him. The fact that she hadn't given him an opportunity to help her both crushed him and sparked his tenderness. "Anka..."

"He kept carving his name into my flesh over and over." She closed her eyes. Her breathing turned choppy again, her skin pale.

"I'm so sorry. You felt your life in jeopardy and you wailed?" he guessed.

"Yes." Her voice cracked. "It just happened. After that, he managed to put a strip of duct tape over my mouth so I could no longer let out the banshee cry, then he grinned maliciously and left me to heal. In the middle of the night, he dragged me from my cell to that family's house and—"

Pale and trembling, Anka dissolved into sobs. Talking about it would eventually be cleansing for her, but right now, she seemed to be reliving the horror. Lucan tightened his embrace.

"It's all right, love. I'm here for you. Let it out." He caressed her back in soothing strokes. "Being taken from home must have been traumatic in itself, but what a terrible blow, to suddenly realize you're a banshee, and to be forced to use your power against your will. How the hell could your parents have kept your origins from you? How frightening and devastating that sudden discovery must have been in that terrible circumstance. Bloody hell."

She swallowed, gaped for a long moment. Then she wrenched out of his arms and leapt off the bed, throwing her little robe around her naked body and curling in on herself, as if she sought to hide from him. Lucan stared, confusion plaguing him. What the devil was wrong? Pacing furiously to the far side of the room, Anka looked back at him with stormy eyes, dragging in a breath as if it would help her find her courage. But for what?

"Love?"

"Oh, God! You thought..." Panic tripped across her face again, followed by guilt so terrible, he could see it crushing her. "This is why you will hate me. This is why the youngling growing inside me will be all I have left of you after today."

In the past, Lucan would have waited for her explanation, reluctant to spook or upset her more. He was still reluctant, but he wasn't about to leave all the responsibility on her back. The past few days had taught him to fight for her with everything he had.

He jumped from the bed and stalked to her, cornering her against the wall and gripping her silk-clad shoulders. "Don't tell me how I'll react or feel. I could never hate you, nor ever imagine leaving you. Give me your troubles, Anka. We will work through them together."

She tried to shake off his hold. Lucan was having none of that. He gripped her tighter, raised a brow at her, and waited.

"All right, then." She swallowed nervously. "Mathias's terror didn't prompt any self-discovery on my part. I've known I'm a banshee my whole life."

Lucan stared at her beautiful, beloved face. He heard her words, but they simply did not register. How could they? Because if she'd said what he thought she had... "Why didn't you ever tell me?"

"And risk losing you?" She bowed her head, shook it. "I was too afraid."

"So you kept this knowledge from me during our *entire* mating?"

Anka's eyes slid shut. She nodded, a little furrow creasing between her brows as she frowned. "I felt as if I had to. Try to understand—"

"Understand what?" he snapped. "That you lied to me for over a hundred fucking years?"

Lifting her lashes, she locked her gaze with his. "If that's how you want to see it, yes. But you know that there are still hunters willing to sell a washerwoman to the Council for profit! Those women—most have done nothing, yet they are shuttled off to camps where they are rarely seen or heard from again. So many have sought our extermination. Can't you understand my fear?"

He gripped her tightly and shook her. "So you imagined I would sell you to monsters likely to imprison or kill you? God, Anka! Did you actually believe that?"

She shook her head. "I never thought that you'd allow me to be taken by hunters or tell anyone my secret. But I didn't want to burden you with the terrible truth. Growing up, my mother urged me every day to keep our secret, above all else. She never breathed a word of the truth to my father in all their centuries together. She said we could *never* tell *anyone* our true origins."

Lucan sucked in a sharp breath. As much as he hated to admit it, her mother hadn't been totally wrong. There were plenty among magickind who both feared and loathed banshees for the death they often left in their wake. But he would never have allowed anyone to detain her. He would have taken her secret to his death. She must have known that.

Or maybe she didn't.

Fury sizzled like a river of fire in his veins.

"I'm not just anyone, Anka. I was your *mate* for over a blasted century. Even after all that time, you still didn't trust *me* enough with the fucking truth?"

In his arms, Anka trembled. She bit her lip, then ran her tongue over the abused flesh. Fury and desire both blindsided him. He wanted to toss her on the bed, rip that robe off of her, and fuck her into oblivion as much as he wanted to make her hurt the way he did right now.

"Lucan..." She placed a trembling hand over his chest, right over his heart, and goddamn if his flesh didn't burn with the need for more of her touch. "I was afraid to tell you because then you would know how unworthy I was of you. Your family is of greater consequence, your uncle on the Council. I feared that if you knew, you would—"

"What? Spurn you? Leave you? Cast you aside for some

Councilman's daughter who could add more consequence to the family name?" When she tried to look away, sobs wracking her, he shook her as if that would make her understand how deep this betrayal ran. "Damn it, witch! Did you never trust in my love? I would *never* reject you for your birth, unlike those thick, paranoid idiots among magickind who fear the very sight of a banshee."

"I'm sorry." Her voice was small.

"Sorry? That's it?" He crossed his arms over his chest. "For over a century, I believed with every beat of my heart that you knew you could count on my love. I counted on yours. But you didn't trust me at all, did you? Not enough to tell me your secret, not enough to believe that I would protect you from Mathias, not enough to love you no matter what. Having so little faith in me as a mate must have made your decision to live with Shock so much easier." He grimaced bitterly. "All the while, I tried to worship you. You merely schemed to keep your little secret."

"That's not true! I loved—"

"You didn't love me! You couldn't. Not if you thought me so shallow that I would break our bond over the blood you'd been born with."

"I didn't know what to t-think." More tears ravaged her face, and he tried to be unmoved by them. "I felt so inferior, so unworthy. I-I couldn't bear to give you any more reason to regret taking me as your mate."

"I never did, Anka. Not until this moment."

Her face fell; she looked stricken. He almost wanted to take the words back. Almost, but he didn't.

"Lucan—" She reached out for him, her face pleading.

"No!" he roared, pulling back. "Why would you want to touch me at all when it's clear you've always lacked respect or confidence in me as a worthy mate? You saw my privilege and what, decided I was a shallow prat? Was that what you believed?" An incredulous growl erupted from the depths of his chest. "You assumed that I would never truly love you unless I believed you to be my equal?"

"That's not it. I wanted to be your truest love, not your deepest regret. I never wanted to tell you because…then you would know I wasn't good enough for you. You always touched me so gently, were polite to a fault, advised me on what to wear, how to speak, who to befriend. I always knew you were trying to present me in the best light for others so that you'd have no cause to lament Calling to me, so I couldn't imagine telling you that I'm a banshee."

Lucan reeled back. "You thought my guidance was for appearances? That I give a fuck all what others think? It was for *you*. You seemed lost half the time, afraid. I was trying to help you find your way. I was…" He dragged a hand through his hair. "I was a fool."

"You weren't trying to make me into what you wanted?"

"Bloody hell, no, witch! There were times I missed that girl I met, the one with spark and fire. She'd been replaced by a demure, polite stranger. I thought you wanted a gentle wizard for a mate, one who would treat you with deferential adoration. Sometimes I gritted my teeth because all I really wanted to do was throw you against a wall and fuck you into next week."

Her plump red lips formed an *O*. Even as he fought the urge to pound a hole in the wall, Lucan ached to cover her pretty mouth with his own and ravage her.

"I-I didn't know."

"Clearly, I've been in the dark about a number of things myself." He clenched his fist as anger bottled up inside him. The pressure kept building until he feared he would explode and say something he couldn't take back, do something he would forever regret. "Goddamn it! I can't stay."

He zipped around and strode for the door. Anka's delicate fingers wrapped around his arm. Desire sparked deep inside him. Her touch seared him down to his soul.

"Let go."

"Please…don't leave! This is my worst fear come true. This is why I never told you."

Her face crumpled into grief, and her anguish shredded his heart. Shutting her out was killing him, but if she had so little faith in him, what did they have but a tainted past and a coming youngling? He was too angry to talk now. Too stunned, too hurt, too furious.

"Let. Go."

She jerked her hand back, shrinking away at the look on his face. Then her own anger seemed to take hold. She clenched her fists and faced him defiantly. "You said you don't care that I'm a banshee, yet here you are, walking out the door the moment I confess."

"I don't give a flying fuck that you're a banshee. I care that you lied. I care that you didn't trust me with the truth. I hate that I now must question whether our mating was only good in my head."

Anka gasped, her eyes flaring with fury. "No, most days it was a dream come true. I loved you so much. I even broke my childhood friend's heart and made him endure a hundred years of celibate misery because I was impatient to be mated to you. Every day, I couldn't wait to wake and see you smile. Every night, I looked forward to being the witch in your arms, feeling your touch. I used to pinch myself, half-convinced that my joy couldn't possibly be real. Don't you ever think I didn't love you! Or that I didn't trust you. Don't you *dare* take my insecurities and my futile wishes that I could be perfect for you and toss them back in my face!"

Half of him wanted to rail at her and make her understand his rage. The other half...blast it, that primal part of him wanted only to shove that thin little robe away from her beaded nipples, push her against the wall, and remind her who she belonged to.

But even if he did, the lack of trust would still be there, widening the chasm between them.

"Anka, if you trusted me totally, you wouldn't have hesitated to tell me for a moment. I would have known the truth decades ago. If you truly believed that it wouldn't matter to me, you never would have kept it from me." He shook his head, crumbling inside. His whole fucking world was falling apart again. "Without trust, we have nothing."

Blast it all, he couldn't look at her now, the colors of her signature ripe with his Call and his youngling, and to love her so completely…only to find that perhaps he didn't know her at all.

He ripped his arm free from her grip and turned away.

Anka raced around him, standing between him and the door, her face pleading. The pain there nearly tore him apart. "I love you. I trust you, with my life, my heart, my protection. I swear it."

Everything inside him quaked. His fists clenched. His gut clenched as if he'd been stabbed. How fucking badly he wanted to believe her… "Words are easy, Anka. They mean nothing."

"I'll prove it. Tell me how, and I will. I have no more secrets, nothing left to hide. I can't strip myself any more bare for you. I've given you everything, I swear it."

But she was wrong. She wasn't stripped bare. She hadn't given him everything. That robe covered her. He wasn't inside her. But as badly as he wanted her, what would taking her to bed again prove? She would welcome him. Her peaked nipples alone proved that. And fuck, he could smell her pussy. The juicy, ripe flesh would be plump and needy, waiting just for him. No denying how urgently he wanted her again. She was an addiction, a disease with no cure.

Fucking her now would prove nothing but it would make him feel damn good—until he remembered that they had no trust left between them.

Mitchell Thorpe's voice rang in his head. The hours they'd talked about trust and control, and the essential need for them in any sort of power exchange. And as an idea rolled through Lucan's head, he smiled.

If Anka wanted to prove her trust, then by God, he'd let her try.

"Take off your robe, get on the bed, and spread yourself wide for me."

She blinked at him, wide eyed. "Lucan?"

"Do it now, or I leave. Your choice. Either do as I say and prove your trust, or I walk out and everything is over."

Her whole body trembled as she stared at him, trying with all her might to decipher his thoughts. Or maybe she was willing him to be merciful. That wasn't going to happen. They needed his resolve more than she needed his compassion.

Finally, Anka swallowed and unbelted the silken robe. The flimsy black scrap fell to the carpet. The sight of her lush, naked body, even after spending an entire night wrapped around her, nearly undid him. Slowly, she backed to the bed and lay across it, arms and legs spread.

He sauntered over, forcing himself to move slowly, control his temper and think carefully before he acted. At the foot of his bed, he stood between her spread legs and stared, his eyes heavy-lidded. Carnal fire singed him down to the core. He would demand everything from her. If she gave it, maybe…maybe they could talk.

"What is your least favorite implement of punishment? You'd better tell me the truth."

"I-I don't know. Shock most often used a crop. I'm certain I would hate a whip. No one but Mathias has ever used one on me. They terrify me."

He knew nothing about wielding one, but it would both take her to the edge of her fear and force her to decide whether she genuinely trusted him.

With a snap, he conjured a whip. A tightly braided leathery strip, black, long and lethal-looking. He coiled it in his fist and held it up to her. Instantly, Anka gasped at the sight, her eyes wide and pleading. "No. Please…"

"Make your choice. Either stand up, walk to the wall, and put your face against it or get dressed and leave. Choose now."

"Lucan…"

"You trust me or you don't, Anka. Will I really hurt you?"

"You're angry." She sniffled back fresh tears.

"I'm in control of my temper. I would never lift a finger to you in anger. Ever. But I can tell you that until the stars fall from the sky. You could tell me you believed me, but you have no more faith in me now than I do in you. So pick."

He watched Anka quiver in fear as she got to her feet. She glanced at the robe, and for a moment, he felt sure that she would put it on and go.

"If you touch that robe, we're done."

She turned to him then, her beseeching gaze nearly unraveling his good intentions. If he let her put any sort of barriers between them again, Lucan feared they would be impossible to tear down. She had to give him her trust or they had no business being together.

Just when he thought for certain she was going to grab the robe and shelter herself with it, she headed straight for the wall. Stunned and a bit elated, he watched the sun streaming through the window glow off her bare skin as she swayed toward the wall, then stopped, placing her forehead against it. She clenched her fists. God, she was terrified. Lucan couldn't miss the fear bouncing off of her. Again, some stubborn, lovesick part of him wanted to coddle and protect her, make the whip go away and hold her. But inside, he still reeled in disbelief that she'd kept such a huge bombshell from him for a century. They wouldn't survive another hour if he couldn't believe that they could build trust again.

Lucan followed her to the wall, stopping behind her. He couldn't resist the urge to press against her, rub his throbbing shaft into the cleft of her backside. Damn it, how badly he ached to touch her again.

"Good, Anka. Are you afraid?"

"Y-yes."

At least she'd been honest this time. He wanted her to know that he appreciated how difficult it was for her to make herself vulnerable to him. It raised his hopes a bit, showed that she trusted him on some level.

"Thank you for that."

"Lucan." Anka spoke his name like a plea as she eased back against his chest, arching her head to rest on his shoulder.

Their gazes connected, and the jolt kicked him all the way to his soul. He itched to touch her, cast aside the whip, and simply feel his way over her body until she surrendered and he possessed her. But trust must come before comfort, before reassurance, before pleasure.

He brought the whip up in front of her, and she gasped, tried to shrink away. She looked furiously for an escape, but between his body and his arms trapping her against the wall, he didn't give her one. "You know what this is, Anka. You know what it can do."

She looked at him over her shoulder, her lips quivering as she held in tears. But she nodded. "Yes."

"You know the pain it can give."

Anka squeezed her eyes shut as if she could stop the horrific memories from bombarding her. "Yes."

"I want to be clear. You're giving yourself over to me and this whip now?"

She looked like she fought for courage. "If that's what it takes to earn your trust again, y-yes."

Her voice trembled, but she fought hard to give him what he needed, and the man inside him reveled. Not only must he believe that she would give him all her problems in the future, she had to know that she could.

Lucan uncoiled the whip slowly, letting it slide over the skin of her back and arse. She sucked in a harsh breath and tensed. But she didn't say a word as he smoothed it over her nape, trailed it over her shoulder, let it drape between her breasts.

"Still afraid?"

"Yes."

Of it or him? He had to answer that question, get her to separate them in her mind so that she could focus on him alone.

He retracted the leather, gripping it by the handle, then set the rest of the coiled length in front of her. "Touch it."

"W-what?"

"Touch it. Put your fingers around it. Caress it. Explore it."

She hesitated, her fists clenching defiantly.

"Do. It," he commanded.

Bowing her head, she hunched her shoulders as if bracing for an explosion of pain.

"Relax," he whispered in her ear. "Breathe. Then touch it."

She gave him a shaky nod, then released a long breath, drew in another. Finally, she uncurled her fingers and reached up, her hand creeping toward the leather dangling in front of her. As she closed in, she hesitated, yanking her hand back to her chest protectively. Then she shook her head, steeled herself, and reached out again.

With one finger, she dragged down its length until she fingered the popper at the end. Then she moved back up, tracing from the knotted tip to the length gathered in his hand.

"Does that hurt?" he asked softly.

"No."

"Can the whip itself hurt you?"

"No." The up note in her voice made that sound as if that was a revelation to her.

Behind her, he smiled a bit. She was listening and trying. Anka cared for him at least a bit. That he believed. But he couldn't take part of her affection or something that only seemed like love on the surface. He needed it all, including her trust.

"Curl your hand around it."

She did without hesitation, and his smiled deepened. As she squeezed it, he felt an odd pride glimmer through him. If nothing else, maybe he was easing some of her fears. Maybe he could help her exorcise a ghost or two that might aid in her recovery.

"Did it bite you?"

"Of course not." Her voice sounded even surer than last time.

"So is it the whip that hurts you or the man?"

The moment his lesson became clear, she tensed again. "The man."

"Exactly. You passed the first hurdle so beautifully, don't retreat now."

"I-I'll try."

She'd better do more than try. "You have too much determination to let fear defeat you, Anka. You wanted to fight against a madman in a bloody war for your vengeance. Where is *that* woman?"

"Buried under fear." She leaned her forehead against the wall and dragged in deep breaths.

"What's the worst I can do to you? If I hurt you, you have only to grab your robe. I will back away instantly. You'll be free to go."

"It wasn't like that with Mathias."

"But I am not him."

Slowly, she nodded. "I know that."

Did she? Time to determine just how much trust she had in him.

Lucan uncoiled the whip again and wrapped it around her hips, sawing it gently back and forth over her skin, nudging the slick folds of her sex and the little bud in between. She sucked in a shocked breath, and the smell of her arousal perfumed the air all over again, nearly dropping him to his knees.

Licking his way up her neck, so hungry to be inside her, he raised the whip up her abdomen, then under her breasts, lifting them up just slightly with the strong leather. She moaned.

He nipped at her lobe. "The whip feels good, doesn't it?"

"Yes." The word sounded more like a moan.

It went straight to his cock, and he ached to melt against her again, fill her with his throbbing flesh, and make her admit that she'd distrusted him. But he'd never really, truly know if she would trust him tomorrow if he didn't see this through now.

He drew the whip over her breasts, letting the braided leather graze the hard red peaks. Anka slapped her hands against the wall, the pleasure clearly catching her off guard. He did it again and leaned around, watching intently as she bit her lip.

"No, don't hold in your moans. I must hear those. I need to know how you feel."

Her lip slid free from her bite. Then he dragged the whip across her nipples once more. She scratched at the wall and groaned.

How beautiful that sound. How sweet her budding trust. Lucan found himself trembling with the power she was beginning to give him. A little at a time, yes. But she was trusting him with her worst fear, not begging, not screaming. Just believing that he would never hurt her. He wished to fuck that she had trusted him this much with her secret long ago.

He rolled the leather up the swells of her breasts and wrapped it around her neck, gently drawing her head back against his shoulder once more. If she fought him, it would cut off her air. If she didn't, he would tell her exactly how beautiful he thought her, how much she was pleasing him.

Anka hesitated only an instant, then she arched her neck in offering, her gaze fluttering up to his, her eyes wide and luminous.

"That's it, love. When you put yourself in my hands, you look radiant. You're trembling again. Are you afraid now?"

"No. I ache. I want you."

Honesty rang in her voice, and Lucan had to fight the urge to celebrate, to grab her and shove every inch of his aching shaft inside her. She was truly trying to work through her fears and give herself over to him. He must focus on Anka and her needs now. If he met hers, they'd definitely get to his.

"We're not done yet." He backed away slowly. "Stay against the wall, face pressed to it."

She went tense again but complied. "All right."

"Remind me what hurts you, the whip or the man?"

"The man."

"That's right." He backed up another few paces, then paused. "Will I ever truly hurt you?"

"No."

"Never," he corrected. "So I stand here behind you, whip in hand, ready to strike. Are you nervous?"

"Yes. My head is telling me that I've nothing to worry about, but experience is screaming at me to run."

"You had a terrible, traumatic encounter with Mathias. I'm forcing you to face it and trust me. I'm not asking you to let go of something so terrible yet. Only time will enable you to do that. But are you truly afraid that I'll do something to cause you pain when I lash at you with this?"

Anka paused for a long moment. "Not…really. Perhaps only because you've never—" She stopped abruptly, then ventured, "Or have you?"

"Taken a whip to another for sensual torture? No."

From his conversation with Mitchell Thorpe, he was aware that using this implement wasn't something to be undertaken lightly or without a great deal of experience. If he didn't have magic on his side, Lucan never would have attempted it without significant practice. He took protecting Anka very seriously.

"I want you to trust me, Anka." No need to add the "or else." It hung there, unspoken but understood.

This pause was longer, but finally she nodded. "I do."

"Good." He cracked the whip at his feet, letting the sound fill the bedroom.

Anka jolted as if he'd struck her, then she stilled, going into a trembling silence. The sound scared her, clearly. Likely, it brought back terrible memories.

"Last chance. Grab your robe or tell me that you're prepared."

Her fingers curled into fists, and her body tensed. "I'm ready."

Lucan let her wait for long moments. He tested the weight of the whip in his hand, gauged how much magic he'd need to make his point without truly hurting her. And he let her think. If she worked this out in her head, she would know that he would never harm her.

Raising his arm and the whip, he flicked his wrist, tempering the blow with his magic and muting the cracking sound for her. The leather barely caressed her backside, the popper sliding over her skin like a whisper of a kiss.

Slowly, her head turned, and she met his gaze. "Lucan?"

"If you trust me, turn around and let me finish."

Without another word, she faced the wall again. He repeated the process, grazing the other cheek of her arse with a slow brush. Then again. And again, never giving her more than a gentle skimming across her skin. With every lash, she relaxed, the tension leaving her shoulders, her fists uncurling. He could almost see her trust growing, and it filled him with pride. It made him goddamn ravenous for her

He planted one last lash in the place he knew would give her pause, the lightest touch yet over her lower back, a glancing sweep across the scars there. She stiffened. Then the whip was gone, and she let out a deep breath, all tension draining out.

"Do you want me to do it again?" he asked, curious for her reply.

"If you wish."

No pleading with him to stop. No begging him to cease pushing at her comfort level. Just…acceptance and an olive branch of trust.

"If I did, do you think I would hurt you?"

"No." Her response was automatic

He smiled and dropped the whip, prowling toward her and shoving off his jog pants. As they hit the floor, he reached Anka and grabbed her thighs. "Spread your legs."

Again, she complied quickly, and a fresh, pungent wave of her tangy scent hit his nostrils, making his mouth water and his cock weep. Bloody hell, this woman undid him every single time he came near her.

Reaching around Anka, he took her breasts in his hands and breathed across her neck, then bent his legs and nestled the fat head of his cock right against her slick opening. He paused.

She whimpered and wriggled, trying to work his length inside her. He pinched her nipples hard to get her attention, and she gasped. Then he nipped at her earlobe. "Stay still. I'm not ready yet. I have some questions."

"Hurry," she pleaded.

He grabbed a fistful of the glorious blonde curls trailing down her back and yanked at them. "Once you've answered me, Anka. Not before. Will you keep your secrets from me anymore?"

"No."

"Will you ever fail to tell me important information again?"

"No. I promise," she sobbed. "I'll tell you anything you want to know."

"Do you trust me?"

She nodded. "Yes."

Lucan didn't hesitate; he had to know. "Do you love me?"

"I always have."

Her words flowed over him like honey. "Let me hear you say

it."

She glanced over her shoulder, their gazes fusing, her eyes glossing over with tears. "I love you."

Fuck, he couldn't resist anymore. He gripped her hips and, with a roar, thrust in deep inside her.

Gasping and scratching at the wall, she cried out his name. He felt her get instantly wetter.

"This is what you wanted all along, isn't it?"

The flush crept up Anka's skin. She stood, her pussy wet and open as she panted with each and every one of his thrusts. She'd surrendered her pleasure entirely to him, his to grant or withhold. The power was heady. It swelled inside him, a thrill all its own adding an edge to the considerable bliss already thrumming through his blood.

One hand gripped her hip. The other he slid between her legs to rub the little needy bundle of nerves, completely hard and desperate for his touch.

"Answer me, Anka!" he growled in her ear.

"Yes. I've fantasized about feeling the force of your desire and giving you everything..."

And he'd been too gentle to take it before, just as he hadn't been strong enough to save her or fight for her once upon a time.

That time was long fucking gone.

He pressed her into the wall, her breasts plastered to the blue paint as he shoved into her like a piston, fast and hard, no stuttering, no respite. Just a thorough pounding into the tight fist of her pussy.

The telltale fluttering of her folds told him that her end was near. The burn of the coming climax razed his ability to hold back. It heated, pooled, started to overflow. *Fuck*! This time, just like every other damn time, she was going to dismantle him. With her, he couldn't hold out. Every instinct inside him demanded that he come deep inside her and mark her again. It didn't matter that she was already expecting his youngling. He wanted to do it once more.

But he wanted to feel her pleasure first.

"Come now, Anka," he growled in her ear. "Right fucking

now!"

He'd barely gotten the words out when she cried out in a strangled, low-pitched groan, her nails digging some of the paint from the wall as her entire body jerked and her knees started to buckle.

Holding her up with a hand around her waist and another between her legs, he let the convulsions of her sex work their magic. He grazed her clit to draw every ounce of ecstasy from her body. He gave her a hoarse shout, then the swirling knot of tension inside him released like a geyser, taking his resistance and sanity with it.

He blinked back into consciousness moments later to find his forearm braced against the wall above Anka's head and his shaft still buried inside her wet heat. *Jesus*! A wave of dizziness rolled over him, and he withdrew from her, staggering to the bed with his arm wrapped around her. Together, they fell on the mattress and dissolved into a heap of arms and legs, flesh pulsing with energy galore.

Exhaustion pummeled Lucan. He closed his eyes, wondering how the fuck to process everything that had happened this morning. Besides a growing youngling, Anka had given him her trust today. Was that enough for him? For them to rebuild their love? Or was her confession simply a hundred years too late?

Chapter Sixteen

Lucan lay sprawled on his back, sleeping fitfully near her. He'd dozed off without curling into her, without touching her as usual. The meaning wasn't lost on her. Show of trust or no, she'd kept something vital from him for over a century. The wound wouldn't be easily or quickly healed.

For the past hour, she'd been staring at the ceiling, contemplating the future, the youngling growing inside her, and her place in the Doomsday Brethren. She knew exactly why Morganna had zapped her with the fertility spell. When Lucan heard about her conversation with Morganna, he would see the ancient witch's plan—and likely object. Anka didn't want to further damage their fragile relationship. She loved Lucan. At one point, he'd loved her, too. Likely, he did still, at least on some level. Unfortunately, she didn't think staying out of this fight was an option.

She had to get to Bram. He was a scheming prat at times, but a bloody smart one. He would see reason.

As she rose from the bed, a groan broke the silence. Lucan stretched and rolled over. He opened his eyes and sought her out immediately. "Where are you going?"

She knew when she answered that it would likely start another fight, but she refused to lie if trust was going to be an issue between them. She took his hand. "I need to see Bram."

"Why?" He sounded suspicious, with good reason.

"Well, first, I think I left my mobile somewhere in his house."

"Rest." Lucan rose, deliciously naked. "I'll bring it to you."

Something inside of her wanted to yield to him and allow him to take care of her, but that was a fantasy. They lived in the reality of war—one in which they were fighting for their very existence. "I also want to talk to him about the ways I can be useful to the cause."

He frowned, already adopting a protective mien and looking like a warrior. "You're pregnant now. You can't fight."

If they lived in a better world, she would try to help in the background and not go for the jugular of the man who had nearly destroyed her. But even if Mathias had no further plans to make her life hell, she was pretty sure Morganna was cooking up a scheme or two. Anka's revenge was no longer the only thing that mattered. Lucan and their youngling must be more important. She had to work not only on avenging her past, but growing their future.

"I can't sit in the corner like a helpless little girl. It won't work."

She made her way to the closet, wondering if she'd find any of her old clothes still inside. When Anka flipped on the light, she found everything exactly as she'd left it, neatly arranged and pressed, ready to wear. The sight of her clothes totally undisturbed touched something deep inside her. Lucan hadn't moved on. He hadn't even tried, really. She choked on a lump of emotion and turned to find him standing arm's length away, watching.

"You kept everything?" He'd never thrown out her things in a heartsick rage while wishing her to hell?

He regarded her with solemn blue eyes. "I always hoped you would come home."

That made her heart swell, her knees go weak. She pressed a tentative hand to his chest. "Do you still feel that way?"

His expression looked unreadable, closed. "I Called to you. You're having my youngling."

She shook her head. "You Called to me in desperation, to keep me alive. I'm having your youngling because Morganna willed it. Neither fact means that you want me here."

Bloody hell, so much had happened between them. Could they ever mend their relationship enough to be happy together again?

He grabbed her fingers and kissed them fiercely. "Do not tell me what I want, Anka. I *know*."

She worked up the courage to step closer. "There are still obstacles between us. I realize that we didn't communicate enough when we were previously mated. I allowed my insecurities to silence the truth because I feared losing you. Since then, given all that's happened with Mathias and Shock…I'm not certain how we put ourselves back together."

His mouth pursed tightly. "Have you given up on us, then?"

With her clothes still hanging in his closet and her heart still belonging to him? "No. It won't be easy, but…" A terrible thought occurred to her. "Have you?"

"I'm angry and hurt that you kept the truth from me. I'm saddened by your insecurities. I never imagined that you felt less than comfortable. I never want you to feel anything but special. Only time will tell if we can truly rebuild the faith we once had. But right now, I've no intention of letting you go."

Relief swept through her. She released a pent-up breath. She'd been more than half afraid that her betrayal would eat away at Lucan's feelings for her. "Then we'll get through this together. But now, I must talk to Bram."

"Why? The bastard sent you back to Shock and tried to come between us. I'd rather not give him another opportunity."

Her face softened. "He also asked you to train me so we could spend time together and work out our problems, didn't he?"

Lucan grumbled. "He's still the last person either of needs to see now." He stalked up behind her, blocking her path. "You're not fighting, Anka. That's final."

"We may not have that choice." She tore a T-shirt and a pair of jeans from hangers, then ducked under his arm and marched to the dresser to pull out some clean knickers and a bra.

Morganna had given her the special gift of this youngling—for her own purposes, yes. But Anka resolved to protect it at all costs. That meant taking matters into her own hands before someone else took them from her.

Lucan grabbed her arm. "You will not risk our youngling for your revenge."

Giving up on revenge would be logical. Bind to Lucan, focus on her coming youngling, and put the past behind her—yes. She would try. But if she gave up the vengeance altogether, would she always be bleeding and furious inside? Would she be raw and broken and unable to move forward if she didn't at least have some hand in bringing Mathias to his knees, the way he'd brought her to hers? What kind of mate would that make her to Lucan? What kind of mother to their precious daughter?

"That's not my plan," she promised.

"Bollocks! That willful look on your face says otherwise."

Lucan was worried, and rightfully so. He'd lost everything once, too. Now they both had even more to lose. "I will trust you to take care of us. Isn't that what you wanted?"

His glower told her that he didn't like having his words used against him. "Good. Then stay home. I'll put a protection spell around the house—"

"Because that worked so brilliantly last time," she said as she struggled into her clothes. She knew the words would wound him, but the truth mattered more than sparing his feelings, no matter how scathing. "We can't sit idle, Lucan. This is bigger than what we want. Come with me to talk to Bram, and I'll explain."

She exited the bedroom as Lucan was sliding on his jeans and searching for a shirt.

"Explain it to me now!" he shouted.

If she did, he would only object to her plan. Undermining him wasn't her objective, and she didn't want to risk her youngling. But they didn't have the luxury of sitting idle. And as much as she wished otherwise, Anka wasn't sure she could face her future before being at peace with her past.

"Come with me. I swear, I'll explain there."

Anka tried to teleport out of the house. Lucan's magic blocked her.

He smirked. "You're not going anywhere."

"You're not being reasonable. I have some information about Morganna that Bram and the others must know, and I only want to explain it once."

"So you can find some way to get involved. No."

She drew in a breath, trying to keep a lid on her temper. "I understand your need to protect, but now isn't the time to behave like a bloody brick wall." Lucan was doing a damn fine imitation, raising a brow and still refusing to budge. "Right, then. I don't want to do this without you, but since you won't even listen, you're forcing me to go on my own."

He could magically restrict who teleported in and out of the house. But once outside, he wouldn't be able to block her. She strode out the bedroom door, toward the front. From the foyer, she spied Caden kissing Sydney in the kitchen.

"Stop her!" Lucan demanded, hopping into his shoes and carrying his shirt.

Anka didn't wait to see if little brother followed. Marching outside the house, she emerged into crisp morning air and gray skies that, not surprisingly, portended rain. She stood ready to teleport out when someone grabbed her wrist. She whirled.

Caden glared at her with narrowed eyes. "Let's get one thing straight. If you break his heart..." Suddenly, he fell silent. His jaw dropped in astonishment. "You're carrying his youngling?"

"Indeed. And you'll do what if I break his heart? Beat me up?"

"No." He looked quite cross. "I'm not the sort to hit females. But I will do everything in my power to stop you from leaving now. You and Lucan need to work your differences out. He's been fucking miserable without you."

She had heard that Lucan and Caden were quite close now. She wasn't keen to come between them, especially when Caden had sacrificed so much to care for Lucan these past few months.

Her gaze softened. "I've been unhappy without him and I've no desire to hurt him. We'll work it out, I swear. But he must see reason. Get him to Bram's." She tugged free of Caden's hold as Lucan came bounding through the front door.

"Anka!"

She teleported away before either of them could say another word.

As she emerged onto Bram's lawn, she threw out her chime. A scant moment later, the barriers eased to admit her. A *whoosh* sounded behind her. She cast a glance over her shoulder. Lucan and Caden were hot on her heels.

"Anka!" Lucan shouted, his blue eyes pinpoints of fury. She was definitely going to get an earful. "You are *not* fighting."

"Not unless I have to," she tossed back and entered the house, darting for Bram's office.

The air resounded with Lucan's and Caden's magical calling card. They sent it quickly, more than once.

She reached Bram just before he let the brothers in. His head snapped up. In an instant, his eyes widened. "I'll be bloody damned. You're—"

"Expecting a youngling, yes. Lucan knows. I need you to gather everyone and listen to me for ten minutes. If you let Lucan stop me before I've explained, I may not be able to help the cause."

Bram sent her a considering stare. "You can't help anyway. I've put the war over my friends more than once, and Lucan despises me now because of it. If I let you fight pregnant, he'll bloody kill me. The answer is no."

"I know how to release Morganna's potion—and maybe kill Mathias at the same time."

Pushing out of his chair, Bram leveled a disbelieving stare at her. "What?"

Lucan's and Caden's chimes continued to sound incessantly.

"Is there a reason you're not letting them in?" Sabelle called down the stairs.

"In a minute!" Bram shouted and turned back to her.

"You heard me," Anka answered. "Let Lucan and Caden in, then gather the others. I'll explain."

He hesitated, shrewd blue eyes dissecting. "All right, then. I'll give you ten minutes. If I'm not convinced, you'll go home with Lucan and stay there until the youngling is grown!"

As Bram sent an urgent text to all the warriors, he admitted each who arrived inside the protections surrounding the manor. Lucan and Caden barged in, several others right behind them as Marrok made his way down the stairs, to the office.

"This is how you trust me to take care of you? Running out and not listening to a bloody word I say?" Lucan's expression thundered, dark brows slashing over angry blue eyes.

"I'm only asking that you listen to me." She placed a hand over his drumming heart. "I have information that everyone needs to know, and I only want to say this once. Please."

A muscle ticked in his jaw. "You're not telling everyone about every*thing*, are you?"

Anka bit her lip. She understood Lucan's reservation about telling a roomful of people about her bloodline. Anyone with a future ax to grind could report her, and she'd be dragged away forever, tortured, then likely killed. But if they were going to save magickind, then her one life couldn't be more important than all the others.

"Fuck me!"

At the sound of the familiar, furious bellow, Anka turned. She peered up into familiar sunglasses, taking in Shock's grim, taut mouth. As he stood in the doorway, glaring, he looked ready to tear apart the mansion's roof with his bare hands, shingle by shingle.

"You're carrying his youngling?"

Even from behind the sunglasses, she saw Shock's stare was as focused as a laser. He looked stunned...and shattered.

Nerves knotted her stomach. "As you can see."

He zipped around to find Lucan hovering ever closer.

"And you Called to her," Shock said. "But Anka hasn't spoken the Binding yet?"

"I haven't," she murmured, feeling Shock barge into her head.

There really hadn't been an opportunity to Bind to Lucan. They needed more time to work through their difficulties and learn to communicate better before they both committed to forever. And she let Shock know it. She owed him the truth.

Lucan curled an arm around her. "But she will."

"Children!" Bram whistled, getting everyone's attention. "Anka has the floor now. No one—and I mean no one"—he glared at Lucan and Shock—"interrupts. Or I'll throw you out. Go ahead, Anka."

She stepped into the middle of the circle of warriors and reached deep for her courage.

"Thank you, Bram. As you all know, we must have three beings to retrieve the potion that will kill Morganna: blood from the lines of both Merlin and Nimue, which we have in Bram and Mathias, and a second generation washerwoman." A general rumbling of assent rolled around her, and she pressed on. "Our problem has been finding a banshee who is also a mother, correct?"

After another rounds of nods and grunts, she risked a glance at Lucan and Shock, who stood side by side. Lucan remained tense, ready to pounce all over her if she confessed her secret. Shock looked like he had a whole lot of questions about what else she planned to spill.

Sending Shock a slight, reassuring shake of her head so he knew that his secret would remain with her, she addressed the others. "We don't have that problem anymore."

Silence stopped the room. The wizards looked at one another, clearly wondering how she could make such a claim.

"Anka..." Lucan warned.

Caden slapped him on the back, none too gently, as a reminder of Bram's gag order.

"As you can see, gentlemen, I'm expecting a youngling." A stunning surprise every time she thought about it. She would protect this little life with her dying breath. But first, she had to make sure the world her daughter would grow up in was as safe as possible. But if she got revenge against Mathias in the process, so much the better.

Bram narrowed his eyes. “You’re expecting, yes, but Merlin’s magic is strong enough to discern that you’re not a banshee. Pretending won’t work.”

“I’m not pretending.”

The entire room came to a dead stop. No one moved, spoke. Breathed. They all stared—except Lucan and Shock. They uttered the same curse in the same moment.

“You could wail now and kill us all?” Ice finally asked.

She shrugged. “I suppose.” When he and Duke both backed away, she held up her hands. “Until Mathias took me, I had never wailed. It was a terrible, wretched experience, and I have no interest in ever using my voice that way again.”

“So you want Mathias and me to take you with us to release Morganna’s potion?”

Leave it to Bram to skip being spooked by the odd girl and get right to the practical.

“She’s staying home,” Lucan insisted.

Anka shook her head. “You can’t put your hands on Morganna’s potion without me.”

“That was the reason for Morganna’s fertility spell?” Clearly, the wheels in Bram’s head were turning quickly. “She knew you were a banshee?”

“Right away,” Anka answered. “But I pointed out that I was not a mother and, therefore, was of no use to her.”

“So she fixed that for you. Brilliant.” Bram’s eyes narrowed. “But how did she know that releasing the potion would require a second generation washerwoman? Merlin would never have allowed her to discover that information.”

“I told her.” At the collective incredulous stares and growls around her, she scowled. “I had to give her some useful information or else she was coming straight for you and Sabelle.”

“Bugger,” Bram muttered.

"Morganna is potentially even more dangerous than Mathias, Anka," Lucan implored. "Come home and let me protect you."

Anka wanted to scream. The truth was in front of Lucan. Why couldn't he see it? "That's impossible. She knows my face, my bloodline…and that I'm now carrying a youngling. She needs me and she knows it. She will find me, and it won't matter who gets in her way. As long as she perceives that I'm merely a part of the combination to unlock her potion, she'll mean me no harm."

Lucan clenched his fists. He looked like a truck had hit him, but he was no longer arguing.

"Are you suggesting that we simply give the potion to her?" Bram's question left no doubt that he thought she'd lost her mind.

"The two of us, along with Mathias, must retrieve it." She swallowed realizing how close she'd have to be to her tormenter. He would comment about her pregnancy, deliver more veiled threats. Mathias would realize that he could make Lucan weak again if he harmed her. He would scare the hell out of her and enjoy every minute of it. Damn it, she hated being vulnerable, but she could do nothing now. "I said nothing about giving Morganna the potion, however. In fact, I have a plan to use it to destroy her and Mathias."

Caden cut in. "Why risk you, the youngling, and my brother's ire to stop her? Why not let the potion stay hidden?"

Turning, Anka addressed him. "You mean beside the fact that Morganna won't let me? For two reasons: First, the Doomsday Brethren can't fight both Mathias and Morganna at once. And don't forget, we can't retrieve the potion without Mathias. As long as Morganna is threatening to expose us to humans, she's a greater threat. Am I wrong?"

"Not at all," Bram returned.

"We need that potion." Anka smiled. "Second, I don't think for one minute that Mathias wants to play nice with us for the good of magickind. The moment that potion is free, he'll enact whatever scheme he's brewing in his head and double-cross us. He'll try to leverage the potion to control Morganna."

Bram crossed his arms over his chest. "I've already considered that. Go on."

"I've got an idea to both get the potion down Morganna's throat and trap Mathias."

"Truly?" Bram raised a brow. "Two super villains in one day. How many battles have you been in, Anka?"

"Don't you dare belittle her, you sodding dimwit," Lucan snarled.

Anka sent him a grateful glance, then directed her attention back to Bram. "None, I admit. How many nights have you spent in Mathias's dungeon?"

"Are you suggesting that you know him better because he tortured you?"

Anka nodded. "Better than you think. I'm not stupid. His biggest weakness is his vanity. He resurrected Morganna, never imagining that she would be too powerful for him to control. If we play on his arrogance, he'll never suspect that we're one step ahead of him."

"Are you certain you really want to be involved?" Bram asked again, glancing up at Lucan. "He may think otherwise, but Lucan is my friend. He'll perish in every sense of the word if the worst happens to you and your youngling."

"Morganna isn't going to let me sit this one out. My life will hardly matter if we allow her wreak havoc at will. She will kill innocents and expose us to all. Then what?" she challenged, looking at Lucan. "You must let me play my role."

"If I don't?" Lucan crossed his arms over his chest.

Lucan was calling her bluff. Anka threatening to leave him or face Morganna anyway would accomplish nothing. She loved Lucan, no matter what issues they had to work through. Unfortunately, they had a war to win first.

"Then your youngling will grow up in a very dangerous world—if she gets to grow up at all. And her mother will be quite unhappy."

Lucan shook his head with an agitated sigh. "Bloody hell. All right, under one condition: The moment that potion is free, you teleport away, back to safety. No questions asked."

Anka hesitated. She desperately wanted to deliver Mathias one blow, preferably the fatal one. But with a youngling coming, she had to look forward, not back.

"Agreed. I'll leave administering the potion to Morganna in the hands of others. I will try to avoid fighting. But I think I know how to trap Mathias."

"Do you?" Bram challenged. "Tell us."

"We'll need everyone here first. Every witch, wizard, and human we trust. And the Untouchable. We especially need her."

"I don't want Felicia in the middle of this," Duke objected, glowering. He might be stylish in his pricy designer suits, but he could be intimidating as hell.

"No one wants to be in the middle of this," Anka argued. "But with Felicia, we'll have a chance. Without her, even though Morganna and Mathias aren't pals, they might team up to destroy us. Take away their magic and we have a fight that's two against many. *Then* we have a chance."

No one argued with that logic, though Lucan looked as if he wanted to try. Frustration poured off of him.

She slipped her hand into his. "I'll do everything in my power to stay safe, but you know this isn't going to go away if we do nothing."

With a sigh, he wrapped his arms around her. "I don't like it. But you're right."

Anka smiled up at Lucan. He really was the most beautiful man she'd ever seen. And one of the best inside, as well.

"Oh, vomit," Shock muttered beside her.

Please try to be happy. I'll keep your secret. And I'll always be here if you need me.

"Yeah, yeah," he grumbled. "Same to you."

Shock got her message loud and clear. He wasn't in mate mourning. He wasn't even terribly bitter. Her instinct that she wasn't the mate of his heart had been right.

Someday, you'll find the perfect woman for you. She'll complete you, put a smile on your face, and pull your head out of the bottle. I'll be thrilled for you.

Rolling his wide shoulders in his black leather jacket, Shock grimaced. "I'd rather decapitate myself with a razor blade."

"Want help?" Lucan quipped.

But it lacked the hate that had backed his words before.

"Fuck off," Shock groused.

"Wait," Bram objected loudly enough to get everyone's attention again. "If Felicia is there, none of us will be able to use magic, either. I don't know if that's a good idea."

Anka pulled away from Lucan and turned to Bram. "That's the dilemma. We need to give Felicia a crash course in trusting us all. Without that, the plan won't work. And we must be quick. Morganna isn't going to wait long to find me. Another day or two at best, then…I'm afraid we're in for a war."

Lucan pressed a damp towel to his face and tried to keep his calm. Duke and Marrok had taken aside the human ladies, Sydney and Kari, to drill them in self-defense. Olivia worked in a corner with a spell book, reading feverishly to understand more advanced magic. All of them were doing well. That's where the happy news ended.

Felicia sat curled up against the far wall, eyes closed, mind obviously focused as he, Shock, Anka, Caden, Ice, Sabelle, the twins, and Bram all took turns trying to use their magic. Raiden had insisted Tabitha sit this battle out, given her coming youngling. They all agreed.

The poor Untouchable looked small with her knees curled to her chest and her petite frame dwarfed by so many warriors. Felicia had let the witches past her trust barrier within an hour. Anka and Sabelle both managed to turn lights off and on, conjure objects, and use magical defense spells easily. Anka had even shown a bit of her impish side and grown a thick floor of Bermuda grass inside Bram's ballroom, complete with insects. Predictably, Bram had objected. But he hadn't been able to magically make the out-of-place fauna disappear and restore the wooden floor.

Time was running short. They'd been at this for nearly twenty-four hours, stopping only briefly for food and a few hours' sleep. Despite the frustration, all the wizards kept trying. Lucan bit back the urge to yell at Felicia that he'd never hurt her. Shock hadn't held back at all. Caden diverted himself with a hanging punching bag. Ice joined him. Even Bram was unraveling.

"What the fuck do we do if we can't make this work?" Shock asked.

Lucan hesitated. He had no idea why the wanker was talking to him.

"Oh, bury the fucking hatchet already." Shock sounded somewhere between exhausted and annoyed. "You're going to get the girl. I'm free. Now we can all shit unicorns and rainbows and be happy or whatever."

"Sounds fun." But he still didn't understand why Shock was asking him anything.

"Honestly? Ice will hate me forever, which is no loss to me. Bram annoys the fuck out of me. Your brother…" He shrugged. "Don't know the git at all. Seems high-strung. The twins are off in their own world. If they weren't related, I'd think they were having a bromance. That leaves you."

Shock usually didn't want to talk at all, but Lucan decided that he could play along for a minute. "Caden, Ice! Stop punching that bloody bag and see if Felicia needs anything. Take five."

He walked to the far side of the room, and surprisingly Shock followed. Anka watched with a frown, but he stayed her, holding up a hand. For once, she listened.

"So you don't absolutely loathe me anymore. Splendid. That all?"

"Oh, I wouldn't say that. But Anka will always be important to me, even if she loves you for some reason I can't understand. If I have to make nice with you in order to see her, I will."

"But she isn't the mate of your heart."

"Apparently not." He peered around the room, looking anywhere but at Lucan, as if the whole conversation was too uncomfortable. "I've been sober for a few days now. New clarity and all that shit."

"Enlighten me, and I might be more inclined to let you see Anka now and then."

Shock scowled. "Oh, God, you're one of those touchy-feely types who wants a bloke to spill his guts? Oprah in a wizard's clothes? Fuck. All right. What do you want to know?"

"Why fixate on Anka?"

"Brilliant. That's a really simple question to answer, you sodding idiot." He shook his head. "She's beautiful. And she's really decent. Kind. I've known her most of my life. She keeps secrets. She's loyal."

"But you never had the mating instinct with her. You never Called to her until I was interested. When you feared you would lose her, that's when you acted."

"Thank you, Dr. Freud. I'm pretty sure all that mating instinct stuff is rubbish, so I picked a witch I thought I could tolerate for the rest of my life. She's still a female above all others in my eyes. And yeah, having a few months to rub your nose in the fact that Anka slept in my bed was fun. I especially liked reading your tormented mind."

Lucan tensed. Just when he thought Shock wasn't a complete wanking bastard, he said something to prove Lucan wrong.

"Go fucking crawl back into a bottle and leave me alone." He moved to stride past Shock and resume work. No time for this stupid chitchat anyway.

Shock grabbed his arm. "I only climbed in a bottle because I got tired of reading Anka's mind every time we fucked. All she thought about was you. And the only time I could tune her thoughts out was when I was pissed drunk. Happy?"

Incredulity slid through Lucan. "What?"

"If you didn't hear it the first time, you deaf plonker, I'm not repeating myself."

Shock had just admitted, more or less, that he'd known all along Anka wanted her former mate. That he had never really loved her as more than a friend. Was the sky falling, too?

"No, Chicken Little." Shock heaved an annoyed sigh. "I like her and I thought, why should the Privileged prat get the girl all the time?"

So Anka had been a prize to win. He'd meant for her to level the field between the two of them. He'd wanted to win, not because he loved the girl, but because he hated to lose. Stunned didn't begin to cover Lucan's reaction.

Lucan looked to Shock for confirmation. The big wizard merely shook his head. "Oh, sod off, you annoying barmpot."

With that, Lucan knew he was right.

Shock swung away and headed back toward Felicia and the other warriors. Lucan stopped him. "You can see Anka. She cares for you. I'll never take something away from her that makes her happy. You'll never threaten her safety." And Lucan knew that, once he and Anka were mated, she could never touch Shock again. "I won't stand in your way."

Big shoulders taut, Shock stopped in his tracks and turned. "Thank you. Now really, fuck off."

Lucan laughed as he watched the other wizard walk away, sending Ice an obscene hand gesture just to pick a fight. And what do you know, it worked. He rolled his eyes at the two wizards rolling around on the mats like angry children, then wandered over to Felicia.

Kneeling in front of the Untouchable, he stared with concern as she rested her forehead on her knees, shoulders slumped. He looked at Caden. "Go get Duke. She's had enough for now."

Felicia's head popped up. "We have to keep going. I have to make this work. It's just that, I'd already had time with Sabelle and some of the other ladies in Swansea. And…trusting men is so much more difficult for me."

He remembered that Duke once had a devil of a time coaxing

this reluctant beauty to believe in him. "We'll work it through. Don't put too much pressure on yourself."

"Everyone's safety is in my hands. You, your brother, Bram, Anka...the youngling. I can't let you all down." Her eyes filled with tears of frustration.

"It will wait five minutes." Lucan bent and scooped her up in his arms, despite her protests, carrying her to her concerned mate. "No need to kill yourself. Rest up a bit."

"But I'm putting you all in danger with every moment I delay. I don't know why I can't...let my guard down." She slapped her palm to her forehead.

"None of that," he scolded gently. "We'll pull through. I have faith in your ability. You should do the same. Hello, Duke."

Felicia's glowering mate approached them and held out his arms. Lucan slid the small blonde into them, and she curled up into Duke's chest. "You don't have to coddle me."

"I do," Duke disagreed. "Part of the job description when I signed on to be your overprotective mate. I'm sorry, sunshine. You're stuck with me."

She smiled tiredly at Duke, then turned back to him. "Thank you."

"Take a few minutes." Lucan slid a glance up to Duke. "I think she skipped most of her lunch."

The wizard narrowed his dark eyes at his little mate. "Felicia?"

"I wasn't hungry."

Duke sighed. "You need your strength."

Felicia rolled her eyes, then turned her glare Lucan's way. "Tattletale."

Lucan smiled. "Guilty. Now eat."

"Indeed. Lucan only has your best interests at heart." Duke scolded. "I daresay he's more concerned about your wellbeing than you are."

Watching the two walk away, Lucan smiled wistfully. Would he and Anka fall into such a closely bonded relationship in the future? Could he recover from her perfidy and simply believe her again? Staying angry with her would be easy—and pointless. She'd been afraid and insecure. Neither of them had communicated well. Now they had to move forward, and he only had two choices: either be mad and walk away, miserable for an eternity, or try to understand her fears and help her, then see what the future brought them.

No contest. He wasn't about to let her go. But one worry nagged at him. Would she ever open up to him fully and let him inside her head and heart?

Everyone around them had taken a break, it seemed. Caden sought Sydney, pulling her onto his lap to ask about her self-defense training. Sabelle stood between Ice and Shock, zapping them both until they broke apart with a curse. The twins were still fist-bumping and roughhousing in the corner, Kari looking on with a laugh. Bram sat with his back propped against the wall, eyes closed, stealing a quick nap.

A presence brushed behind him. A familiar scent. His heart raced.

"Sneaking up on me, Anka?"

"No, I…" She shook her head. "What did you say to Shock to rile him? He's been trying to beat Ice to a bloody pulp, and Ice was having none of it."

Of course not. "I made him admit that his love for you is one of friendship. Then I told him that I wouldn't stand in the middle of that."

"Oh, you tried to be the bigger man." She smiled softly. "No doubt that truly annoyed him."

"Precisely."

He wrapped his arm around Anka, and she slid into his embrace, wishing desperately that they were alone. He ached to talk with her, reestablish some of their old intimacy. No way he'd turn down an opportunity to share pleasure and energy with her. He moaned, barely resisting the urge to rub up against her, his jog pants tighter than they had been a few minutes ago.

"Anka, I know this is terrible timing, but the past few months have taught me that there may never been a good time again. I won't put off important discussions with you. Why haven't you spoken the Binding to me?" Lucan wasn't sure he wanted the answer. But he needed it.

Her smile fell. "We've had so little time to work everything out."

"You could speak the words now, and we would have the rest of our centuries to do that."

She swallowed. "You only Called to me again because you thought I was dying."

"Is that what you think?" He shook his head. "I would have spoken those words anyway."

"Even after everything? I wasn't sure you still wanted me. I've been less than perfect—"

"I don't need perfection, just honesty."

"All right. Honestly, I'm concerned for two reasons: Having the mate bond blasting from both our signatures makes us a target again. Mathias and Morganna both will know where you're vulnerable again. They may use it against you."

Lucan shrugged. "It's possible, but they already see my Call in my signature and my youngling in yours. Even without the complete circle of the mate bond, Mathias already knows that you're my weakness. I don't think keeping the words to yourself will make a bit of difference. What's your other reservation? I know your heart has chosen me."

Anka hesitated, obviously mulling over his question. Lucan felt as if he'd been holding his breath for hours, waiting for her to speak those precious words to him. And still, she remained mute. He sensed there was more to her reluctance.

"Anka, the truth. All of it."

She sighed. "I can't help but feel as if I'll always be a disappointment. I'm a scarred banshee from a barely respectable family. You could do so much better."

Hell, she still felt unworthy. They would work on that little by little, day by day. He could kick his own arse for correcting her through the century of their past mating, when he should have been telling her every day that she was wonderful exactly as she was.

Lucan cupped her face in his hands. "But I can't. You are my mate, Anka. Always. I was falling apart without you. Your gentle spirit, your unexpected sense of humor, your kindness, and the way you think of others. Love, I'm brought back to you again and again because you're *you*. You're the woman I fell in love with. No time or distance or event is ever going to change that."

She nodded, her amber eyes filling with tears as she flung herself into his arms. "You're not angry anymore?"

"What good does being angry do me? Hanging onto it doesn't get me what I want, which is you. But I expect absolute honesty in the future or there will be hell to pay. Am I clear?"

A sob escaped her. "Thank you. I will always try to be what you need. I'll never keep secrets again, I swear." She pulled back to caress his cheek, looking into his eyes. Love shined from her face. He'd seen this expression once before, radiant and hopeful. She wanted to speak the Binding.

"I've got it!" Bram leapt to his feet and shouted across the room suddenly, so loudly his words echoed around the big ballroom. "I've had a dream…a vision of the future. I see now. I know precisely where to find the potion. Everyone gather 'round. Quickly! We haven't much time."

Chapter Seventeen

Within a few hours, every member of the Doomsday Brethren and their mates sat at Bram's enormous dining room table. They'd all gone their separate ways to charge their energy, and Anka blushed remembering the thorough, toe-curling loving Lucan had given her. Every touch had been eager, grateful…and desperate. They both knew that if things went badly, this could be their last time.

In theory, tonight's mission was simply to retrieve the potion, but Bram's vision foretold of a battle where both Morganna and Mathias would be present and likely fighting against them. The wizard didn't often have such premonitions, but when he did, they were spot on. She wished to hell Bram would have dreamed the outcome so she knew what to brace for.

When she and Lucan had retreated to the bedroom they'd shared as mates, Anka had yearned all the way down to her soul to Bind to him, but she'd waited. Now wasn't the time to be impetuous or selfish. Mathias likely still had a malicious desire to weaken the Doomsday Brethren. If they managed to retrieve this potion and make Morganna drink it, Mathias would still be their enemy, while she and Lucan would be an even riper target now that she expected his youngling. If she spoke the Binding today,

Anka couldn't help but feel that, regardless of what Lucan thought, she'd be holding up a neon sign, advertising their vulnerabilities to Mathias.

Now the warriors had reconvened for dinner, knowing they must refine their plan. Shock was a no-show thus far. That worried Anka a bit. The others could say many things about Shock, and they might even be right at times. But when her safety was involved, Shock always put her first.

"I don't like it," Ice said. "None of the wizards are yet able to use magic around Felicia. I think she should stay behind."

"I'm sorry," the Untouchable murmured.

Felicia looked so miserably guilty. Anka's heart went out to the woman.

"I'm not blaming you." Ice tried to soften his expression, but it still looked like a cross between a scowl and a glower. "I'm simply stating fact."

"Even if you can't use your magic around Felicia, Anka and I can," Sabelle pointed out. "And neither Morganna nor Mathias will be able to. We still have the upper hand."

"It's too dangerous." This time, Ice didn't bother to hide his snarl at all.

Sabelle raised a brow and looked ready to go toe-to-toe with him. "It's as safe as a battle is going to get."

Caden jumped in. "I agree with Ice. It's too risky. That puts the onus of containing and killing Morganna, and possibly battling Mathias, too, on Sabelle and Anka. It's better to leave Felicia at home and hope that our combined magic is strong enough. We're warriors. We've trained for this for months. You're talented witches, but you're not prepared."

"That's crap!" Sabelle insisted. "You haven't been able to trap Mathias since Zain brought him back, but you're going to add Morganna to the mix and suddenly succeed?"

Marrok leaned back in his chair and crossed his arms over his massive chest. "If Morganna and Mathias have not their magic, then think on this: Neither is versed in the human ways of war.

Between the magic of your females"—he addressed Ice and Lucan—"and all the combined fighting prowess in this room, 'tis likely we can force Morganna to drink the fatal potion. Then, mayhap, Ice can poison his sword with his blood and end Mathias."

"I can help to trap him so you can stab him, Ice," Anka suggested. She would offer herself as bait, if she must.

"You're having a youngling," Lucan thundered. "You promised to teleport away as soon as we obtain the potion. Have you forgotten that?"

"Of course not, but—"

"No buts." Lucan shook his head. "If you're no longer there, and none of the warriors can use magic, can we truly expect Sabelle's magic alone to defeat both Morganna and Mathias?"

"Fuck, no!" Ice growled.

"Won't they be much like humans without their magic?" Anka argued. "I know I promised to teleport away, but if they're disabled…shouldn't they be easy to defeat?"

"In theory," Lucan pointed out. "Felicia disables Mathias's magic. We know that from the night he attacked Duke's ancestral home. But we don't know for certain about Morganna's. We're assuming her Untouchable powers will work on that bitch, as well, but who knows?"

"I agree," Duke seconded. "Too much is unpredictable. Anka, this fight is too dangerous for you and the youngling. And what's to prevent Mathias from finding some way to kill Felicia? He must be within a hundred yards of her for her to disable his magic. He's not stupid. He'll have guessed we'll have her near and be prepared with some human weapon, I suspect."

Yes, there were risks, but these overprotective wizards weren't seeing the bigger picture.

"Mathias is vain," Anka argued. "He will never believe that anyone, least of all a group of females, can best him."

"Possibly," Lucan conceded. "But is getting your revenge worth risking your youngling?"

The question was a slap to Anka's face. "We've been over this. Our daughter has no future if Mathias and Morganna are still here to wreak havoc."

"Enough debate." Bram stood, finally having enough of this argument. "Felicia, are you willing to come with us and continue trying to let these wizards through your Untouchable defenses? If they can use magic around you…Mathias might be expecting it, but he'll still be powerless. And in case Shock is a spy, he'll have reported back that we've been unsuccessful performing spells around Felicia thus far."

"Then why not wait a day or two to see if we can, in fact, be successful?" Raiden asked.

"What if Morganna loses patience and does something to expose us to humankind again?" Bram challenged. "We'll have a potential genocide on our hands, a twenty-first century witch hunt. I have no doubt she'll soon seek out Anka, then threaten to kill all those we hold dear until we lead her to the potion. If we grab it first, maybe we have some prayer of stopping or killing her."

"But if we know Mathias will grab it and use it to try to control her, why are we playing into his hands?" Lucan asked.

"If we do this as I'd like, Mathias will be dead and his plans won't matter." Bram turned to the Untouchable. "Felicia?"

She turned her blue eyes to Duke, then gave him an apologetic glance before facing Bram again. "Yes. I'll keep trying. Always."

"I believe in you," Bram assured. "You came through for Duke at the last possible moment when you faced Mathias previously. I believe you'll find the trust in time again."

"You're certain Morganna will be there?" Caden asked.

"She was in my vision. Either she's figured out the location of the potion on her own or she's watching our every move. I expect that she will make this plan somewhere between difficult and impossible. So we must be prepared for anything. As for Mathias, I've got another trick up my sleeve. This should be fun."

Lucan resented the hell out of Bram demanding that he follow along on this last minute jaunt. And he would happily tell his former friend to sod off...except he didn't like the thought of Bram scheming without supervision. If Merlin's prick of a grandson was going to let him in on whatever the hell he had brewing in his head, Lucan would follow.

Bram pulled an enchanted rock from his pocket, mumbled something, then threw it. With a satisfied nod, he made his way out of the dining room and away from the others. Lucan followed, feeling Bram's assessing stare on him.

"I see you're still angry with me."

Lucan raised a brow at him. "Furious, actually."

"And you'll never believe that I sent Anka to Shock to keep her safe?"

"You could have sent her to *me*."

"She wouldn't have gone."

"How do you know? You didn't try that tactic," Lucan argued.

"She was barely speaking to you at the time." Bram pinned him with a glare.

"We would have worked through it. You simply wanted a spy. Admit it."

"Gladly. Yes, I needed one. The only person I trust Shock with is Anka. He will always have her best interests at heart. I'm certain that's of some benefit to him, though I'm still figuring out exactly what. But he will do anything to keep her safe. I gave you the opportunity to train her because I know you two belong together. I wish she'd had more time to learn to fight, but the mission is upon us now. And soon she will Bind to you, and you have a youngling on the way." Bram smiled tightly. "You're welcome."

Anger poured through Lucan like fiery-hot lava. "Morganna did more to bring us back together than you did, you manipulative wanker!"

Bram opened his mouth, but before he could unload whatever piece of shit argument currently defiled his brain, a magical chime sounded. Light and tinkling, a bit old-fashioned.

"Ah, there she is." Bram raced to the front door and admitted his doddering Aunt Millie.

She patted his cheek with a wrinkled hand. "Hello there, dear boy." She smiled Lucan's way. "And you, too. How is Anka?"

"Very much alive and pregnant," Bram supplied.

Millie looked as if she wanted to ask who had done the deed, but couldn't find a way to express the delicate question. Lucan saved her the trouble. "With my youngling."

She smiled brightly. "So you are the mate of her heart. How lovely."

Yes, he was. Supposedly. Then why hadn't Anka spoken the Binding this afternoon when they'd been alone and he'd been deep inside her, exchanging love and energy?

"What can I do for you, my sweet nephew?" Millie asked. "Do you wish me to look at Anka?"

"I need a bit of binding magic."

The little witch pursed her lips. "You know the restrictions."

"We'll have her consent," Bram assured her.

"What the hell are you doing?" Lucan demanded. If this involved Anka, and Bram was once again taking matters into his own hands, Lucan swore to God he'd rip his former friend into tiny pieces.

"Something designed to help us with two problems at once."

Lucan didn't like Bram's smile at all. "This better have nothing to do with Anka."

"Absolutely nothing except to make her safer," Bram assured. "You'll fancy this."

The other wizard guided Millie with a hand at the small of her back. Within a few steps, Lucan realized they were headed down to the dungeon. Bram waved open some of his magical protections, then sealed them again once they'd passed the barrier.

Nodding to some of the new guards he'd put in place since

Zain's last escape from this place, Bram approached the magical cell with its lone prisoner, Rhea.

Mathias's favorite play toy and courtesan pouted, elbows propped on her pale knees as she sat on the wooden bench inside the cell. She wore black lingerie that couldn't possibly be legal, even inside the bedroom. Sleek dark hair fell in waves past her shoulders. With her dark, slumberous eyes, so-red lips, and sinful body, Rhea looked like the devil's mistress. Essentially, she was. She also looked damn near drained of energy, her magical signature fading and weak.

She stood at their approach. Her full breasts barely fit inside her peek-a-boo corset. Her knickers were nearly nonexistent above legs that went on forever. She was a beautiful witch, yet Lucan almost couldn't bear the sight of her.

"What do you want?" she demanded.

"I'm here to make you a deal, Rhea."

"I've no energy for that. The last surrogate you sent me gave me so little," she whined, then looked Lucan's way. "I'd hoped you brought me another in this one." Lucan felt her stare dance all over him, undressing him, then she rolled her eyes. "He's quite lovely, but mated. How does that help me?"

"You won't need energy for this, dear. All you have to do is say yes. My aunt will take care of the rest."

Rhea looked at them both with suspicion. "I don't have to agree to anything."

"You don't," Bram agreed. "Unless you'd like to be free."

She jumped to attention, then narrowed her eyes. "What's the trick?"

"I want to tie your fate to Mathias's. It will be very nearly like you're mated."

Her lips parted. Her eyes brightened, and Lucan could see that the idea of being mated to Mathias appealed to Rhea. *Sick woman.*

"What do you mean?" she asked suspiciously.

"Well..." Bram wandered closer to her cell and brushed his knuckles up her arm. "If we tie your life force to his, then at the end of tonight's meeting with Mathias, if he follows the rules and colors inside the lines, you'll be teleported immediately to wherever he is. You'll be free."

"What about your magic? Won't it keep me here?"

"I've given you my word and my consent that you'll be released under these circumstances. It will be part of the magic in your binding."

Rhea bit her lip. Lucan could see she very much liked that idea. "What's in it for you?"

"You're his reason to behave. I happen to know that he misses you a great deal. I think he will be a good boy this evening if we give him proper incentive. That's you."

"If he cooperates tonight, I'm free? No tricks?"

"Precisely. What do you say, dear? I'll be a bit sad to see you go. I've so enjoyed our chats."

She narrowed her eyes. "I've told you nothing useful."

"But you've been adorably stubborn. I see why Mathias is so taken with you."

She smiled at the thought. Then, as if realizing that she was giving too much away, she wiped the expression from her face. "If he doesn't cooperate?"

"Then you're no worse for the wear. You simply remain here. Your choice." Bram shrugged as if it was of no consequence.

But Lucan sensed the tension in the other wizard's frame. He definitely had something in mind.

Bram sent her a flirty smile. "I almost hope he's a prat. More time for us together."

Rhea rolled her eyes. "Shut it, wanker. I hate it here, and you know that. You're mated."

"Doesn't mean I'm dead when I see a pretty witch." He winked. "What do you say? The potential to go with Mathias or stay here with me?"

She hesitated, clearly working through everything he'd said in her head. Finally, she nodded. "I'll take any chance to get out of here and be with Mathias again. What do I need to do?"

"Have anything of Mathias's with you?"

"Why?"

"It will be much simpler to bind your fates."

She gave him a suspicious glare. "Are you performing the spell?"

"No. My sweet, little aunt will. She's full of heart magic."

Mille stepped forward. "It's all right, dear. You won't feel anything, and everything Bram has told you is true. If your fates are bound, then as soon as Mathias upholds his part of the bargain, you'll be transported from here and returned to his side. It's much easier to perform the spell if you have something of your beloved's."

"I keep a small vial of Mathias's blood 'round my neck." Rhea gently tugged on a silver chain.

"Lovely." Bram's aunt was trying not to grimace at the macabre jewelry. "I'll need you to hand it to me willingly, then we're set."

Rhea scrambled to do as she was bid, handing the little vial, chain and all, to Millie.

The older witch tried not to flinch as she took it. "Whatever you offered of your beloved's, I'll need the same of you." When Rhea looked confused, Millie supplied, "Blood, dear."

"I'll help," Bram grabbed her wrist, then dragged a finger across her palm, cutting her a bit deeper than necessary with his magic.

Rhea hissed. Blood pooled in the sensitive center of her hand, then ran between her fingers. Millie opened the vial and poured a bit of Mathias's blood over hers, murmuring a few words over Rhea's palm. As Lucan watched, mesmerized, a small blip of light was his only clue that the spell had taken effect. Wizards were notoriously bad with heart magic. The tiny bit he'd tried…disaster. Bull in a china shop. Millie might be small and worth little on a battlefield, but right now, she was a goddess.

"It's done." The little witch smiled, then waved her hand over Rhea's to stop the bleeding.

"Thanks much, Aunt Millie."

"Think nothing of it, dear." She patted Bram's cheek, then turned to leave the dungeon.

Lucan followed with Bram right beside him. The moment they left the dungeon and Bram secured the magical protections in place again, Lucan turned to the other wizard. "What the devil was that about?"

Bram smiled widely, clearly savoring his maneuver. "Do you think for a moment that Mathias is going to play by the rules?"

"Are you daft? Of course not."

"Exactly. I'm certain he could care less about Rhea or anyone but his own ambition. But I told her the absolute truth. She's free if he follows our rules. Since we both know that won't happen, she merely stays here. But the best news is, if we manage to kill Mathias, then she dies, as well."

Nursing an idea of his own, Lucan made his way out of the dungeon and peeked into the dining room, hoping to find Anka with the rest of the people gathered there. Her seat sat empty.

With a frown, he leaned down to whisper in Sabelle's ear, ignoring Ice's scowl. "I need a favor."

"Sure." She glanced at him over her shoulder, her blue eyes expectant. "What is it?"

"I need your help with a spell. Just in case."

Lucan didn't want to prepare for this possibility, but he could rule nothing out. If Felicia couldn't get there in time, if her Untouchable powers didn't work on Morganna, if Anka couldn't—or wouldn't—teleport away when she should, he had to give her a way to defend herself. Mathias would likely come after her for his own malicious pleasure. No way was Lucan letting his mate be taken again.

Sabelle rose under Ice's watchful gaze. The wizard's green eyes narrowed, promising slow, extensive pain if Lucan touched one hair on Belle's head. Lucan held up both hands. As lovely as she was, he had no designs on Bram's sister. Anka had his heart…and Bram would be one terrible brother-by-mating. Hell, Ice probably deserved an award.

In the library, Sabelle quickly found what he needed. He tore the page from the book, scanned it, then handed it back to her. "That is precisely what we need. And you can perform this, if necessary."

"Of course."

Lucan smiled. He wanted to thank Belle with a kiss on her cheek, then decided it would be better not to incite Ice just now. Instead, he escorted her back to the dining room.

"Have you seen Anka?" he asked her as he seated her again.

The lovely witch hesitated, as if she'd rather not answer, before finally admitting, "Shock arrived about ten minutes ago. He'd obviously just received a great deal of energy from someone. Anka seemed perfectly content with that fact. Then they had a cryptic conversation, something about Shock being full or not." She shrugged apologetically. "No idea what it meant. I only know that he said he wasn't and they disappeared upstairs."

Upstairs? Nothing but bedrooms up there.

After thanking Belle, Lucan left the dining room, taking the stairs two at a time, anxiety gnawing at his gut. He arrived on the landing in time to see Shock emerge from one of the bedrooms with a loose, satisfied swagger. Anka followed, looking pale and bracing herself against the wall. She closed her eyes and heaved in a deep breath. Lucan felt his temper come unhinged.

Storming over to the pair, his gaze darted between Shock and Anka, the kick in his gut reminding him that because Anka hadn't spoken the Binding to him, she was free to do anything she wanted with Shock. Anything at all. Succumb to every lascivious, raunchy, wicked demand the wankstain had.

Fuck, Lucan felt sick to his stomach. Anka claimed to love him. He was the mate of her heart. She would give birth to his youngling. And yet…she'd disappeared into a bedroom with her former lover.

"What's this?" He stared at Anka, willing her to speak some truth that wasn't going to kill him. Instead, her legs crumpled under her, and Lucan lunged to catch her in his arms as she fell to the floor. He turned to Shock with an accusing glare. "What the fuck did you do?"

The other wizard's face closed up immediately. "Don't panic, Sir Galahad. She's all right. I told her to lie down. Stubborn witch doesn't listen."

"How do you know she's fine? What did you do to her, damn it?"

Shock growled. "I said she's all right already."

"I don't care what you said. This whole 'he who must not be fucked with' persona might scare others. Me? I don't give a shit what you think you can do to me. If you threaten her—"

"After everything I've done for her, you can accuse me of that with a straight face?"

Lucan unclenched his fists. Slowly, he backed away. Shock would never harm Anka. He cared. He might even need her in some odd way. Or at least Bram had hinted as much. Bram might be a scheming prat, but he was a smart one. But Anka's safety wasn't Lucan's only concern.

"That doesn't mean you didn't slide her between your sheets," he snapped.

But Sabelle had mentioned just minutes ago that Shock arrived at the manor brimming with energy. Lucan saw no hint of Anka's energy in Shock's signature now.

"I wish." Shock hadn't touched her, and his expression said that he sorely wished otherwise. "Don't I fucking wish. But you won that battle, so back the fuck off."

"Sorry." Lucan was forced to admit he'd been wrong. He sighed, cradling Anka against his chest. "What's wrong with her, then? Did something happen?"

Shock grimaced. "No. Really, give her ten. She'll be right as rain. Where's Bram been? I need to talk to him. Mathias is getting antsy."

Before Lucan could stop it, his memory flashed a picture of heading down to the dungeon with Bram to talk to Rhea.

The other wizard snarled in his face. "What did they discuss?"

Lucan intentionally blanked his mind. "Does Mathias care about Rhea much?"

"Mathias doesn't give a piss about anyone."

As he'd suspected. "Then there are no worries."

"Fucking wanker," Shock muttered and stalked off, jogging down the stairs in his leathers.

Lucan watched him go with mixed feelings. He didn't like Shock, or trust him much, but the way he'd behaved with Anka proved that when he was loyal, he was loyal to the core. Too bad they couldn't transfer some of that allegiance to the Doomsday Brethren. They could use someone fearless *and* reliable with connections to both sides.

There would probably be a month of full moons before that happened.

Anka roused in his arms, her dark lashes fluttering up over her amber eyes. When she realized where she was, or more precisely who was holding her, she gasped. "Where's Shock?"

"Gone downstairs. What were you doing with him?" Lucan tried to keep the accusation out of his voice, but feared that he was falling miserably short.

She squirmed in his arms until he set her on her feet, carefully keeping her near in case she needed his support. Anka hesitated in answering him for such a long time, Lucan feared that she'd refuse to speak at all. Yeah, so much for honesty. Finally, she drew in a resigned breath.

"I can't tell you that. And I'm sorry, truly. He's kept my secret since my childhood. In exchange, I agreed to keep his. I chose to tell you and the others mine so that I was no longer deceiving you and I could be helpful to the Doomsday Brethren. But I can't divulge his, not even to you. I owe him too much. If you're angry with me and can't accept that, I'm sorry."

The speech stunned him, and he watched, open-mouthed, as she headed for the stairs on wobbling legs. Jolted into action by her unsteady gait, he jogged to her and made her hold the rail with one hand. He gripped her other arm.

He tried not to feel shut out, betrayed. It didn't work. Instead, he focused on getting her downstairs safely. *Then* they'd have a nice row.

"You're not steady enough to fight tonight."

She didn't look at him, didn't pause. "I'll be all right. Surely Shock told you that."

And he was simply supposed to trust Shock? Lucan scrubbed a hand down his face. "Yes. But Anka, after everything that's happened, you're asking me to just…believe him?"

Anka paused, her pale curls swinging over her breasts, still tightly encased in a T-shirt. "No. I'm asking you to believe me. And to trust that I know I'm going to be perfectly well to fight. You want me to trust you, but you have to do the same in return. If you can't trust me to be truthful about that …" She blinked up at him with such regret in her eyes, his heart lurched. "I love you, but maybe it's best that I didn't speak the Binding."

Bram called everyone back to the dining room to await Mathias so they could ostensibly share the plan with him. Anka fidgeted in her seat. Lucan sat beside her in silence, scowling at his former best friend—before turning his silent glower on her. Clearly he didn't like what she'd said earlier, but she couldn't take it back. She wouldn't even if she could. She owed Shock too much, and Lucan had to understand that. If he didn't…God, she couldn't be caught between them again, forced to choose. It hurt too much.

The more Bram talked—Anka wasn't listening as she should—the more Shock looked ready to crawl across the table and throttle him. In fact, Shock and Lucan might not agree about much, but it was clear they both violently hated Bram's insistence that Mathias go with them to the site where Merlin had hidden Morganna's killing potion. But Bram overruled them. Without Mathias, there was no way to know if the potion was still in its place.

Lucan turned to her during a lull in the conversation around the table. "Are you truly all right to fight tonight?"

"Of course." She was nervous, but she refused to burden him with that. But she had fully recovered from her few minutes with Shock.

"Anka..." The warning in his voice couldn't be mistaken. "Don't lie."

Honesty. Right. She couldn't forget that. "I'm worried. Every time Mathias comes near me, I break out in a cold sweat and freeze. I fear that I won't remember my part in time. Or that he'll know he can take advantage of my fright. I don't want to be the weak link."

"I'll be there with you. I won't let you falter."

"I'd give my life, Anka." Shock's voice was a low rumble across the table. Clearly, he didn't give a shit who heard him. "You know that."

She gave them both smiles that she meant to be reassuring. She did feel loads better knowing they would be nearby. But she also knew that she had to stand on her own two feet and not let Mathias intimidate her. She would not be the one to deliver him any blows once he double-crossed them, but she'd get to play a role. That would have to be enough. Lucan and the others would carry through with the plan, and if it went off without a hitch, they would hopefully rid magickind of its worst villains and they could live safely and happily ever after.

"Any other questions about the plan?" Bram demanded.

No one said a word.

"Perfect. Does everyone remember what to—"

A chilling magical chime rang over the room. Anka gasped. She knew exactly who that belonged to.

"Mathias?" Sabelle asked.

Bram grimaced. "The arsehole is early. Why?"

Good question. She looked over at Shock, who merely shrugged.

"Can't you read his mind?" Lucan demanded.

"Not without him knowing. He's adept. There are

consequences."

In other words, Shock would be exposed as a Brethren sympathizer? Anka frowned, wishing for once that she could read Shock's mind herself. He'd let her in on most of his deepest secrets...but he'd kept more than a few for himself.

At her thought, he raised a brow over his shades, but didn't say a word.

Pushing back his chair with a curse, Bram rose to admit Mathias. Anka wanted to tackle the unscrupulous bastard, scratch and scream and punch him with her bare fists until she beat him to a bloody pulp. Her rage at his atrocities hadn't gone away, and she didn't know how to make the searing pool of acid in her soul stop boiling, how to look forward, rather than back. The youngling in her belly was months away. It hadn't yet made her sick or kicked in her womb to serve as a physical reminder of her "delicate" state. But Mathias and her need for vengeance were right here, right now. She felt that pounding strongly inside her.

Lucan caressed her arm, the sweep of his palm soothing. "Relax. Don't let him know that he bothers you or he'll only use it to get under your skin."

"I can't help it," she whispered. "I want to kill him!"

"You think I don't?" he challenged. "I'd love to cut off his balls, shove them down his throat, and watch him slowly choke to death. But the time will come. You will not go unavenged. Trust me."

Bram returned with Mathias, and Anka wanted to slap the smarmy smile off of his deceivingly handsome face. He gave a jaunty wave to the gathering as a whole, seemingly amused when every mated male dragged his female a bit closer, Lucan included.

Mathias sent a questioning stare Shock's way. "Fancy meeting you here."

"Imagine that," Shock quipped.

Then Mathias's gaze settled on her, following Lucan's arms wrapped around her.

"I see congratulations are in order. You and MacTavish are going to have a youngling. Isn't that fortunate?"

Anka bristled. Mathias had some trick up his sleeve. He always did.

"You're early," Bram said.

"You'll understand that I'd like to know a bit more about our mission here today before we go."

"We're going to retrieve the potion. I suspect Morganna is watching that location, waiting for us to make a move. We have all the necessary elements now, so we'll venture there together. I'll be bringing Marrok, Caden, Ice, Sabelle, and Lucan for backup. They'll watch over us as we retrieve the potion."

"Sabelle?" Mathias slid his gaze over to Ice. "Teaching your mate to fight, then? She's so delicate. Aren't you worried that she can be easily broken?"

Ice's scowl shouted that he was ready to crawl across the table and rip off the wicked wizard's head. "I'll have her back, rest assured."

"And I'll have Anarki at the ready." Mathias smiled, as if he knew that provided no comfort whatsoever and he liked that fact.

"Once we've retrieved the potion, we must make sure Morganna imbibes it. We've no idea when and where she will be," Bram lied. "But when we find her, we'll have to do what we must to force it down her throat."

No one breathed a word about Bram's vision, about Morganna awaiting them at the site.

"Of course. Since we'll be retrieving the potion today, does that mean the lovely Anka has finally confessed her true origins? You were all daft not to see it before, you know."

"Excuse us for not having any experience with banshees." Bram bristled. "And if you knew, you might have given us a clue."

Mathias shrugged. "That was my test, to see if you would figure out all the clues and keep up your end of the bargain."

"We couldn't do anything without you," Anka pointed out. "There are no more children of Nimue, just as there are almost no washerwomen left in existence. We must work together."

"That is true. And Bram, being a most noble Rion of the great

Merlin's bloodline, did as promised and contacted me. We'll work together well, I'm sure. Under one condition."

Anka longed to tell Mathias to shove his condition and go straight back to hell, but they still needed him. And this plan might seal the evil bastard's fate. That would be worth any discomfort she might endure now.

"What?" Bram snapped.

"When we retrieve the potion, I think you should give it to me."

Marrok snorted. "'Tis far too convenient to leave such with you. Why should we do something so daft, you swag-bellied miscreant?"

"Because Morganna does not trust you at all. She wants to kill your leader. But she considers me something of a pet since I'm the one who resurrected her. I've let her believe that I'm helping her find the potion."

At the end of the table, Marrok visibly shuddered, no doubt remembering his repugnant time in Morganna's bed.

"Sorry," Bram said without a hint of apology. "I'm not giving it to you."

"How will you catch her off guard to give her the potion, then? Do you have another plan? I can do it in bed, as she sleeps unaware. I have ways of compelling her to swallow it." He glanced at Shock. "If you have a better idea, let's hear it."

Anka didn't understand the dangerous role Shock played as Mathias's right-hand man or even whose side he was genuinely on, but she knew better than to dig too deep, especially now. Both he and Lucan would heartily object, and she didn't dare do more to attract Mathias's attention now that she was pregnant.

"I'll concede, but I've got a condition of my own," Bram grumbled. "You must follow all my rules and directives as we retrieve and administer the potion, or the deal is off. Otherwise, how do I know this isn't simply a ruse?"

Mathias narrowed his eyes in warning. "I came to you for help, if you'll recall. I want the bitch gone."

No one could argue with that.

"All right. I'll give you the potion," Bram grumbled, as if

conceding against his better judgment and will.

Anka watched, almost certain that Mathias had just fallen into some trap of Bram's.

"Lovely. Where are we going?"

"Well, Nimue was the Lady of the Lake. We'll start there."

With that, everyone in the group stood. There was nothing left to negotiate. The only thing left to do was teleport to the site where Merlin had likely hidden the potion an eon ago and hope that they managed to end Morganna, contain Mathias, and all make it back alive.

Chapter Eighteen

The wizards all bid a tense good-bye to their mates, except for Sabelle, who ventured out into the twilight with them. Anka teleported with everyone to a quiet district in Somerset, near Glastonbury. The body of water looked placid, surrounded by tall willows weeping into the lush grass. An old stone bridge with three arches sat in the distance as the setting sun skipped its last few rays across the water's glassy surface. In the distance, fog clung to the sea's shoreline to their west.

Anka frowned, rubbing her hands up and down her arms. It was cold here. There was something about this place she didn't like. She could almost hear past ancient battles echoing across these plains, smell the running blood sinking into the soil. Of course, Mathias being beside her didn't help her imagination at all. Uneasiness settled deep as they reached the banks.

"This is a river," Lucan pointed out, hovering behind her and wrapping an arm around her to lend her his body heat. "Not a lake."

"One of the many ways Nimue kept her location hidden from others who would hunt her," Mathias quipped. "She was quite crafty."

A trait that had clearly passed down the line.

Shock closed in behind Anka, as well. “Need a coat?”

She shook her head.

“I know you’re cold.” Even when she didn’t look at him, she felt his agitation and concern. Poor Shock. He’d tried so hard to take care of her in every way. In the end, he still wound up alone.

“I’ll be all right.” She glanced at him over her shoulder, her expression an apology.

His face closed up, fast and tight. Clearly, he didn’t want her pity.

“Are you certain?” Lucan frowned as if he didn’t like her answer, either.

Anka tried to send him a reassuring smile. The cold she felt was deeper down, something inside. Dread. Fear. A coat wasn’t going to fix that.

“What now?” Ice demanded.

“We spread out in case Morganna arrives unexpectedly,” Bram said.

“Agreed.” Mathias snapped his fingers, and an army of Anarki appeared on the river banks. “Where shall we position them?”

“Right there works.” Bram looked ready to grind his teeth into dust. “Ice, Lucan, and Caden, get on the opposite side of the river. If we must fight Morganna, we’ll have soldiers on both banks. She’ll have to go through them to get the potion.”

“Unless she uses trickery, which she’s good at. Shock, stay with the others.” Mathias pointed toward Ice, Lucan, and Caden. “That’s the best use of your talents.”

After the four of them teleported across the river, Bram addressed the remaining members of the Doomsday Brethren. “Marrok, Sabelle, Raiden and Ronan, fan out and head for the bridge. If we have human company of any sort, they’ll likely arrive from there. Sabelle, send the others at home a text to keep them at the ready in the event we get a visit from the evil bitch, will you? They can join us, if need be.”

Sabelle pulled her phone from the pocket of her jeans and quickly tapped out a message. Anka knew that was the signal to

Duke to be prepared to teleport Felicia here to surprise Mathias and contain Morganna. The next text would bring the Untouchable here.

"Splendid. Anka, Mathias, we'll head into the water."

Anka frowned. "Into? It's January. That water can't be much above freezing."

"I expect not." Bram eyed the water. "Can't stay in long without using magic or dying of hypothermia. Ready?"

"Of course," Mathias assured. "But before we wade in, do we have a spell to utter? Must we join hands or raise some magic together? What did Merlin say?"

"Nothing." Bram shrugged. "So I'm going to guess what he intended, based on what I know of my grandfather. Mangy old coot. Half-crazy, he was, at times."

Brow raised, Anka leveled a glance at Bram. *Crazy like a fox, perhaps. Crazy like his grandson.* No doubt, Bram was up to something.

Mathias smiled. "Once we've obtained the potion? I teleport out with it, try to find Morganna, then report back once she is dead, yes?"

Even to Anka's ears the plan sounded preposterous. After all the evil Mathias had inflicted on them, did he really believe they were that trusting? That stupid? He must, for he smiled smugly. Anka longed to slap the smarmy smile off his face, but she managed to refrain—barely.

"Of course," Bram returned smoothly. "Shall we?"

As they stepped up to the water's edge, Anka shivered both from the cold and Mathias hovering so closely beside her. She looked across to the opposite bank and caught Lucan watching her intently. He might appear relaxed with his feet apart and his hands clasped in front of him, but she wasn't fooled at all. He didn't want her near Mathias. His big, warrior-hard body was poised for a fight, and he would leap to her rescue at a moment's notice. Shock's stance wasn't much different.

Nerves dive-bombed Anka. She patted her still-flat belly. It would be months before her youngling would change the shape of her body, but life was growing inside of her. She didn't want to do anything to risk that, but she certainly hoped they could neutralize Morganna, if she appeared. And that somehow, someway, Mathias paid dearly today for his sins. No matter how much she told herself to look to the future, that need for revenge still flickered and burned inside her.

Anka waded into the river between Mathias and Bram. The nearly freezing water quickly surrounded her up to the knees. Anka gasped, feeling the chill surge up her body and roll through her blood. Bram reached out to steady her, but she shook him off. She couldn't look weak, or Mathias would find some way to use it to his advantage.

"I'm a-all right."

Bram snorted. "And I'm Guinevere."

"Nay, you wretch. Her face was much fairer than your ugly mug," Marrok laughed as he walked to join the others on the bridge.

She, Bram, and Mathias sloshed deeper into the water until it engulfed them to the waist.

"Submerge," Bram demanded, clenching his teeth. "Merlin would want us completely drenched in Nimue's waters before we ask this favor."

The task just got worse and worse. Not only did she hate the cold, but her magic simply wasn't as strong when she was spending all her energy shivering to stay warm. A glance up at Lucan proved that he wasn't any happier about this and looked ready to object. But she couldn't heed it. This must be done.

Holding her nose, Anka sank under the icy waters, dousing her shoulders, face, and head. The chill seeped under her skin, all the way to her bones, as she came up with a shuddering gasp. Beside her, Mathias and Bram both emerged, looking wet and stark and determined.

"I am Bram, son of Merlin's line. I have come to claim what he left behind." The wizard conjured a blade and cut into his palm, allowing several drops of his blood to plop into the lake. Then he reached across her and handed the knife to Mathias, prompting him with a glance.

Memories assailed her, of the terrifying wizard clutching a knife before carving his way into her flesh, laughing as she screamed while he etched his name into her bloody skin. Pushing down her fear, she sidestepped him and drifted closer to Bram, wrapping her arms around herself for comfort.

"I am Mathias, son of Nimue's line. I have come to claim what Merlin left behind."

At Mathias's uncertain expression, Bram nodded, forming a silent okay with his fingers. Mathias repeated Bram's gesture, slicing into his palm. He curled his hand into a fist and squeezed until several drops of blood splashed into the cold, dark waters.

The two wizards both turned to her expectantly. Shivering from both cold and terror, she took the blade from Mathias and drew in a ragged breath. "I am Anka, washerwoman, daughter of a crone, mother of a maiden, come to ask the spirits to release what Merlin left behind."

Bram smiled his silent encouragement. Cutting herself seemed barbaric and stupid, but so much of the ancient magic was tied up in blood, and she knew it would verify their identities to the spirits guarding the potion.

With a wince, she gouged her palm. Blood oozed from the wound. She turned her hand upside down, watching the slow drip of blood into the placid river, then disappearing into its depths.

Anka pocketed the knife and stood, waiting for whatever happened next. The river went utterly still, as if every creature all the way down to the moss held its breath. Quiet hushed over the land as the sun finally sank under the horizon and night enfolded them in its moonlit embrace.

Suddenly, the water rippled, starting against the banks with a gentle lapping, gradually becoming a disturbance, a choppy churn, then a violent wave that peaked over the banks. In the middle of the river, a geyser streamed, shooting high in the air in front of the three of them. The silvery moon backlit the spray, which rose higher and higher until it rivaled the towering, ancient trees around them.

Slowly, the geyser receded until it was nothing more than a tranquil fountain. At the top of the jet, a little crystal vial danced. Mathias lunged for it, but the spirits controlling the cascade delivered it right to Anka's hands. She grabbed the little bottle, holding the chilled glass in her shaky grip.

"I've got it." But what the devil did Bram want her to do now? Give it to Mathias, truly? That was the plan...but if she gave the vial to him, he would only slip through their fingers to threaten them another day, this time with Morganna by his side. Then Anka feared what they could do to her and the rest of the Doomsday Brethren.

Where was Felicia? She was supposed to be here already.

Out of the corner of her eye, she spied Sabelle surreptitiously texting, giving Duke and Felicia's "go" signal to teleport here. Anka sucked in a breath. *Hurry*! Until they arrived, she had to stall.

Anka stared at Mathias. She didn't have to work hard at all to pretend fear.

"Little witch..." Mathias tried to gentle his voice, but she saw the impatience behind his icy eyes, in the tense flick of his fingers as he gestured to her to give him the potion. Anka had little doubt that he would have taken it from her, but she could feel Bram near, watchful and ready. Mathias had to play nice. For the moment.

"Don't come near me!" Anka shouted.

On the banks of the river, Lucan glared at Mathias in silent warning, his face full of wrath, looking like an avenger just waiting for an excuse to slaughter the stain on magickind.

"Give me the potion," Mathias demanded.

"No!"

Mathias looked past her to the Doomsday Brethren's leader. "Bram?"

"We agreed to give the potion to him."

"I know," she all but pleaded. They *had* agreed...but Anka noticed that Bram hadn't actually ordered her to hand it over.

She clutched the bottle tighter to her chest.

Eyes narrowed with malicious intent, Mathias zipped his stare over to his battalion of lifeless Anarki soldiers. An instant later, the dark army, row upon row of Anarki as far as the eye could see, suddenly awoke. Like a group of zombies suddenly zapped with life, they turned and headed toward the river with menace.

Mathias had given them the mental command to fight. This was his declaration of war.

Anka screamed and braced herself for an onslaught, shoving the little bottle into her dripping jeans and whipping out the knife she'd stowed in her pocket. Magic wouldn't kill Anarki. She was going to have to hack her way through them.

"Call them back, Mathias!" Bram ordered.

"I think not. You promised me a potion." He turned to Anka, his stare drilling her with fury. "Give it to me or face them."

As one, Ice, Caden, and the twins all teleported to the bank in front of the advancing Anarki, human weapons at the ready, shielding her from their advancing march. From his position at the bridge, Marrok charged toward the fight, clearly ready for battle.

The sudden clash of blades and the hoarse cries of warriors filled the night. Nervously, Anka watched the battle rage. Five soldiers with a river at their back against hundreds of Anarki. Who could survive those odds? Yes, they could employ magic—at least for now—but even then, were there too many Anarki to fight? Dread slithered through her veins.

Suddenly, Lucan was gripping her arm and putting her behind him as he watched the Anarki advance. "Go!"

A moment later, a *whoosh* filled the air. Anka turned, looking around for Duke and Felicia's arrival. The Untouchable would save them from hell breaking loose or at least prevent Mathias from using more of his magic to destroy them.

Instead, a witch stood on a hill not far from the river, her flowing platinum hair shimmering in the moonlight and blowing in the chilly breeze. She wore a dress straight out of the sixth century. Her signature blared brightly like a neon sign.

"Morganna," The name fell from Anka's lips.

Dear God, they were doomed.

Bram had envisioned the ancient witch here, and he'd been

right. What the devil would happen now? A battle of epic proportions, she had no doubt.

Mathias's head snapped around, and he fixed narrowed eyes on Morganna's slight body in the distance, her hair and dress flapping in the breeze. Lucan's and Shock's stares both followed.

This plan was quickly going to hell.

Anka shoved the potion deeper into her pocket, trying not to alert Morganna that she had the vial. But Morganna's violet gaze zeroed in on her instantly. A gust of cold wind blew through Anka, also delivering a blast of malicious fury. The strong gale nearly dropped her to her knees. Even though she shivered, she refused to bow to Morganna's not-so-subtle warning.

"Give me the potion, washerwoman. You owe me for the gift growing in your belly."

"Leave, Anka!" Lucan shouted.

Teleport away. She'd promised Lucan that she would remain safe for their youngling. She must keep the potion safe, no matter what, or Morganna would plague them forever.

Anka knew that, after the huge secret she'd concealed from Lucan for so long, he needed to know that he could trust her. But if she left now, was she consigning her friends—and the mate of her heart—to die? This vial was their bargaining chip. She must decide quickly how best to use it.

"Stay here, Anka," Bram said. "She'll only follow you and corner you when you're alone."

"You don't know that, Bram. Now, Anka!" Lucan barked. "Keep our youngling safe."

Her mind raced. In the battle with the Anarki, Ice and Caden both withdrew their wands. She wasn't sure why, since Anarki were immune to magic. But they must have some plan. That would help the effort, but who would fight Morganna and Mathias?

Another *whoosh* interrupted the scene. With a spooked glance to her left, Anka spotted Duke and Felicia standing not ten meters away on the bank of the river, near Shock.

The Untouchable would neutralize Morganna and Mathias—a

relief, yes—but she would also prevent Caden, Ice, and the twins from using magic to fight the Anarki. *Bloody hell*! Now what? The handful of warriors had no prayer of defeating a battalion of Anarki alone. Mathias had given his brainless minions the command to fight, and they would continue to do so. Now that he could no longer use magic to command them to stand down, the only way to stop them all quickly was to kill Mathias.

"An Untouchable?" Morganna screamed suddenly.

"Anka," Bram instructed. "It's all right. Remember our deal. Give the bottle to Mathias."

Now? Voluntarily approach the man who had ravaged her life, her body, her mind, and give him the tool to control magickind's most powerful witch for his use? She glanced Lucan's way, not surprised that he looked ready to tear his former friend's head from his body.

Why did Bram want her to give the potion to Mathias? Because Morganna would then attack the evil wizard? Because they would be upholding their end of the bargain? Uncertain, one scenario after another whizzing around in her head, Anka played along and nodded, her insides quivering with fear.

The sounds of clanging swords and growled curses split the air. So much was happening so quickly. The outcome of a battle had never been less certain. Anka wanted to live, wanted to see her precious youngling born. Bram had a plan; she had to believe it would work.

With a shaking hand, Anka held out the potion toward Mathias. He took it from her with a greedy swipe of his hand, then shoved it in his coat pocket. His nearness horrified her, terrified her. She wanted to stand tall and brave and fight him, but memories overwhelmed her. She shrank back, a thousand flashbacks of the worst days of her existence pelting her unmercifully. All she could think about was putting as much distance between herself and him as possible.

But half of the Doomsday Brethren were fighting an army by themselves. Lucan glanced between her and his friends, clearly torn.

When Caden took a blade across the shoulder, Lucan leapt into action, joining the fray.

"Anka!" he yelled, command roughening his voice. "Go!"

Save herself, he meant. Disappear. Stop dividing his loyalties and let him help the others fight the Anarki—probably to their deaths. That's what he wanted her to do.

But she couldn't leave all of her friends and loved ones to die.

A shrill scream split the air. Anka startled, her stomach knotted in fear as Morganna clenched her delicate fists. Fury twisted the witch's face into a murderous visage as she belted out her displeasure. "Where hast thou come from, Untouchable? Be gone with you!"

"The Untouchable is not leaving, Morganna," Bram shouted. "Been waiting for us to retrieve the potion, have you?"

"For centuries. 'Tis mine, you spawn of Merlin! Mathias, give it to me!"

"Come get it," Bram drawled.

"Having the Untouchable here wasn't part of our agreement, Rion," Mathias snarled over the raging battle on the riverbanks.

"A little insurance policy." The smile Bram sent Mathias was anything but comforting. "I had a suspicion that Morganna would appear, and here she is. She cannot teleport away. Neither can you. So if you'd like to chase her down and give her that potion now, we'd all be happier."

But Anka knew Mathias had no intention of doing so. He'd rather control Morganna's awesome power than destroy it. Bram's smug grin indicated that Mathias was fooling no one.

Mathias cursed viciously, then turned to Anka, his evil eyes promising pain and suffering. He grabbed her by the arm. She gasped at his cruel hold, but couldn't break free.

"Send the Untouchable away or I will start killing you all, beginning with the pregnant washerwoman." He grabbed Bram's blade from her pocket and held it to her chest. "I may not be able to use magic to kill now, but this knife will cut through muscle and bone to reach her heart just as easily."

Anka trembled. The last time she'd been in Mathias's clutches, she'd been his victim. This time, she refused to go down without a fight.

Thinking back to the little bit of training Lucan had given her a few days ago, she elbowed Mathias in the stomach. With a grunt, he loosened his hold on her enough that she could break free. Then she whirled, raising her hand and curling her fingers to shove the heel of her palm into Mathias's nose. A satisfying geyser of blood erupted, along with his yelp of pain.

He dropped the knife and grabbed his face, blood pouring out from between his fingers. Anka picked up the glinting blade before it sank to the bottom of the dark waters and she held it up at Mathias, threatening him with it.

Above his splayed hands and the red, running blood, his eyes narrowed. "You won't hurt me."

Anka raised a brow at his muffled words. "Don't doubt that I will, every bit as much as you hurt me."

"Mathias!" Morganna shrieked, sounding as if she was in agony. "Get the Untouchable gone. Now!"

Anka didn't dare spare a glance at the other witch. She kept her focus on Mathias as he advanced on her. Suddenly, Lucan broke away from the battle and dashed to her side, shoving her behind him, his stance threatening.

"Are *you* going to fight me?" Mathias laughed. "You'll go into mate mourning as soon I rip your bond apart again, more like."

"No, I will fight for her to the death, preferably yours."

Before Mathias could deliver the scathing retort Anka felt sure sat on the tip of his tongue, Morganna screeched again. "The potion! I must have it, Mathias..."

Her pitiful whimpers resounded over the *clang* of the battle. Lucan stood by protectively as Anka glanced up at the witch, then gasped.

Morganna's hair had grown a foot and turned an utterly dingy gray. The hollows of her cheeks were sunken into the bones, the flesh around her eyes deeply lined. She looked feeble.

"What's happening?" Anka wondered aloud.

Bram turned to the witch. "Where's your beauty gone, Morganna? Magic been holding you together? Oops, no magic here now..."

The ancient witch whipped her hands in front of her face. They'd suddenly become the gnarled hands of an old woman, with spotted, wrinkly skin and brittle nails. Morganna screamed, the sound so blood-curdling and shrill that Anka had to cover her ears with her palms or risk having her eardrums burst. Everyone else did the same.

Anka's mind raced. Could Felicia kill Morganna simply by standing here and disabling the magic holding the old bitch together? Could it be that easy to rid magickind of her scourge?

Did she dare leave it to chance?

Shivering in the freezing water, the cold January wind blowing over her wet skin, Anka pocketed Bram's knife again and lunged around Lucan to tear the vial of Merlin's potion from Mathias's coat pocket.

He protested and grabbed for her arm. Lucan snapped brutal fingers around Mathias's wrist in warning. "You will never touch her again."

"Bring that back to me, you stupid bitch," Mathias barked at her over Lucan's shoulder. "Or I will enjoy hearing you beg me to rape you again, knowing this wanker will suffer and lose his mind once more with every moment that passes."

"Mathias!" Morganna's piercing cry sounded desperate and wobbly. Anka glanced at the witch again to see that she'd aged half a lifetime in the past thirty seconds.

"Bugger off, Morganna. I'll get the potion eventually. I have to put this bitch in her place now."

"You swine!" Morganna cried, then began to run as quickly as her aged, unsteady gait would take her.

Where the devil was she going? Anka didn't understand the old witch at all until Morganna finally disappeared on the far side of the hill and into the nearby field. A cyclone-like wind descended next. Then poof, Morganna was gone, having teleported away the moment she moved beyond Felicia's Untouchable defenses.

"Fuck!" Mathias yelled. "Double-crossing viper!"

Anka blinked at his curse. So Mathias had planned this all along. He'd used the Doomsday Brethren to procure the potion. Once successful, he'd be holding the one thing that would have made Morganna bow to his commands. With her as his minion, he'd planned to rule and enslave magickind with the most awesome power ever, save Merlin's.

Together, the Doomsday Brethren had foiled their plan.

But she didn't doubt that Mathias had more tricks up his sleeve.

"There went your partner in crime, Mathias?" Bram ribbed him. "Did you think I hadn't guessed? You knew exactly who and what you needed to retrieve the potion. She knew precisely where to find it. You waited until you thought you had everything …but you didn't count on us being smart."

Mathias's eyes narrowed, not on Bram—but on her. He was going to lunge for her again. She yanked the steely blade from her pocket and crouched, battle ready.

"Lucan!" Caden called from the battle on the riverbank behind them. The cry was desperate, panicked.

Anka didn't dare look, but Lucan did—and he swore.

"Anka, please go. You promised. My brother needs me."

Or he was going to die at the Anarki's hands. She heard the unspoken words in his voice.

But if she left them now, they'd be down one warrior. She might not have much training, but she and Sabelle alone could use their magic around Felicia. Time to start saving the others before it was too late.

"Go help Caden." She shoved him toward his brother. "Sabelle and I will manage."

Lucan sent her a hard stare, torn and worried and furious all at once. "Anka…"

"Trust me." She looked him right in the eyes. "I know I haven't always given you reason to, but please. I can do this and stay alive."

He stared, so obviously torn.

"Brother!" Caden's voice sounded weaker, even more desperate.

"Go," she urged Lucan.

"I love you." He darted off into the fray, pulling some nasty firearm from the small of his back.

"Brave," Mathias commented with a sickening smile. "But stupid. You can't fight me. I scare you too much."

"Sabelle!" Lucan called out to the lovely half-siren as he joined the battle. "The spell. Use it now!"

Sabelle hesitated a moment, then nodded, her pale hair shining in the moonlight.

What spell? Anka had no time to wonder before Lucan punched one hooded monster, then shot another right between the eyes. Black blood spurted everywhere.

"Let me hear your voice, Anka. Unleash it," Lucan commanded.

She gaped. He wanted her to wail? "I'll kill everyone!"

"Trust me. I've worked it out. Do it!"

As Mathias lunged at her, one hand reaching for Bram's knife, the other trying to cover her mouth, she didn't have time to question Lucan. She simply had to take a leap of faith and believe he could save her, the same way he had to trust her to stay alive.

She opened her mouth and began to shriek, her wail high and sharp and loud. Instantly, Mathias crouched down and slapped his palms over his ears. The rest of the Doomsday Brethren looked blessedly unaffected.

"How are you bloody doing this with an Untouchable here?"

"Wailing isn't magic," Bram gloated. "And my sister can use hers to shield us even with Felicia nearby. Enjoy your slow, painful death."

Sabelle was sheltering everyone else with a spell? That Lucan had prearranged? Hope filled her.

Black blood from Anarki carcasses began to ooze down the grassy banks and seep into the river. The sound of gunshots echoed in the night. Blades clashed. The desperate sounds of combat and pain surrounded them. There were still too many Anarki for all the wizards to fight. Sabelle cast an anxious glance at Ice, who fought off three hooded monsters at once, determination tightening his face into something battle-hard and raging. How long could that last when he and the others were outnumbered fifty to one?

Anka jerked farther away from Mathias. She had to kill him quickly. Besides Sabelle, she was the only other person thus far who could use her magic with Felicia present. Neither of them had the skills to fight one person in hand-to-hand combat, much less a flipping army. And Sabelle couldn't stop protecting the others from the washerwoman's wail to pull out some warrior-like magic, or all their loved ones would die.

Ending Mathias for good was their only hope.

How the devil was she going to do that? Her mind raced as she watched Bram curse, then grab Mathias's hair at the back of the head, slamming the incapacitated wizard's face into a nearby boulder. Anka heard a sickening crack of bone. Mathias screamed in pain, but Anka kept wailing, high and clear, her voice ringing in the night. Mathias crumpled into the freezing water, his ears bleeding. Before the splashing had even subsided, Bram leapt to the banks, pulling some nasty gun from his pocket and pointing it at the Anarki. Seconds later, a shot rang out, and another Anarki fell.

Anka risked a glance over her shoulder at the battle on the banks. The odds were better with seven trained warriors—but it was still hopeless—bullets whizzing, blades resounding, and shouts echoing. Mayhem ruled. Unless she killed Mathias, she might lose everyone she held dear, especially the father of her unborn youngling, the wizard she loved.

She'd been Mathias's victim once. She refused to be one again.

Sharpening her wail, she prowled closer to him. He tried to crawl away, and looked in Felicia's direction, but Duke stood sentry over his fair mate. He seemed to be torn between protecting her and helping his brothers in arms.

"Sunshine," Duke implored her, grabbing her shoulders. "Please, love. Trust them. All of them. Because you trust me. No one will let you down. They *need* their magic."

Anka drew in a bracing breath, silently imploring Felicia to believe in all of them.

"I-I'll try," the Untouchable promised.

Suddenly, Mathias dove toward the opposite bank. Once on foot, he might be able to sprint away until, like Morganna, he teleported beyond their reach. It might alleviate their problem today, but he'd only come back again and again and again, like a pesky insect. She had to squash him now. Eventually, her wail would kill him, but it was a slow process. The more time she gave him to plot and scheme, the more likely he would find a way to escape.

Using her magic, Anka quickly teleported to the edge of the battle. Still screaming out the deathly howl, she searched for Ice. She found him defending the western side of the melee, parrying two Anarki with a blade in his right hand. In his left, he held a gun and popped off shots, hitting one black-blooded goon after another. The temperature among the dead beings was even colder than the river.

When she approached Ice from behind, the big warrior didn't hesitate. He tossed a glance over his shoulder, and they made eye contact for a split second. She drew the blade from her pocket, holding it up. He frowned, then nodded, and she knew he recalled that when he'd battled Mathias for a seat on the magical Council, he'd discovered that his blood, pure of heart and intentions, was incorruptible—and poison to Mathias. Anka had to hope that held true today.

"It's all right. Do what you need," he shouted above the din.

Wincing as she wailed, she sliced the blade along his thigh, not too deeply, but he still froze for a moment as she dragged the blade through his flesh. She coated one side of the knife in his blood, then flipped it over and whisked the other side of the blade through the bleeding incision, until the knife dripped red.

Suddenly, Lucan managed to light up the riverbanks with

blazing strips of flames, even as Mathias tried to crawl away. Anka had seen him use that power before. Lucan could light a blaze to set the world on fire when he must.

On the field across the river, Anka saw that Felicia had closed her eyes, focusing on heeding her mate and allowing the wizards to use their magic. She was letting people in, trusting them to use their powers for good. *Thank God*!

Smiling, Anka teleported back to Mathias. She hoped like hell that her little plan worked.

As she appeared again behind him, Mathias scrambled to find some way out of the river and away from her wailing. She couldn't let that happen. But the sight of him crawling in fear satisfied her bruised soul deeply. After all, he'd made her swallow all pride, forced her to get on her hands and knees and come to him, despite her bleeding and humiliation. Now the tables were turned.

Mathias turned to avoid the fire barrier and tried to crawl back to the other bank, to disappear into the battle. Anka blocked his pitiful attempts at escape, trapping him between her unforgiving blade and Lucan's fire at his back. Behind her, she heard a giant crack like thunder. Anka glanced behind her and saw a rain of bullets falling from the sky, each hitting an Anarki in the head. Then Caden quickly multiplied himself, using the power that only he possessed to create an army that rivaled the number of Anarki. The battle expanded, louder, more brutal—but much less one-sided.

Quickly, the Doomsday Brethren fought their way to the south edge of the fight and waged war until they forced the Anarki to retreat right against the river. Then Lucan set the grassy bank ablaze. Caden's cloned soldiers controlled the east and west perimeters of the battle, immune to the flames. Soon, the soulless Anarki had nowhere to turn without stepping into a Doomsday Brethren blade or the funeral pyre Lucan had made. Then the slaughter began, Anarki gaping and howling as they flailed in the fatal trap and died.

But nothing could cover the sound of Anka's wail.

Mathias scrambled to his feet, covering his ears again. "Stop it, you banshee bitch! Shock!"

Anka stared at Shock, mentally warning him not to interfere between her and Mathias. He stood impassively.

Satisfaction roiling thick and hot through her veins, she approached Mathias. The blade she clutched in her hand still dripped with Ice's blood. Never before had she been a violent woman, but with deep satisfaction, she shoved that knife as deep into Mathias's belly as she could.

He grunted, and his eyes bulged in pain. He hunched over and his skin faded to gray as the poison of Ice's purity sank in. Straining for a breath of air, he groped around his torso for the handle of the knife. Anka merely twisted it deeper, vengeance thrumming through her.

The moment was so bloody sweet.

"That's for Ice's sister, Gailene," Anka stopped wailing long enough to say.

"Shock!" Mathias demanded. "You've served me…"

He nodded, his dark head and sunglasses bobbing. "I know exactly what to do."

Mathias collapsed onto his back, and the knife slid free. He clutched the open, bleeding wound in his stomach with one hand and tried to cover one ear with the other as he writhed on the ground in agony. "Good. Yes… Hurry!"

Shock was all stealth as he approached Mathias.

"Don't!" Anka warned her former lover, her friend, raising her blade high. He'd better not try to save the fucking rapist who had nearly destroyed her, not after everything she and Shock had meant to one another.

"Calm down, Anka. This is for the best."

"For you to save him? No!" She'd stopped wailing and she knew it. She couldn't afford to argue with Shock now, but to believe that he would help Mathias after everything the monster had done to her… It bloody hurt.

"It's all right," he promised.

Shock lunged—but not to take Mathias away. Instead, he dove toward her and plucked the potion out of her pocket. Then he ran as if the hounds of hell chased him.

"Shock!" Anka screamed after him.

They needed that potion. Morganna would come after it again, no doubt. What would they do if Morganna's demise wasn't in their hands? How would they coax Shock into giving it to them so they could end Morganna for good?

Before she could even think about chasing Shock, Mathias grabbed her ankle in a surprisingly strong grip and pulled her roughly to the ground. She fell with a hard crash into the river, careful to keep the blade out of the water. She needed whatever was left of Ice's blood to finish this bastard off for good.

And she needed to keep wailing.

She gathered a breath to begin her song again. With maniacal eyes, Mathias shoved her against his bleeding body. "Fucking shut up, banshee. No more!"

Shaking her head, Anka wailed louder, until he released her. She would not bow. She would not give in. She would not let him hurt her—or anyone else—ever again.

Mathias covered his ears and scrambled back. She got to her feed and advanced on him like an avenging angel, knife raised above her head.

"The first stab was for Gailene." She stood over him, legs spread, and stared, putting the same fear into him that he'd once wielded over her with such merciless delight. "This one is for me."

Mathias gaped at her with something Anka never thought she'd see in his eyes: genuine fear. Knowing that she'd served justice and struck a blow to all those who had been wronged by this monster—Ice, Tabitha, so many of the magical families he'd slaughtered—Anka didn't hesitate.

She plunged the blade deep into his heart and wailed the sharpest notes yet of her banshee song. Within seconds, he fell limply to his back, icy eyes stark and wide and unseeing. Behind her there was a giant thud as the Anarki, powered only by Mathias's life force, fell as one to the ground. Lucan raised his hands like an orchestra conductor to grow his fire. The Doomsday Brethren all scrambled away to watch the cold, hooded figures burn in one giant pyre.

The fire hissed and crackled, but a moment later, a violent tumble of air cycled directly beside Mathias. Then Rhea appeared, sprawled out, stabbed, and ears bleeding, every bit as lifeless as the evil bastard she'd adored.

Sabelle teleported over to her as Anka's voice cracked into silence. Bram's sister knelt to the pair and touched their skin. "Dead."

Bram jogged over to check the bodies himself. His face broke out into a grin that widened into a full-bellied laugh. "Tying their life forces together worked. How bloody perfect!"

Ice patted him on the back. "Two for one. I'm impressed."

Anka ignored them, looking for Lucan. Suddenly, he emerged from the middle of the snarling blaze and hit her at a dead run, wrapping his arms around her so tightly, she knew he would never let go. "You did it, love. You killed the notorious Mathias d'Arc with nothing more than a blade, a little blood, and your very special gift. I always knew you were incredible, but now…so will the world."

Anka slipped her arms around his neck and pressed kisses to his face. "We all did it. Together, we rid magickind of the worst threat in centuries. I don't care if anyone knows my role. I only care for peace. And love. Would you take me to your house?" She looked at him with her heart in her eyes. "I mean, to our home?"

Chapter Nineteen

Gratitude warred with dizzying happiness as Lucan lifted Anka into his arms, tight against his chest. "Of course, love, home is where you belong. I'll never let you leave me again. I will fight for you. I will die for you. And I will love you every day."

Wet and shivering, covered in mud and blood, and fresh from dispensing justice, this wasn't the Anka he'd fallen in love with over a hundred years ago. This Anka had endured hell and walked through fire. Like a phoenix, she'd risen from the ashes stronger, better. He had a deeper understanding of this woman, her fears, her sorrows, her needs. Lucan swore to God he'd do whatever he must to fill her up, heart, body, and soul everyday for the rest of their centuries. This Anka was more dear and beautiful than ever.

As he made to teleport away, he looked up at the small audience who had gathered around Mathias's and Rhea's bodies. He thanked God that, save a few nicks and scratches, they all looked no worse for the wear. Sabelle's eyes watered with happy tears. Ice, with his arm slung around his pretty mate, sent him a nod, as if congratulating him on a job well done. Marrok lifted his sword in salute. Bram sent him a superior smile, as if to suggest he'd known Lucan would be reunited with Anka all along. Lucan wasn't sure he was ready to forgive Bram yet. But he'd gotten his woman back. In the end, nothing else mattered. The twins flashed him a wry grin. Yes, the wicked duo knew exactly what he and Anka would be doing next.

"Have fun. And don't do anything we wouldn't do," Ronan suggested with a waggle of his brows.

Raiden laughed. "Don't worry, mate. That leaves you with plenty of options."

Since the wizards had shagged their way through most of the UK for decades?

"Most assuredly," Duke drawled, holding a tired but glowing Felicia to his side.

"Splendid advice." Lucan grinned. In fact, he couldn't wait to get started.

In his arms, Anka laughed. God, it was good to hear that sound again.

Caden clapped him on the back and sent Anka a gentle smile. "You deserve it. Both of you. Love well and forever."

"I'd like that." Her voice shook, but this time it wasn't from the chill, Lucan knew. She trembled with emotion.

"I'd love that." Lucan held her closer. "Like I'll always love you. Let's go."

Anka caressed his face, love shining from her amber eyes. "Take me home."

Lucan kissed the tip of her nose, then closed his eyes and pictured their bedroom. Moments later, they stood in the middle of the room they'd shared during the mated years of their past. He lowered her to her feet, pulling her to his chest. She tilted her head up to meet his kiss. Lucan couldn't help himself. He covered her mouth greedily with his own. His hunger for her would never be sated. His love for her would never end.

Suddenly, she pulled back, gaze downcast, putting distance between them. He gazed at her with concern.

"Can you forgive me for not telling you the truth sooner?" she whispered.

"Love…I was hurt that you felt you couldn't trust me with the truth or believed for a moment that I didn't see you as worthy. Never doubt me again. I will always be here. Just as I will never doubt you again. You will always be my moon, sun, and stars."

The yearning to believe him softened her tear-filled eyes. "Even if I'm a banshee?"

He cupped her face in his hands. "Especially because you're a banshee. You saved us today and did something incredibly brave. Something that saved lives. Something magickind will celebrate forever. I couldn't be more proud. I know I'll be proud of our daughter, as well."

Anka placed her hand over her stomach. "Thank you for the gifts of your love, your seed, and your forever."

"Forever?" He searched her eyes.

Anka smiled shyly. "As I become a part of you, you become a part of me. I will be honest, good, and true. I heed your Call. 'Tis you I seek. From this moment on, there is no other for me but you."

Forever.

Lucan didn't wait for a shower or dinner or even another breath. He picked Anka up, pinned her to their bed, and made their clothes disappear with a snap. Moments later, he sank deep inside her, wordlessly promising her that he would be her mate, her lover, her friend, and her heart for the rest of their centuries. With her soft, welcoming body and her passionate cries through the hours of loving that night, she vowed to be the same to him.

As the sun rose, his body was sated, but his heart would never stop hungering for her. He held her close, her head resting on his chest. He couldn't take his eyes from her delicate face, swollen lips, or the crescents of her dark lashes against her pale skin.

He kissed her forehead. Sun streamed through their windows as her lashes fluttered open, and she met his gaze with a devotion that clutched at his heart. Lucan held her tighter. A new dawn. A new day. A new beginning for them.

"I love you." He kissed her gently.

"I know," she said softly. "I finally believe that. Never doubt again that I love you, too."

Photograph by Marti Corn

About The Author

Shayla Black (aka Shelley Bradley) is the *New York Times* bestselling author of over 30 sizzling contemporary, erotic, paranormal, and historical romances for multiple print and electronic publishers. She lives in Texas with her husband, munchkin, and one very spoiled cat. In her "free" time, she enjoys reality TV, reading and listening to an eclectic blend of music.

Shayla has won or placed in over a dozen writing contests, including Passionate Ink's Passionate Plume, Colorado Romance Writers Award of Excellence, and the National Reader's Choice Awards. *Romantic Times* has awarded her Top Picks, a KISS Hero Award and a nomination for Best Erotic Romance.

A writing risk-taker, Shayla enjoys tackling writing challenges with every book.

Connect with me online:

Website: www.shaylablack.com
Facebook: www.facebook.com/ShaylaBlackAuthor
Twitter: www.twitter.com/@shayla_black

Also from Shayla Black/Shelley Bradley:

EROTIC ROMANCE
The Wicked Lovers Series
Available now:
WICKED TIES
DECADENT
DELICIOUS
SURRENDER TO ME
BELONG TO ME
"Wicked to Love" novella
MINE TO HOLD
OURS TO LOVE

Sexy Capers Series
Available now:
BOUND AND DETERMINED
STRIP SEARCH
Coming soon:
"Arresting Desire" – HOT IN HANDCUFFS Anthology

NAUGHTY LITTLE SECRET (as Shelley Bradley)
"Watch Me" – SNEAK PEEK Anthology (as Shelley Bradley)
DANGEROUS BOYS AND THEIR TOY
"Her Fantasy Men" – FOUR PLAY Anthology

With Lexi Blake:
THEIR VIRGIN CAPTIVE
THEIR VIRGIN'S SECRET
Coming Soon:
THEIR VIRGIN CONCUBINE

PARANORMAL ROMANCE
The Doomsday Brethren Series
Available now:
TEMPT ME WITH DARKNESS
"Fated" novella
SEDUCE ME IN SHADOW
POSSESS ME AT MIDNIGHT
"Mated" – HAUNTED BY YOUR TOUCH anthology
ENTICE ME AT TWILIGHT

HISTORICAL ROMANCE
(as Shelley Bradley)
Available now:
THE LADY AND THE DRAGON
ONE WICKED NIGHT
STRICTLY SEDUCTION
Coming Soon:
STRICTLY FORBIDDEN

CONTEMPORARY ROMANCE (as Shelley Bradley)
Available now:
A PERFECT MATCH

Continue reading for a brief excerpt for

Tempt Me With Darkness

Doomsday Brethren, Book 1

Chapter One

Present day England

Beside the lush banks of a pond, a woman beckoned, familiar. Yet Marrok of Cadbury had never seen her face in his life.

Vivid grass and multicolored flowers rioted around her. A cityscape towered in the background. None of that held his gaze rapt. Her bare-to-the-skin nakedness and dangerous beauty did.

The woman's sable hair swept over one pale shoulder, curling under the swell of a generous breast topped by a berry nipple—and framing a birthmark he knew well.

She no longer possessed the platinum tresses into which he'd once thrust his hands. Her new face was delicate—higher cheekbones, pert nose, pillowy mouth—but the siren could not disguise herself from him. Black lashes fluttered over violet eyes that had long haunted his nightmares.

Morganna.

Lust crashed into him, a battering ram to the gut. Need stiffened his cock. He wanted her as he never had, with a frightening desperation. Bollocks! Was he daft enough to let her lure him to further doom?

Acid hatred mixed with clawing desire. He tried to look away, but his gaze caressed her small waist, her curved hips, the moist flesh between her thighs glistening. Luminous, her smile coaxed him to touch her, challenged him to walk away.

Marrok didn't—couldn't— do either.

Morganna bewitched him more now than she had on their wind-drenched night of shared pleasure an eon ago.

The strawberry mark low between her breasts brought back memories of pale moonlight surrounding them as he'd succumbed to temptation and tupped her senseless. For that mistake, he'd paid dearly.

With the last fifteen centuries.

Mist swirled around her like the mystical fog of legend, as if caressing her. Though she was deadly, Morganna in this new form captivated him. Today, society had clinical terms for his obsession. He cared not. Getting the treacherous bitch to release him from his hell . . . nothing else mattered.

With an alluring curl of her fingers, she summoned him. Marrok gritted his teeth. To yield would only mean further torture. But his body betrayed him, inching closer, his cock swelling painfully. Cursing, he closed his eyes.

If he must resist her to be free, he feared he was doomed.

Marrok opened his eyes as a fresh rush of desire slammed him. Want was a luxury; this woman he *needed*. The feeling was as new as a baby's first breath . . . and as welcome as the plague. And likely illusory, merely one of Morganna's tricks.

Though he dug his fingers into his thighs, her haunting eyes pleaded with him. Marrok very nearly surrendered to the urge to touch her.

Then she waved her hand. Suddenly, she clutched to her naked breasts the ornate red book he knew meant the difference between his life and death, and she backed away.

Nay!

Marrok launched himself at her. They fell to the ground in a tangle of breaths, arms, and legs. The book fell beside them, its maddening lock still firmly closed.

Before he could grab it, she latched slender arms around his neck and arched, distracting him with her lush curves.

"Marrok, love me."

Her plea spiked his fevered lust. He ached to sink deep into her. But he had to resist this fatal woman. Somehow.

"Release me," he growled.

She clung tighter, then writhed against his erection. By God, she was wet. He was on fire for her. A heartbeat from explosion. A mere moment from forgetting how treacherous she was.

"Open the book!"

"You want me." Her whisper made him shiver.

Why deny that? A waste of time and breath.

As she wriggled under him, lightning chased across his skin. Like a fool, he thrust against her and groaned. The need to utterly possess her screamed through him. Later, he'd remember all the reasons he could not.

Marrok dropped his hands to her thighs and pried them wider. "If you tempt me thus, you will take what I give you. All I give you."

"Anything."

Morganna's nipples burned his chest as he lifted her legs over his arms. From one instant to the next, his clothes melted away and he poised himself at her entrance.

Groaning, he buried his face in her fragrant neck. Incredible. Inevitable. More intoxicating than ever. Marrok had sworn never to touch Morganna again—a promise he had kept for centuries—but now . . . he *had* to be inside her.

"Everything . . ." she encouraged.

As he surged forward, Morganna grabbed the book. Desire chained him; he could not move, not even to snatch it from her grasp.

With a wave of her pale hand, Morganna unlocked the volume. The cover fell open, revealing a hint of its pages, as she faded away.

"Give it to me!"

He shouted at fog. She—and the book—were gone.

Again, she'd used her power against him. Desire sizzled deep but he was, as ever, cursed. Desolation slashed him, leaving his soul to bleed.

His anguish made no sense. He'd never mourn Morganna's loss. He would, in fact, spit on her grave if she had one.

"I am the key." Her soft entreaty swept through the wind. "Find me."

Marrok dragged himself to his feet, suppressing a primal scream. He must hunt her. That cityscape behind the pond he recognized as London. There, he could find her. His torment would never end without that book—and without a taste of her flesh.

Around him, something rattled. Marrok sat up with a startled gasp, his bed rumpled, eyes wide. Panting, he scanned his surroundings. Bare walls, carved bed. A sword beside his hand. Glock under his pillow.

His cottage, not a mist-draped clearing. No Morganna.

The book! Marrok whipped his gaze around. On his bedside table rested the leather-bound tome. The vehicle of his never-ending torment, the key to his freedom, was still here and still locked.

It had been but a dream.

Or perhaps a message? Though it had been centuries, Morganna had once enjoyed reaching from her exile to taunt him in sleep. He dared not disregard the message—she had returned to this mortal realm as an ethereal brunette, able to unlock the volume and intent on thieving it.

He rose, determined to find the sorceress in her new disguise. She alone could end the torture of his ages-old existence. Shadow and torment her he would, until she granted him what he wanted most in life.

Death.

A sharp rap against the cottage's front window startled Marrok—the same sound that had awakened him. He hadn't had a visitor in a decade, and preferred it that way. Guests were both unexpected and unwelcome.

Marrok slid the book into the safe hidden beneath loose floorboards in his bedroom, then took up his sword and stalked down the hall. As he slid around the corner, his heart raced with the anticipation of impending battle. Morning sunlight seeped through the window, illuminating dust motes and casting a human shadow onto the gleaming wooden floor.

If someone had come to take the book from him, he would greet them with bloodshed.

Marrok crept forward, crouched for attack. The shadow disappeared. A faint crunch of footsteps outside replaced the silhouette. He slipped toward the door silently, weapon in hand.

Hey, freak of nature," a familiar male voice called from outside, punctuated by another knock. "Are you in there?"

Heaving an annoyed sigh, Marrok yanked the door open to find a nightmare nearly as bad as the one that had awakened him. Golden hair spiked above sleek brows and wicked blue eyes. A glittery Hollywood smile belied the gifted wizard's immense power. Bram Rion. Marrok groaned. Now he would never have any peace.

"Are you calling *me* a freak of nature? Coming from you, that is rich."

"If today is your day to conduct beheadings, count me out." Bram flashed the million-dollar smile that had seduced magickind into seeing things his way for four hundred years. Marrok frowned and propped his sword against a nearby wall.

Bram paused outside. "Are you going to invite me past the magic circle guarding your place, or must I continue to stand on the mat?"

"If I do not?" Marrok challenged, raising a dark brow. He was heartily tempted not to. The magical coxcomb amused him at times . . . but Marrok didn't dare trust him.

"If you don't let me past, I can't tell you something juicy . . ."

Bram would not go away until he spilled his secret, though Marrok cared little what the wizard had to say. He must find Morganna in her new guise, then force, coerce, or beg her into unlocking that accursed book and setting him free.

"Enter," he huffed.

Bram stepped inside and shut the door behind him. "You look like hell. Did you sleep in yesterday's trousers?"

Marrok stared at his rumpled chinos. "Did you come all this

way to be my mum?"

"If you need one . . . " Bram shrugged, mischief lurking in his eyes.

"What the hell do you want? Say it and be gone," Marrok demanded, striding to his room to snatch a fresh T-shirt and old jeans out of a drawer. Then he trekked across the hall to his bathroom.

Bram followed, lingering outside after Marrok slammed the door in his face.

After donning fresh clothes, he turned to a mirror and slid a brush through his dark hair. Ancient eyes stared back at him, filled with misery, anger, and thwarted lust. He *did* look like hell.

"To talk to you," Bram said through the door. "You know that only something gravely important could bring me to the Creepified Forest."

"Important to magickind." Not necessarily important to him.

"Since I'm the only friend you have, it's important to you,
as well."

"I have no friends." Marrok pictured Bram gritting his teeth. He smiled.

"All right, then. I am the only living being who knows of your immortality and still speaks to you."

Marrok grunted and reached for his toothbrush. "I am not interested. I must hunt."

"The local market too civilized for your Dark Ages upbringing?"

Marrok wrenched open the bathroom door, staring at Bram as if he were a bloodsucking insect. "Is magickind so starved for a comedian that you suffice?"

Bram sighed. "I really have come for a reason."

Though the wizard loved to antagonize him, Marrok knew the darling of magickind would not visit without cause.

"You will only pester me until I give in. Why are you here?"

"Because I've had a vision."

Vision. Being in the same room with anything or anyone

magical was enough to give him hives. Having Bram around was like a permanent case of leprosy. "Why tell me? You must have a magical healer for this sort of thing."

"Because when it comes true, it will involve you."

"I involve myself in nothing." He shouldered past Bram and headed for the kitchen.

"And all of magickind knows it. Ever heard of the Book of Doomsday?"

"Nay."

"It's also called the Doomsday Diary."

His uninvited guest placed his hand on Marrok's shoulder. Immediately, he sensed a tightening under his forehead, then between the temples. Bloody hell, the bastard was trying to sneak into his thoughts. Marrok jerked away and slammed a mental door between them.

Bram reared back in surprise, speculation on his face. Clearly, humans were often unable to block him from their minds. But Marrok hadn't survived half of forever without learning a few tricks.

"Never have I heard of the accursed book by either name. Do not touch me or attempt to invade my head again, or I will slice you in two."

"It would be amusing for you to try, human." The wizard snorted. "You've never seen the book? It's red with gilt inlays, and is small, ornate, and very old."

That sounded like . . . Marrok shoved the thought away, lest Bram read it. No reason to add fuel to his fire.

"You *do* know something." Excitement revved up Bram's face. "All magickind knows of the Book of Doomsday. It's part of our folklore. I thought you might know of the book because it was created by my grandfather's nemesis."

"I did not know Merlin well. Why should I know of his enemies?"

"Well, Morganna was your lover."

Marrok grimaced. "You have confused a one-time sating of lust with a real bond."

"She's the reason you're immortal. She cursed you with the book, didn't she?"

By hell's fire, how could Bram know that? "I know naught of it."

"You're lying."

"Shove off!" Marrok stomped to the door, opened it, and gestured with a wave.

"A moment more . . ." The wizard sent him a sober stare. "I want to share my vision with you."

"Of ?"

"The future. Watch."

"Keep your visions to yourself, you droning codpiece."

Bram ignored him, grabbed his arm, and waved a hand in front of his face. A picture appeared before Marrok's eyes. He fell into it, unable to back away.

Nighttime. A darkened home, once sprawling and lovely, now decayed. A small mass of people walked toward it. Some were clad in gray robes trimmed in red. Others wore normal dress and oddly vacant stares.

Intrigued against his will, Marrok peered closer, then reeled back in shock. The people in robes dragged the others toward the house with ropes about their necks. The air of excitement surrounding the berobed was palpable.

"Who are the people dressed like friars?" he asked.

"Definitely not clergy. They're part of the Anarki."

Marrok flinched. Even in his isolation, he'd known of the chaos and fear they created in their rise to power two centuries ago.

Once inside the run-down manor, a man in robes waited in an empty room, surrounded by a circle of flickering candles. His face obscured, he hovered over the still body of a naked man who, if human, looked to be about thirty.

"Who lies there?" Marrok asked Bram.

"Mathias d'Arc."

Even a seasoned warrior like Marrok shuddered at the name.

Mathias was the magical equivalent of Genghis Khan, Caligula, Vlad Dracula, and Hannibal Lecter rolled into one. Cruel, clever, hedonistic, rapacious. Brilliantly evil. A wizard of great power and no conscience, Mathias wouldn't be happy until everyone in his path was either enslaved or dead.

"What are the Anarki about?" Marrok hissed.

"Watch."

As the group entered the shadowed room, they formed a circle around the candles, pushing some of the entranced people inside, closer to Mathias, who lay still as death.

The robed wizard who had been waiting stood at Mathias's head and raised his arms. "We, the Deprived, have waited centuries for this night. The Privileged will hear our thunder and feel only terror until they give us all they've denied our kind. Until the 'Social Order' laws prohibiting any with 'undesirable' traits and bloodlines from holding vital positions are dissolved, they will know war and pain and death. They do not know that we, the faithful, have waited for salvation. Tonight, our patience will be rewarded."

A cheer went up from those in robes. The others were silent.

From a distant part of the house, a clock chimed low and loud, gong, gong, gong . . . Twelve times. The room seemed to hold its collective breath. Then silence. Mathias's eyes opened wide. Around him, the candles flickered. His followers gasped.

The ceremony leader knelt, then whispered reverently,

"You've returned!"

"My faithful Anarki . . ." Mathias's voice was thin and strained. "My sleeping draught fooled the Brethren but you believed in me. They thought me dead?"

"Very much so," the first replied.

"Excellent. Did they all pass into their nextlife?"

"Within days of your sleep."

"Your name?"

"Zain Denzell."

Continue reading for a brief excerpt for

Mine To Hold

On Sale June 5, 2012

Mine To Hold

"Please, just let me go. I know best, really. If you'll . . . do this for me—"

"You mean leave you now, just like I did after I touched every inch of your body and got deeper inside you than any man ever has? Leave again simply because you asked me to? Because you think you know best?"

Tyler advanced even closer, and suddenly, the door to his bedroom was at her back. He planted both of his large hands on either side of her head and leaned in. Her heart picked up speed viciously. That woodsy, testosterone-oozing scent swamped Delaney, and her legs trembled beneath her. She flattened herself against the door . . . but Tyler kept coming closer, leaning in, his green gaze darkening, drilling into hers.

"How well do you think me listening to you worked out last time?" he challenged.

Terribly. Eric had eventually screamed that Tyler slinking off only made him wonder how long they'd been fucking each other. Her protestations otherwise had fallen on completely deaf ears. The positive pregnancy test had been the death knell of their marriage.

By then, Tyler had been long gone, and she'd missed him so much.

Delaney closed her eyes. "This is different."

"Yeah. It's worse. Seth could lose you for the rest of his little life. *I* could lose you forever instead of for two years. No. Last time I saw you, I listened to you about everything. This time? It's my way."

Tyler took her face in his hands, cradling jaw in his big hands. His stare zeroed in on her mouth. He pressed the length of his body against hers. The thin T-shirt she wore did nothing to protect her from the blistering heat of his body. He notched his heavy, steely erection against her mound. Delaney's heart stuttered.

And then his lips hovered right above hers, his head cocking to the side as his gaze ensnared her. He lowered his mouth so, so close. She curled her fingers into fists at her sides so that she didn't wrap her arms around him, her legs around him, and beg for everything he could give her—safety, comfort . . . feverish desire, shattering pleasure.

He exhaled against her mouth, parted his lips. God, she couldn't breathe. Already, she wanted him desperately. If he kissed her, it would only make everything ten times more difficult.

"Don't," she whispered.

He hesitated, dropped his head near her ear. "*My* way, Del."

Then Tyler nipped at her lobe with his teeth. A shiver wound through her, all the way to her toes.

She didn't get in another breath before Tyler's lips took hers, at first hungry but searching, as if testing his welcome. The past, his long list of conquests, the pain between them—all instantly obliterated in the comfort of his solid embrace. His aching familiarity. There was no way she could stop the acceptance bubbling inside her. Her lips turned pliant, seeking.

An instant later, Tyler groaned, bulldozing his way into her mouth. His heat crashed over her, inside her, surging low in her belly—then spearing deep between her thighs. The warmth of his breath as he seized her mouth and shoved her lips farther apart with his own burned her up. His arms twisted around her body, jacking her tight against the inferno of his taut muscles and steely cock.

She gasped into his mouth. He went deeper, even as his palm worked under her shirt, branding the suddenly feverish skin of her back, holding her against him without a breath of air between them.

Without conscious thought, she whimpered, her body melting into his, hands fisting his T-shirt, then clutching his shoulders to drag him closer. She opened wider for the hot thrust of his kiss. Needed it. Tyler gave it to her, then grabbed her thigh in one hand, slung it over his hip, and pressed harder against the needy spot throbbing between her legs. She moaned.

Then Del caught herself.

No, no, no . . . Please let the response shimmering inside her be like a mirage on a hot highway, glimmering with promise. Not real.

Because if it was, she was in a whole world of trouble.

But it felt all too genuine, too intense. It had been so long since she'd experienced the tug and pull of attraction, that agonizing want making her sink against a man's body.

Now wasn't the time to be distracted. Her life—and her son's—were on the line.

Delaney tore her lips from his and turned her head away. She'd love to push him aside and tell him that he didn't affect her in the least. But her trembling and panting were dead giveaways, along with her heart galloping madly in her chest. Tyler wasn't stupid or blind. His stare was all over her, weighty and scorching, cataloging her reactions. Her breath hitched at the thought. Her only consolation was that he was breathing hard, too.

Don't let him kiss me again. If he laid his lips on her now, she'd be toast.

Gently, he tucked a finger under her chin and forced her to look at him. "Del?"

What the hell did he want her to say? Was he looking for permission to continue?

She shook her head. "Don't do that again."

A muscle in his jaw ticced. "Why did you come to me? Honestly."

“I had nowhere else to turn. Please don’t make me regret it. Just . . . watch Seth for me. I’ll be back as soon as I can.”

With that, she twisted out from beneath the solid warmth of his body and turned, yanking frantically at the door knob. Damn it, she had to get free before she did something with Tyler that she’d regret.

With a low curse, he stepped back and let her go. Then she was in the hall, running toward the guest room as if she was on fire.

Because she was, and Tyler had done that to her with a single kiss. And Del had no illusions; he’d let his bedroom her leave because he’d chosen to. If he ever decided to put his hands on her again, chances were he wouldn’t release her until they were both utterly sated—because she wouldn’t be able to find the strength to tell him to let her go.

MINE TO HOLD